DownFallen

By

R. J. Larson

For permission requests, please contact: rjlarsonbooks@gramcoink.com

Printed in U.S.A.

Cover design by: Kacy Barnett-Gramckow
Background and images: Shutterstock.

Books by R. J. Larson:

Books of the Infinite
Prophet
Judge
King
Realms of the Infinite
Exiles
Queen
And
DownFallen
Coming Soon:
Valor

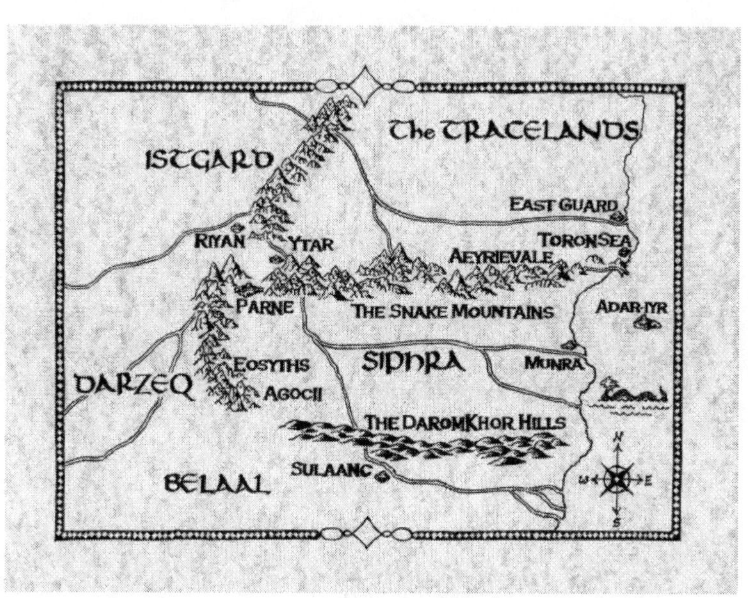
The TRACELANDS
ISTGARD
EAST GUARD
RIYAN
YTAR
TORONSEA
AEYRIEVALE
PARNE
THE SNAKE MOUNTAINS
ADAR-IYR
SIPHRA
MUNRA
EOSYTHS
DARZEQ
AGOCII
THE DAROMKHOR HILLS
SULAANC
BELAAL
N
W
E
S

Character List

Corban Thaenfall **Cor**-ban **Thane**-fall\ Renegade Siphran lord, son of Siphran rebel against Infinite.

Matteo of Arimna \Matt-**tay**-O\ Youngest son of King Jonatan of Darzeq.

Arimna \Ah-**rim**-nah\ Capitol of Darzeq.

Darzeq **Dar**-zek\ Nation ruled by House of Jonatan, ostensibly faithful to the Infinite, prey to political infighting.

Cthar \Sith-**are**\ Princess of Kaphtor. Mother of Jonatan, Grandmother to Matteo and Anji.

Kaphtor \Kaff-**tore**\ Realm beyond the sea, west of Darzeq, devoted to ideals of self-worship venerated in Chaplet Temples.

Valsignae **Val**-sig-nay\ Queen of Darzeq, wife of King Jonatan. Matteo's mother.

Anji, Lady Rhiysa **An**-jee \ **Ree**-sah\ Princess of Darzeq, only niece of Jonatan, wife of Ekiael

Dalia Hradedh **Dal**-ee-yah Raided\ Daughter of Lord Roi Hradedh of Tragobre

Ekiael \Eh-**Ki**-ay-el\ Devout and honored high priest of Darzeq.

Araine \Ah-**Rain**\ Prophet of Belaal.

Belaal \Bell-**A**-el\ Kingdom southeast of Darzeq, formerly ruled by a dynasty of god-kings.

Parne \Parn or **Parn**-ay\ City-state east of Darzeq

Ela Roeh **El**-ah **Roe**-eh\ Prophet of the vanquished city-state of Parne.

Chapter 1

Corban Thaenfall awoke to the sight of cobwebbed, smoke-colored ceiling beams, and straightaway the truth gnawed into him, as fierce as a starved dog attacking a carcass—he could not escape himself.

Not that he hadn't tried. More than a month's fugitive journey through the Snake Mountains and the Tracelands had landed him in this pit of a rented room in Istgard, but hadn't erased abhorrent reality. Running wouldn't redeem the Thaenfall name. Wouldn't restore life to the old man who'd perished last month in ToronSea. Wouldn't blot out the memory of his love, Araine, vanishing as she lay dying beneath his grip—after she'd uttered the only word that could make him hate her.

Infinite.

Corban mentally edged away from the fateful precipice of saying His name. Surrendering would accomplish nothing. He'd remain the son of a rebel Siphran lord, without estates, without honor, without hope of making restitution for his crimes. Forever denied the peace Araine had sought for his sake. No. He must not think of her.

To dream of Araine was to invite the madness of remorse and grief. He'd never see her again. Yet why should he mourn her? She'd betrayed his trust. She'd lured him toward the Enemy who'd wrought his downfall. By every established measure known to mortals, she'd deserved the hatred he could no longer summon.

Foolish love now overruled cold-eyed vengeance, and he must pay the price of his ungoverned rage. In truth, he'd wrought his own ruin. Now, he must live with Araine's absence, and he must reach a truce with his war-torn soul. Therefore...

Corban rubbed one hand over his face and shook away sleep's bleariness, flung himself off the creaking, warped wood-framed bed, and winced. Movement pained him, as if he'd lost a fight, or won badly, which might have happened. He must give up his attempts to drown his thoughts with strong drink. All his muscles burned as he crossed the rented room within three steps. Resisting pain, he slowly scrubbed, rinsed, and plied his razor over his stubbled beard. While wiping his face, Corban scowled at his grim, warped reflection in his polished silver travel mirror. At least he wouldn't terrify the locals quite so much now.

Not that he cared.

He shoved the mirror into his leather knapsack, worked three coins from within his money-belt, scratched the flea-bites on his shins, donned his overtunic, then buckled on his boots, sword, and long dagger.

By the time he'd pinned on his mantle and snatched his gear, his stomach was growling its beast-like hunger, and he needed water before his sleep-dried tongue fused permanently to the roof of his mouth. He unbarred the door and stomped down the creaking, uneven wooden stairs. In the decayed, cramped hall below, the puffy-faced innkeeper smoothed his sparse grease-clumped hair and affected an equally oiled smile. "All's well, sir?"

Corban glared, silently daring the man to say another word. The innkeeper gaped and then shut his mouth, wisely deciding not to demand another coin for the dusty bug-ridden excuse of a closet he'd rented to Corban as a—for lack of a better word—room.

Outside, the spire-decorated city of Riyan met Corban's gaze, pleasant as an idle old minstrel dozing in the sun, and

Corban shielded his eyes from the light. What a decorous air this new regime had cast over Istgard's reputedly riotous capitol! His sources had lied through their rotten teeth. This was not a city where a renegade nobleman could hide, nor earn a living by more adventuresome means.

Likewise, signing himself into the local militia was out of the question. He'd be trapped by rules, boredom, and fleas. Nor would he pledge himself to safeguard some bumptious pack of traveling merchants as they journeyed from city to city. The monotony of continuous back-and-forth between those cities would tempt him to jump from the nearest cliff.

What, then, should he do?

The question weighed Corban's steps and added to his glum mood as he entered Riyan's aggravatingly cheerful marketplace. The vendors who glanced up at him swiftly looked away. Wise men. He was in no mood for banter, and clearly his antipathy heralded his way as a warning fanfare. He purchased a small jug of fruit juice, fresh rounds of bread and grilled meat from a silent, hurried vendor and ate his breakfast as he walked to the city's stables.

The grizzled stable-keeper—wiping a fly-beset mare's eyes—greeted Corban with a slight bow and then muttered to a brawny stable-hand, "Saddle the gray."

"As if we'd others to worry about," the hand retorted as he trudged deeper into the stables. "Thank all the gods I'm nearly done here!"

The stable-keeper called after him, "Be grateful for the silver you've earned, Aki! I've given you more than your share for the little work you do!"

"You don't see half of what I do, old man, and I'm paid for less!" From the depths of the stable, thuds and a clatter emphasized the hand's fury. Soon, the aggravated huff of Corban's gray was answered with a ferocious 'thwap!'

Repeatedly. Definitely the sounds of a man thrashing a horse—and not just any horse, but Corban's splendid gray, Ghost.

Corban gritted his teeth as he set down the remains of his breakfast. He must resist reaching for his dagger. He could *not* slice the stable hand apart. Wasn't it enough that Thaenfalls were known and sought in the Tracelands and Siphra for murder and attempted murder? He must not add Istgard to the list.

A stream of muted oaths followed as the hand led Ghost to the stable door. He dropped the reins and huffed at the stable-keeper, "I'm away to Darzeq for real money. You can tend this sty alone, old miser!"

His silvered eyebrows lowering, the stable-keeper tied the mare, then growled, "Go, and Istgard's well-rid of you!"

Fury-maddened, the stable hand snatched a long, leather vest from a nearby wall-peg. As he struggled into the garment, he snarled at Corban, "I'll take my coin for tending your beast!"

Would he indeed? Corban grabbed the man's vest, lunged into him, and then flung the wretch into the muddied street. Before the fool could collect his wits, Corban drew his short sword and held it ready. "Leave before I take off your nose and ears! You can thank me for sparing your life—I'll pay no man for mistreating my horse."

The stable-keeper pitched a tarnished coin at the still-supine offender. "Aki, I'll pay you to go! 'Less you'd like the magistrate's men to lock you away."

Aki grabbed the old silver coin and stood, casting a wary, sullen glare toward Corban, then slunk away, his vest dangling ludicrously from one shoulder.

Corban sheathed his sword, pulled a quarter-dram of Tracelands' silver from his money belt, and tossed it at the stable-keeper, who caught it neatly. As the man articulated a half-hearted protest, Corban said, "That's for the feed and the lodging. Tell me about Darzeq. How does that lack-wit expect to earn better wages there?"

"Word is that gold's hirin' forces in Kiyrem, in Darzeq."

"To serve whom?" Hearing his own question, Corban almost sneered at himself. Ironic that he was still principled enough to care about his potential master's reputation. Absurd, considering his own corrupted name and lowered status.

The stable keeper shrugged. "None know. Payin' gold—need a man ask more?"

Yes, always, a man should ask. However, payment in gold was worth considering. And Darzeq had potential. Chiefly that it was farther from ToronSea and Siphra.

Farther from Araine, if not from himself.

Corban turned toward Ghost, who waited in trained, elegant, ground-broke patience. "Time to leave."

He tied his gear onto Ghost's saddle, mounted, and then goaded the beast southwest. Toward Darzeq.

Matteo of Arimna, youngest son of Jonatan, King of Darzeq, forced down his hasty morning meal of bread and chilled fermented milk, brushed crumbs from his new tunic and leggings, shrugged his formal gold baldric over his shoulder, buckled a ceremonial belt and dagger about his waist, and then fastened his cloak with the required insignias and gold pins.

It wouldn't do to face Queen-Grandmother, Cthar, while unfed and informally attired.

Why had he been summoned? More to the point, why was Cthar awake so early? This couldn't be good. Had Darzeq's most grand lady heard about Dalia?

Matteo shoved his feet into his new boots, nodded to his servants and slaves, and then faced himself in the mirror, straightening, soldier-like. He placed a plain gold circlet on his head, and frowned. "What do you say, Abiah? Do I pass inspection?"

Abiah straightened Matteo's mantle and stepped back, tension easing visibly in his lined brown face. "More than pass, sir. If the queen-mother dislikes what she sees, then she must dislike her own son—and herself."

Matteo exhaled, but not from relief. He loathed being ever-compared to his lord father and Cthar all in the same breath, and one day, he'd tell others so. Summoning dignity, he thanked Abiah and sped from the room, his sword clattering faintly against his gold-studded belt.

His boots, however, thudded too loudly over the gleaming amethyst marble floors. Listening to his own racket, Matteo scowled. For once, he'd like to arrive in Queen-Grandmother's rooms without warning. Just startle her and watch her leap like a frightened hare.

However, nothing ever seemed to startle Cthar.

Cthar's chief guard, Gueronn, nodded slightly as Matteo approached—and in truth Gueronn could do little more than vaguely nod while ridiculously clad in full ceremonial gear. He might overset that too-lofty gold-crested helm. Had Cthar ordered new and specific honorary attire for Gueronn alone? If so, the king would be displeased, for discretion was not one of Cthar's strengths, and Gueronn was rumored to be Cthar's love.

Muting his misgivings about the man, Matteo motioned at Gueronn's new helm, conveying sympathy for Queen-Grandmother's latest whim. "A new decree?"

Gueronn grinned, his gray eyes and white teeth gleaming in his tanned, blonde-bearded face, betraying his rogue-nature. "Nothing unbearable, sir. Thank you for your concern."

Gueronn announced Matteo, then allowed him inside Queen-Grandmother's private reception room. Matteo entered, bowed, and paused, glancing obliquely at Queen-Grandmother.

Cthar—clad in sumptuous embroidered linen robes and eating her morning meal—placed her slender rock-crystal cup on the polished stone table, then motioned Matteo to approach. Fatigue blurred Queen-Grandmother's features this morning. Yet, at almost sixty, she was magnificent, her slim, proud face still regal and painted, her glowing olive skin etched with only the faintest lines, her eyes golden and fringed with dark lashes framed by imperiously lifted black eyebrows and long, glossy black curls.

No woman in the entire realm of Darzeq resembled a grandmother less. Which was why Cthar's painted likeness adorned every street in Arimna, to Father's vexation. It was bad enough—according to Father—that she'd foisted his own likeness onto every coin when he first wore Darzeq's crown, but she must make her staring presence felt at every turn when he rode through the capitol. Such self-worshiping images were apt to become objects of unconventional worship, and to an extent, Cthar's celebrated beauty stylishly mitigated her personal controversies.

Cthar's golden eyes glinted as she studied Matteo—her gaze so intense that Matteo bowed to avoid at least one instant of inspection. Had she heard of his communications with Dalia?

Queen-Grandmother pointed to a footstool, and Matteo sat like a trained pup. An overdressed fool.

His regal grandmother arranged her flowing white gown in elegant lines as if that singular task was all she'd planned for this morning. At last, she looked down at Matteo and spoke, direct as the linear folds she'd just arranged. "I've been considering your future and the influence I might have upon your life. Among the family, you most resemble your father and me. How much alike are we, I wonder?"

Matteo kept his voice gracious. "Lady, I protest. How can anyone be like Father, or you?"

"How, indeed?" Grandmother smiled, the tiniest of creases showing near her black-rimmed eyes. "But tell me plainly, Matteo, what is most important to you?"

Dalia. Her name instantly winged into Matteo's thoughts. Followed by, "My family. My lord-father, my mother, my brothers, you—of course—and the Infinite."

Queen-Grandmother's smile turned bland and her voice sweetened. "What a dutiful answer. Yet I've no doubt it's the truth."

Clearly his answer hadn't pleased her. What had she hoped he would say?

She sighed and flicked at a fold in her gown. "Be that as it may, I wondered and decided I should speak to you this morning. A whim. Perhaps one I should ignore. Never mind, Matteo. Return to whatever you were doing."

Braving her irritation, Matteo asked, "Lady, have you heard from our lord, the king?"

Cthar sniffed and looked away—evidently a mother unhappy with her royal son, the king. "Of course not. He's in Port Bascin, hunting, fishing, and ignoring us completely."

Flicking her long, graceful hand, she dismissed Matteo without another word. Matteo bowed, then fled. The interview was done—and so easily. Not to mention pointless. But who could understand Cthar? Her Kaphtor-born reasoning remained incomprehensible to all who were Darzeq-born, Matteo included. Why couldn't Cthar be more like Mother? Grinning at the thought of surprising his mother and stealing some of her breakfast, Matteo sped to her rooms.

Darzeq's Queen Valsignae, despite all her royal blood, never affected hauteur. The instant Matteo was announced, Mother stood and called to him, "Matteo! Come in and sit down. Why are you prepared for Alvir's party so early?"

Matteo frowned. He'd nearly forgotten the naming day celebration for his second brother this afternoon—a feast in the garden. "Queen-Grandmother sent for me, so I dressed properly."

Valsignae briefly cast her gaze toward the gilded roof-beams as if pleading for grace from the Infinite, their own Creator. "The queen-mother quarreled with your father again before he left. Let's not speak of her." Valsignae sighed, then smiled. "Have you eaten?"

"Not enough, so thank you." Matteo bent and kissed his mother's softly curved, tawny face. "Any news from Father?"

"None." Valsignae settled onto her floor cushion again and picked at her breakfast of fruit, bread, and cold lamb. "But we must remember that when the king's hunting and fishing, he rarely pauses to write letters, not even to me—and I'd like to believe he's fond of me."

Matteo grinned, tore off a chunk of bread, added some meat, and dipped his snack into herb-flecked olive oil. "You know he loves you."

Valsignae nibbled a bit of the cold roasted meat, swallowed, then shrugged. "I'm thinking of surprising him with a visit. Matteo, would you like to accompany me? Sheth's agreed to go."

"Sheth?" At the mention of his long-absent third brother, Matteo swallowed his mouthful, abandoned his food, and stood. "He's finally returned from Belaal?"

"At dawn." Valsignae smiled and selected a summer peach. "Though I shouldn't have mentioned him. Obviously, you're about to run away just as I've settled in for our visit."

"Don't worry. I'll return!" Matteo kissed his mother in farewell and then dashed through the echoing corridors to the garden. If Sheth was home, then he'd undoubtedly detoured to stay overnight in Tragobre to visit with Roi Hradedh. Perhaps he'd have news of Dalia.

Every palace had its secrets, and Anji—niece of King Jonatan—crept through one of her favorite childhood secrets now: the hidden passageway behind the false panels in the king's rooms. Ancient, musty, and barely lit, with miniscule vents pierced high inside the stone outer walls of Arimna's palace, the passageway was known only to the king, his queen, and his children, and Anji as the royal family's much-indulged only girl.

Ordinarily, Anji would never dare to intrude upon the king's chamber, but he wasn't in residence, so she was quite safe. Why bother to wait for an audience after the king's return in order to present a worthy petition from two of his favorite subjects?

For the sake of her husband, Ekiael, Anji would presume upon royal favor. Anyway, it wasn't as if she and Ekiael were requesting wealth or any such nonsense for themselves—this was a plea on behalf of Ekiael's assistants, his priests, for improvements to their living quarters near the Infinite's Holy House. Jonatan was devout. Surely he would allow them a grant of some sort....

Holding her breath, Anji pressed the framed secret doorway panel at the end of the passage. If only Dalia could be with her in this little sortie. Anji sighed, missing her childhood friend for the thousandth time. But Dalia might make her laugh and give them both away. Smiling, Anji waited in the musty darkness. Hearing no servants' voices, she gently eased open the secret door. Within her, Anji's unborn child fluttered for the first time, as a tiny bird struggling against terror. Anji smoothed at the tiny tempest, her delight warring with perplexity. Sweet little one, why such tumult? Why...

Anji stared about the king's chamber. At unreality.

Jonatan, King of Darzeq, lay crowned and robed, bizarrely wizened and motionless upon his fully made bed. His royal robes rested in perfect order, redolent of embalming spices, his waxen brown hands folded and bound over his unnaturally concave belly, and ... his sunken eyelids sealed shut. With glue, visibly dried and darkened beneath his long lashes.

On the floor beside him, arranged on tarps, four servants lay unmoving, their hollowed-out bodies bound and glued—all four freely dusted with a white powder that turned their brown skin to murky ash. Unlike the king, their faces were contorted, as if they'd died in agony.

Oh, those poor men! And dear irascible King Jonatan. What had happened?

Pressing a protective hand over her agitated baby, Anji retreated, fearing to breathe, her throat too dry to rattle out even a squeak. Anguished tears blurred her gaze as she closed herself within the hidden corridor, then stifled sobs of grief.

Adored Creator...dear Infinite, what must she do? What was her wisest course?

The king was dead. Days dead and embalmed, and no one knew. Except for a handful of now-dispatched servants. And, unfortunately, Anji and her frantic unborn child.

Chapter 2

Matteo pretended a glare down at Sheth while they strolled through their favorite haunt, the most ancient walled garden in Arimna palace. They were halfway through the garden's main rose terrace—its formal pavilion set with a long table for their feast—and Sheth hadn't said a word about Dalia. On the way home, he'd undoubtedly stopped off at Tragobre Fortress, Dalia's lord-father's magnificent primary residence, to rest and catch up on news while returning from Belaal. Yet Sheth's thoughts were evidently wandering amid unknown realms. And he was hacking at the bushes with his ceremonial dagger, testing its gleaming edge amid a shower of fallen roses and scattered petals.

Matteo shoved his third brother and then snatched the dagger, bidding for his absent attention. "Give me that! I know you must have stopped at Tragobre. Where's my letter from Dalia?"

Sheth's golden eyes widened in the afternoon light. "Be patient! And don't cut yourself on those edges—I've just had that blade sharpened."

Matteo snorted, rolled the blade in an edge of his light mantle, and tucked it safely beneath his filigreed sword belt. "Am I a child that you ought to warn me? No! I'll return this when you hand over my message. Don't make me thrash you for it!"

Sheth retaliated, swiping Matteo's hair. "What if I thrash you? Ever since you surpassed me in height, you've become far too belligerent. All the same, your future is as sealed as any note."

"So you say." While Matteo smoothed his hair, Sheth fished a sealed parchment square from the leather pouch slung from his belt, then dangled it just beyond Matteo's reach. Dalia's silver-gray wax stamp gleamed, impressed over a slender green cord.

Matteo lunged for the long-desired letter, but before he could open the seal, Sheth raised a warning hand. Servants entered the garden, lugging serving ware, pitchers, and trays of food toward the pavilion. Clearly wary of being overheard, Sheth motioned to a vine-screened arbor at the far side of the garden.

The instant they were hidden by the shadowed vines, Sheth scolded quietly, "Matteo, seriously, this flirtation must end. What could you two possibly hope for? Your marriage petition would be refused by the lords of the First Forum and Dalia would be punished for overreaching her rank, never mind how high her lord-father's placed. You'll both suffer!"

Matteo mentally shoved away the thought. "Sheth, no lectures. Not yet. I love her. You know I do—as she loves me. It's no flirtation, so please allow us to hope. I might yet persuade Father to approve the marriage petition."

Sheth shook his head. "According to the law, you're no mere lovesick boy. You're a bargaining tool. A game-piece to be moved about by Darzeq's will."

"I'm no boy, and I'm certainly not a game-piece. If I'm involved, shouldn't I have some say in determining the game's moves? What if I wish to dictate the bargain on my behalf?"

"Matteo, you have no voice! No wish of your own. You're merely an instrument. Everything you possess is granted to you by the First Forum, and every lord in Darzeq will vote against you through the First Forum if you rebel. And, unless he wants to risk inordinate fines, so must Tragobre, regardless of how much he loves Dalia as his only child. Live with that understanding as best you can. We've all been forced to accept this, believe me."

"Which is why you're not married—the First Forum can't even decide whom Tarquin should marry, much less agree on wives for the remaining six of us."

Sheth grimaced at the truth of Matteo's observation, then shrugged. Matteo couldn't blame him, considering some of the candidates nominated by the First Forum for Tarquin and Alvir. Who wanted to be bartered off to some foreign land that might turn hostile? As for bringing foreign princesses into the country... Darzeq was understandably wary after years of dealing with Queen-Grandmother's caprices.

All the more reason to consider domestic marriages. If only the lords would finally agree on something! Matteo scowled. Never mind. Sheth might be mulish, but Matteo and Dalia could win over Father, and *he* could deal with the lords of the First Forum.

Shaking off his aggravation, Matteo broke the silver seal and opened Dalia's note.

Love, Sheth's promised me on his honor to deliver these words, though he's warned me it will be the last time he serves as our messenger. Know that all my thoughts are with you and I look forward to visiting with you at the winter festival this year. I'm now dragging myself off to more studies with Master Tredin and our beloved Sophereth in Kiyrem, though Sophereth writes that the city is overrun with riotous men rumored to be mercenaries.

My lord father has sent inquiries to Kiyrem's authorities and to the other members of First Forum concerning the probable mercenaries, but has received no reply, and Sheth—being newly returned from Belaal—has no idea why mercenaries would suddenly swarm a dull academic town on the eastern border. Has our lord the king heard anything of this dissolute invasion? I pray that you and all your brothers are well. Please wish Alvir a blessed naming day for me. I'll send his gift as soon as I'm permitted to visit the Kiyrem markets—you know how unpleasant Sophereth is when she suspects mischief.

Send me word of your wellbeing as best you can with help from your servants, or bribes. Do not leave me stranded in Kiyrem with no letters from you for the next six weeks, or I'll surely go mad for lack of your promises that you love me still.

May the Infinite bless and protect you until we meet again.

Written this day by my hand at Tragobre,

Yours forever, Dalia.

Matteo frowned down at Sheth, who was brooding, leaning against a wooden pillar. "Sheth, what about the mercenaries? Is Dalia in danger?"

"I don't believe so. However, it's worrisome. Why would anyone would be recruiting mercenaries in Darzeq? I wrote to Father from Tragobre, and I've sent an inquiry to the First Forum." Sheth shot a wary glance at Matteo. "It's odd that I haven't heard from Father. Has anything else happened while I was gone? Anything that concerns you or the family?"

"No. Why?"

"Because the god-king of Belaal now has a pretty new diversion. Araine, Prophet of the Infinite—or so she claims. While I was visiting the king, she prophesied against me."

Indignation and a whisper of dread raised Matteo's defensive hackles. "What? How dare she!" Matteo hesitated as a worse prospect came to mind. What if this young woman was indeed a blessed voice for the Mighty One? "Do you believe she's a true prophet?"

Snapping a leaf off a nearby vine, Sheth tore at it, scowling. "My impression was of a lovely, sheltered young woman who believes her own visions. Moreover, she was beset with hiccoughs for half of the time I saw her, and Bel-Tygeon treated her like an amusement more than a true attendant. It was difficult to accept her as a prophet. And yet...."

"Yet you wonder?" Matteo resisted swatting the shredded leaf from Sheth's hands. "If she's the Infinite's own prophet ... what if her visions are true?"

Sheth exhaled and scattered the shreds over the walkway. "I hope her visions aren't true. I admit I'm uneasy."

"Well?" Matteo prompted, though Sheth's expression was so disturbed that he feared to ask, "What did she predict?

"Disaster. My death. Danger for our entire family. She begged me to remain in Belaal. To send warnings to you all, commanding to you flee. To hide."

Hide!

The silent word resounded within Matteo's thoughts as if spoken by another, and his very soul seemed held, encased in chilling, unyielding ice. He sucked in a sharp breath, ignored the chill, and forced his voice to work, to tell off Sheth. "If you'd sent a warning, we would have left Arimna days ago. Why didn't you?"

Straightening, Sheth shook his head. "I refuse to believe the girl is a prophet. She was about your age—too young for a prophet—and she was peculiar!"

"Too young?" Matteo's chill vanished, heated by indignation. "No prophet's ever too young if the Infinite's Spirit is present. Anji told me that Parne's prophet wasn't much more than a girl, and she ever predicted the truth, including the downfall of her own people."

Even as he spoke, Matteo suppressed a shudder. The city-state of Parne had been founded by a particularly devout sect of the Infinite's followers, which had departed from Darzeq generations ago and crossed the mountains to the east—pledging to be permanently rid of Darzeq's corruptions. Yet Parne, despite its former purity and fervor, had fallen. Was Darzeq next? Had the Infinite abandoned His faithful, including Darzeq, despite His pact with Ancient Darzeq?

Sheth tore at another leaf. "Parne's prophet is now exiled to another country for her pains, if she's still alive. Our traders have returned from beyond the mountains, declaring Parne's a poisoned ruin. All the same, Anji's too wrapped up in her high-priest husband's thinking. As much as I like Ekiael, he's got some far-fetched ideas. I trust the Infinite—the One-Who-Sees—and you know it, Matteo. But when a strange girl predicts the ruin of your family and foretells your own death, you might question her judgment!"

Matteo comprehended his viewpoint and his agitation. Perhaps it was safer to back out of this debate. "I apologize for ranting at you. I'd..."

Voices interrupted from the garden. With laughter and beckoning whistles. Matteo peered through the curtain of vines and glimpsed their remaining five brothers—all dark-haired and richly garbed—as they approached the garden. A pack of happy troublemakers on a search mission. Tarquin, Alvir, Efraim, Boas, and Melkir were clearly prepared to feast and celebrate Sheth's return and Alvir's naming day. Loudest of the five by sheer force of his age, twenty-eight years, Tarquin bellowed, "Sheth! We know you're here—you've been slaughtering the flowers again!"

Melkir, nineteen, thin and slouched as a tree-pruning hook, yelled, "Don't make us hunt you to ground!"

"Go on," Matteo urged. He grinned at Sheth, and then sat on one of the arbor's sheltered stone benches. "I want to read Dalia's note again."

Sheth swiped at Matteo's shoulder. "Don't run away. We'll talk later."

"Ask the others about the mercenaries," Matteo urged. "It's odd that we haven't heard of them here in Arimna."

Matteo frowned at Dalia's letter. Was she in danger? Unease chilled Matteo again, prompting him to pray. "One-Who-Sees-Me, watch over her!"

Why would mercenaries gather in such a remote town as Kiyrem?

Abandoned by her servants and the guards who'd escorted her safely to Kiyrem, Dalia Hradedh of Tragobre overturned her leather backpack onto her fleece bedroll within the narrow confines of her whitewashed cell. She'd best settle in and make this place home again, so why delay unpacking? It wasn't as if she had much to do except wait for classes to begin. Dalia shrugged and looked around. With the exception of some dust and spiders, the place was as clean as she'd left it seven weeks past. And quiet. In truth, all Kiyrem had seemed peaceful this afternoon while she and her servants rode through the town.

Had the supposed mercenaries departed?

Perhaps her lord-father's messages, threats actually, had somehow aided Kiyrem.

According to the locals, the renegades had poured into Kiyrem the past month and proceeded to drink the city dry and bash countless doors and quite a few citizens. Dalia growled beneath her breath, irked by the thought of such pointless destruction within Kiyrem's ancient and revered city walls.

A sharp rap sounded on her cell's oak door. Visitors already? Dalia turned and flinched.

Tall, gaunt, linen-swathed, and so cleanly shorn that Dalia was convinced that the man polished his scalp, Master Tredin glowered at Dalia from the doorway. Formidable as ever. And soft-footed. Dalia hadn't heard a whisper of noise at the master's approach.

She bowed, accepting her role as mere student—particularly when she noticed Tredin's wife, the equally tall and ever-feared Sophereth, standing just behind him.

Sophereth's bronzed face puckered thoughtfully and her keen, dark eyes flicked criticizing glances from just over Tredin's shoulder at the thin, impassable window and the whitewashed wall of Dalia's cell.

Oh, scaln's breath! Inspections so soon...

Dalia cleared her throat and addressed her visitors. "Sir. And lady. Good afternoon."

His tone dry and crisp as old parchment, Master Tredin asked, "Have you declared it good, young lady of Tragobre?"

Dalia held back a grimace. She should have known better. Master Tredin usually challenged even the most polite and banal statements. Not daring to smile at the cold-faced master-scribe and his wife, Dalia shook her head. "I only wish your afternoon to be pleasant, sir. Yet you dictate the actual state of your current mood, therefore I await your decree."

"As if I rule the universe." Tredin scanned Dalia's cell for infractions that would undoubtedly be noted in Dalia's formal records. Dalia could almost see the elaborately detailed report now, written in Tredin's exacting scribe lettering: Spider on the wall—an ordinary garden gray. Two grains of sand on the floor. Needle-sized splinter in the window's narrow shutter. The air sullied by dust motes from Dalia's overturned pack.

Tredin's thin brown nostrils flared. "We received your lord-father's ... expressions of concern. You will write to him this evening and assure him that the mercenaries have departed, and that his precious lady-heir is safe in Kiyrem. But first, put away your gear. After which—!" Tredin rapped his knuckles fiercely against the door. "You will polish this oak until I can see my reflection. You've no servants here, young lady."

Dalia bowed her head. "As you say, sir. It will be done."

"As if I rule the universe," Tredin repeated, drier than before.

Had she actually heard self-mockery in the master's tone?

Sophereth cut through Dalia's wonderment with a snap of her long fingers. "Get that spider off the wall."

Dalia slapped her curved hand over the spider and glanced back at the doorway just as Tredin and Sophereth departed, their footsteps silent as air in a tomb. Cautiously, Dalia lifted her hand and peeked at the now-skittering spider. "Your humble heritage has saved you," she murmured as the tiny creature made its desperate zig-zag charge for the open window. "If you'd been poisonous, I'd have smashed you flat. Be gone!"

She smiled and walked her fingers along the wall, hurrying the gray toward open air and safety. Perhaps this final year would be an improvement over the last three years. Master Tredin had actually scoffed at himself—an unheard-of occurrence. Better yet, the mercenaries had departed.

To where?

She must write to her parents, and then to Matteo. But first, she'd polish the door.

Dalia rummaged through her gear and hauled out her required supply of rags and oily beeswax polish. Donning appropriate solemnity, she went to work on the massive oak door while continuing her prayer. Infinite, Most Holy, by Your will, let my winter here pass quickly.

Let me leave this place and marry Matteo. Somehow...

Finished re-reading Dalia's letter for the tenth time, Matteo sighed, folded the parchment neatly, and tucked it behind his wide, gold-studded belt, near Sheth's dagger. He ought to return the dagger to Sheth. Indeed, he ought to go join his brothers. The Dreaded Seven, as the servants called them—a title they'd supposedly never heard, but of which they all approved.

Dark haired, brown-skinned, and royally attired in white, gold, and variants of Darzeq's purple, Matteo's brothers were indisputably princes of the realm and true sons of Jonatan. Matteo was proud to be numbered among them. Even if they were laughing without him, hovering near the pavilion-shaded table and picking at the food—all their favorites. Jellied fruit lozenges, leaf-wrapped marinated cheeses, black rice fried with olives, cold relishes, massive portions of grilled meats, and enough soft bread to pave the entire garden if the Dreaded Seven chose to do so. As they might.

Matteo and his brothers rarely ate quietly, and a private family feast such as this one promised every breach of formality and etiquette frowned upon by Queen-Grandmother. Alvir flung a dark leaf-wrapped chunk of cheese at Sheth, who got even by striking him with a jellied lozenge—which was sludgy from the day's warmth. Boas yelled, "What are we waiting for?"

Sheth turned toward the arbor, obviously planning to fetch Matteo. Sighing, Matteo stood. Just as Anji ducked through the wall of vines on the arbor's opposite side. Matteo glanced at her—his usually joyous and pretty cousin, the ever-present bane and blessing of his childhood.

Even from this distance, Matteo noted his cousin's swollen eyes, and her dark curls spilled from her wide headband, as if she'd been tearing at them in despair. Worse, Anji's gait was furtive. A wary, fearful pace as she hugged her mantle close. The last time Matteo had seen Anji in such a state, Great-Aunt Pinni had just died.

In her delicate condition, Anji must be protected. Matteo frowned. "Anji—?"

Anji shushed him with a silent, imperious upraised hand, and tears slid down her pregnancy-softened face. She snagged Matteo by the arm and whispered, "I've been looking everywhere for you! Be brave...."

Sheth sidled into the arbor, halted, and stared. He'd always been fond of Anji. Protective as if she'd been their own sister. Anji hesitated, then motioned him nearer. "Sheth, how can I even speak? The king's dead. He's been dead for days, and no one's said a word to the family. ... I saw his body! He's robed, crowned and embalmed, in his own chamber!" Sniffling moistly, her voice almost squeaking with panic, Anji pleaded, "Who'd do such a thing and simply not tell us! Why? What's happening?"

Matteo recoiled, actually leaning away from his cherished cousin. This could not be true. It was a joke. Some elaborate jest of wax and wood created to terrorize the family, and Darzeq. He glanced at his brother, then stared. Sheth seemed immobilized, his face shock-drained to grayness—a man living a nightmare. He swallowed, then rasped, "Anji, you're very sure?"

"Yes. Don't you think I recognize our dear lord-king? Not to mention the scent of embalming spices from royal funerals!" Her hands trembling, Anji plucked a formally sealed parchment from her embroidered money purse and confessed, "Forgive me! I broke the rules and went through the secret corridor from Great-Aunt Pinni's rooms, thinking the king was gone. I meant to leave this petition from the priests in his empty chamber. But it's not empty! Four of his servants are dead and embalmed on the floor beside him—all sealed within the chamber!" Fresh tears welled in Anji's dark eyes and slid down her face. "Why would the king be dead and no one told? Did someone kill him?" She pressed one hand to her belly, and whispered, "Even the baby knows something horrible's happened—it's fluttering wildly, as if it's trying to escape!"

His voice horror-laced, Sheth whispered, "Araine of Belaal's prophecy... 'Save the youngest!'"

Sheth grabbed Matteo's shoulder and Anji's shoulder, shaking them so fiercely that Anji stopped weeping. "Matteo,

Anji, listen to me! We're all in danger, and I'm going to warn Tarquin and the others to flee. You two—you *three*—are the youngest! Warn Mother! Disguise yourselves and leave Arimna now. Hide in some obscure, defensible city—Eshda! Take Mother. Go to Eshda and stay hidden until you know it's safe to return! If I survive, I'll send a letter to Dalia with instructions. Do you hear me? Go now, Matteo, promise me!"

He shook Matteo again, his grip bruising, his golden eyes so huge that Matteo nodded despite his shock. Before Matteo could protest, Sheth departed, sidling through the arbor's sheltering curtain wall of vines and shrubs. Debating the wisdom of following his older brother, Matteo stared hard through the obscuring curtain of vines and hedges, while Anji hugged him, sniffling again. Together, they watched as Sheth dashed to the pavilion and spoke to Tarquin, Alvir, Efraim, Boas, and Melkir.

Different as they were, Matteo's brothers reacted the same. All turned ghastly with shock, then recovered, their hands flexing over golden dagger hilts and sword hilts, ready to fight, Sheth among them. Tarquin, Darzeq's acknowledged heir, snarled, "Whoever did this, we'll kill them!"

Matteo nodded silent agreement, one hand shifting to his own sword. Before he could excuse himself and join his brothers, Anji whispered, "It's obvious they didn't know either! Matteo, what does this mean?"

Even as Anji spoke, the garden's gates were flung open, north and south. Soldiers—more than twenty strange warriors, with swords and spears drawn—charged inside, their dissimilar plate armor and chain mail clattering in heavy unison.

Led by Gueronn, Grandmother-Queen's personal guard. Ready to kill.

Matteo gasped. "Assassins!"

And his brothers were badly outnumbered. He started to shove away the vines, to enter the garden and join his brothers.

But Anji dragged him back with all her might, half-sobbing, whispering fiercely, "No! Remember the prophecy! We're obeying Sheth!"

Matteo hissed, "Stop!" He tried to shake off his cousin. But Anji clung to him, and they both stared, aghast as the renegades surrounded the pavilion. Gueronn and two other soldiers aimed spears at Tarquin.

The heir dashed away the first soldier's spear with his sword as his brothers yelled and rallied to Tarquin, sides and back, struggling to protect him against the onslaught. Gueronn himself ran Tarquin through with a spear, though Sheth landed his sword against Gueronn's forearm, gashing it—just as another guard ran Sheth through.

Sheth... Tarquin...

Anji dragged at Matteo as his brothers fell one by one in the massacre, their blood spilling over the garden's pavings and the feasting table.

Alvir... Efraim... Boas... Melkir... He must warn Mother. Save her...

Hide!

Snatching his cousin by the arm, Matteo fled through the arbor and out the other side, while Gueronn bellowed his triumphant battle cry over the royal slaughter.

Chapter 3

Tears of rage and grief blurring his path, Matteo lunged into the gardeners' shed, snagged three grubby cloaks, and then shoved his leather-shod feet into battered, oversized, oiled-leather boots. They must disguise themselves. He pushed a cloak at Anji.

She donned the cloak, stifling sobs.

Catching his breath, Matteo whispered, "We warn the Lady Valsignae and fetch her to the temple! Will Ekiael help us?"

"Of course he will!" Anji gulped down her tears and twisted her hair into an obscure knot beneath the cloak. "I'm ready."

Could they evade the assassins? Matteo plotted an escape route. "From Mother's rooms, we'll head for the Keyhole Gate, then down past the ponds and out through the carters' yard."

He and his brothers often visited the ponds, and they'd sometimes disguised themselves, then sneaked out of Arimna Palace through the carters' yard and the gate beyond, returning later after exploring the city, with no one seeming the wiser.

Matteo stared through the shed's slats and listened hard. In the distance, Gueronn and his men were laughing, obviously celebrating their feast of royals. Over the bodies of his brothers.

Matteo gritted his teeth, then fought sobs. How could he tell Mother and effect a quiet escape? Surely Valsignae would cry down the skies!

They crept outside, and Matteo latched the shed's door, praying silently. Infinite, let no one realize that they'd escaped wearing gardeners' gear! In unspoken agreement, they entered the palace through the gardeners' door, and then darted through corridor after corridor until they reached the musty, linen-shrouded rooms favored by Great-Aunt Pinni until her death. At the far corner of the smallest chamber, Anji opened a section of carved paneling, and they both stole into the secret corridor, Matteo closing the concealed door quietly behind them.

No one would find them here. Great-Aunt Pinni had jealously guarded this room until her death, and the servants vowed that Pinni's rooms were haunted and fit only for gathering dust. Even the queen-mother, Cthar, was ignorant of the corridor, for Pinni had loathed Cthar and privately called her, "That wretched-foreign female." Only Anji and Matteo and his brothers shared this secret with his parents, and the rules were strict. The corridor was used only by the royal children on invitation from the king and queen, and for dire emergencies, such as this.

Here and there, tiny high-set sheltered vents spilled light from the outside into the grayed, dusty corridor, allowing Matteo and Anji to see each turn. At the forth turn, they reached the panel accessing Valsignae's rooms.

There, before he touched the panel, Matteo heard the screams.

He gripped Anji's arm and they waited, statue-still, then hugging each other as they listened to Valsignae's servants wailing. Pleading. Then silenced, one by one. Men's low voices filled the sudden hush, and Matteo dared to press his ear against the wooden panel. One man spoke above the others, his voice cuttingly harsh. "Tell Gueronn the queen's dead. Time to bury this lot."

Mother...

Matteo slumped over in the hidden corridor, smothering his unspent screams.

At dusk, their gems and rich garments bundled together like laundry, their heads scarved in grubby old linen drapes from Pinni's rooms, and armed with empty, fish-pungent baskets stolen from the palace ponds, Matteo and Anji merged with a small crowd of traders, laundrywomen, and carters who were being herded from the palace grounds before the gates were locked for the night.

Drab cloaks gray within gray, they kept to the shadowed edges of Arimna's broad streets. Walking as if nothing were wrong. Feigning stoicism, as if Darzeq was as calm and normal as it appeared.

As if most of the royal family hadn't been slaughtered.

Matteo's throat threatened to close. To suffocate him. He wished it would. Until he gripped his parcel more closely within his musty cloak and felt Sheth's gold dagger press into his side. Why hadn't he returned Sheth's dagger to him? Not that he'd be alive.... Each of his brothers had used their swords and daggers during the massacre, yet they'd died by sheer force of numbers—by pikes and spears wielded by ruffians.

Where had those murderers come from? He'd recognized only Gueronn, his grandmother's beloved. Were they the mercenaries from Kiyrem? Had Gueronn hired those men? Or had Cthar?

Queen-Grandmother's imperious face turned to Matteo in his thoughts. Hauteur tinged Cthar's voice as she whispered in his memory, "How much alike are we, I wonder?"

Matteo stared, recalling his grandmother's painted face once more, seeing himself weighed and measured by that one question. Had Cthar decided then that Matteo would die for his dutiful and heartfelt answer?

His voice almost inaudible, Matteo growled, "I'm nothing like you!"

Aunt Pinni had known Cthar's true nature.

Rage clawed into Matteo, demanding reaction. Yet he walked onward, climbing the stone street's gradual rise, his gaze fixed on Darzeq's golden House of the Infinite. Surely the One-Who-Sees knew the truth behind his family's destruction. Infinite, guide my steps as I walk Your path, taught by my parents.

Give me answers, and a plan to claim justice from those who killed my family.

At last, Anji led Matteo to the right of the vast temple complex, into the residential area inhabited by Darzeq's priests. Even through his dazed grief, the simplicity of the lesser priests' homes startled Matteo. Any of these domiciles would easily fit into his main chamber in the palace. Moreover, he saw no servants among the lesser priests' homes.

The lack of servants brought Matteo's thoughts back to his own servants. Had they survived the massacre? If Gueronn had killed Abiah.... But Gueronn's men had killed Mother's servants, after Mother....

Fresh grief sent draining tremors through Matteo's limbs. Clearly recognizing his distress, Anji gripped Matteo's arm as they approached the high priest's comparatively modest mansion. "I was supposed to return ages ago. By now, Ekiael's probably frantic with worry."

As they neared the mansion's tall, shielded iron-studded gate, one of Ekiael's sentries spied them through the watch-portal and called over his shoulder to a comrade inside, "She's returned! Tell the master she's safe!"

He unlocked the gate and hurriedly bowed Anji and Matteo inside. "Lady, your lord-husband was about to fetch you from the palace himself. Why didn't the servants bring you home? Why are you clothed like some laborer?"

Anji shook her head at him. "Beni, spread the word quietly. No one's to go to the palace tonight. In fact, send word to the priests that they might be summoned to the meeting chambers."

"Yes, lady." Beni bowed to Anji, then glanced at Matteo and gaped like a fish snagged from a pond. "Lord Matteo, what...!"

Anji hissed, "Sst! Beni, hush! You never saw him—it means your life! Do you hear me?"

"I hear," Beni muttered. But he studied Matteo so earnestly, so worriedly, that Matteo retreated. He'd break beneath that kind man's gaze. Benumbed, he followed Anji's lead as she set aside their baskets and guided Matteo onward through the formal entry yard.

Fine as it was, this mansion had been a step down for Anji from the grandeur she'd been accustomed to as a child in the palace. Yet she'd fought for months to marry her beloved Ekiael and live here—a fight she'd won the previous spring in the First Forum, because she'd been a mere royal cousin and female. A triumph Matteo had hoped to mirror when he petitioned for marriage to Dalia this autumn.

At the far side of the yard, Ekiael himself opened the grand entry door and rushed down the steps to meet them. Though powerfully built and ten years older than Anji, Ekiael looked distraught as an abandoned boy. "My love! I was ready to seek you myself whether it was proper or not. What...?"

His steps slowed as he stared at Matteo. At their rough clothes and anguished faces. Without a word, he swung his big arms around them both, hustled them up the stairs and into the mansion's hall, then barred the door behind them. After glancing around to be sure no servants were nearby, he rasped, "What's happened?"

Matteo managed, "My parents ... my brothers ... were massacred!" His voice failed and he shook his head as images of the massacre returned, raw and agonizing as if he'd just seen them. Anji hugged Matteo fiercely as she told Darzeq's high priest of Gueronn's murderous attacks.

Ekiael tore his outer robes and then raised both big fists as if he could battle Gueronn and the renegades himself. He swept his arms around Anji and Matteo once more, practically carrying them across the formal stone-tiled hall. "Down to the meeting chambers! We'll send for the others and make plans!"

Matteo shivered in the dark, hidden chambers below the temple complex. This day's horrors clawed him, shook him as predators might toy with prey. To still his tremors, he braced himself and clenched his cold hands into fists as Ekiael faced his shocked lamp-bearing priests.

Ekiael's resonant voice echoed against the smooth stone walls, though he spoke quietly. "If the queen-mother has incited this butchery to seize Darzeq, my friends, we're next! She's no supporter of ours. Pack your belongings, seal the temple and your homes, and abandon Arimna by dawn. Those who follow the Infinite will flee as soon as they see that the temple is sealed."

One of the older priests glanced at Matteo and asked, "What of the prince? If he's the only survivor—"

Ekiael lifted one broad hand. "As my wife has advised, our prince—our king!—must not be mentioned!"

Our king.

The words sent a shudder through Matteo's guts. Never! Father and Mother and his brothers could not be dead. This was not true. Yet Ekiael continued, death-serious. "Matteo of Darzeq was never here. You know only that I commanded you all to lock and seal the temple and scatter. Believe me mad if you wish, but go to your own cities until I—and only I!—summon you to return for service. I would rather send you all away and look a fool, than see you and your families slaughtered as supporters of King Jonatan's family. May the Mighty One shield us all!"

Matteo exhaled as Ekiael blessed and then dismissed his priests. Did Ekiael believe Cthar to be such a threat on Matteo and Anji's word alone? Or did he have other reasons to suspect her potential for treachery? Ekiael retrieved his gilded lantern and then nodded Matteo toward the dim stone steps again. As they climbed up the passageway, returning to his mansion, Matteo asked, "Are you convinced that my grandmother is plotting to seize Darzeq?"

Ekiael paused in the stairwell. "Yes. My lord, your lord-father honored his mother as the Infinite commanded, but their relationship was never easy. Cthar was brought to Darzeq as a marriage clause in a trade treaty, much against her will."

"I know this," Matteo pointed out. "Everyone does. My grandmother made no secret of her scorn for Darzeq and her preference for her homeland." According to Cthar, Kaphtor was the epitome of a beautiful and sophisticated realm. A glorious sea-faring kingdom worthy of emulation and adulation throughout Darzeq—an ideal Darzeq's citizens and kings had never appreciated.

The high priest grunted. "What you don't know is the extent of her scorn. She's fought the king beyond reason to bring Kaphtor's ways to Darzeq. The Chaplet Temple for example..."

The Chaplet temple. Matteo scoffed, remembering the place. Cthar's attempt to venerate Kaphtor's principles of limitless free will had taken shape in the form of an opulent circular temple near the heart of Arimna. Darzeq's citizens used the place to exercise and relieve their dogs after Cthar's fundraising attempts for upkeep had failed.

Ekiael snorted and shrugged his big shoulders. "She's never forgiven us for refusing to love her edifice to self-worship. Worse, she hated her husband for not supporting her cause more fully. But he knew the Chaplet temple was unpopular and contrary to the Infinite's will. Not to mention a waste of public money—money that bore your lord-father's likeness at her insistence. Abandoning the Chaplet was one of the few wise decisions he made, along with leading our King Jonatan away from Cthar's teachings. If she'd been given her way, Darzeq would now be morally and financially corrupted."

Matteo nodded, but gritted his teeth as he contemplated Cthar. How could such a woman be his own grandmother? How had he allowed himself to be deluded? In his own defense more than Cthar's, Matteo said, "Yet, she loved my lord-father, the king, which is why I trusted her."

"Which is why I believe she didn't kill the king," Ekiael agreed. "He was her own offspring—part of herself—therefore she bowed to his bidding as king. Apparently the instant he died, she was freed to do as she pleased. And it evidently pleased her to kill your brothers and take control of Darzeq."

Anji half-turned on the step above Matteo, making them all pause. "But at the cost of others' lives—her own grandchildren among them? No sane woman would do such a thing!"

Ekiael shook his head. "Most likely she feared Tarquin would lock her away or have her reprimanded for some political or personal reason. Therefore we must find a haven for Matteo—and allies to defend his cause as our king." Ekiael motioned for them to hurry up the stairs.

Cause? King? Never... This was impossible. Matteo climbed the stairs, seeing the steps in a numbed daze. He would wake in the morning, and there'd be no cause; his parents and brothers would be alive, and this day a vanished nightmare.

Holding two of Ekiael's horses in check, and wary of being caught, Matteo glanced sidelong at Ekiael, who nodded to the guard in the city gate's night-shadowed dimness. "Eki of Port Zamaj, leaving Arimna for home. With my wife and our stable hands." He motioned to Anji, Matteo, and Beni, who was crooning to another pair of horses.

The guard looked them over. Matteo dared not meet his gaze directly for fear of being recognized. But the guard grunted—evidently aggravated and not the least suspicious. "You and half the city. Hand over the pass fee, then go."

Pass fee? Matteo frowned. Father had forbidden the pass fee almost a year ago, after Arimna's poor had protested outside the palace gates. But Ekiael shrugged. "Four pieces of silver?"

"A quarter-weight of gold."

Ekiael huffed. "A quarter-weight? Do you think I'm a lord?"

Unmoved, the guard said, "You've two stable hands, and four horses. Pay or stay."

Muttering beneath his breath, Ekiael dropped two bits of gold onto the guard's scale. The guard watched the scale settle, then he tipped the gold into his palm and yelled toward the gate, "Pass!"

Arimna's massive wood-and-iron city gates opened beneath the first hints of dawn. Following Ekiael and Anji, Matteo and Beni mounted their horses, rode out of the city, and met up with Ekiael's household near a designated field. To cover their identities, Ekiael had sent his household through the city gates a few at a time. He greeted them all and motioned them to ride onward. To Anji and Matteo, he said, "We stay alive, seek allies, and oust the usurper!"

Corban nearly spat at Kiyrem's guard who controlled the city's gate. Since when did any man pay to leave a city? No such fee was required in Siphra. Mastering his clawing, snarling temper, he produced the required coin, shoved his seriously depleted money pouch behind his belt, and nodded to the gatekeeper. "Which way did the other hired soldiers ride?"

"South and east toward Arimna. You can't miss it," the guard advised. "Just don't drown in River Tinem along the way. Good luck catchin' the others. Bad lot all."

Bad lot, eh? Then, he, Corban Thaenfall, murderous son of a failed assassin should fit right in.

He chirruped to Ghost, urging the horse southeast, while willing aside his own growing doubts about entering Darzeq.

Chapter 4

Tragobre Fortress rose above the shore of the River Tinem North, a stone-spired crown firmly set upon a hill overlooking the beautiful garden-clad town below. Matteo eyed the grand fortress warily as Ekiael guided their wearied cavalcade over the high five-arched stone bridge spanning the river's wide, sparkling surface. Dalia's lord-father was obviously in residence; Tragobre's crimson banners, embellished with golden fortresses, rippled in the warm evening breeze.

Matteo held the edge of his hood to prevent it from being caught in a sudden gust, and then ducked his head. Two days after the massacre, he was still averting his gaze from everyone. His grandmother's distinctive pale amber eyes—Father's eyes—had become an inherited curse, too easily recognized by half the realm. However, Roi Hradedh, Lord Tragobre, would remember him instantly, though they'd not met for several years.

Might he count on Tragobre's support? What if Darzeq's most honored lord disbelieved Matteo's story?

Matteo snatched back the first unravelings of panic, which picked at the edges of his thoughts.

If Lord Tragobre refused to support Matteo, then he must conceal his wounds and move on quickly. Surely other lords of the First Forum would mandate punishments and sanctions against his family's enemies.

Yet... If the lords of the First Forum believed Matteo, would they condemn and execute Cthar as well as Gueronn? If only Cthar might be proven guiltless, that Matteo's own bloodline would be exonerated—a vain hope, most likely.

Four times, they were halted by guards on the way up to the fortress, and four times Ekiael convinced the guards to allow his household through by revealing his embroidered golden belt with its priestly insignias and talk of urgent matters involving Tragobre's own safety. Who needed to know that the "priest Eki" was actually Darzeq's high priest?

Roi Hradedh's servants met them in his central yard, greeted them politely, and led away their horses—a gesture of courtesy that clearly set Ekiael on edge. Lugging his personal stash of gear, which none of the servants were allowed to touch, Ekiael approached Anji and Matteo and muttered, "The one thing about seeking help here is that we're trapped if he decides to imprison us and turn us over to the First Forum—or worse, to Cthar's questionable mercy. Pray that Lord Tragobre's merciful, even if he rejects our pleas."

Infinite, One Who Sees, reveal the truth to Dalia's father.

If Lord Tragobre rejected Matteo ... scorned his plea.... Matteo set aside the fear and shouldered his own knapsack, which was packed with his few possessions: his purple-and-gold robes, his gold-stamped boots, and his clasps, pins, and insignias—protected inside one of Anji's own jewel boxes. Yet Matteo still wore his gold-studded belt, which held Dalia's note and Sheth's dagger, all hidden beneath a plain linen sash, and concealed by his drab cloak.

Tragobre strode out to the yard and his dark eyebrows lifted at the sight of Darzeq's incognito high priest. Braving his rejection, Matteo looked Dalia's father directly in the face, waiting for him to notice Matteo's presence. Dalia's warm brown eyes and striking features were hinted at in Roi Hradedh's face, but he lacked Dalia's welcoming candor. Within a breath, Tragobre caught Matteo's glance and stiffened like a man facing a viper.

Hopefully Tragobre's reaction was merely due to the shock of Matteo's amber wolf-eyes.

Tragobre motioned to a servant and when the man neared, he muttered a few terse words and nodded the man away.

The servant hurried toward the gatehouse. To order it closed and barred? Matteo clenched his jaw as Tragobre said, "Please come inside."

No welcome there, despite the "please."

They followed the proud lord inside. Lady Sona of Tragobre, slender as Dalia, with flowing curls and sweet features, met Ekiael and Anji kindly. "Welcome, my lord and lady. Why does Darzeq's high priest and his Lady Rhiysa honor us with a visit?"

Tragobre waved aside her gentle question with a warning hand and a silencing glance. Lady Tragobre instantly stepped aside, but her huge eyes widened when she saw Matteo. She bowed to him, and Matteo reciprocated. If only they could talk. If he could enlist Lady Tragobre's support....

In forbidding silence, Tragobre led them through the great hall and up a flight of stairs, into a closed, dim, windowless room. Anji clasped Matteo's arm and then drew near and whispered, "Whatever happens, we won't leave you!"

What if death happened? Disquiet seeped past Matteo's numbness. He hugged his cousin and warned, "If it endangers your life, don't stay. I won't risk you!"

He dared not say more; Tragobre was watching. And he'd evidently heard enough to become alarmed. He tensed further, his gaze a cutting force. "Has something happened to my daughter?"

Matteo caught his breath and kept his voice steady. "No, my lord. Last I knew, she was on her way to Kiyrem. It's my brothers. And my parents."

He lifted his cloak to reveal Sheth's dagger, partially concealed by the wide linen belt. To Matteo's mortification, stabs of grief broke his explanation into jagged pieces. "We were ... in the garden ... celebrating Alvir's naming day...."

Tragobre listened, his stone-gray eyes flickering as Anji and Ekiael added their stories to Matteo's. Ekiael warned, "My lord, if the queen-mother did hide her son's death and plan this rebellion, then the First Forum must act and seize power to support our new king."

Tragobre's wide mouth compressed into a thin, tensed line, then he shook his head. "We have the vote, sir, but not the army. You're inciting a civil war—"

"Yes," Ekiael interrupted sharply. "I'll fight alongside any warrior to save the king!"

Dalia's lord-father snarled, "High priest or not, you won't raise your voice to me beneath my own roof!"

At once, Ekiael inclined his head, contrition and courtesy smoothing his features. "Forgive me, my lord. My voice was raised against the rebels, not you."

Tragobre snapped his attention to Matteo and Anji once more. "These men who invaded the garden. Were they mercenaries?"

The mercenaries from Kiyrem? Matteo swallowed. "I wondered if they were. Dalia was worried—"

"*Dalia* was worried?" Tragobre lifted one eyebrow. "How would you know? Have you been writing to my daughter, sir? And she to you!"

"Yes, my lord."

"Do you have any of her letters about you?"

"One." Matteo slowly withdrew Dalia's last note from the money purse supplied by Ekiael's own wardrobe. Tragobre held out his hand—a silent, unyielding demand. Answering the great lord's hostility with a deliberate show of devotion, Matteo kissed Dalia's written words then handed them over.

Tragobre scanned the message, folded it, and tucked the parchment within his own tunic. Before Matteo could request Dalia's letter to be returned, her father said, "You believe you are asking for my help, sir. But what you're actually requesting is blood. My daughter's and my own. This is not a decision I'll make lightly. You may rest here for the night, but then you'll leave in the morning."

Shamed heat warmed Matteo's face. Fury-strengthened, he glared at Tragobre. "I'll accept that burden, my lord. If my royal father's line is to die, then I'll go. I love your daughter, and I don't want to risk her life. But what I'm truly asking for is justice! And honor! Where's the outcry for my family and our king?"

"Time will tell, sir. Until then, you must wait."

Dalia's father swept from the room and slammed the door, the thud striking Matteo as a weapon. Ekiael placed a heavy, consoling hand on Matteo's shoulder as Anji hugged him.

Ekiael said, "Sir, you've spoken as a king. Whatever Tragobre answers, I pledge you my life, if it's needed. Listen, we'll leave tomorrow and strive to gather true allies and regain the crown!"

Regain the crown.... For Jonatan's youngest and least-prepared son. Matteo's stomach clenched, then hollowed as if he'd been eviscerated—kill from a hunt.

Despite his chilling reception, Tragobre provided Matteo with a small chamber, a puffy bedroll, two coverlets, a full water pitcher and a basin, a basket of fruit, dried meat, grain cakes, and a chamber pot. A chamber pot with no lid.

Matteo frowned at the supposed convenience. Warm as the day was, he could easily imagine the ripening odors he'd inhale by morning. Disgusting. Didn't this mighty fortress boast at least one privy?

He donned his light cloak and sneaked out of his chamber. Evening's crimson rays slanted in through the high windows in the wooden-beamed roof above. By the echoes of voices, the servants were setting up tables downstairs in the hall for the evening meal, which would exclude Matteo, Ekiael, Anji, and their household. Matteo supposed it best that they remain hidden, being such dangerous guests, yet he would have much preferred Tragobre welcoming them openly, in brazen defiance of his lord-father's enemies.

Clearly, that wouldn't happen.

Matteo shoved aside the thought, paused in the upper passageway, and sucked in a deep breath. Well, if Dalia's father did boast a privy reserved for the upper chambers, it must be clean, for Matteo couldn't catch a whiff of it. Hesitant, he studied the nearby doorways, blind arcades, and niches in the walls. Nothing. If he didn't find something soon, he'd have to give in and use the inadequate chamber pot.

A man's low, respectful voice beckoned. "Sir?"

Startled, Matteo turned. Dalia's own steward, Petr, studied him quizzically, his hazel eyes wide as if he doubted his senses. "My lord Matteo? You're here?"

Was Dalia here? As Petr bowed, Matteo gave up hope for that joyous notion. No, Dalia would certainly be in Kiyrem, preparing for her final half-year of schooling. Kiyrem's famous school and restrictive masters didn't allow students to bring servants. Even the wealthiest students, such as Dalia, must wait upon themselves and perform menial labor.

Matteo smiled, but raised a quietening hand. "No one's supposed to know I'm here."

Petr shrugged his narrow shoulders and muttered, "We all know we've guests, sir. Now I know who, and I'll not breathe a word."

Trusting Dalia's servant, Matteo asked, "Petr, if I scratch out a small note, would you deliver it to her in Kiyrem?"

The thin servant straightened. "For you, I'd manage, sir—yet forgetting I'd seen you."

His kindness, the loyalty of his tone.... Matteo swallowed, grateful for even the humblest ally. He'd beg pen and parchment from Ekiael. For Dalia's sake, he'd beg. "Thank you, Petr. Now, where's the nearest privy?"

Matteo rode with Ekiael's household along the dusty, summer-heated road, grimacing as sweat trickled irritatingly down his back beneath his borrowed garments. If Ekiael's household were smaller, Matteo would have suggested riding through the woods to their right—at least the shade would offer some relief from the heat.

Four days of travel had brought them nothing except a worrisome lightness to Ekiael's money pouch and such exhaustion that the entire household had become snappish and irritable.

Beni rode past Anji and Matteo, his earnest gaze fixed upon Ekiael, his grizzled eyebrows fretting creases all the way up his forehead.

Why was the man suddenly so worried?

Anji leaned toward Matteo and muttered, "Something's wrong. Is someone ill?"

Matteo glanced over his shoulder, at the remainder of Ekiael's household. To a man, they were so glum that he didn't want to know what they were thinking, or what they feared. Ekiael eased his horse back and waited for Anji and Matteo. As soon as they were within earshot, the burly high priest muttered, "Beni suspects we're being followed by watchers in the trees alongside this road—he's observed consistent movement within the woods as we've traveled today. The next town's Port Agen. We'll shelter there and decide our safest course."

Anji briefly closed her eyes, as if praying. Then she said precisely what Matteo was thinking. "Sheth told us Eshda was easily defensible."

"We'll consider Eshda later." Ekiael's brusque tone deepened. "After we're certain we've not been followed and found. For fear of that, let's hurry."

Port Agen announced itself with wafting odors of drying fish and dank heaps of canvas spread over the rocks edging the narrow, sandy riverbank far below the main road. Small boats, too, rested on the shores on both sides of the river, where men scraped and painted the hulls and bellowed curses at each other.

The atmosphere remained unchanged as Ekiael led his household into the town's center.

Low, weather-worn houses of wood and stone faced the river, and the long, sand-strewn main road was fronted and supported by a rough-mortared freestone wall that evidently shielded the port from potential floods.

The citizens were quite suited to their town, all blunt, weather-worn, and roughhewn. Even the children were bellowing at each other like packs of little dissenters. Matteo glanced away from several youngsters, who heckled Ekiael's entourage—children were far more apt to comment loudly over Matteo's startling scaln-yellow eyes. Best to look away.

While most of his household rode toward the stables, Ekiael chose the ostensibly cleanest public house, dismounted, and helped Anji down from her horse. As Matteo shouldered his knapsack and Anji's, Beni led their horses off a short distance. Ekiael murmured, "Inside, before the watchers spy us."

The stone floor proved surprisingly clean, and the plastered walls and polished tables added reassurance that travelers might be temporarily safe here. Until Matteo briefly glanced across the room at the massive fireplace—tended by a bored, sweating youth, who was searing fish on a footed iron griddle over the flames—and at a cold-eyed man seated adjacent to the fire. The man eyed Anji, then stared at Matteo as if he might harbor a plague. Or a reward.

Had he been recognized?

Matteo shifted his gaze to the floor and willed himself to remain calm. He sat at a bench along the wall with Anji while Ekiael ordered and paid for food from the house-owner. Ekiael took a share of food out to Beni, then returned to eat with Anji and Matteo. He prayed, then nudged a plank of sliced bread and a dish of olive oil at Matteo. "Eat! How will you claim justice if you're dead?"

No doubt the food was well-prepared, but since watching his brothers die at their own feast, Matteo's appetite had vanished. Beside him, Anji murmured to Ekiael, "My love, we'll try. Grief robs mourners of any taste for life."

Matteo studied his cousin. Anji looked thinner. They'd both lost weight, and Ekiael was correct. Matteo craved justice for his family, but to claim it, he must survive. He challenged Anji. "I'll eat if you do."

They broke off pieces of the bread, dipped them in the herbed olive oil, and Matteo willed himself to swallow bite after bite. When the owner finally brought the charred fish and cold fruit juice to their table, Matteo dutifully forced down his share.

If only that baleful patron near the hearth wouldn't persist in watching them. Matteo mistrusted the man. Why was he wearing those heavy armguards and that faded crimson leather over-vest, which was padded as any battle gear? Yet, despite his thinness and unshaven whiskers, he appeared to be a man of some social standing, not a ruffian, or one of Gueronn's mercenaries.

Unlike the four men filed into the public house, striding like braggarts and clattering their swords. Louts and bullies, all of them. Too similar to the men who'd invaded the garden and butchered his brothers.

Worse, they were watching Anji, Ekiael, and Matteo as closely as predators stalking prey.

One of the men tossed a coin in the air, then caught it. A large coin undoubtedly bearing Father's image. Despite his resolutions to remain calm, a fine sweat prickled over Matteo's skin.

Infinite, One Who Sees Me, let my fears be unfounded.

He stared down at the remains of their meal.

Corban studied the plainly clad young woman, intrigued more than he'd been at any time since Araine's disappearance. Much as this soft-eyed lady tried to remain unnoticed, seated between her two male protectors, she didn't blend within this rustic backwash of a port. He'd venture that she wasn't even the daughter of some native landed nobility. No, not in the least. He could smell highborn, even when highborn needed a bath, as she obviously did.

Why was this young lady here? Why should she try to hide herself? She'd failed. Her pretty olive-skinned face and lustrous eyes, her air of reserve, those beautiful hands and her proud bearing were all too striking to go unnoticed in any setting.

And, obviously, he wasn't the only one interested in this young woman and her companions. The four travel-roughened men who'd just entered this wayside public house and seated themselves were blatantly staring at the noblewoman and her companions. The rustics markedly studied the younger man—also, highborn, Corban noticed. A wary young man, with the most peculiarly amber eyes Corban had ever seen, though he'd swiftly glanced away as Corban studied him.

A diffident, cautious lordling, just old enough to merit being called an adult.

The young nobleman bore Corban's curiosity and the four brutes' stares for a while. But at last, he leaned toward his companions and murmured something. The burly man nodded.

They stood, gathered their gear, and turned to depart.

But three of the four who hadn't bothered to order food—reached for their swords as their leader tossed his coin again and caught the gleaming disc midair.

What scheme lurked in waiting?

Corban watched. Prepared.

A sickening coil of fear tightened about Matteo's lungs as the coin-tosser stood and approached, smiling, while his three companions drew their swords. They'd been recognized, and he was to blame. Worse, until Ekiael's household rejoined him, they were outnumbered. Would these men, these mercenaries, run Matteo through as his brothers had died? And Ekiael, Anji, and Beni alongside him? No. This would not happen. If they dared....

Matteo slid his free hand inside his cloak, gripped the dagger's pommel, and eased it from his belt.

Chapter 5

Corban watched the young highborn woman and her comrades close ranks as the leader of the four asked, "Did you think you'd escaped, one week out from Arimna?"

The burly man scoffed. "Escape? From what? We're a family, journeying together, sir, and our concerns are none of yours, so back away."

"Family?" The leader of the four laughed. "Ah, I believe in families remaining close in all situations. Don't you agree, O prince?"

The diffident youth lifted his chin, turning coldly hostile. "You're mistaken."

Brandishing his coin, the leader snarled, "This says I'm not, sir, so don't bother. Foreigner I might be, but I've been in Arimna long enough to recognize the face on this coin, and your eyes! I've seen the king. Now, what'll we take back to Arimna? Captives or corpses?"

The youth glared at him, his pale eyes flashing, reflective even in the dim room. "Kill me and you'll have nothing but a paltry sum as a reward and your companions might butcher you for that at the first chance!"

"No doubt they might. Unless we spend it first." The troublemaker tucked away his coin, then unsheathed his sword, its metal hissing and flashing in the suddenly quiet room. The house-owner retreated, motioning his curious kitchen staff away. Near Corban, the hearth-boy had stopped tending the fire and faced the commotion, staring eagerly, even as he furtively reached back toward an iron poker.

A deferential-seeming man entered the public house, his shadow filling the doorway, drawing all attention. Not looking away from the sword-wielding renegades, he announced, "My lord, we're a-waiting. All of us!"

A bluff from a loyal servant? Before Corban could decide, the respectful servant and the burly man both drew their swords. Corban stood, dagger drawn.

One of the four charged the servant, sword lifted. The servant roared, parried the initial blow, then tangled with the attacker even as his master slashed toward the hostile leader. As they fought, the soft-faced woman flung a table on its side as a makeshift defense—but a third aggressor snagged the young nobleman's arm, hurling his knapsack to the floor.

The youth resisted briefly, but as Corban charged toward the fray, the young man leaned fiercely into the brute instead of running. His assailant yelled and dropped to his knees. The fourth man lunged for the nobleman, but Corban attacked, fury-strengthened as he spun the man away and pulled his blade along the miscreant's throat. The fourth's sword fell, ringing to the floor, followed by the bleeding corpse. A scuffling behind Corban made him turn, his bloodied dagger aimed toward the noise.

The hearth-boy blinked, dropped his iron fireplace poker, and grinned. Corban turned back to the lordling, even as his burly protector was reaching for him. The assailant lay at the young man's feet, holding his belly, a pool of blood spreading, staining his boots. The brute's gaze faded and his hands relaxed. Had this diffident young nobleman killed him?

Corban stepped toward the nobleman. "Sir..."

Through a slash in his blood-stained cloak, the lordling shifted a crimsoned dagger toward Corban. Prepared to attack him.

Corban stepped back and bowed slightly, hoping to ease his fears. "Are you well?"

The youth wiped his dagger on the dead man, then shook his head, his expression a terrible combination of grief and rage that Corban knew all too well. "No, sir. But thank you for your help and your concern."

The soft-eyed woman hurried toward them. "Cousin, let's leave before the local authorities arrive." To Corban, she said, "Sir, thank you. Don't risk yourself for us any further, lest the mercenaries attack you!"

Corban shrugged at the young woman's warning. He'd been searching for the talked-of mercenaries in order to join their ranks, but perhaps he'd been wrong. Perhaps he'd found the side he ought to fight for. "Thank you, lady. I'm not inclined to sit still while renegades interrupt a decent meal."

He looked across the bloodied scene at the burly man, who knelt in the doorway beside his fallen servant. Without quizzing his own impulsive decision, Corban hurried to help the nobleman carry his servant from the doorway before they were all found and questioned by the authorities. Behind them, the house-owner finally found his cowardly voice and huffed, "Who'll clean up this mess? Who'll answer when we're questioned about these deaths?"

Corban flung his coin pouch at the man. "You will! Take the last of my silver and that of the dead, then hush. These villains got what they deserved for attacking peaceable citizens while you stood by and did nothing!" As the house-owner retreated, Corban crouched beside the brawny nobleman and his servant, who was feebly patting away their hands and muttering. Corban strained to hear his fading words.

Exhaling, the servant pleaded, "Master, I'm done. Save him ... go...." He sucked in a thin breath, his eyelids flickered, then he stilled.

The big man rested a hand on his servant's forehead and whispered, "Depart in peace, to the One Who Sees. Beni, may your death be avenged."

"Sir," Corban muttered, "I'm a stranger, but let me help you. We must leave."

Only a few days in Darzeq and he'd killed yet another man. Plagues! He'd be running for the rest of his life! Corban gritted his teeth, restrained his ire, and helped this stranger rush his servant's body from the public house.

The man hissed, "To the stables, sir, and thanks. Have you a horse? You must escape!"

Yes, well, he'd proven himself quite adept at escape. Corban tightened his grip on the body and slid a glance toward the young noblewoman and the lordling who followed them down the sand-driven stone street. "Yes, I've a horse, sir, in that stable. Let's hurry."

As they entered the stables, scuffing through the straw, the young nobleman said, "I should stay here and give myself up. How many more will die?"

The burly man grunted. "Do you believe she will stop with your death, sir? I think not! For Darzeq's sake, it's best to fight on and claim justice!" He helped Corban swing the body atop an unsaddled horse, watched by a small crowd of stable hands and servants, who drew near, their mouths agape, eyes huge. The young lady waved off the stable hands and beckoned the servants, who were apparently part of her household. "We've been found—we had to defend ourselves. To your horses. Now!"

The servants shoved away hunks of bread and meat that they'd apparently been eating, and then rushed to re-saddle their horses. Corban followed their lead, but he told the nobleman, "If I need to escape, then I'll follow those who know this realm. With your permission, lady, and yours, sirs."

The big man nodded. "Permission granted. With a warning—they're after our blood. You ought to escape from us as much as them."

"Thank you. I'll consider your warning later, if we've time."

Guiding his wearied horse toward their next hoped-for refuge along River Tinem North, Matteo glanced ahead at Beni's rider-less horse. Guilt swathed him yet again like the shroud he should be wearing—dead as his brothers and parents. Because of him, they'd buried Beni last night in furtive haste, as if he'd been a criminal. As if they were all criminals.

This was a nightmare that would not end. No, this nightmare had just begun. And as Ekiael had pointed out, his own death wouldn't end the destruction.

Would civil war begin in Darzeq?

Wars had been fought over far smaller causes, and Cthar's desires could destroy Darzeq. Unless Darzeq's First Forum came together for once, settled upon its core ideals, and ousted their upstart foreign-born queen. Matteo could no longer think of Cthar as his grandmother. He only hoped he could persuade Lord Iydan, his next potential ally, to offer him aid.

Bringing her horse alongside Matteo's, Anji flung him a wearied, gloomy look. "What do you think? Will Lord Iydan match his power to the queen's?"

Recalling the ever-gracious Lord Iydan—named Magni Ormr—Matteo said, "Iydan's ever been the king's ally in the First Forum."

Lord Iydan's noble, ancient bloodlines and diplomatic ways would prove invaluable if he chose to ally himself with Matteo's cause. He closed his eyes briefly, praying. Mighty One, let it be so!

They rode onward, crossing into Iydan's lands, and finally halting before the first of Magni Ormr's gates, sending a servant to request shelter for the night.

While they waited, Matteo surveyed the Ormr clan's chief honor, the fortress he hoped to might be his refuge. Unlike Tragobre's towering fortress, Lord Iydan's main stronghold sloped gently upward from the Tinem North's main road toward an elegant hilltop manor shielded by two extensive decoratively arcaded curtain walls—one low wall halfway up the hill, the other higher, nearer the manor. Impressive as Iydan was, it was only one of many retreats owned by the powerful Ormr clan, for Magni Ormr's wealth was second only to Tragobre's.

If Magni Ormr took in Ekiael's household and Matteo, they'd be secure against any army of mercenaries. If.

The wait stretched on, shaming them all. Even Corban, the proud stranger who'd rushed to Matteo's rescue in the public house at Port Agen, seemed discomfited and glanced about as if he'd rather be anywhere else.

At last, Thaddeus Ormr, one of Tarquin's childhood friends, rode through the gate and over the dry moated bridge, followed by ten horsemen armed for a skirmish. At the bridge's entrance, Thaddeus halted his horse, but didn't dismount, his straight, lean form hinting at ominous formality. His guards urged their restive chestnut and bay horses in a half-circle off to his right.

He nodded to Ekiael, but he stared at Matteo as if doubting his existence. Of course, they hadn't seen each other for more than a year and he looked like a ruffian—not the least bit royal, therefore Matteo couldn't blame him for that disbelieving look and tone. "Matteo?"

"Thaddeus." He urged his horse forward to meet Iydan's heir and to halt alongside him to talk. "Is your lord-father not in residence?"

Thaddeus cleared his throat. "He is, sir. But we've received disturbing news today, and he's chary of all visitors."

Matteo's throat constricted, and his heart threw in an extra beat, marking his fear of the unknown. "What news?"

Slowly, Thaddeus withdrew a parchment from his belt and leaned toward Matteo, explaining as he offered the document, "The First Forum's been disbanded by order of the crown."

Matteo stared at the parchment, stunned. Only one other person could remotely claim enough authority to disband the First Forum. Cthar. Rage welled within, heating Matteo's face as he spoke. "By order of the crown, *not* the king!" Clearly, Cthar was rushing to consolidate her grip on Darzeq.

Thaddeus hesitated, "We've also heard rumors of rebellion, and ... Matteo, how is your lord-father, the king?"

He braced himself and tried to speak swiftly, without remembering. Still, his voice snagged mid-sentence. "He's passed from this life ... as have my brothers and my lady-mother. Anji and I alone escaped the massacre."

Thaddeus looked agitated enough to fall off his horse. He shook his head, and his carefully combed brown hair actually strayed forward onto his tawny face. "Massacre? They're all dead? Tarquin? The king too? It's ... impossible."

"Yet it happened." Matteo forged ahead, enunciating his words. "Anji and I took refuge in a gardeners' shed, then inside my aunt's abandoned rooms. My lord-father died first—we don't know how. The Queen-Mother's own guard led mercenaries throughout the palace in Arimna and slaughtered my family. We believe she intends to rule Darzeq."

Thaddeus hissed in protest, "She's foreign-born! She'll bring her kindred to Darzeq!"

"That's our fear. Thaddeus, beg your lord-father to hear me! To send word to Lord Tragobre and the others, urging them to form an army and act! She won't be able to fight off all of you."

"If she has the southern lords under her feet, she will," Thaddeus argued. "My lord-father will do nothing until he's sure—"

"Which means you're sending me away!" Matteo allowed his bitterness to sharpen his words into singular darts. "I'd hoped for shelter from one who played armies and hunted with my brothers for all these years beneath my royal father's care!"

A shamed look slid over Thaddeus's gracious features. He pleaded, "Matteo, this isn't my decision. My own lord and father has barred all visitors. Until we know which way the southern lords sway in this matter, we dare not commit lives to battle against Arimna. We won't win against its garrisons and the southern lords combined—you know this!"

Ekiael rode forward, causing a stir among Thaddeus's guards, and making the young nobleman straighten. Thaddeus nodded toward Darzeq's high priest, equal to equal. "Sir, I'm not quarreling with the prince, only following my lord-father's orders."

Unappeased, Ekiael challenged, "This prince is now your king! He's Jonatan's only living son! What if your lord-father's orders allow others time to find the king and kill him? What then? You'll be foreign-ruled indeed! Trust me, sir, those foreigners won't tolerate your political and spiritual leanings, and every lord of the First Forum will be cut down, one by one, and their properties parsed out as rewards to the new loyalists. Mark me, you'll regret not sheltering your king! The One Who Sees sent a warning weeks ago, and it was ignored. As a result, the royal family's all but destroyed!"

Thaddeus clenched his fists, angered enough to raise his voice at Darzeq's high priest. "What warning? We've heard nothing!"

Ekiael bellowed in return, "A new prophet, Araine of Belaal, warned Prince Sheth to remain in Belaal and send messages to his family to scatter and hide! He refused to believe the young woman, and look what's happened! Do you think your lord-father's behavior is hidden? His cowardice is seen by The Mighty One! Remember that when your family is staring at ruin! And pray your king survives."

As Ekiael turned his horse aside, huffing to match the beast, Matteo lifted a hand toward Thaddeus and spoke quietly, praying they could at least part on fair terms. "Sir, any of my brothers would have bowed to the wishes of their lord-father under similar circumstances. As would I. Believe me, I understand. But I pray you and the other lords of the First Forum will unite and resist this foreign-born queen. When you do, please seek me out. If I'm still alive, I'll join the battle! Until then, please, demand justice for the murder of Darzeq's royal family, I beg you! Speak for me where I cannot go!"

Thaddeus exhaled and bowed his head. When he dared to look at Matteo again, the full definition of remorse was written upon his expression. "Matteo, I'm sorry! If this decision were mine, you'd be inside our hall now, honored and defended, but I've nothing to say in the matter. Where will you go now?"

"I don't know."

"Has Dalia heard of the massacre?"

Had the whole realm heard of his love for Dalia? "By now, I hope she has—her parents know. But we must leave. Please, sir, speak for me wherever you dare."

He turned his horse away and nodded to his brothers' friend one last time. Thaddeus bowed. Ekiael groaned a noise of complaint heavenward. Anji sniffled. Matteo offered his cousin a reassuring nod and urged his horse onward.

Where to now?

Why ask what he couldn't answer? Matteo willed himself to appear proud and undaunted as he rode away. Let Thaddeus tell his father and Darzeq's other lords that he'd shown spirit. Courage to match any of The Dreaded Seven and their king.

Corban rode after Darzeq's rejected king, his thoughts reeling—mind-numbed as he hadn't been for months. And it wasn't just the confirmation that young Matteo was truly Darzeq's rightful king. Another name spun through his thoughts instead.

Araine. Prophet of Belaal.

She could not be his Araine.

He was mistaken to leap to such a wild conclusion simply because her name was also Araine. Yet, if only it could be true.

Much against his will, Corban's soul sent an unspoken appeal toward The Unnamed One. The Infinite, whose presence seemed so ever near. If she could be yet alive....

No. He was wrong. He would never see Araine again.

Chapter 6

Watched by Sophereth and her assistants, who were shepherding the school's girls into the whitewashed lecture hall—Dalia knelt in Matteo's old, accustomed place set against an eastern wall. It comforted Dalia to think of him as she occupied this rough mat and listened dutifully to Master Parnemedes reciting his traditional welcome to the new students. Though Dalia wished Parnemedes would liven up his speech. Half of Kiyrem's students failed his classes simply because they couldn't stay awake during his lectures.

Pinching her wrist, Dalia focused as the reedy, drawling Parnemedes recited in the low monotone-drone that guaranteed listeners would war against dozing off. "... in addition to this, scribes must be honorable, impartial, and diligent to record the truth without adding their own opinions, or worse, opinions of some paymaster—for then they are nothing but scribblers of invented histories...."

Dalia pinched herself again. Just as a nap threatened, the school's youngest master, Kurcus, sidled into the room, his scholar's face gawping, astonished as a hooked fish snagged from his placid stream. Moving stealthily, as if creeping would prevent everyone in the room from staring all the more, Kurcus handed Dalia two parchments—one sealed and inscribed from Tragobre, the other from Matteo, opened and half-crushed.

Kurcus had read and besmirched this note from Matteo?

Dalia longed to wring the master's neck as a poulterer would a scrawny bird's. Yet, to be fair, the school was pledged to prevent students from receiving notes from unapproved correspondents. At least Kurcus had actually handed her the parchment. Dalia bit her lip. Hard. She must behave; Sophereth was suspicious. Smoothing Matteo's note—so recently touched by his own hands—Dalia read.

From Matteo of Darzeq to Dalia of Tragobre, in Kiyrem,

Beloved, I've no time to write anything but the terrible truth. My lord-father is dead and embalmed—days ago, without our knowledge—and my lady-mother and brothers were massacred in Arimna by the Lady Cthar's own guard, Gueronn, and his mercenaries. Anji and I have fled with her lord-husband, seeking allies for our cause. If I do not survive, know that I cherished your beloved presence in my life. Pray for us and for Darzeq! I shall send word to you at the first chance—we are riding north to Iydan and possibly to Eshda. My love is ever yours,

Matteo of Darzeq, written by my own hand at Tragobre.

Dalia stared at his clear, Kiyrem-trained script, unable to comprehend his news. Tears blurred the letter, and she closed her eyes hard, refusing to allow herself a much-needed fit of weeping. The king and Matteo's brothers couldn't be dead. Nor the queen.... Yet Matteo's own handwriting proclaimed this news, and Matteo wouldn't jest about such deaths to save his life.

She opened her eyes, mopped fresh tears, read the note again, and shook her head. Master Kurcus stood beside her, blatantly reading the note once more, his expression still hooked and brought shockingly to ground.

Fighting to organize her thoughts, Dalia sniffled, dabbed her eyes with a corner of her mantle, then took a deep breath. Matteo had been at Tragobre Fortress. For how long? Why hadn't her parents compelled him to stay, instead of dashing off to Iydan lands? As if Lord Iydan had the gumption to do more than look formal and prance around as ambassador to Belaal. Surely Father could be of more assistance to Matteo!

Master Parnemedes was also staring, his droning lecture conspicuously dangling, unspoken and unfinished. Dalia bowed to him and retreated from the stone hall to the school's central courtyard, trailed by Kurcus. In the sunlight, Dalia turned and scowled at the distraught master. "Do you wish to read my lord-father's note as well, sir?"

Kurcus protested, still flustered, "Lady Dalia, it's hardly my fault that I was compelled to read that first contraband note, and you know it. But is the note true?"

"It must be. It's Matteo's writing, and he would never set ink to parchment with such a tale if it weren't true." Particularly not relaying the massacre of his entire family. Oh, beloved Infinite, how could this be true? Dalia blinked down another freshet of tears and gulped. She must be coherent, for Master Tredin swept from the hall, his expression and words thunderous in the evening's slanting sunlight.

"Kurcus, your contract can be revoked for halting a lecture so conspicuously—don't think Parnemedes won't mention it. We'll have to listen to him for weeks concerning this slight. Young lady, are you well? You look green."

Dalia handed him Matteo's note, warning, "Sir, I'm leaving. I'll take Matteo's letter and leave Kiyrem the instant you've finished reading it."

"Leave?" Kurcus spluttered. "Why ... you can't! It's ... it's forbidden and dangerous! Clearly the mercenaries have been unleashed upon Darzeq!"

Sophereth had joined them, gliding from the lecture hall, regal as any royal. "What's fetched such disorder? Sir?" She looked her husband in the eyes. Clearly unwilling to speak the appalling news aloud, Tredin handed her the note. Sophereth read it and placed her free hand at the base of her throat as if she could free herself from the near-strangling grip of such ghastly events.

As her teachers stared at each other in horrified silence, Dalia swallowed her unspent tears and held out one hand. "I'm leaving. Now. Give me his note and permit me to pack my gear as you send for the guards."

Tredin recovered and glowered at her, his most severe look—just short of threatening a beating. "We don't feed you tripe, young lady, so why are you talking it? You are forbidden to leave."

"By whose order? I've the emergency funds my lord-father placed here for me. I'll hire guards and then go. Forgive me, but I must find Matteo."

Sophereth cut her off with a testy glance and a meaningful nod toward Lord Tragobre's note. "What do your parents say?"

What if she didn't wish to share Father's news with them? Dalia hesitated, then opened the note. Best to thrash it all out now. Her teachers would know the truth soon enough.

Father's slash-ridden script sprawled across the entire parchment, betraying his agitation when he'd written this note.

Daughter,

By now you've heard the news from Lord Matteo concerning Arimna—I know he has corresponded with you—and now you know the king, the queen, and the young Lord Matteo's brothers have all perished. While I perceive your tender sympathies toward Lord Matteo, I require you to think coldly and practice restraint. Tragic as this news is for us, and for Darzeq, we cannot commit ourselves to action until we know that the southern lords will also support his cause.

To commit our household and all Tragobre's people to Lord Matteo's defense—and to protest what has happened without knowing the truth—is to risk our lives, perhaps in vain. Until we have proof of the assassins' identities, we must watch, wait, and remain impartial. Furthermore, I forbid you to communicate with Lord Matteo, lest you be reckoned a traitor. Again, with all the love and concern I bear as your lord-father, I command you to think coldly and practice restraint. For your own safety, remain in Kiyrem until I summon you.

Your lady-mother sends her love and greetings and expects that you write her soon.

Farewell.

By my own hand, written and sealed.

Roi Hradedh, Tragobre

Dalia held the note carefully, lest she lose her temper altogether and tear it to bits. Yes, as Father had commanded, she would try to think coldly and practice restraint. But how could her lord-father restrain himself so callously, then judge Matteo as a liar and possible traitor, after everything Matteo had suffered? Worse, Father had evidently turned him out of Tragobre fortress with no help. All this while ignoring the fact that Matteo was the rightful king!

Dalia growled her frustration, folded the note and bowed to her teachers. "I'll remain—for now. But, with your permission, may I be excused today's lectures? I must go to the market."

Sophereth nodded, and actually appeared sympathetic. "Yes. I'll accompany you."

Dalia hid a protest by allowing herself a bout of tears. By the time she finished her shopping, Sophereth would think Dalia an absolute zany. Short of confessing her plans, how could anything but insanity explain her intended purchases of seven-dozen lengths of parchment, endless windings of cordage, numerous pots of ink, and an entire box of wax wafers? Well, for Matteo's sake, Dalia could endure being named a zany, for she wouldn't confess her plans.

And if anyone interfered with Dalia's strategies to help Matteo, then she'd set the wax afire and flee to Eshda.

Swiping her sleeve across her wet face again, Dalia followed Sophereth out of the courtyard. Eshda. Yes, she must go to Eshda.

Corban sat near Matteo, Anji, and Ekiael, sharing the coarse journey cakes of grain, fruit, and nuts that had become the staple of their fugitive route from River Tinem North. Corban had enjoyed the cakes well enough, but after several days of eating the things almost exclusively, he was craving seared meat. Stews. Roasted vegetables, and fresh hot bread—none of which would leave him picking seeds and dried fruit from between his teeth for the remainder of the night.

As if he'd been saving the fruit and seeds for snacks.

Finished, Corban shoved the last allotted grain cake into his knapsack, then studied the others, who'd been wearied to silence. Matteo was staring up at the stars and brooding, Anji was leaning against Ekiael, and Ekiael was finishing his ration of journey cakes, gently encouraging the exhausted Anji to do the same.

Corban guessed that Ekiael was some sort of priest to this unknown deity—the One Who Sees. Or the Mighty One—Ekiael prayed using both names. However, for a priest, Ekiael was a sensible man, good with a sword, and a kind enough master that his servants followed him on this bleak journey without complaints. But, for the first time on their journey, they were risking a full night of rest. With the sun setting and with his own emotions becalmed enough to talk, Corban asked, "Sir, Priest, what do you know of Belaal's prophet, Araine?"

Ekiael shook the few crumbs from his full robes and shrugged. "I don't know much, sir, except that her name is Araine, and she's never been mentioned until Lord Sheth returned from Belaal."

Matteo cleared his throat and looked from the stars to Ekiael and Anji, then to Corban. "All we know, sir, is what my brother Sheth told me just before he died. Araine, Belaal's new prophet, warned my brother not to return to Darzeq. Apparently, he resisted her suggestion, and she pleaded with him to warn us that disaster was about to strike us all, and Sheth would die. She also warned him to save the youngest. Me, Anji, and her baby. This much, Sheth did—forcing me to swear we'd run. And hide."

Like a coward.

Corban heard his unspoken thought at the end, and Matteo's rueful expression emphasized his supposed failing. Did the young man regret being his family's sole survivor? To distract him, and to satisfy his own curiosity, Corban asked, "Did he mention this Prophet Araine's appearance?"

Darzeq's uncrowned king rubbed one hand over his face as if he'd rather not remember his last conversation with his brother. "Sheth described her as my age. A lovely, sheltered young woman who believes her own visions. Belaal's king obviously believes her as well, for she is his official Prophet of the Infinite."

"May His Name be blessed forever," Ekiael added, as Anji murmured drowsy agreement.

The Infinite. All the breath left Corban, drawn away by the cold shock of that Name—the last word he'd heard Araine utter before she vanished.

Infinite.

Apparently not noticing Corban's shock, Ekiael mused aloud, "Speaking of blessing, Corban, thank you for joining us though we're a motley band of refugees. You embody your name."

Relieved by the distraction, Corban mustered a breath. "My name? My parents named me Corban because my hair was black when I was born—that's all my name means. Black-haired."

"In your country, perhaps," Ekiael agreed, his words a pleasant rumble in the darkening evening. "However, in Darzeq, in the language of the priests, 'Corban' means, 'a gift from the Infinite—one that is consecrated to Him.' Interesting..."

Consecrated to Him? No. A feverish chill crept over Corban's flesh and he suppressed a shudder. Was this why he felt so pursued? Did the Infinite intend to claim his heart? His soul?

"I'll continue with 'dark-haired.'" The words escaped Corban before he could halt them. Noting his listeners' shocked gazes, he explained, "The Infinite wants nothing to do with me."

To the Infinite, Corban argued, *Why should You? Everything I've loved is gone—to You! Don't You have enough? Why should You call to me?*

Almost fatherly, Ekiael interceded, halting Corban's inner spate of fury. "This is where your battle begins. You must accept that He loves you as His own child. Until your last breath, His hand and His Spirit are extended toward you. It's not weakness to believe in Him and accept His call—it's courage!"

"As you say, sir." To cut off the discussion he'd so foolishly instigated, Corban drew his cloak around himself, settled into the coarse ground-cover and closed his eyes, seeking sleep. Yet inwardly his battle raged amid a silent storm.

Even as a calm, quiet voice beckoned.

Will you be My servant?

Follow Me.

A tap at her cell door startled Dalia from prayers. Barefoot, she stood, gathered her gown and robe, then opened her door and peeked outside.

Sophereth lifted an eyebrow at her, as if still concerned for her sanity. Dalia's stomach knotted its dread as Sophereth slipped into her cell and looked around, her searching glance finally resting on the heap of parchment, wax, cords and ink, all stashed in the far corner of her stark, lamp-lit cell. "Are you well, young lady?"

"No. But I must endure, and so I shall." Matteo needed her.

"Are you not writing?"

"I will. I could write volumes concerning my grief, yet never express what we've lost."

"Volumes." Sophereth looked skeptical. "You've enough parchment there to write your own library."

"Perhaps by the time it's finished my mourning will be done."

Sophereth looked over Dalia's head, toward the narrow shuttered window, her gaze seeing beyond it briefly, to another time and place, to some grief of her own. "Mourning is never finished. It's the tide of an ocean, the current of a river overflowing, then ebbing once more. Your task is to navigate those waters throughout life. And to find the strength to swim. If you need help amid the current, you come to me, young lady. Do you hear me? Never enter deep waters alone."

Dalia's throat burned as her eyes stung then welled with tears. How cruel-sweet of this dour schoolmistress to make her cry, and then hug her and pat her back tenderly as if Dalia were a child again. To make her think of the king and queen, who'd ever been gracious and pleased to see her. To make her think of Matteo's brothers, who were so like the brothers she'd never had. And to make her think of Matteo, abandoned....

As Dalia's sobs faded, Sophereth stepped away. But she gave Dalia a warning look. "If you've any fears, young lady, come find me, no matter what hour of the day or night."

"Yes, lady. Thank you." Dalia wiped her face and worked up a half-smile to reassure her doubtful teacher.

As Sophereth closed the door, Dalia paused to question herself. Was she right to sail into this course she'd decided upon amid the overflowing currents of her furious grief? Would her actions help Matteo, and Darzeq?

Perhaps she should instead ask herself if it was right to allow Darzeq to continue in ignorance, leaving Matteo bereft of family, friends, allies, and justice.

Exhaling, Dalia gathered her supplies, sliced the lengths of parchments into roughly halved squares and opened her travel desk. To pay out her grief and to fight for justice, she must wield the weapons of a scribe—an anonymous scribe.

Mourn, Darzeq! Your noble king and his sons have fallen.
Weep as the yellow-eyed queen rejoices, this sovereign of the Chaplet Temple.
Darzeq, who will demand justice when the venomous she-scaln feeds upon your remains?
Who will lament for your six golden lords, slaughtered by her word?
Your future slain by her ambition.
Must the mighty stand silent, shamed and stripped of honor, while Darzeq's uncrowned king, calls for shields and swords?
Darzeq, remember your glory....

Scrawling her grief and outrage onto parchment after parchment, Dalia wrote the lament, then copied it repeatedly, signing each note, For Matteo of Darzeq.

One Who Sees, protect him!

A jolt snapped Matteo from a sound sleep. Who had swatted him awake? He lifted his head and looked around. Ekiael's men—the entire household—lay sleeping exactly as he'd noted just before closing his eyes. Ekiael, Anji, and Corban also slumbered on just as they'd been.

Only the stars had shifted, and dawn's first golden hues seeped through the fringes of the trees around them—revealing the dark silhouettes of perhaps ten approaching warriors, their weapons readied. Too near for Ekiael's household to flee to their horses and escape unharmed.

Matteo rolled over and shoved at Corban, then Ekiael, calling out. "We're found! Seize your weapons!"

Chapter 7

A rude shove jolted Corban from the depths of sleep, and Matteo's voice reached him thorough a dream-muddied haze. "We're found! Seize your weapons!"

Found.... Corban rolled over, stood, and drew his sword, its blade's gleam too harsh in the morning light. Sleep's dullness muddled his thoughts and his stance. If he must fight now, he'd already lost.

Not daring to close his eyes against the blinding dawn, and the surreal shadows outlined within, Corban prayed in silent desperation.

Infinite, save us! Help me.

Matteo stood and drew his sword—its glittering ceremonial insignias seeming to draw the morning light, to declare his identity to the approaching assassins. Corban stood, wavering on his feet, obviously sleep-dazed. But then he shook his head and straightened, turning cold-eyed and alert. Beyond him, Ekiael stood as a wall before Anji, who braced herself like a small soldier, though she had no weapons.

Matteo challenged the invaders who'd entered the small clearing, their faces and swords now visible. "Identify yourselves!"

A stocky, grizzle-bearded man yelled, "We are defenders of the crown! Identify yourselves!"

Before Matteo could defy them, Ekiael bellowed, "We are peaceable citizens! Since when does Darzeq attack its own people?"

"If they are declared traitors, they must die," the stocky man snarled. "We are seeking Matteo of Darzeq and his companions, who slaughtered four men in Port Agen."

Matteo flexed his fingers over his sword's grip, readied. No one had spoken his name in Port Agen, yet these men knew he'd been there. Undoubtedly they'd been sent by the queen, and were comrades to the fallen four in Port Agen. One of the men caught Matteo's gaze and motioned one leather-guarded hand. "Him."

Cthar's traitorous yellow eyes had giving him away, of course. Why had he looked at the mercenaries? Yet he couldn't hide forever. Matteo nodded to the discerner, his intended killer. "Yes, it's me. And what do you care, mercenary? Did you help to massacre my brothers?"

The mercenary offered a mock bow, widening his eyes, speaking through bared teeth. "We all have our orders, Lord-prince Matteo. Ours is to bring your corpse to Arimna, and yours is to die."

This man had helped to kill Tarquin and the others. Matteo ground his teeth and wrenched open the front of his tunic, baring his throat. He spat toward the man, then cried, "I am Darzeq's king, thanks to you and your murderous comrades! If you kill me, then take my corpse to the degenerate queen-mother and tell her I spat on her name and yours, if you dare, you stinking scaln! If you survive! Otherwise, may your guts rot and serve as pickings for animals!"

Roaring a guttural battle cry, the mercenary charged toward Matteo, followed by his comrade-mercenaries. Ekiael's household converged as one force. And, in silent answer to the mercenary's battle cry, Corban raised his sword and brought its pommel down like a stone onto the maddened mercenary's helmet, felling him with one lethal strike, crumpling the man's helmet into his skull.

Even as the mercenary dropped dead before Matteo, Corban swung his sword upward in a vicious arc and speared a second mercenary, then flung the man's body toward two others, hurtling all three to the ground, where Ekiael's household guards finished them.

Corban charged the remaining six, raging his own battle cry, an unstoppable force—leaving Matteo no choice but to follow.

Corban slashed toward the fifth mercenary, seeing with perfect clarity the man's startled flinch, his too-slow reaction to the killing flash of the blade. Corban felled his enemy with one cut to the neck, drew in his sword to avoid the young king, then spun about, knowing his next target approached, sensing with exactitude where his blade must angle and shear as it met enemy flesh. The sixth fell, and three others fled, pursued by Ekiael and his men. The last man, the leader, stood his ground, sword held almost plow-like as if he hoped to take Corban with a gut-piercing thrust—too slowly.

Corban drove his sword down onto his foe's blade, shoving its tip toward the morning-damp ground, then he lunged and bashed the hilt from the man's grasp onto the grass. Tramping down the man's sword, Corban lifted his own blade and drove it into his adversary, dispatching him within a breath. Silence reigned in the field. Corban wiped his blade and stared about, seeing the answer to his fragment of a prayer—his first half-trusted plea to the Infinite. He'd sped the thoughts toward the Infinite with no hope. No surety that he wasn't being a pathetic fool.

This, then, was this His answer? This bizarre swiftness...

"Why?" Half-dazed, Corban turned and looked about. Matteo was staring at him—a young man gawking at something too mysterious to believe. Corban scuffed a booted foot at the tenth mercenary's trampled sword. "Weapons and wealth to the victors. What we cannot use, we'll sell."

Still gazing as if Corban were an apparition, Matteo lowered and then sheathed his gleaming, unused sword. "Are you wounded at all, sir?"

Corban returned his sword to its scabbard, and then moved his arms and legs to show Matteo that he was unharmed. "If I've a scratch, sir, I don't feel it."

The king gusted out a disbelieving breath. "What are you? Those men fell before you like sheared grass and shrubs—all of them root bound and unable to escape you."

Now, Corban felt the first weakening in his legs. His arm muscles quivered as if drained of blood. Though he suddenly longed to do nothing but collapse and rest, he braced himself and held his ground. "Those men were slow, sir."

"No." Matteo shook his head. "They weren't. You were too fast. Beyond any fighter I've ever seen, and I've seen enough, I guarantee you. My brothers and I often attended the champion fights in Arimna."

Overwhelmed by the tremors, Corban sat and concentrated on breathing. Ekiael and the others were returning, victorious, yet hushed. All staring at Corban, exactly as Matteo had stared. But Ekiael kneeled before Corban, placed his sword between them, then lifted his hands and gaze skyward. "Mighty One, You-Who-See-Us ... hear the praises of Your servants! We thank you for blessing this man to Your purpose and our help! May Your Name be glorified through his service to You!"

Corban covered his face with his hands, struggling to master his disgraceful weakness and confusion. How could this be true? He, Corban Thaenfall, had bowed to his Enemy, the Infinite, for *one* breath of a prayer during a sleep-blurred panic.

Then, inexplicably, he'd felled five men in an impossibly short time. Now he'd returned to his previous state of exhaustion. Accepting divine intervention was more logical than trusting his own sleep-deprived perceptions.

Why had he surrendered? Even briefly ... to Him. In Siphra, he'd be attacked for such a betrayal of their goddess, Atea.

"Sir?" Anji's gentle voice compelled him to look at her. She knelt beside Ekiael, her soft lovely face fretted with genuine concern. "Clearly you're shaken, and you must rest. Please, would you drink a tonic if I prepared it? We can't offer you much, just honey water with olive-leaf extract—but it should help until we've time to prepare or buy a full meal."

Reduced to tonic-taking, Corban nodded, all pride cast off.

He wouldn't risk another prayer.

As Corban rested and Ekiael's servants packed the mercenaries' weapons, hunting gear, cloaks, and coins under Anji's quiet leadership, Matteo walked with Ekiael to saddle their horses. Ekiael murmured, "There's something of a prophet in you, Sire. You wished those mercenaries' bodies picked apart by animals, and so it shall be. It'll be days before anyone finds them in this remote place."

"It was a chance wish, nothing more." And he wanted to think no more of his foul temper. Casting a backward glance at Corban, Matteo changed the subject. "My lord-priest, what did you think, when you saw him fighting?"

Ekiael snorted and retrieved a fleece pad, settling it onto the nearest horse—never mind that the padding and horse might be mismatched. "When he attacked those first five men ... I couldn't believe it. He didn't seem mortal. I'm convinced that the One-Who-Sees sent Corban to us for a purpose—perhaps for Corban's own soul's benefit and our survival. Who can know all His ways?" He flopped a blanket onto the padding, then paused. "Are you uneasy about him?"

Matteo lifted what he hoped was the appropriate saddle onto the horse. "I've wondered who he truly is. We know nothing of him, yet he's willing to fight for us. By his behavior and apparel—worn though it is—he appears highborn, not an ordinary mercenary. Furthermore, Anji trusts him. And, clearly, the Mighty One has some role planned for him. For all of us." Checking the girth straps, he added, "I hope he stays. After this morning, however, I'd never fight him."

He cinched the girth strap, wound its excess securely through the loops, as his brothers had taught him, and then moved on to help Ekiael with the next horse. "If we're continuing north, then we've a few more strongholds and lords to petition."

"If we dare," Ekiael groused. "By now, every lord who's enough of a lord to pose a threat to the queen has likely heard that the First Forum is dissolved. We should approach the remaining lords when we're well-rested and prepared to flee as they backhand us. I don't trust any of them."

Matteo grabbed another saddle, matching it to the current horse's bridle. "Then we take refuge in Eshda."

"Why Eshda?"

Good question. Matteo shrugged. "Sheth mentioned Eshda. He said it's defensible. That tells me we've some sort of stronghold there, ready and waiting."

Ekiael frowned as he threaded the saddle's straps through its iron cinches. "Yes, there's a stronghold, held for the crown by a steward. However, it's been out of favor for more than thirty years, and with good reason. Eshda's a burning land, and even the water must be cooled before it can be consumed. I'd wager Eshda's steward doesn't yet know what's happened."

For the first time since being chased from Ormr's stronghold in Iydan, Matteo allowed himself a sliver of hope.

"All the better. We'll take possession of the place in my lord-father's name, and in my own, and we'll pray it's as defensible as Sheth believed."

Then, with any blessings, he might receive letters from Dalia.

One-Who-Sees-Us, bless her. Save her from this disaster that's befallen me.

Dalia nodded to Sophereth's dubious, pink-faced assistant as they halted outside Kiyrem's Hall of Scribes. "Wait here, please. I'll return directly." Armed with her parcel and her money purse, Dalia entered the building's plain stonework antechamber. Two scribes looked up at her from their cushioned seats, and then returned to work, writing letters dictated by their clients, who sat nearby. Beyond the scribes, Dalia spied the local couriers, all slouched and napping behind pillars as they awaited commissions. She approached the eldest, an ordinary man who could have been any properly armed wayfarer on the road. "Sir?"

The man raised black, caterpillar-fuzzy eyebrows at her, seeming astonished. Dalia stepped away from the others, cradling her parcel. Was she right to do this? To become an anonymous scribbler of deliberately offensive pamphlets? Not to mention sending this ordinary man off on such a dangerous mission? "Do you have time for an extended mission, sir?"

The courier bowed and spoke quietly—the voice of a man used to keeping confidences. "For you, young Lady Hradedh, I do."

Dalia almost stepped back. "You know my name?"

"Lady, anyone in Kiyrem who doesn't know your name ought to be flung outside the gates after double the pass-fee."

She liked his kindly expression, the way his brown eyes crinkled at the corners. Returning his smile, she warned, "I beg you to forget my name now. Even my face. I am anonymous for this mission to the realm. Have you heard the news?"

The black-caterpillar eyebrows lifted and the courier's face brightened, though he clearly tried to mute his gleeful reaction. "Are you to marry our Lord Matteo?"

Our Lord Matteo. The man spoke like a subject loyal to the king—an avid follower of the royal family who delighted in Kiyrem's open secret of Dalia and Matteo's love. Did she dare confide in him further? "Eventually, we hope. But these notes have everything to do with his wellbeing. Please betray no emotion. Just listen...."

She told him everything, grateful that her murmured warning snagged only once, and that she was able to swallow the tears that threatened and blurred her vision. She even dared to recite her dreadfully penned lamentation in a whisper, which he strained to hear. By the time she'd finished, the courier's eyebrows had merged in a frown, and his kindly smile tightened to cold, suppressed fury. "If this is true, lady, I'll take half the pay for the honor of spreading this news. That foreign woman's been a thorn in Darzeq's rump since the day she set foot in our land!"

"Thorn indeed." What a rebel-heart lurked here! Dalia handed the man a drab, heavy little bag of coins. "Most men would charge double the fee, sir, which is what I'll pay. Half now, half when you return. I've calculated your journey and so will expect your return within three weeks. Go down the river road, as far south as it takes you, and begin posting your messages there. One to each city gate at night. Avoid being seen, and please be safe."

"May the Mighty One shield us," her courier murmured. "Farewell for three weeks, Lady Hradedh."

He departed, the first soldier in her anonymous insurrection against Cthar.

One-Who-Sees, thank You! Please, protect us all.

Finished with his evening meal of seed cakes and dried meat, Corban stood, sauntered over to Ekiael and sat beside him in the grass. The priest was watching Matteo, who sat cross-legged in the dusk, quietly conversing with Ekiael's guards. Corban nodded toward the young king, seeking answers to his private plague of questions. "I've seen a dynasty wiped out in Siphra's own revolution. Few mourned, apart from my family and other like-minded individuals. Despite our anger, the remainder of Siphra's people continued life almost as usual—and one of my own cousins actually married the new king. Kings come to power and then die, ultimately forgotten. Why is this young man's line so vital?"

Ekiael gazed up at the stars as if seeking the answer. At last, he said, "His father's bloodline must survive, for it's the Infinite's sign to us—His promise of grace toward Darzeq and to every mortal who's ever drawn breath. A sign that He loves us though we are weak and imperfect and don't reciprocate His love. Through this downfallen dynasty, the Infinite will ultimately send a high-king to save us all. Then, it will be known that He-Who-Sees is faithful to His people and His promises endure forever."

"And what of us who aren't His people," Corban demanded. His words sounded testy—sharp even to his own hearing. "Those of us who declared Him the enemy?"

"You are the ones who declared your Creator an enemy, sir. It's a one-sided battle you're fighting, and you won't win. Yet He offers you limitless grace! Call to Him, and you'll find mercy, Corban. Haven't you sensed the Infinite's Spirit waiting for you?"

Yes. And following with a persistence that gnawed at his conscience, even as it riled his blood. Corban muted an inward growl of frustration. He disliked this … feeling obligated to answer to the One he'd scorned and loathed for most of his life. Nevertheless....

Darzeq's high priest added, "Not to mention His willingness to answer your first breath of a true prayer toward Him. Many of the faithful would envy you, including me. Except that I'm too grateful for envy. You've been a blessing to us."

As Corban glared toward the grass, Ekiael shifted, then mused aloud, "I wondered why it should be so. Why you, a haughty highborn lord—and don't deny it—a hater scornful of others, should be granted an answer so swiftly, while many of us have prayed for what seems ages. Is it due to your own nature? Your impatience and pride, perhaps? How great He is to see all our faults and turn them to His own good, in His own time! How amazing that He accepts us the instant we first call to Him."

Accepts? Corban shook his head. To be divinely accepted, with an alarming swiftness that the goddess Atea had never once employed, was unimaginable.

He bowed his head toward Ekiael, then stood. "Excuse me."

Corban stalked away. To his chagrin, the priest's words lingered, humming and buzzing within his thoughts like aggravatingly bright and persistent insects. Scowling, he swatted them off. And he complained in silence to the Infinite. Did I ask to be accepted by You? Did I ask to become Your weapon?

He'd prayed only for safety.

He'd never asked to become this priest's example of divine favor and acceptance—an unnerving, burdensome and virtuous status he'd never be able to uphold in Darzeq.

He would stay only until the king was safe in Eshda, then he'd depart Darzeq forever.

Chapter 8

Swiping raindrops from his face, Matteo glanced over his shoulder at Ekiael's household—the bedraggled, rain-soaked lot—and he pitied them all. He didn't deserve their loyalty. Had it been only four days since the morning attack? It seemed they'd been riding for years.

Half-ready to surrender, Matteo exhaled a plea to the sullen, midday skies. "Infinite, grant us favor! Let Lord Losbreq and his people offer us shelter."

If Losbreq refused them entrance to his fortress, then their plan was to huddle down wherever they might shelter for the night, cross the northern branch of River Tinem again in the morning, and head for Eshda. But after Eshda, what then?

He'd be the uncrowned king of a burning city in north-most Darzeq. He'd—

Matteo's bay shook out his wet mane, disrupting Matteo's gloomy thoughts with a spattering of droplets. Matteo smoothed the bay's wet coat, then urged him ahead to join Ekiael, Anji, and Corban at a curve in the muddied road. In silence, they rounded the curve, cleared the trees, and Ekiael grunted at the view. Qamrin's fortress glowered down upon them from beneath its murky blanket of clouds, its banners clinging in sopped ropes to the staffs above Qamrin's conical slate-roofed towers.

They rode up the muddied road, which gave way to a graveled incline, leading to a barren stone path that ended beneath the gatehouse. Ekiael, being naturally gifted with the loudest voice called up, "Greetings! Matteo, son of Jonatan, requests shelter—with the Lady Anji Rhiysa and Ekiael of Arimna and his household!"

Matteo studied the guards above, lurking behind the bow-loops, evidently consulting with each other. One bellowed, "Matteo, last-born son of Jonatan of Darzeq?"

Biding for patience, Matteo lifted one hand in greeting. "Yes, I am Matteo of Darzeq. Will Lord Losbreq offer us shelter?"

Silence answered, merging into an interminable wait that terminated with a bellowed challenge. "Who are you, Matteo of Jonatan, that I should risk all for you, when another wears the crown and commands the garrisons in Arimna?"

Cthar had already warned and subjugated Losbreq? Matteo nearly ground his teeth, feeling his heartbeat quicken to a near-killing speed. He yelled toward the crenellated tower above, "For how long, ask your lord-master, does he bow to that foreign queen? Will he kiss the feet of her relatives when they bring their self-crowning beliefs to Darzeq? Will he rejoice when his lands are taken—when he is paraded like a tamed beast through Arimna to the Chaplet Temple? Support my cause and be rewarded, not ruined!"

Another chafing silence answered, broken by the renewed spattering of raindrops pelting Matteo's cloak and the stones around them on the road. Then, a downrush of arrows slashed from the tower, cutting past Matteo's horse and spiking the ground. To his left, Anji screamed as Ekiael fell to the ground, an arrow angled down into his chest.

Corban motioned to the servants, yelling, "Ride! Return to the river road and wait!" He steadied Ghost, who curveted amid the turmoil. The instant he was sure his startled horse wouldn't trample him, Corban dropped to the ground and rushed toward Anji and the fallen Ekiael. Matteo joined them and, together, they grabbed Ekiael, who was desperately wheezing for air. The burly man waved them off, sucked in a harsh breath and rasped, "Horse!"

As Corban caught the priest's skittish horse, Ekiael dragged himself to his feet, aided by Matteo and the tearful Anji. Still wheezing, the big man wrenched the angled arrow from his chest, motioned them all toward their own mounts and helped Anji back into her saddle. "Ride!" He lumbered to his own gray, mounted it stiffly and wound the reins through his fists. "That was a warning shot. Let's away before it's serious."

Matteo argued, "Wasn't an arrow to the chest serious enough?"

"I'm alive, Sire, and that's enough for now!" Ekiael turned his horse aside, waiting for the king and Corban, his temper visible, yet controlled. The priest seemed well—merely ashen and winded from the fall. Corban obeyed and remounted Ghost, to follow Matteo.

The king called to Ekiael, "Are you bleeding?"

"We'll decide later," Ekiael snapped. "First, let's get you to a safe distance."

They returned to the river road, and urged the household north, all of them looking back now and then to be sure they weren't pursued. By the time Corban felt reasonably certain that Lord Losbreq had remained holed up in his keep, Ekiael was grumbling loudly enough to reassure his entire household. "Call me deluded; I should have known! Losbreq agreed with your lord-father politically and honored him as Darzeq's king, but never liked him."

Anji huffed, "Sir, why didn't you tell us?"

Ekiael waved one broad hand, conveying frustration. "I was trying to remain hopeful."

Matteo threw Corban an impatient glance then called out to the priest, "Might we be hopeful that you'll survive your wound?"

"Oh, rest yourselves, you worry-warts!" Ekiael halted and pulled off his cloak, unbelted and loosened his outer tunic, and then removed a quilted vest that would have smothered any man. A gold breast-plate garnished with jeweled plaques and inscriptions gleamed at Corban, startling him with its brilliance. The priest handled the breast-plate like the amazing treasure it was, unbuckling it only halfway to loosen another vest and tunic beneath, revealing his wound. "It's nothing. See? One thorn-stick and a bruise." He motioned to Anji, who drew her horse alongside his, eying the wound dubiously.

The Lady Anji sniffed, her soft face provoked. "We must get a poultice on that."

"Later."

"I disagree. True, it doesn't look like much, but even that small cut can fester. Are you certain it's not deeper?"

"It's a nick. A mere skin-flap wound. Let's ride."

She persisted. "A poultice of honey and—"

"No!"

Matteo called to him, "Cousin-priest, we *can* take an instant to tend your wound. We're wasting precious time arguing."

"We are indeed, sir." Ekiael tugged his inner vest together. "Therefore, we'll hurry."

Anji warned, "I give you until nightfall before you're grumbling that you ache and that your thorn-stick wound is oozing." Softening her tone, she asked, "May I help you with your vests and cloak?"

They traded sharp looks, knowing looks such as attuned couples share, and Ekiael began to laugh. "No, my little warrior, but thank you. I believe it's far safer if I piece myself together on my own."

Anji's expression eased and she laughed at him in turn, then shook her head fondly. Blushing.

Corban envied their joy. He would never know such affinity with a wife. He'd killed that chance by condemning Araine.

Anji guided her horse toward Matteo and Corban, and she threw them a wry glance. "He's right. His breast-plate blunted the arrow's impact, so it's only a skin-flap dangling down, and the blood's minimal. Darzeq's high priest will survive."

"In fear of his pretty wife," Matteo teased. "Anji, I didn't know you were such a monster."

She pretended a scowl. "Don't test me, sir."

Corban would have added a pleasant taunt of his own to the conversation, but his thoughts dwelled uneasily upon her words. Darzeq's high priest...

He'd fought his way into the household of Darzeq's high priest. He'd pleaded to remain in the company of the ruler of Darzeq's followers of the Infinite. To protect them. Worse, he liked Ekiael and his wife.

The irony galled enough to gag him. As soon as the king was safe, he—Corban Thaenfall, the murderous renegade and former enemy of the Infinite—would depart Darzeq forever.

Sophereth rapped sharply at Dalia's doorway, then strode inside, frowning. "I'm told you sent out a stack of letters. Many letters. To whom?" Dalia sighed inwardly. So, despite being commanded to remain in the street, the attendant had spied upon her at the couriers' station. To be fair, she shouldn't be surprised—spying, albeit subtly—was the young attendant's job. Dalia nodded to her unhappy teacher. "Yes. I wrote to a number of friends in the south who will be concerned for the king and Darzeq."

As for friends, Dalia liked to think she could befriend almost anyone in the realm. Except Cthar and Gueronn, so she hadn't exaggerated much. Might the Infinite forgive her for stretching the truth just a bit? Though she was sounding much like a politician, which might be treading dangerous waters....

She bit her lip and focused on Sophereth, who was scolding softly: "We've been too lenient with you because of your grief and our shock at the news from Arimna. Now, because you've taken advantage of our indulgence, we're returning to our usual habits. No more excursions and certainly no more notes to anyone unless I read them first. With the exception of letters exchanged with your lord-father and your lady-mother. Do you hear me?"

"Yes, lady."

Sophereth marched to Dalia's too-narrow window and closed the shutter, slapping down the lock. "Don't think me any less concerned, nor too severe. Grief can work alarms of the mind, and impair the judgment of even the most rational, reasonable people. And you, young lady, will be the first to admit that you bear an impetuous streak—a brash thread in your otherwise reliable and kindly nature."

"Yes, lady." This was true. Dalia admitted to all that her character certainly mingled Father's brashness with Mother's amiable sweetness. However, Mother could become fierce if pushed too far. Even Father stepped away from Mother then and negotiated from a safe distance. Dalia looked up at Sophereth again. "Am I confined to my cell for this week?"

The matron narrowed her gray-eyed gaze, and then shook her head. "No. You'll be in my company instead, from the instant you're dressed in the morning until you fall asleep at night. I'm watching you, so treasure your sleep. It'll be the only solitude you possess for the next week."

"Yes, lady."

Sophereth gave her a final, assessing look, then skimmed out of the cell and barred the door. Dalia sat on her narrow pallet, perfectly resigned, and prepared to wait.

For whatever chaos, confusion, or turmoil her notes might unleash.

Mighty One, had she been too bent upon scrawling outrageous pamphlets against Cthar to consider all the implications? Had she somehow overestimated herself? Could she actually trust the courier?

Time would reveal the truth. Until then, she would wait and pray.

"One-Who-Sees-Me, if I've been foolish, please forgive me and use my foolishness for good, and for Matteo and Anji. Save them, please. Save Darzeq."

Wearied and sickened, Anji stared ahead at the peculiar landscape of Eshda. No wonder the royal court rarely visited this place. Writhing green trees edged stark fields and muddled stonescapes unlike anything she'd ever seen. The land was beautiful in an appalling way. Heat threw invisible waves through the air just like tossed stones rippled the fish ponds in Arimna Palace.

Just ahead of her, Ekiael's wary horse picked about as the fused and brittle soil crackled beneath its weight. To the distant left of the road, the ground was scorched black in some places and fractured, glowing red-hot in other places. Equally formidable, gruesome scaln traps marked the landscape here and there, wire snares entrapping the horrid beasts' burned corpses, tainting the air with sultry decayed-flesh stench. The men and their household stared about, hushed. Even the horses were quiet. Not picking at trees or grass as usual, and if any horses wished they could tiptoe, these horses did.

Ahead of Anji, Matteo coughed, as did Ekiael. Corban, riding nearby, loosened his mantle and dampened it with his water-skin. Poised to pin the fabric over his face, he warned the others, "We ought to cover mouths and noses at least."

A brief wash of fumes hit Anji, half-smothering. A sooty residue filmed gray over their faces and irritated their nostrils and throats, even as their stinging tears slid downward and left streaks trailing on their skin. To Corban, she said, "Thank you, my lord, for your wise suggestion."

Anji doused a scarf with a few precious drops of water from her water-skin and tied the mask over her face. If only she could cover her stinging, watering eyes and dampen down her nausea. An unforgivingly warm wind slithered over their household, and in the distance flames puffed to life and then vanished as the wind stilled. Sucking in a breath, Anji straightened, then stretched, trying to adjust herself in her saddle. The baby kicked delicately, and she rested one hand over the tiny, beloved disturbance. Lord Corban leaned forward, his cool gray eyes suddenly wide and intense above his mask. "You're with child, lady? Are you ill?"

"Yes. And, no, I'm not ill. Just worried for my dear husband."

"As any caring wife would be," he agreed, a certain bleakness in his tone hinting at some heartache of his own.

Matteo rode up beside her, his masked-renegade appearance deepened by the bitterness she glimpsed in his golden eyes. He nodded toward the soaring stonework fortress perched on cliffs at the far side of the barren stone basin. "There's what's left to my lord-father's line. A stone crown over a kingdom of ashes. The very mouth of the inferno."

What could she do but encourage her cousin? Anji smiled. "It's surely to our advantage that Eshda's been neglected for all these years. We can pray it's mostly forgotten—indeed so neglected that we'd be welcomed by the castellan. Am I right, my lord?" She raised her eyebrows at Corban, who looked grim enough to be an executioner, mask and all.

Corban slowed his horse and half-bowed with the easy grace of a nobleman well-practiced in courtly situations. "As you say, lady. Yet if they look upon you without welcome, they deserve besiegement without mercy. Perhaps you should appeal to the castellan on our behalf."

"I shall, my lord. Thank you." She returned his half-bow. Truly, he was almost as handsome as Matteo. Who was this Corban Thaenfall? Not that she wasn't grateful for his noble presence, but he was truly a man of secrets. Furthermore, if she weren't so madly in love with her darling Ekiael, she'd be intrigued by Corban's reserved demeanor, which hinted at some irresistible mystery.

Matteo's eyebrows lifted, and he nodded at Corban. "Excellent idea, my lord. Anji, I agree. You speak to Eshda's castellan for us. Perhaps you'll succeed where we've failed."

Muffling her laugh behind her scarf, Anji shrugged at her cousin. "I'll try to merit your hope, sir." She urged her horse forward to speak to Ekiael. Her poor love—he must be so tired, hunched down as he was in the saddle. "Beloved…."

Her words faded as Ekiael turned his head to look at her, his lagging movement, dulled glance, and uncovered fever-flushed face all striking her breathless. "You've a fever. Why didn't you tell me? Is it your wound?"

Ekiael rubbed one big hand down his face and exhaled then stiffened, as if catching his breath was a chore. "It didn't seem serious—until now."

"Didn't seem serious?" Hadn't life trained him yet? All fevers were serious! Anji pressed her legs into her horse, sending the pitiable animal into a gallop toward Eshda's stone gates, high above. Even as she rode, she planned her words. Don't mention fever—they'd be barred. Don't mention assassins, battle wounds, or a potential siege….

She reached the stone entry bridge and halted her horse a safe distance from the open gap left uncovered by Eshda's upraised drawbridge. There, she pulled down her scarf, uncovered her hair, and called out to the guards above, "Help! My lord's injured, please!"

When the guards looked down at her from the towers above, Anji called out, "I am Anji, the Lady Rhiysa of Arimna, niece of our King Jonatan! Please, open the gates!"

One of the guards lifted a javelin, his wary motion infuriating her. Anji yelled, "Are you a man of honor? Set aside your weapons and open these gates for Darzeq's princess! *Now!*"

Chapter 9

Anji held her horse still beneath the gate's massive woven iron portcullis. She would not move forward until her husband and their household had joined her. But she fixed her most commanding gaze upon the gathering clutch of guards who stared at her from inside Eshda's gates. "Summon your governing lord to greet me, this instant!"

Mercy, but she sounded as imperious as Cthar herself—the loathsome female. No one could wish to sound like her, least of all Anji. One of the guards motioned to an underling, who ran away as if his heels were burning. Anji softened her tone, returning to her usual voice. "Sirs, forgive me. We've had a long journey and I'm seriously concerned about my lord's injury."

A guard, stout as a barrel and riotously bewhiskered, bowed to her. "We are servants of the king and his family, lady, though none have visited for more than twenty years."

"We're visiting now," Anji told him. "However not under ideal circumstances."

Ekiael, Matteo and Corban were approaching, followed closely by the servants. As soon as they'd filed close along the bridge leading up to the gate, Anji led them forward. In the large gold-and-white courtyard, she dismounted and then hurried to Ekiael. "Sir..."

Ekiael descended heavily from his horse, sweat gleaming on his face. He worked up a wry little grin. "No doubt you'll be unhappy that I refused a poultice for the wound, my love."

"Oh, no doubt," Anji scolded quietly. "But let's settle you down to rest and I'll see what's to be done."

As if trying to muster a defense, Ekiael muttered, "It was a mere thorn-stick. Nothing..."

A portly silver-bearded man descended the stairs, his gray robes, silver belt, and black mantle all rumpled, his beard splotched and stained with—Anji suspected—the remains of his past ten meals. Yet his brown eyes were kind, and his smile seemed genuine as he held out his ink-stained hands and bowed. "Lady Rhiysa, welcome. I am Aristo Faolan, lord-governor of Eshda. We are honored indeed. You are the daughter of..." He paused, leading Anji to supply the name of the father she'd lost before she could clearly remember him.

"Prince Malchiel of Arimna, brother of King Jonatan. And—" she bowed her head toward Matteo, who'd hurried to offer assistance to Ekiael. "This is my cousin, Matteo of Arimna, youngest son of King Jonatan."

"Indeed he is." Aristo studied Matteo, then bowed deeply. "Lord-prince Matteo, I would have known you if I'd passed you on any street. You are the very image of your noble father. Come, my lords—and lady—let's tend to your lord's injury." Aristo offered the lagging Ekiael a shoulder. As they walked, Aristo's high forehead wrinkled, and his pleasant voice lowered with worry as he addressed Ekiael. "It's not a scaln scratch is it, my lord?"

Ekiael sighed, sounding much put-upon and weary. "No. It was a mere thorn-stick..."

Aristo smiled. "Good-good. But whatever this wound is, it's festering and fevering your blood. We'll see to it at once." As if to distract them while guiding the too-quiet Ekiael up the curving whitewashed stairwell, Aristo asked in pleasant, bantering tone, "Any scalns along the way?"

"Only one," Matteo's bitterness edged each syllable. "However, we left her in Arimna Palace, regrettably unharmed."

"My lord-prince," Aristo stared back at Matteo now, seeming unnerved. "Let me understand. Does our King Jonatan now keep scalns in Arimna?"

His question halted Matteo, who looked as if he'd swallowed bile. Anji understood his sudden hush. He couldn't say the words—that his revered parents and brothers were dead. Clearly, she must speak for him.

Anji hugged Ekiael's arm, grateful for the pause allowing him to rest in the stairwell. "That's why we're here, good Aristo. The aforementioned scaln is a mortal—Queen-mother Cthar. She's opened her claws to attack the royal family. The king is dead, as is the queen, and all their sons, save one—Matteo of Jonatan."

The lord-governor of Eshda stared at Matteo, shaking his head. "How can this be, my lord? You alone remain of the king's sons? And the king is dead?"

His voice raw, Matteo said, "I wish it weren't so, my lord. If giving my life would bring back even one member of my family, I'd offer it now. But if you doubt my veracity, my lord, then you should set guards outside my door until you can verify my story."

"No, my lord. You are too distressed to be lying. It's just so much evil to take in." Shaking his head, Aristo drew Ekiael's arm over one shoulder and nudged him up the stairs. "Now, my lord, onward. To our second-best chamber. But you, my lord-king Matteo of Darzeq...I have keys for you. The best is yours, as it was your own father's. His chamber awaits, and I believe you'll find some of his hunting garments locked away. May our Mighty One come to your aid. I was just writing letters today to friends in Arimna, seeking the latest news. Clearly, I should have written weeks ago. We are quite removed here."

Matteo said, "I beg you to finish your letters and send them. I need to know any news from Arimna as well—but please don't mention that I'm here. Not yet."

At the top of the stairs, Aristo shoved open a sizeable oak door, elaborately fretted and shielded with gilded ironwork, the hinges groaning only faintly. He guided them all into a small linen-shrouded chamber. Anji hurried to sweep the linen covers from the bed, then returned to help Ekiael unfasten his cloak and vests. "My dear love, now you can rest. I'll tend you myself, and you will obey."

Ekiael nodded a hand to his chest. She'd never seen him so worn and ill and quiet—her delightful, usually boisterous husband. May the Infinite cure him. Praying in silence, Anji lifted off his hidden gold vest and the padding beneath and tenderly set them aside. Ekiael dropped into the bed, sighing amid the scents of aged sachets and heavy, long-untouched bedcovers. "You rule here, my love."

"I order you to recover your strength." She kissed his feverish, bewhiskered cheek. "We need you, healthy and ready to take on the realm!" She opened the front of his tunic and gasped. In the center of his broad, well-muscled chest, a bubbling, grotesque violet-crimson split had replaced the small red gash she'd seen just a few days ago. "Lord Faolan, what do you say?"

Aristo studied the wound and frowned. "If he's not been scratched by a scaln, this is close enough to it. Those livid streaks are worrisome, but perhaps my lady-wife's healing concoction alone will cure it. I'll flame-cleanse a blade, and—as a precaution—I'm sending up servants with wine and tar to use if needed."

Tar? Aristo was planning to carve and seal the wound. Looking away from her husband, Anji sat on the bed, clasping Ekiael's hand. He seemed to be dozing, and for this she was grateful. Otherwise, he'd be distressed when she fainted.

The instant Matteo and Aristo departed from the chamber, with Aristo calling orders to the servants, Anji slumped over, closing her eyes. Praying to remain conscious.

Still seeing Ekiael's festering purple-and-crimson wound in his thoughts, Matteo hurried down the spiraling stairs, just keeping up with Aristo, who was bellowing for kettles of water, fires in the hearths, and food for Eshda's noble guests. The servants, all men now clad in Darzeq's golden vestments, hurried to obey.

Matteo bent slightly, asking, "My lord, have you seen anyone recover from such a dark wound before? It's too close to his heart. I fear we'll lose him."

"This will be among the most disquieting wounds we've tended in Eshda, yet we'll persevere." Aristo nodded Matteo through a stone-arched doorway into a lamp-lit hall. He produced a broad flat-plated key, slapped it into the lock of a shadowed door, then tugged open the door. Snatching a lamp, he explained, "This is my wife's medicinal closet. She was forever tending wounds my men inflicted upon each other during practice. Have no fear. I've experience in these matters, thanks to her—she was trained by her family's physician and insisted that because we are so distant from physicians and cities, I had to learn her ways. I'm not a true nobleman, understand. It's a good thing too. Otherwise, a number of my men would be crippled or dead from their own cures."

Matteo gathered his wits and his manners. "If I may ask, what happened to your lady-wife?"

Aristo paused, his ink-stained fingers resting upon a shelf. Drawing a breath, he reached for a small silver dish and set it upon an old richly polished table. "A riding accident. She was determined to ride down to the village near Lost Lake for a visit three years past. We'd just finished preparing Eshda for your lord-father's possible visit and she needed time away. I said I would follow. But I finished a letter to your lord-father instead. As she rode toward Lost Lake, a fissure broke open in the road. Her horse took the brunt of the steam and survived long enough to throw and trample her. She lingered three days. Enough time for us to make our farewells, and to pray."

Aristo's sorrow seemed to fill the small room as a tangible thing, a reflection of Matteo's own grief. "I'm sorry, my lord."

"Yes. Well, Sire, none of us walks through this life without pain. Some endure more than others, and I still consider myself blessed. In joy or woe, the Infinite abides with us still in our fallen, finite world. This room is one of the places within this fortress where I yet feel her near. It's just as she left it, and I'll keep it so." He withdrew a wooden box from a shelf, opened it, and began to dole an odd, glittering golden mixture into the silver dish. "Sire, when you're ready, I'll show you the armory, and you may begin to plan for battle. Three years past, your lord-father believed we'd be at war with Istgard, and I prepared Eshda to be his headquarters near the border during the threatened war. We remain prepared for an extended siege."

"I'm grateful. Then you believe we've told you the truth?"

"Concerning the Lady Cthar's violent takeover?" Aristo shut the box with a deliberate thud. "Yes. What else can I think when you and the Lady Rhiysa arrive with Darzeq's wounded high priest? I also know that The Dreaded Seven truly loved their parents—for Eshda is remote, yet I remain somewhat informed. Your grief is clear, sir, and Eshda is yours to command."

"Thank you." Matteo exhaled his relief, blessing the threatened invasion that prompted Father to prepare Eshda for war. That year, Matteo had been sixteen, immersed in Kiyrem's routines, friendships, and rivalries with other young noblemen of the realm, and making comrades of the sons of Eosyths. That year, Dalia had arrived in Kiyrem. He'd been shocked by her added height and beauty. And by her joyful smile, as she walked into the lecture hall amid the other girls who'd just arrived for schooling, had stolen his breath. He'd never imagined scrawny little Dalia as anything but Anji's bothersome childhood friend, until that year. A good year.

While Aristo was grieving here in Eshda.

Aristo, who expected him to plan for civil war.

Matteo brooded, staring at the golden crystals on the silver dish, while Eshda's lord-governor returned the box to its shelf, grabbed a collection of leather straps, and then removed a puffy linen packet from another box. Thus far, Matteo could only count upon Lord Aristo's support. And Anji's and Ekiael's, if Ekiael survived.

However, Cthar, the proud and foreign usurper-queen, was bound to add to her list of offenses. She'd killed most of Darzeq's ancient royal line. She'd dissolved the First Forum. She would certainly restore licentious self-worship in the Chaplet Temple.

What would she do next?

He must anticipate her future missteps. After they'd saved Ekiael.

As they traversed the great hall, Corban joined them. Before Corban could say a word, Aristo nodded at him. "Good, my lord. You can help us hold down Darzeq's high priest while I clean his wound."

Corban's dark eyebrows lifted, but then he nodded. "I was about to ask his condition. If you've need of me, I'll help."

They returned to Ekiael's allotted chamber and found a small fire in the stonework hearth, with a kettle steaming above the flames. On the bed, Ekiael lay sunken in a restless sleep, with Anji seated beside him, wan, but prepared for Aristo's treatment. Darting a fearful look at Ekiael, she pleaded, "Will it hurt him much?"

"Yes, lady, unfortunately. But I've a few remedies for the pain." Aristo poured warmed wine into a bowl and added the linen packet, stirring the packet. At last, seeming satisfied with the medicinal mixture, he nodded to Corban. "My lord, please help me tie up our priest."

An odd, self-mocking look passed over Corban's face, but he followed Aristo's directions with swift, neat efficiency, binding Ekiael's ankles, knees, and wrists. As they cinched the cords, Ekiael stirred, frowned, and opened his eyes. "What's all this?"

Her voice as gentle as the tiny caress she gave his face, Anji said, "It's a surgery, my lord. Your wound is beginning to rot and must be cleaned. We're all here with you, including me."

"I'd rather you weren't, my love," Ekiael muttered. He flicked a glance at Aristo, who approached with his bowl of medicine and the soaked linen packet. "My lord-priest, this may help you to endure the pain, or it might not. But at least we'll try—it's extract of poppies and mandrake. Is there a chance you'll try to bite me?"

Sweat beaded on Ekiael's forehead. "Yes."

Aristo sighed. "Then after you've taken a dose of the soporifics, we'll temporarily gag you. Not dignified, but it works."

Grim-faced, Ekiael drained the cup. Then Aristo bound a leather strap over Ekiael's mouth as the priest growled his disgust.

Taming her flaring curls with pins and twists of ribbons, Dalia nodded to herself in the mirror. She must look tidy and ladylike, for this day she'd certainly face punishment for her recent actions.

Her brave courier, if he was the worthy man she believed him to be, should have returned to Kiyrem the day before. Honor demanded that she pay. Moreover, she had to know if he was safe. She'd paid him, yet if anything happened to the courier, the fault would be hers entirely. Chin up, she scooped the remainder of her year's allowance into her purse, crept from her cell, marched down the corridor and rapped smartly on Sophereth's chamber door. The best and finest thing was to tell the truth. She must appeal to Sophereth's integrity.

The instant Sophereth opened her door, one hand on her unpinned coiled and braided hair, Dalia announced, "Lady, I've a debt to pay."

"Do you indeed, young lady?"

"Yes, please. It's a matter of honor. I gave my word to the courier that I'd return today."

Sophereth spiked slender carved-shell pins into her coiled braid and covered her head with a veil. "Then I'm going with you, and I'll witness the entire transaction."

"As I expected." Dalia smiled. "There'll be less to confess later if you accompany me."

The lady-scribe frowned, studying Dalia as if trying to decipher her. "You are a peculiar girl, Dalia Hradedh. Nevertheless, come along. Let's see what mischief you've been up to."

Sophereth gave instructions for morning lessons to her assistant, then motioned for Dalia to follow her from the school. They proceeded through Kiyrem's morning-busy stone streets like mother and daughter, heading directly to the Hall of Scribes. Inside, Dalia frowned and scanned the grayed hall until she glimpsed her courier. She smiled and approached him, with Sophereth following her, shadow-close. "Sir!"

He stood and bowed to Dalia, offering her a pleasant smile. "You're as timely as you said you'd be, lady. Thank you."

"You're safe, and I'm thankful," Dalia murmured. "Any trouble at all?"

The man subtly tugged at the neck of his tunic, revealing a raw-scabbing graze, so near his jugular vein that Dalia winced. Beside her, Sophereth twitched visibly. But the messenger grinned. "Only the kiss of one arrow, lady. Mercenaries, such as those who vandalized Kiyrem a few months past. I escaped them just south of Arimna."

Dalia longed to hug him. She gave him the last of her entire year's allowance and a smile instead. "Thank you! With all my heart."

The courier winked, charmingly flirtatious. "One day, I shall tell my grandchildren that the loveliest young lady in Darzeq offered me her heart. Until then, lady, I'll vanish."

"May our Mighty One shield you!" Dalia beamed at him, even as Sophereth dragged her away. "It's wise of you to vanish, and more than I'd hoped. Remain well, good sir!"

As they walked through the streets, Sophereth finally spoke. "These were not mere letters of consolation, young lady—you'll never convince me otherwise. What did you write for him to deliver elsewhere?"

"About sixty copies of a rough-shod poem to be tacked to all Tinem North's city gates and fortresses at night," Dalia confessed. "Not quite a poem."

"Sixty!" An exasperated closed-mouth sigh flared Sophereth's thin nostrils.

"Yes, sixty. It took that long before my emotions were settled after news of Darzeq's loss." Moreover, she'd calculated that sending a courier with more than sixty notes would require pawning her boots and hair pins—an option she'd considered.

Dalia's teacher eyed her, seeming the embodiment of winter. "Recite it."

Oh, this would be a failing mark indeed. Dalia glanced around. No one was near. Resigning herself to the fool's corner, she recited the doggerel she knew all too well. "'Mourn, Darzeq! Your noble king and his sons have fallen. Weep as the yellow-eyed queen rejoices, this sovereign of the Chaplet Temple. Darzeq, who will demand justice when the venomous she-scaln feeds upon your remains?...'"

She finished the poem and dared a glance at her teacher. Sophereth's eyes were huge and unblinking, and she moved toward the school as if sleepwalking. But then the lady-scribe huffed, cleared her gaze, and quickened her pace. "Well, young lady, you've called for a revolution. Or at least your own death if the queen-mother catches you."

"I know it's true, lady."

"You've possibly sentenced the entire school."

"Not if we win, lady."

"There is *that*. But with no guarantees." Sophereth lifted her chin, composed as Cthar herself. "Come along. We've plans to make, and I must write an understated and discreet letter to your lord-father. You're mighty cool about this, I will say!"

"I await my punishment."

"If I punish you further, it will become conspicuous and noteworthy," Sophereth huffed. "It will also call attention to the fact that I know you've done something worth punishing. In fact, perhaps I shouldn't write that letter to your lord-father, but simply drop you before Tragobre's gates."

Father would lock her up forever. Unless... "They'll attack him, lady, and he had nothing to do with my insurgency. Surely we might agree on some other plan?"

"I surmise that you've another plan, young lady."

"Yes, and I pray you agree it's wise, given my previous recklessness. The new king has gone to Eshda, with Darzeq's high priest and my beloved friend, Anji, the Lady Rhiysa, princess of Darzeq. I'll go attend her there."

"I'm not inclined to reward misdeeds with the very thing the miscreant desires."

"Yet it's a logical move, lady. If the king is in Eshda, his supporters should join him there."

"We will discuss this when we return to the school."

Inwardly, Dalia pleaded with her Creator, *Please, don't let them send me home!*

She could almost hear the future clattering of armor as Cthar's soldiers approached Tragobre's gates, prepared to attack.

In a secluded counseling cell, Master Tredin listened to his wife, then stared at Dalia, so formidable that she could only stand and await his verdict. At last he said, "You won't be the first fire-starting student from Kiyrem. Yet history has taught us that it's best and safest to remove you from our vicinity."

"Meaning?"

"I'll write a short note to your lord-father, politely explaining that despite your excellent work as a student, you must return home."

Dalia sighed, envisioning an army of bloodthirsty mercenaries calling for her death.

Chapter 10

Matteo removed an emptied tray from Ekiael's bed and placed it on a nearby table. "You're looking better."

"I'm useless," Ekiael grumbled. "We've been here a week. I ought to be out and about, bestirring the entire kingdom on your behalf."

"There'll be time for creating an uproar later," Matteo sat on a corner of the bed, willing back his own edginess. "Until then, please rest. We're just grateful you're recovering."

In a chair beside the bed, Anji smoothed her husband's beard, then held his hand. "Yes, listen to our king, my lord. If I'd lost you..." She paused as if she couldn't finish the terrible thought. Recovering, she smiled. "Such a blessing that we've ended up in Eshda, in Lord-governor Aristo's care. Someone should reward him with a true title and rank—he deserves to be more than a castellan."

A swift tap on the door made them turn. Anji called out, "Come in."

The door to Ekiael's bedchamber creaked open. Corban stepped inside, his expression mask-like. Aristo followed him, personally carrying fresh bandages and a small casket of ointment for Ekiael's wound. Aristo smiled. "Time for a fresh plastering of pine tar and honey."

"Could be worse," Ekiael retorted. "You might tell me that's my breakfast!"

Anji laughed. "You *are* recovering, my love, if you're teasing Lord Aristo after he's saved you."

Matteo smiled at his cousin's joy, and he nodded to Aristo. "My lord, you've become a hero to my cousin, and to Darzeq."

"Thank you, Sire, but I don't deserve praise," Aristo protested. "I merely used my knowledge to help him, and I'm grateful that my wife insisted I learn."

Anji stood and backed away from the bed, allowing Aristo room for his bandages and ointments. "Nevertheless, you're our hero, and I believe the Infinite sent us here specifically for your healing gifts. Someday, I pray we can reward you."

"Your thanks are my reward, lady." Aristo peeled back the layers of gauze over Ekiael's chest and nodded. "I'd say that's mending. No inflammation or oozing."

Ekiael cut him a false-threatening look. "Ask me if the wound's itching."

Unperturbed, Aristo dolloped ointment over the patch of abraded raw-pink flesh. "Itching is good. Scratching is not. Therefore, leave it alone, sir, because it's healing." He applied a fresh bandage over the ointment, then nodded to Anji. "If we must tie him up again, lady, to prevent him from scratching his wound bloody, please tell me and I'll do so."

"There." Anji returned to Ekiael and kissed him. "What was I just saying? Aristo Faolan is a hero indeed and ought to be named as a true lord of Darzeq. As should Corban."

Corban shrugged. "Lady, I'm pleased that you believe so, however, I believe I've done nothing extraordinary. In dark times, the desperate must become their own heroes."

"Unless a hero is sent by the Infinite, of course." Anji smiled at Corban, and he answered with a brief smile of his own. But Matteo noticed silent disagreement in the nobleman's shifting stance and the way he folded his arms as he leaned against the decorative stonework framing the fireplace.

To divert them all, Matteo asked, "Anji, when might a king summon the First Forum outside of Arimna?"

Clearly remembering her history lessons with Sophereth, Anji recited, "During war, plague, or under extreme national duress." Her eyes brightened. "Why? Are you summoning the

First Forum to join you now that Cthar's dismissed the ruling lords?"

"Yes. I'm also officially sending out writs against Cthar, offering a reward for her capture or her corpse, exactly as she's offered for mine. If matters escalate to an actual war, then so be it."

"Good! Let's send for them all!" Anji leaned forward in her chair. "I'll write every summons if I must. Except that we don't have the royal seal."

"We have a seal." Matteo removed Sheth's dagger from its sheath. The gold pommel, set with a replica of their lord-father's seal, gleamed in the morning light. "I'll seal my notes with Sheth's dagger, and I'll be sure every lord in the realm realizes it. My family will *not* be forgotten."

Corban unfolded his arms and straightened. When Matteo looked at him, the imposing nobleman nodded. "The names of the fallen must be properly honored, O king. Indeed, I've been in a similar situation. Therefore, I'm willing to write a few letters to your laggard supporters. When do we begin?"

Facing the blank parchment on the table before him, Corban dipped the carved ivory writing stylus in his allotted ink jar and wrote, "*By order of Darzeq's rightful King, Matteo of Darzeq, you are summoned to the autumn council of the First Forum to discuss Darzeq's future.*

Due to unrest within the realm and the foreign queen's treasonous seizure of Arimna, the autumn forum will be gathered in Eshda. Attend and be acknowledged as true possessors of the lands you hold in fealty to my lord-father, and to his fathers before him, and let us deal with the usurper in Arimna.

Sealed by my hand, and by my brother Sheth's sword—Sheth, who was murdered by order of Cthar of Kaphtor.

Matteo of Darzeq.

Across from Corban, Matteo wrote note after note, wielding a gilded stylus as a painter might use a brush, and without scraping mistakes. For a king, his writing was remarkably clear, swift, and flawless—out-inking Corban's more leisurely approach. After his fourth note, and Matteo's tenth, Anji gathered the parchments and took them to her table to seal them. Corban tossed down his ivory stylus scowled. "Lord-king Matteo of Darzeq, you're a born scribe."

Matteo wiped the stylus, then set it down and grinned, glancing at Corban's four notes. "My lord, I'm a student of Kiyrem, trained by Master Tredin, who thinks nothing of caning laggard students. Even sons of kings aren't spared thrashings—I can personally attest to this."

"No king of Siphra would tolerate such rubbish."

Darzeq's king shrugged. "I was the youngest of seven, and Tredin was unimpressed by royalty by the time I was sent to Kiyrem. However, I'm told that my eldest brother, Tarquin, was spared canings because he was the heir. Beatings aside, my lord, I assure you that anything you've written is greatly appreciated."

From her table, busy folding letters and melting wax, Anji added, "Also, my lord, you've fine writing, for a nobleman."

"Kindly crumbs to the beggar, dear lady." Hearing his own sarcasm, Corban scowled inwardly. One day, his sharp-felt pride would carry him too far. "Please forgive me, lady. Thaenfalls are an arrogant lot."

Anji poured heated wax over a parchment and rested the dagger's insignia-embossed pommel in the silvery pool. "You're too harsh with yourself, my lord—there's no need to apologize."

From his bed, Ekiael added, "In fact, we should apologize, my lord. We're glad for your presence, but you must be bored. We're not the best company right now."

Corban stretched briefly, then reached for another square of parchment. "Thank you, sir, but I'm hardly anyone's 'best' company ever. You're being too generous." And he, the disgraced Corban Thaenfall, was being an ingrate. Why did their kindness irritate him? Did he feel that he didn't deserve gracious treatment? Or was it part of the irascible and restless Thaenfall nature that he must instigate conflict in order to feel truly alive? Why couldn't he settle himself and simply enjoy this time of calm? Instead, he wallowed in this ignoble ferment of discontent with the Infinite. Why should he be accepted and esteemed for something the Infinite had done through him? Where was the glory in that?

Corban paused and shot Darzeq's high priest a glance. In the past, he would have gladly shot such an ambassador of the Infinite with arrows and rejoiced over his death. Now, he aimed questions instead. "Sir, during our travels, you stated your opinion that the Infinite has accepted me on the merit of a single instant of trust—"

Ekiael snorted. "I didn't state some temporary mortal opinion, my lord. I stated the truth. He accepted you and listened the first instant you actually called to Him."

"If I may be bold, sir." Corban leaned back in his chair, striving for calm, and the words to state his opinion with clarity, yet without offense. "The idea chafes at me, because it makes no sense. I have been His enemy. I attacked those who followed Him, and I rebel against Him even now, which makes the Infinite a fool."

"Not if He loves you." Ekiael's entire spirit brightened—visibly and exasperatingly overjoyed. For the first time in a week, Darzeq's high priest looked animated and ready to take on the entire world, even abed. Ekiael beamed at Corbin. "What will mortal love not do? It's the greatest emotion of all, my lord, able to drive us all to the most far-flung heights or depths, depending upon the type of love, be it self-love or selfless love."

Ah, wonderful. A priestly lecture. Corban squelched a sneer and listened politely. Oblivious—perhaps willfully so—Ekiael continued, "How much greater, then, is the love of He-Who-Sees-Us! He understands your failings perfectly, and yet He loves you, He seeks to shelter you and offer you solace and balm for your wounded spirit, my lord. To ignore His immeasurable love is to misunderstand Him entirely."

"Yet He's not above using me to further His causes."

"You mean to save you? And the king and my wife, not to mention me and my household? When you called to Him, He was able to use your weakness to reveal His strength, for which we are all grateful. Do you regret that He used your nature and abilities to save us all?"

"Of course not. However, the manner of—"

Ekiael's voice flowed on—sounding caught in the currents of his thoughts. "To love immeasurably is to serve immeasurably, my lord. The Infinite guards, protects, and defends those He loves through countless ways that often make no sense to mortals. The true question is, are you His servant? Or are you your own servant?" Before Corban could speak, Ekiael lifted his hand gently. "Your answer should be to the Infinite alone."

Very well. He was his own servant. He would abide here for a few more days to finish the task he'd undertaken. But then he must leave.

Though he'd ostensibly worshiped the goddess Atea in Siphra, and he'd enjoyed her rites and defended those rites politically, Thaenfall pride had never permitted him to actually bow to the goddess. He wasn't about to serve as some pawn to the enigmatic Infinite now.

Finished with her evening meal of lentils, barley, leeks, and tough boiled greens that had proven a slimy test of her self-control, Dalia carried her wooden bowl across the school's whitewashed dining hall—just as Sophereth motioned her toward the hall's entry. Kurcus nodded to Dalia from the entryway, his puny face scrunched and blinking as if he'd just sipped vinegar.

What had she done now? Had Tredin and the other masters concluded that she actually deserved some punishment for writing all those notes? Beneath her breath, she prayed, "Infinite, defend me!"

Dalia hurriedly rinsed the bowl in a water basin, dropped it into the kitchen tub, and then hurried toward Kurcus, who spun about and marched from the hall, clearly expecting her to follow like a scolded child. As Dalia furtively wiped her hands on her heavy linen gown, someone gripped her shoulder from behind, making her jump. Sophereth frowned down at Dalia, her silence promising retribution for any infractions. Dalia exhaled, her heartbeat quadrupled. If Kiyrem's teachers wished to terrify their students to death, Sophereth was well along on that path. Why couldn't the woman make some noise when she walked?

Sophereth hissed. "Kurcus, who summoned the young lady?"

"Her lord-father."

Father? Dalia halted in the corridor, dread-seized. Sophereth dragged her onward. "This must be his response to our official letter of dismissal. Let's face him together, young lady. He might have a few harsh words for me, as well as for you."

Oh, it would be more than harsh words. Father would have plans for punishment.

A swarm of excuses buzzed in Dalia's thoughts—plaguing her to tell half-truths. To evade. To justify her actions with self-serving pleas. None would do. Not when facing Roi Hradedh of Tragobre. At least he wouldn't kill his only surviving child. She hoped.

Dalia smoothed her unruly hair and kept her shoulders back as she approached the tiny meeting room reserved for irate visiting parents. Kurcus stepped aside and bowed. Dalia prayed for survival and entered the plain, whitewashed room.

Father, burly and travel-musty, instantly shoved a parchment at Dalia's face, halting her. "What's *this*?"

Dalia glanced at the too familiar words. *...Weep as the yellow-eyed queen rejoices...*

She had only herself to blame. The courier had obviously tacked the doggerel to her lord-father's gate—the one little oversight she'd left out of her instructions. Father, above all people, would know her handwriting. "It's doggerel, sir. I was grieving."

Father's mouth cinched to a tight short fold in his squared face. Then he growled, "Tell me there are no copies!"

Dalia poured out the truth in a scared rush. "There are sixty copies, my lord. Enough for most of the cities, towns and strongholds along the Tinem North's river road. As I said, I was furious with grief."

"And now you're doomed. I pray no one else recognizes your writing. Otherwise, you've guaranteed your own death and your parents' deaths." Roi Hradedh flapped the note at Sophereth. "Did you know of my daughter's political suicide?"

Sophereth's voice remained level, but her eyes were huge as she stared at the parchment. At last, she said, "I knew after the fact, my lord. I demanded the young lady's confession when I learned she'd sent out a packet of notes with a courier. We sent you word at once."

Father lowered the parchment and closed his eyes—a parent counting to ten. Twenty. Thirty. He finally took a breath and released it. "My girl, your studies are finished. It's time to plan your marriage, *if* anyone will have you."

Marriage? Dalia's breath caught unpleasantly. "Marriage to whom?"

"Ormr Magni's youngest son. Or Thelon Stradin from Khombados province."

Dalia winced, trying not to recall Thelon Stradin's smirky little face. "Thelon Stradin is an incurable cheat and his lord-father hates you—I heard him say so. Also, Ormr Magni's three younger sons gambled after lessons."

Sophereth faced Dalia, clearly appalled. "They gambled here? And did young Stradin actually cheat on his tests?"

Thelon had copied Matteo's work—a fact Matteo had told Dalia in strictest confidence. Unwilling to answer or to retract the truth, Dalia met her teacher's gaze. Let Sophereth sort out matters. She'd certainly have more time now that Dalia was being removed from school.

Sophereth bowed to Roi Hradedh. "Excuse me, my lord. I'll leave you alone to confer with the young lady."

Sounding as appalled as Sophereth, Father asked Dalia, "How did I ever offend Karvos Stradin?"

"Thelon said you spoke against Lord Karvos during the spring Forum two years past."

Father huffed. "It was the Forum! We're supposed to argue matters through!"

"Obviously, you soundly bested Lord Karvos, sir."

"Of course I did!" Roi looked near to adding more details, but he clenched his jaw, re-folded the scrap of doggerel and returned it to his money pouch. "Enough. I'm staying here in the guest rooms overnight and we'll leave at dawn. You'd best pack your gear. And—!" He gripped her shoulder, clearly done with any quibbling on her part. "Unless you want me to lose my temper altogether, you will remain silent unless I ask you a question. And you'll confess everything to your mother, and to whomever you marry. Furthermore, I *will* select your lord-husband! Do you hear me?"

Practicing unspeaking obedience, Dalia nodded. Yet her thoughts protested marrying any "whomever." She loved Matteo. How could she overcome this obstacle? To the Mighty One, she pleaded within her thoughts, *Is this Your will? Have I been so unpardonably wrong that I must be punished?*

Worse, how could she plead to marry Matteo if Father refused to allow her to speak?

As dawn's golden rays slid over Kiyrem's walls, Dalia rode her beloved little mare, Grainia, among Tragobre's servants, following Roi Hradedh to Kiyrem's gates. Father tossed silver at the gatekeeper, who hurriedly opened the massive doors and then retreated, allowing them all to pass.

Outside Kiyrem, Dalia caught her breath, grateful for her first glimpse of open land and skies for the first time in too many days. The city's perch overlooking the quiet river valley couldn't be more enthralling, while the distant mountains to the east were so ruggedly perfect and majestic that she longed to turn toward them instead of Tragobre and marriage to one of the younger gambling Ormr boys.

Perhaps she could ride off into the mountains and live among the Eosyths. One of the Eosyth's most honored young men, Nikaros, son of Lord Levos, had studied for several years with Matteo, and they'd become friends. A good and handsome man, and formidable in archery practice; if Dalia weren't so in love with Matteo, she'd have been smitten with Nikaros.

Near the base of the roadway leading to the river valley, a band of soldiers rode onto the summer-dried track, all of them cold-faced as if readied for battle. As they approached, the leader lifted his hand, and his followers amassed themselves in a wall-like unit, blocking the road. A fine sweat misted over Dalia's skin as she drew Grainia to a halt. This lead soldier looked fit to kill anyone who said a cross word to him. Surely he'd execute her instantly if he knew what she'd done.

To Father, the leader said, "Kiyrem is to be locked and searched until we find the reprobates who distributed treasonable notes throughout the realm. Therefore, state your names and business. Why are you leaving Kiyrem?" He looked directly at Dalia, his gaze a cutting force. "You are a student of Kiyrem?"

"Yes. I was." Dalia swallowed. He would know she was lying if she tried. And when he searched Father, this soldier would find the very parchment she'd written...

This, then, was how she would die. Executed like a criminal before the gates of Kiyrem.

And Father would die with her, unless she confessed.

Chapter 11

Before Dalia could say a word, Father interceded smoothly. "I am Roi Hradedh of Tragobre, and this is my daughter, Dalia. I'm removing her from school, as education seems wasted upon her."

Dalia gaped at him, word-slapped. Wasted? What—?

Roi continued, "I deemed it best to marry her off while she's still able to find a husband, and I wish him well!"

Tears stung Dalia's eyes and slid down her face, shaming her. Was Father so furious with her that he must insult her to this stranger? This was worse than if she were a pitiable little wretch of five years. Certainly she must look it. Dalia bit her lower lip hard, trying to mute a sob. Not for the world would she allow Father to hear her. She slid a despairing glance at the soldier and saw his expression had utterly changed. The man pitied her.

Oh, insufferable!

But the soldier waved them onward and they divided their ranks, allowing Tragobre's household to pass.

Dali could feel the soldiers all staring at her as she rode past. She sniffled, totally wretched, as she likely deserved.

Her household servant, Petr, rode up beside her, his kindly middle-aged face all sympathy for her misery. Sweet man. At least she had one ally here.

As they turned toward the River Road, Father motioned Dalia forward. The instant she drew her horse alongside his, Roi said, "Nicely acted."

"I wasn't acting, my lord. You insulted me before those men."

"Well the ruse worked, particularly since you deserved some shaming, and we told the truth. However..." Father glanced over his shoulder, up the slopes toward Kiyrem. Sounding sick with dread, he muttered, "You'll be identified soon. Thanks to your foolishness, our lot is decidedly cast against the queen. We can't return to Tragobre—we'll be overtaken and killed before we ever reach the gates."

This was her fault. How could she lessen this disaster? Braving Father's wrath, she offered, "If I surrender myself and declare the truth—that you had nothing to do with my behavior—"

Roi glared at her. "No! I forbid you to even think of such a thing! Furthermore, do you seriously think *she* will believe me ignorant? I'll die alongside you, my girl, make no mistake. *She's* not above killing all her own grandchildren. I'm nothing to her, while you're everything to me—you and your lady mother." Roi rubbed one hand over his face and then grimaced. "Where is he now hiding? Have you any clues?"

He. Matteo. Dalia caught her breath. Dared she hope...? "Eshda, my lord."

"Eshda?" Father pronounced the word as if she'd said "abyss." He pondered for a breath or two, then murmured, "He couldn't be farther away without leaving Darzeq. And yet there's merit in his choice." Father beckoned Petr, who rode forward at once. Roi glanced back at Kiyrem's walls and said, "Petr, once we've ridden beyond view from Kiyrem, you're to strike off for Tragobre. Warn Lady Sona to gather in all our resources and people, then close the gates against a possible attack. She's not to welcome anyone into the fortress until I return. Promise her that my family's safety and Tragobre's wellbeing are my chief concerns."

Petr bowed, then straightened. "Yes, my lord."

Father reached for his money pouch, removed Dalia's parchment and some coins, then tossed Petr the remainder.

"Don't stop, even for sleep. Pay for fresh horses at the posting houses along the way, and I'll reward you upon my return."

"Yes, my lord. Thank you." Petr glanced over his shoulder at Kiyrem. The instant they rounded a tree-sheltered curve at the far side of the hill, Petr urged his horse away like a streak, heading south toward Tragobre.

Dalia watched her servant depart until Roi asked quietly. "How far up and down the River Road did you send those parchments?"

"From Kiyrem southward, my lord."

"None to the north?"

"No, my lord. My year's allowance wasn't enough to blanket the kingdom with my grief."

Father snorted loud enough that his horse perked its ears. "Obviously, I allowed you far too much." He looked around, and then motioned his guards to turn about. "We'll ride north to evade the queen if possible. And we'll pray with all our might that their hunt for the offending versifier ends in Kiyrem."

Following Aristo and Matteo, Corban ascended the curving stone steps to one of Eshda's armories. Aristo unlocked the chained door and bowed Matteo and Corban inside. "As you can see, Sire, and my lord, we're mightily prepared."

Mightily prepared was an understatement. Corban halted, shocked by the veritable wall of light chariots stacked together in rows at the far side of the armory. Before the chariots, orderly stands of weaponry waited, as did harnesses for warhorses. Royal insignias. Royal banners. And exquisitely sleek weapons such as Corban had never seen, short powerful bows fastened upon gleaming wooden stocks, the metalwork uniformly simple, each sporting latches that Corban instantly realized must serve as triggers to release the short, heavy arrows arrayed with each weapon.

Matteo exhaled. "Crossbows! I saw one years ago, but didn't realize my lord-father had commissioned an army's worth."

"He was wary of them," Aristo explained. "Rightfully so. Those bolts, plain and short as they are, will punch through all armor. They're fearsome weapons in the wrong hands, and easily learned. A farmer's army of these might take down a nation, and we've four buildings of these."

Matteo sobered. "It seems I must resort to such weapons. Is there a similar stockpile in Arimna?"

"Not that I'm aware of, my lord. All were brought here, to be arrayed against King Tek An's threats."

Corban studied the weapons again, intrigued by their sleekness and lethal potential, even as his thoughts warned him against his craving to fight. He wouldn't stay for the coming war. He would not become a living weapon.

Turning away from Matteo and Aristo, he muttered beneath his breath to the Infinite, "How far would You have taken me? Past the brink of war? To my fill of bloodshed?"

He was no servant.

Not even to save others? Corban's thoughts mocked him with the possibilities. He'd been struggling for months to escape his bloodied past. Longing for the chance to offer reparations to the young woman he'd harmed. To redeem his family's name. Was this his chance? Might it lead to an eventual reconciliation with Araine, if she yet lived?

Was she actually alive in Belaal, serving as the Infinite's prophet?

Caught by the idea, Corban gazed ahead, only half-seeing the mountain of dried foods arrayed within bins before him. Unbidden, Aristo joined him and nodded at the stunning stockpile of rations. "Perhaps this seems excessive, my lord.

However it never goes bad. For a meal, you throw these into a kettle full of boiling water—and we've plenty of boiling water."

"You're undoubtedly right, my lord. Unfortunately, I won't remain to partake of this army's food."

Obviously overhearing, Matteo protested, "My lord, you cannot leave us now—we've placed our trust with you, when we've so few to trust!"

Trust from royalty? From the Infinite? Corban pressed one hand against his forehead, trying to rub away a sudden kettle-drum of a headache. "I'm no one you should trust, my lord. I'm a reprobate deserving nothing but death. I'd be a blight to your good name."

"As if my own grandmother's not enough of a blight already? My lord—"

Corban opened his eyes against the headache. "Sire, may you triumph over Darzeq! Yet it's best you triumph without me. I cannot serve here."

Not if it meant bowing to the Infinite.

Matteo appeared genuinely stricken. He lowered his gaze, staring at the stone floor. At last, he said, "If you are determined to leave, at least allow us to supply you well enough to reach your intended destination. Where will you go?"

"Belaal." The word was out before Corban could stifle it. Yet Belaal held his hopes. "I must seek the truth. I must know if I actually caused Araine's death, or if she's still alive."

And if she truly served as the Infinite's prophet to Belaal. Until he saw Araine, his soul would not rest. He'd never find the peace she'd sought on his behalf through more than a year of writing her dangerous little letters. Soul-rending, thought-provoking letters he'd read repeatedly and cherished until he'd learned the source of Araine's inspiration: the Books of the Infinite.

Remembering her letters, Corban clenched his jaw and rubbed a hand over his face, longing to rant against the Infinite.

Composing himself, he listed his complaints in silence. *What chance did I have? You were forever there, calling me! Your pursuit wearies me, weakens me.... Yet I long for the peace Araine's verses brought—much as I hated them.*

What *was* he that he ever-fought such tranquility? That his thoughts warred against his Creator, even as his soul reached warily toward Him?

Aware of Matteo and Aristo both staring at him, Corban lowered his hand. "I'm a living battlefield. I must find peace."

Matteo looked away. "Very well. Whatever you need, we'll supply it from our stores. But are you sure?"

"You don't want me here, my lord. I'm a marauder at heart. A killer. I'll bring no honor to your name."

Darzeq's king half-grinned. "It's honor that forces you to admit these things, my lord. You'll never convince me otherwise. If you must go, tell the Lady Rhiysa first. Don't leave that wretched task to me."

Bid farewell to Darzeq's sad-eyed princess? He'd rather not.

Except that he was leaving Eshda to find Araine.

He must deal with his conscience, and her own verdict concerning his fate. He returned Matteo's grin, with a challenge. "Burden me with that heartbreak, my lord, and I'll demand one of each weapon here as repayment. Sword, spear, and crossbow."

Matteo's smile faded to bleakness. He nodded. "Agreed. Name the weapons; they are yours."

Dalia longed to drop off to sleep after five days of wearisome travel—though that would mean dropping off of her horse, Grainia. Adjusting the reins, Dalia smoothed Grainia's warm, soot-darkened brown neck. Poor Grainia was as wary of the vaporous ash-dusted landscape and this oddly brittle road as was Dalia.

Was this Eshda? Father had been right to scowl over the name. Parts of Eshda certainly looked as if it should harbor the entrance to the abyss. Midday sunlight seeped reluctantly downward through a haze, and the nearest trees looked equally gloomy beneath filmy veils of ashes. Yet Eshda intrigued her. Was a village nearby? What sort of people lived in this uncertain place? Certainly they must be hardy.

Riding ahead of her, Roi Hradedh called out, "There it is. We'll shelter in the fortress for the night."

Peering ahead through the haze, Dalia glimpsed beautiful soaring walls and arcaded stone tracks leading to a high bridge before the rock-gray citadel crowning the cliffs above this smoldering half-forested land. The place certainly held an austere sort of beauty, untouched by its wild, ash-and-soot-smudged surroundings. Was Matteo there? Please be there! Safe and delighted by her unexpected arrival.

Father turned and looked at her, one eyebrow lifted. He motioned Dalia forward, and she obeyed, struggling to mask her eagerness. Roi grunted. "Do you know what your mother said to me when we saw your note on our gate? 'Look what *your* daughter wrote.' And she was correct. In your place, I suppose I would have done the same."

A concession! Dalia bit down a grin. Father continued, "Believe me, I'm not proud of my recent decisions, and I've questioned myself over sending away our Lord Matteo. Yet this place is probably the safest in the kingdom."

Yes. Dalia nodded, allowing him a smile. Roi turned fierce. "Do not hope for what you cannot have! We've been forced to take refuge here until we know Tragobre's safe for us both, thanks to your impulsive behavior, my girl. I intend to keep you locked away, do not mistake me! If I say you shall marry Thelon Stradin, then you will! The First Forum might be disbanded, but it won't be forever, mark my words! If you marry Matteo, we'd be compelled to answer to them all, and it would be hostile work for us both, I promise you."

So much for hope. Still, Matteo would surely be in Eshda. It would be enough to see him, and know that he was safe.

Dalia guided Grainia to the road's left, apart from the others, and gazed up at the fortress until a rankness hit her nostrils, quite apart from the soil's own scorched mineral scent. A scent of roasting rotten meat.

Father made a sour face and looked around. "Scaln traps. At least one's died recently."

The thick gruesome odor was enough to turn her stomach inside out. And apparently she wasn't the only one who felt that way. A solitary rider approached them, coming from the castle. Swarthy and stately, even on horseback, and very well-armed with gleaming spears, blades and such, looking as if he fought against breathing the stinking air.

Smiling, Dalia pulled Grainia further to the left to allow the man to ride past. Undoubtedly, he'd think her a soot-smeared grub.

As the man approached, he nodded gravely to Father, then lifted a swatch of fabric to his lean, hard-edged face. A spare, yet elegant movement such as a nobleman might use. Furthermore, Dalia realized he wasn't as swarthy as she'd believed. Instead, his complexion was dusted with ashes as dark gray as his eyes. Very striking eyes, which widened as he studied her then flinched.

Was she so repulsive?

Dalia banished her smile. She would have sniffed in offense, except that the foul odor increased, and a glottal hissing-gurgling noise caught her attention from the nearby trees. Dalia covered her nose and mouth and glanced toward the dreadful sound, which echoed, then multiplied.

Seething, sinuous, broad-skulled creatures crept toward them from the woods. Leathern-skinned blood-red beasts that seemed vomited from perdition. Stalking *her*.

Riding apart from the others, the slight and exquisite girl smiled at Corban, half-stealing his wits. So like Araine! Corban recoiled—a visceral reaction he couldn't master. Unable to breathe from the shock and from the sudden vile stench polluting the air, Corban tightened the cloth over his nose and mouth, then stole another look at the girl, who'd sobered.

He wasn't mistaken. With those huge light gray eyes, her appealing looks and fragile grace, she could have been Araine's younger sister.

Infinite, why strike me with this girl's resemblance?

Was this some new game to twist his senses?

He glanced away.

Toward a skulking ambush of five skeletal red-skinned beasts that looked as if they'd crawled from a fire instead of the woods. Broad, heavily muscled creatures as sinuous as reptiles, and yellow-eyed... Scalns.

Stalking the girl and her small horse—marking her as prey.

The lead beast charged, and Corban growled, intuitively reaching for the spear slung alongside Ghost's saddle.

No! Infinite, save her!

Chapter 12

Time blurred then vanished as Corban raged, dropped to the ground, and hurtled his spear squarely at the lead scaln's bloodshot yellow eyes. The beast dropped dead before its companions, which cowered and halted just long enough for Corban to slash the second with a lethal wound to its leathery crimson throat. The third slunk about the first beast's corpse, half-circling Corban, its fetid breath reaching him like a surging miasma defiling the air. Threads of venom slid glistening from between the beast's bared teeth as it hissed and lowered its head, gathering momentum to lunge.

Never moving his gaze or sword from the encroaching scaln, Corban reclaimed his spear and flung it with all his might at the third, then slashed at the fourth before it could lunge, felling it as the fifth surged past him ... toward the girl's agitated horse.

She lifted her feet just as the fifth beast raked its claws into her skirts and then downward, slashing bloody streaks into her terrified horse's sides. Corban charged at the scaln's rippling crimson back and wielded his sword two-handed, landing the blade hatchet-like into the base of its muscular neck, driving the beast into the ground.

The girl leaped from her horse as it fell. Beyond her, the shocked nobleman flung himself off his own horse and cried, "Dalia!"

She dropped without a sound, feet first onto the gritty road, then fell forward and caught herself with her hands. Corban scooped the girl away from the dead scaln and her now thrashing horse, then set her on her feet.

The girl, Dalia, gulped audibly and stared up at Corban as if he, not a scaln, were the true monster. To his surprise, she recovered her wits and clutched Corban's hand. "Sir— Tell me you're not scratched or hurt!"

"I'm not." Reorienting himself, Corban took a deep breath and nearly gagged at the stench of five scaln-corpses. Five. He'd killed five scalns and emerged unscathed. How? An impossible feat.

"Grainia!" Dalia gasped and released Corban's hand, turning his attention. She rushed to her quieting horse. "Grainia?"

The sturdy nobleman caught her, holding her back. "Dalia, don't touch her! She's been poisoned."

The girl sobbed, "My lord, how can I not touch her? Those were scalns—she's dying of the wounds! We must comfort her!"

"Just don't touch her," the nobleman admonished. "You know scaln wounds are fatal."

Sniffling, Dalia kneeled near her horse's head. "Grainia, I'm so sorry! My poor girl, you're so brave. I've loved you! You've made me so happy!"

She crooned sweetly until all life and light vanished from her unfortunate horse's eyes. Then she rested her forehead on the darkened road and cried. The nobleman, evidently her father, hugged her. But he looked up at Corban. "Sir, may the Mighty One ever bless and guard you! Name your reward for saving my only child. But *how* did you do it so swiftly? I scarcely had time to leap from my horse—much less draw my sword—and you'd felled them all. By everything that's sacred, I've never seen such fighting!"

Corban shook his head, feeling the sickly aftermath wash over him, casting tremors throughout his limbs. Evidently concerned, the girl looked up at him, tears leaving thin tracks down her tawny cheeks. Her lovely face contorted as she finally perceived the dead-scaln stench. She lifted one hand to her mouth and persisted. "Sir, thank you! Please, won't you accompany us to Eshda and let us tend you? Reassure us that you're not hurt."

He weakened, guilt rendering him unable to refuse this girl's plea. Her tears and entreating gaze were too crushingly similar to Araine's just before she'd vanished.

When he'd judged she must die.

He'd give everything to return to that night and wipe it from existence, just for the chance to be near Araine again, and to control his unfettered emotions, even if cost his final breath.

Looking away from the girl and her father, Corban nodded. Yes, he'd return to Eshda's fortress. Just as well. He'd likely suffer from shock for the remainder of the day. Did he even have enough strength to remount his horse?

Clearly holding similar doubts, the nobleman motioned to two of his servants, who hurried to help—one holding Ghost, the other offering Corban a hand up. Fresh humiliation set him on edge, though he didn't have the strength to act upon his growing internalized fury.

Infinite, what have You done? And why?

Seated behind Father on his horse, Dalia sniffled back tears, then braced herself as Roi called up to Eshda's watchman, "I am Roi Hradedh! I request permission of the king to enter!"

The king. Dalia couldn't think of her darling Matteo as Darzeq's king. Yet it was true, thanks to that wretched Cthar. Was Matteo here? Beneath her breath, Dalia begged the Infinite with all her might, "Please let Matteo be here! Please let him welcome us!"

The guards looked down at Father, then scanned his household. Their attention swiftly focused on the mysterious man who'd fought off the scalns. Someone bellowed from high above, "Lord Corban's returned! Alert Lord Aristo!"

Without further questions, they rushed to open the massive woven-iron gates and then lower the bridge's span.

As the huge gate lifted amid the creaking and groaning of gears, Dalia flung a quizzing glance at the exhausted man who'd saved her. Who was this Lord Corban? She'd never heard of him, but beyond doubt, he was known and trusted here, despite Eshda's formidable defenses. She tugged at her father's arm. "He must be important, my lord—the man who saved us."

"I don't doubt it," Roi muttered. "I hope he's not been poisoned somehow."

"I'm praying not." Losing her sweet Grainia was terrible enough. To lose the man who'd saved her before she'd so much as heard his name would more than add to her grief. Dalia swallowed a fresh sob and blinked hard at the threatening tears. She glanced fretfully at the man once more, but he seemed a-wandering in his own thoughts.

The final spanned section of the bridge lowered, and they were waved across Eshda's beautifully arcaded stone passage. Dalia didn't dare look down at the smoking chasm below. Instead, she fixed her gaze beyond the magnificent gatehouse tunnel to the stone courtyard beyond, which resounded with shouts heralding their approach.

Guards formed ranks on either side of Father's household as they rode into the magnificent enclosed and paved courtyard, its beautiful golden stonework adorned with more graceful, simple stonework arcading. Why had Father scowled at the mention of Eshda? This fortress was truly amazing—set high and clear above the smoldering lands below.

A robust, silver-haired man marched out from the magnificent keep and stood on the stone landing near the sculpted entrance. He folded his arms and watched father's household enter. As Father dismounted and reached up to help

Dalia, a delighted cry made her glance up again at the castle's keep.

Anji dashed past the silver-haired man and swept down the keep's broad stone steps, her mantle flaring and lifting about her as she laughed. Behind her... Dalia gasped. "Matteo!"

She dismounted and slid from Father's grasp, joy warring with her misery. Oh, they both looked older, her sweet lifelong friend and her love. Matteo's face was thinner and somber, despite his smile—she must console him, and Anji.

Snatching up her tattered skirts, Dalia sped to Matteo and Anji, all but flinging herself into their arms, kissing Anji's soft face, then Matteo's rough-whiskered jaw. "You're both here! I didn't dare hope! I've been thinking of you both, constantly."

Anji laughed and hugged her again as Matteo bent to stare into her eyes as if he wanted to study her forever. Dalia touched his face once more. Matteo kissed her cheek, then scooped her closer, dragging Anji into his embrace as well. In his best Master-Tredin style, he mocked, "We know why we're in Eshda, *young lady*! But why are you here?" He lowered his voice to a whisper. "I thought your lord-father disapproved of me. What's happened?"

"It's my fault. I'm in disgrace, and I'm not even supposed to be talking to you. I wrote a bit of doggerel and sent it throughout the Tinem North valley. It made Cthar so angry that she's sent soldiers searching for me. Father brought me here for my own safety."

She'd quite forgotten that Father was watching. Dalia stole a guilty peek over her shoulder. Roi Hradedh shook his head and beckoned her to his side once more, obviously intending to hold her to his ordained punishment.

Matteo pressed Dalia's hand, summoning her attention. Allowing her another chance to gaze into his beautiful, long-lashed golden eyes, which were so mesmerizing that she fought to pay attention to his words. He grinned. "I believe we're all still in disgrace—you'd best return to him. Wait ... there's Lord Corban. I saw him off earlier. Why's he returned?"

Hoping she wouldn't dissolve within puddles of tears, Dalia said, "He ... saved my life, but so remarkably that I doubt he's mortal. Ask him what happened. I'll cry."

Dalia studied the mysterious nobleman, trying to comprehend him. Lord Corban looked away, and it was just as well. Remembering this lord's courage and nearly unbelievable fighting abilities brought poor Grainia's death to mind again. No. Dalia refused to face that grief. Everyone was watching.

Father motioned to her again, more sternly this time, both eyebrows raised. Dalia gave her beloved friends a final hug and then sped to him, returning to captivity.

With Matteo and Anji following, and obviously listening, the portly Lord Aristo Faolan approached, his gracious expression creased with worry. "My lord, forgive me, but was there some trouble? We weren't expecting Lord Corban's return."

Dalia fought tears as Father wrapped one protective arm around her shoulders then nodded to Lord Corban. "We are forever grateful for Lord Corban, sir. He saved my daughter's life. An ambush of scalns charged us as we approached."

The portly lord's grizzled eyebrows lifted, conveying shock. "Scalns? This early in the year? Winter will be early then. They'll hunt everything that moves as they feed for winter. I'll have my men set spike-traps all along the road to thin them out."

If only those traps had been set weeks ago. Dalia looked down at the pavings. Dear Grainia could have been saved.

Too tired to do more than descend from his horse, Corban leaned against Ghost and watched the happy reunion. So the young lady Dalia was a friend to both the Lady Anji and Matteo of Darzeq? Interesting. The way she touched the king's face ... and his fervent kiss to her cheek... They were in love.

Corban masked a bleak scowl as envy welled, followed by renewed self-incriminating fury. He had only himself to blame for losing his own love. Yet Araine had never greeted him with such joy.

Actually, now that he considered Araine's behavior, Corban confessed another truth to himself. He'd believed he'd lost her, yet clearly she'd never been his. Indeed, whenever Araine had looked at him, Corban had seen what no man wished to see: compassion, not passion in his beloved's gaze—unless he'd frightened her, as he had all too often.

In truth, Araine had never loved him. Yet he longed for her still, and he owed her some form of justice. Nothing had changed. He needed to find Araine. He couldn't become involved with matters here in Darzeq. He must continue on his way. Why did he care what happened to these people? Yet he did care. If he left them, would he regret the decision?

As the girl returned to her lord-father, Corban muttered in complaint, "Infinite, why have You brought me here again? Why do You pursue me?"

Dalia looked over her shoulder at him, and Corban brought his gaze back to Ghost, unwilling to answer her silent curiosity. Unable to do more than rest, recover, and complain in silence to the Infinite.

Freshly shaven and wearing clean hunting garments he'd unsealed from one of his lord-father's storage chests, Matteo stepped up on the stone dais and sat at the high table, Anji, Ekiael, and Corban to his right, while Lord Tragobre, Dalia, and Aristo sat to his left—with Aristo subtly directing servants here and there, pouring watered wine for himself and Roi, fresh juice for Dalia and Matteo and a steaming tisane of herbs that Anji had requested for Ekiael and herself.

Ekiael prayed over the bread, blessing the Infinite, and then the servants brought out platters of food—a hurried but welcomed feast ordered to honor Roi Hradedh's arrival and Corban's victory over the scalns.

A small army of guards had been sent earlier to clear the road of dead scalns, which they'd burned, and Dalia's unfortunate little Grainia, whom Matteo had ordered respectfully buried. The guards had sent back lengthy and reverential reports detailing the wounds inflicted on the scalns and the horse, extoling Lord Corban's valor.

Corban refused to speak of the clash when most men would have been boasting.

"Sire," Roi Hradedh complained quietly as they helped themselves to bread and marinated vegetables, "your Lord Corban rejected my offer of a reward, *and* he turned his back on me!"

To excuse Corban, Matteo murmured, "Forgive him, my lord. He's cousin to Siphra's queen and his family's pride is ancient and ocean-deep. He's also called himself a living battlefield, therefore humor him."

Roi puffed out a breath and accepted several slices of richly sauced venison. "I will. If you could see the man fight, Sire ... it was like watching some legend come to life."

"I've seen him fight, and I agree." However, the first time he'd seen Corban fight in that public house against the mercenaries, the man seemed capable enough with a sword, but nothing beyond that of any well trained nobleman. Corban's newfound light-swift speed and exactness with weapons was surely a gift from the Infinite, as Ekiael had declared. To shift the subject, Matteo asked, "Are you calling me 'Sire' because you've changed your mind about supporting my cause?"

Lord Tragobre's frown could have collapsed Eshda's bridge. "I call you 'Sire' because you are indeed the rightful king. As for supporting your cause—" Tragobre exhaled deeply. "We need more of Darzeq's lords bringing their men to your cause before any of us can march. I'll not send my good men off to certain death, no matter how much I honored your lord-father, and much as I might honor you."

Well, that was blunt. Matteo carved off a bite of his venison, resisting his desire to glance at Dalia, who was undoubtedly listening, and remarkably quiet. "You're admirably forthright, my lord, therefore I'll be equally blunt. I've summoned the First Forum to meet here in a few weeks. I intend to require their approval for my marriage. Then I'll ask your formal permission to wed your honorable and beautiful daughter, so please consider my request."

Roi spluttered, "What? No! Think of the added danger you'll place her in. And, may I remind you, Sire, the First Forum's been dismissed! Dissolved!"

"No, it hasn't," Matteo countered. "I commanded no such thing. In fact, I sent each lord including you a personal summons yesterday, with instructions to avoid Arimna and the queen-mother. You're welcome to remain in Eshda until then. As for danger ... we're all in danger here." Matteo leaned forward and grinned at Dalia. "By the way, tell me about this doggerel verse you've written to aggravate my traitorous grandmother. It might become my anthem."

Dalia glanced up at her father, her beautiful eyes so wide and pleading that Matteo wanted to kiss her. Roi growled, slipped a folded parchment from within his belted overtunic, and handed it to Matteo.

Mourn Darzeq... . Matteo's smile faded as he read. Memories resurfaced of his parents and the massacre. His brothers fell again, one by one, butchered by Gueronn and his mercenaries.

Tarquin, Alvir, Sheth, Efraim, Boas, Melkir...

He finished Dalia's anguished tribute in silence and then handed it to Anji.

If Cthar were here— Matteo started to shove aside the thought. But the depths of his silent ferocity acknowledged the truth.

If that she-scaln were here, Matteo would cut her to pieces without regret.

How viciously Cthar-like of him. Would this conflict with his grandmother finally bring out his blood's true nature? Bad enough that he'd been born of Cthar's "self-above-all" bloodline, but had he inherited her tendencies?

Was he ultimately corruptible?

Furthermore, was it wrong of him to enmesh Dalia further within his troubles? Perhaps he should send her away. Hide her, and Anji, among the Eosyths, or in Istgard until Cthar was dead and this "doggerel," as Dalia called it, was forgotten. At least Dalia and Anji would remain safe; he'd be sure of it.

Then, he would deal with Cthar.

Quietly, so that neither Roi nor Anji heard him, Matteo threatened beneath his breath, "Grandmother, your own blood will kill you. If it costs me my life, I'll destroy you!"

Chapter 13

Thirst-driven, Corban drained his cup of the healing tisane, its mild sweetness easing his raw throat. At least the brew didn't taste medicinal. Before Corban could ask, Ekiael refilled his cup, then grinned. "At this rate, Lord Corban, we'll both be perfectly healed by morning. What are you brooding over now, eh? Talk and let's deal with matters before you frighten the ladies."

Corban scoffed and lifted his cup again. "You know my complaint, sir. Why should I say a word?"

"Talking helps." Ekiael waved one hand, becoming cheerfully expansive. "Think of it as a curative for your mind. Talk to me, or talk to the Infinite—we're both willing to listen."

"As if He will agree to my objections."

"As if your objections supersede what's best for our future? Not just yours and mine, Lord Corban, but Darzeq's and indeed the world's future. Unless you know more than He-Who-Sees."

So they must debate? Very well. If he offended Darzeq's high priest, then Ekiael had invited the offense. Yet Ekiael was ever-approachable, and he'd accept most verbal strikes with ease. Corban swallowed and launched into his grievances. "It's as if I'm His captive! He's taken my life in His hands and won't release me. It's obvious that He actually longs to destroy me, or at least drive me insane. If I leave again, He'll inflict some new scheme upon me—some new twist to wrench me about and make me question my every thought. I feel He is here. Constantly *here*!"

"Ah ... Spirit beckons you! Do you know how many priests would half kill themselves to be in your place? The beloved Spirit longs to commune with you, yet you perceive His concern as being hunted because *you* are trying to ignore Him so you can do as you please." Ekiael shook his head at Corban. "Forgive me, my lord, but I'm convinced you want to hear the truth." He folded a small heap of venison within some fresh bread. "Do not apply your nature's traits to the Infinite's, because I guarantee you, His motives are pure, and yours are not. Your senses, on the other hand, are finite, warped by our fallen world, whereas His are eternal and unfailing. Instead, trust Him! Pray and let His nature become as your own—then you will indeed live!"

"As some divine puppet."

"As His cherished son, who has much to learn about communicating with his Infinite Father. Believe me, He waits for you to speak to Him, even if it's an argument. Just be aware that you're not omnipotent, therefore, you cannot win the final argument."

"What if I refuse to speak? What if I refuse everything He requires of me?"

"Then refuse. That decision is yours. However, He will find another who'll obey, and He *will* grieve."

"Unlikely."

"Indisputably likely." Ekiael bit into his meal, clearly delighted to eat actual food once more. When Corban remained silent, Ekiael swallowed his bread and meat and continued, "What Father doesn't grieve over a child bent upon his or her own destruction?"

Anji interrupted their debate with a note. "My lords, look! Dalia wrote this and sent copies throughout the Tinem North valley."

Ekiael took another bite of food and read Dalia's verses as he chewed. Swallowing hard, the priest snorted. "Perfect! I'm sure that this has thrown a few knots into Cthar's royal sash! May the Infinite be served!"

He handed the note to Corban, adding, "I wish the young lady hadn't risked her life with this, but it can't be undone. We're all dead men anyway if we can't convince others to join Matteo's cause. If you're determined to escape us, my lord, you'd best depart soon."

Corban frowned, read Dalia's impassioned verses, then paused. Had that charming young lady truly endangered her life with these words? Most likely. Furthermore, if the queen mother was all that he'd heard, she would gladly see the Lady Dalia garroted and hung from a city wall. Corban glared at the parchment again, remembering his own rage at his lord-father's death in Siphra—a death he'd perceived as tyranny.

Well, here was irony. By defending this wronged young king—a champion of the Infinite—he'd stormed to the other side of the conflict. Nevertheless, he'd found a cause worth venting his wrath over. And why not? If he left Eshda again, he'd likely be diverted by another disaster that would land him here once more. Because *He* had willed Corban here.

To the Infinite, Corban complained beneath his breath, "What *is* Your plan? And why involve me when I'm such an unwilling servant? Speak to me!" A chill ran up his arms as his words faded. What had he done? And yet ...

Corban lifted his cup and mouthed the words again. "Speak to me!"

Under Father's watchful gaze, Dalia marched through the vast noon-bright courtyard, nodding and smiling at the guards. Eshda's fortress was so beautiful—perfect! Simple yet elegant stonework walls and towers framing this huge enclosed courtyard, with its fine buildings. Her gaze strayed to the kitchen, the guard's hall, the laundry hall, and a grand building quite apart from the others, which could only be Eshda's house dedicated to the Infinite.

She started toward the graceful, gold-roofed building. Until the austerely handsome Lord Corban crossed her path, then bowed. Had he deliberately planned this happenstance? Dalia halted and smiled, liking him despite his forbidding appearance.

Corban's grim countenance softened into an almost-smile. "I read your note to Darzeq, Lady Dalia. Well done. Your lord-father was wise to bring you to Eshda, lest you both be stung after bashing such a hornet's nest." He inclined his head toward Father, all courtesy. "Let's turn and walk toward Lord Tragobre, shall we? I've no wish to make him suspicious of my intentions."

Dalia beamed at him, liking him all the more. "Thank you, my lord. I've angered my lord-father enough for now—and the hornets are likely to prove lethal. I'd hate to die while in my family's bad graces."

Corban scolded, sharp as Master Tredin. "You have no business speaking of your death when I took such pains to save your life, lady." Grudgingly, he added, "At the Infinite's behest."

"Thank you, my lord. Truly. I've had a good life thus far, and I strive to appreciate everything—as I appreciated your astonishing rescue. You deserve to become a legend! I'm still amazed."

"So am I," the proud lord muttered. "I confess, it's not my doing at all, but the Infinite's. I had nothing to say about it."

Dalia halted and stared into his stone-cool gray eyes. This lord was shockingly resentful of his Creator. Was he angry that he'd saved her? "My lord, forgive me, but you sound frankly dour when you speak of the Infinite. You don't need to answer me, but *why*?"

For a long instant, he studied her as if debating the wisdom of trusting her with his thoughts. Gruff-voiced, he said, "My past dealings with ... the Infinite ... have been openly hostile. Even murderous. My being frankly dour is a vast improvement."

"No," Dalia shook her head at him. "You cannot be a murderer. I refuse to believe it."

"That's very kind of you. However, it's true. I've spent half the spring and most of the summer fleeing my crime. Now I've resolved to face justice as soon as matters here are settled. I intend to seek out the one I hurt the most, beg her forgiveness, and surrender to justice."

Dalia sighed over this proud nobleman's remorse. "If I could plead your cause to her, I would. She'd forgive you—I hope."

Father was approaching, clearly perplexed that they'd stopped for this seemingly private talk. Dalia smiled and bowed, hoping to dispel Roi Hradedh's exasperation. He might yet lock her away as he'd threatened. Would he allow this conversation to continue? Lord Corban was so intriguing....

Father bowed to Lord Corban, giving silent permission for the conversation to continue. To soothe her curiosity, Dalia asked, "By the way, Lord Corban, you're not sorry you saved me, are you?"

"I'm grateful, lady. This I promise." He studied her again, adding, "You resemble the young lady I spoke of. She was, until the last, the joy of my life. Without her, I have no peace."

How wonderfully his expression changed when he spoke of the young lady he loved! Dalia started to ask about the young woman when Anji's voice drifted across the courtyard. "Dalia! There you are." She approached, smiling, with Matteo following, though he appeared far less pleased. Why was he so serious?

She greeted Anji with a fierce hug, and exchanged glances with Matteo. His eyebrows lifted meaningfully, but his concern faded as he greeted Corban. "Good day, my lord. You're looking much better. I speak for all of us when I say I'm thankful."

"I appreciate your thanks, sir." The haughty nobleman hesitated, as if debating the wisdom of his decision. "As a favor, may I request a few details concerning Belaal's new prophet? Did your brother mention her appearance, her age, anything apart from her name?"

Matteo shook his head, his golden eyes shadowed with regret. "My lord, I've few details to offer. My brother Sheth met her briefly in Belaal. He said that she was young, lovely, sheltered, and beset with hiccoughs. Belaal's king prized her highly as his prophet."

Lord Corban's expression darkened, turning gloomy. He bowed. "Thank you, Sire." He retreated from them, clearly lost in his own somber thoughts—unwilling to enlighten them regarding his interest in Belaal's prophet.

Matteo clasped Dalia's hand, snatching her attention from the intriguing Lord Corban. He inclined his head politely toward Roi and Anji, then led Dalia several steps away. Matteo stopped, then smiled down at her, so wistful that Dalia's heart caught in a small skip of worry. "My lord, what's wrong? Have you received bad news?"

"No. You're here, and I'm grateful. Your safety has been one of my chief prayers since the massacre. Yet I'm worried." He covered both of her hands within his own and murmured, "I'm questioning my wish to marry you. Your life will be all the more endangered."

He was changing his mind about the marriage they'd prayed over for months? "No! My lord, you know I'm not afraid! Why should you be?" She hadn't convinced him; she saw it within less than a blink. She stepped nearer—making Father nervous—and she argued fierce and low: "Won't it be better to present a stable happily married king to Darzeq? With the promise that Darzeq's bloodline will continue? The royal house is all but destroyed! You must offer proof to the First Forum that you look to the future. Surely the Infinite will honor His word to Darzeq that their royal line will ever rule and be honored for the Infinite's Name!"

Matteo's grip tightened, engulfing her hands. "Those are my thoughts as well, love, and I promise you, my feelings haven't changed. If anything, I cherish you more since the deaths. Which is why I need to know that I'm making a wise decision—how can I continue if you die because of me? Lord Corban described himself as a living battlefield, yet he might have been describing me. Give me a few weeks, Dalia, please. Let's face the Forum and wait upon the Infinite's will."

Anything could happen within a few weeks. She might lose him altogether. Before she could muster another word to convince Matteo of anything, he bent and kissed her fingertips, nodded to her lord-father, then departed in silence for the main hall—and for Lord Aristo, who waited on the steps above the grand, bustling courtyard.

Father and Anji approached. Anji hugged her. "Dalia, don't look so sad. I'm sure Matteo will sort out matters; he's overwhelmed and fears for your safety, so we must wait and pray."

Pray? Indeed she would pray!

Father gave her a strange half-bleak look. "It's clear that you truly love each other. Blight! This complicates everything."

Corban turned in front of the huge guards' hall, scowling. Why did he torment himself? The king's description of Belaal's prophet had resolved almost nothing.

Young, lovely, sheltered, and beset with hiccoughs.

Hiccoughs. Yes, Araine had suffered that weakness quite often. However the general description could fit any young woman. Interesting that within days of arriving in Darzeq, after months of flight and escape, he'd heard Araine's name spoken by Darzeq's own uncrowned king, and Darzeq's high priest. What were the true odds of such a chance?

Is this why You brought me here?

No. He imagined the connection.

Was Araine in Belaal? If there was the least chance... If he went to Belaal to request an audience with the king, and to speak to Belaal's prophet, would his time be wasted? More to the point, would he long to kill Belaal's king for taking Araine—if she was Araine—as the royal favorite? For if she was truly Araine, she would undoubtedly become a royal favorite.

Corban growled at the thought of Araine in Belaal's royal clutches—jealous hatred speeding his impulses to murder. Again. He rubbed one hand over his chest, willing his fury-driven heartbeat to slow. He must calm himself before he struck at someone. He couldn't afford to make enemies here. His father had been executed for trying to commit regicide, and Darzeq's king might be less welcoming if that truth became known.

Moreover, he had no right to be jealous of Araine. Hadn't he surrendered all hope of her during their final confrontation? He must bear this thought; he'd brought it upon himself.

He slowed, wrestling with the unwelcome idea—until two guards passed him, carrying a pole over their shoulders, with five crimson leathern scaln tails tacked to the pole like dangling blood-bright trophies.

Other guards stared at the grim relics, then glanced his way—utterly respectful. Not the sort of attention he relished. Corban called to the guards, "Wait! Where are you taking those? Why weren't they burned?"

The tail-bearers halted and glanced at him warily. One finally spoke, reluctance weighing his every word. "My lord, forgive us, but we were commanded to bring these proofs to the great hall. They're to be displayed from the hall's beams among the royal banners—the pride of Eshda. The king and Lord Aristo are determined to honor you."

"No!" Corban stalked past them through the courtyard. He ran up the steps and charged into the great hall, where he found the king somberly conferring with Lord Aristo, who was motioning to the hall's high, smoke-darkened ceiling beams. Corban interrupted them, not bothering to be polite. "Why weren't the scalns' tails burned? They're poisonous!"

Aristo bowed. "Forgive us, my lord, but we don't know that they're poisonous. Furthermore—"

Matteo interrupted, "Furthermore, and sadly, my lord, you're to become a national hero, and it's to our advantage that you're in Eshda. I'm indebted to you beyond measure, and I intend to reward you fully as soon as possible. Right now, I must be content with proclaiming your feats, and I beg you to humor me."

Corban willed himself to don a veneer of patience. A show of tranquility. The attention was unwelcome indeed, but to fight would summon even more attention. "I'm not inclined to humor, therefore I bow to you unwillingly, Sire. Eshda's yours, so command matters as you please."

Darzeq's king accepted his acquiescence, completely ignorant of how rarely Thaenfalls granted such submission. Corban bowed, but before he could turn away, Matteo halted him with an upraised hand. "All this reminds me that I must provide you with garments befitting your courtly status. It's expected of me, and you need fresh clothes—no offense, my lord, but you're beginning to look ragged. If it's any comfort, I don't expect you to be gracious toward the lords of the First

Forum. Just lurk about and glower as you please when they arrive."

Corban almost smiled. "Trust me, Sire, I will glower."

Early autumn sunlight streamed into Eshda's bright, banner-draped great hall, welcoming Darzeq's lords of the First Forum. From his vantage-point on the dais, standing just above the royal guards, Corban muted the First Forum's jubilation, taking advantage of Matteo's command to glare and skulk as he pleased in his new gold-embroidered black robes, selected by Matteo from King Jonatan's own Eshda garderobe. Despite his mistrust of these lords, he must be on his most court-appropriate behavior out of respect to Matteo. If he, Lord Corban Thaenfall, openly honored Darzeq's king, perhaps these capricious lords of the First Forum would follow his lead and seriously accept Matteo as their rightful ruler.

Darzeq's newly arrived lords mingled about below, filling the hall with a buzz of confusion, some of the lords laughing, others studying Corban as if they wished to question him or challenge him. Corban eyed the dubious lords balefully until they looked away. Several actually retreated.

Anji, Ekiael, Dalia, and Roi Hradedh wandered through the crowd as well, greeting friends and speaking graciously to others. Dalia in particular was either teased or frowned upon as she accompanied her lord-father. Clearly, rumors abounded regarding her political activities, and Ekiael and Anji lingered near, Ekiael formally clad in his priestly robes, interceding graciously if a pompous nobleman became too overbearing. Several times, Corban twitched with the violent desire to interfere, to defend this girl who was so like Araine.

Ironic of him. Why hadn't these overwhelming protective instincts taken over when he'd comprehended Araine's 'betrayal'? In truth, he'd held no genuinely protective instincts concerning Araine—he protected her only because he'd deemed her as his possession. Until that last night. He shouldn't have touched her. He should have fled the instant he'd realized she followed the Infinite, instead of giving way to violence against his unfortunate Araine.

An ache took hold, seizing Corban's breath. He drew in a deep breath. As he fought the pain, he prayed, wary yet question-ridden. Infinite ... am I changing? I now see myself as I was, and I am appalled. Why did You have mercy upon me? Aloud, he muttered, "Help me to understand!"

Guards to Corban's right, called the First Forum to order. Matteo entered the great hall from a private doorway concealed by regal purple banners. Corban turned and bowed. Darzeq's new king seemed prepared for his role—no one could fault the young man. Clad in his lord-father's royal purple-and-gold robes, Matteo's regal bearing and his own glittering ceremonial insignias and weapons, all emphasized his rights to the throne, as did his gold circlet, resting in place of his anticipated crown. The forum lords hushed for an instant, then a buzz of talk lifted again.

Matteo glanced around, stepped onto the dais and stood before his father's throne-like chair, which had been brought out of storage. "What do you think, Lord Corban? The majority of Darzeq's lords are in attendance. Anything we agree upon here will become law. If I can win them to my side, I will have Darzeq. My family will be avenged!"

"It's maddening that you're dependent upon an agreement of cowards," Corban muttered. He eyed a blue-cloaked lord who threaded his way through the throng. The man's conspicuous mildness didn't rest well with Corban. The man seemed an actor, deserving a mask in addition to the false-gracious one he wore. Heavily-swathed and soft-footed, the nobleman slowed in the front of the hall, directly aligning his stance with the king's.

All his senses lifting like the bristling hairs on the back of a threatened hound, Corban hissed to the Infinite, "What's this? Show me his intent."

The meek lord smiled at Matteo, bowed ... and slowly, too slowly ... shifted an arm beneath his cloak, lifting a weapon.

An arrow-point gleamed bright beneath Corban's gaze, betraying the man's murderous resolve before the miscreant ever lifted the short bow against the king.

Corban shoved Matteo down into the throne-like chair, then snarled at the false-meek fool, eager to kill.

Chapter 14

Corban seized Matteo's footstool and flung it at the failed assassin even as the man released his arrow. The arrow's midflight 'thump!' against the footstool resounded through the vast hall—just before the footstool smashed into the attacker's face and threw him flat on his back before the entire First Forum.

Two other lords drew their swords in unison, their reflexes far too sluggish, though their intentions were clear. Both noblemen started toward Matteo.

The king's guards stirred, but not quickly enough. Corban snatched one guard's javelin and sent it whistling toward the nearest rebel-lord, taking him down with the impact. Two guards headed for the fallen one and two charged toward the last rebel while the Forum's remaining lords fled to the walls and drew their weapons, prepared to fight.

Ekiael and Roi drew their swords and rushed Anji and Dalia from the great hall, toward the secluded, banner-veiled door beyond the dais, though Dalia lagged, clearly frightened for Matteo.

Matteo called to her, "Go! We'll summon you soon."

As soon as she'd departed with the others, one young nobleman shouted from the far wall, "Let every man place his swords and daggers at the entry and submit to being searched or risk death! The king must be protected, and Darzeq's crisis must be stemmed here and now!"

Dalia hugged Father and bit down tears. She *must* believe Matteo was safe. Truly, Corban protected him with the Infinite's strength. Strength she wished she possessed.

"Dalia." Father tightened his grip around her shoulders and guided her to the spiraling stone stairs. He'd bruise her if he didn't release her soon. Shaking his gleaming sword, Roi whispered hoarsely, "I'm certain the king's safe now. But this is what you'll face, Dalia! Is this how you wish to live? Because it'll certainly turn me silver well before my time!"

She patted his hand. If only she could ease his grip. "My lord, if we can bring all the lords present to a peaceable agreement, that they should support Matteo and oust Cthar, then you've no worries. You'll be years away from silvering."

"Since when have we of the First Forum agreed upon anything of importance?" Roi huffed.

Ekiael turned about on the step above them, eyebrows raised, sword toward Father. "You're implying that the Lady Rhiysa's personal petition for marriage was of no importance?"

Father made a face. "Ekiael, no offense, but you're a priest, not my son or another lord. The Lady Rhiysa's petition to marry you held little actual political significance."

"Well!" Anji took one step down to stand with her husband, her sweet voice indignant. "I'm glad that our lords of the Forum thought we weren't important enough to worry about! Mere princess and high priest."

Father lowered his chin, never good ... he was about to become indignant. "It *might* soothe you both to know that I spoke privately to most of the lords present last spring and mentioned that linking the crown to the temple could prove a commendable way to strengthen the crown's domestic image. And who better to represent the crown than our adored and gentle princess, the Lady Anji Rhiysa?"

Ekiael started up the stairs again. "Thank you, but I don't feel any better."

"I do. Slightly," Anji hesitated, glancing at the doorway to the great hall. "I'm sure Matteo is troubled by the attack, as is most of the Forum. However, I'm certain he's safe with our Lord Corban nearby."

"Lord Corban ... what sort of man is he?" Father nudged Dalia toward the stairs. "His fighting abilities are impossible to believe, yet I saw him with my own eyes. Twice, he's fought like something from a legend. Incredible!"

Ekiael relaxed, clearly forgetting his indignation at the mention of Lord Corban. "It's the Infinite's power displayed through him. How I've blessed the Infinite for sending the man to join my household."

"We're blessed as well." Roi glanced down at Dalia. "If not for him, my daughter would be dead."

Taking advantage of Father's brief doting expression, Dalia begged, "My lord, can't we wait here? Please? I can't leave Matteo."

Roi closed his eyes. Dalia held her imploring glance. When Father looked down at her again, he growled and shook his head. "What am I to do with you? I warn you of danger and you run straight toward it!"

She couldn't blink down the tears quickly enough. "I love him! He needs us near. My lord ... Father—"

"You'd risk us all!"

"Cast me off publicly," Dalia urged. "Go out to the hall and tell the First Forum that you've disowned me. Tell them I'm rebellious and a scapegrace, unworthy of Tragobre!"

If she'd slapped him, Father couldn't look more appalled. "You're my only child! Who would believe me if I disowned you? *I* wouldn't, because it's not true!"

He stared at her hard, as if meeting someone new. "You're truly set on marrying him? On facing war for his sake—and possibly death?"

Matteo. Dalia sighed over the very thought of him. His quiet jokes, soothing presence, and his dear face. Not least of all, his wry smile, and stunning golden eyes.... "Yes. I've already placed myself at risk, so why not? If I can't be Matteo's wife, then I don't care who I marry. I'll never love another man as I love him."

Roi Hradedh, Lord of Tragobre, turned bleak, the light fading from his gaze, like a man at his child's funeral.

From the watch-keep in Eshda's massive gatehouse, Corban fought fatigue to stand beside Lord Aristo as official witness to the disposal of the three traitor-lords who'd dared to turn against their king. The one still-living lord squirmed and fought as he was lifted over the side of Eshda's high bridge and dropped into the smoldering gorge below, while the two other lords—dead the instant Corban struck them—were lifted a bit more reverently and held over the side of the bridge. As the last corpse dropped like a stone into the steaming vale below, Lord Aristo sighed.

"Let there be no others. Our Creator sees that I've no joy in ordering deaths. Yet our king, His anointed lord of Darzeq, must be protected at all costs."

Corban nodded. "I commend you for doing your duty, my lord. Now that the matter's finished, I'll return to the hall and guard the king."

"Thank you, my lord." Aristo bowed to him, his expression wearied as Corban felt. "I'll write the official statements and send word to the families of these traitors—with their possessions. We'll let it be known that the king has no wish to profit by their deaths, though it is his right to confiscate their estates and dispose of their families as he wishes. He's chosen mercy."

Was mercy the wisest course? Vipers' nests, according to Siphran laws established by the former King Segere, must be exterminated, down to the youngest family members. Corban frowned. "May his mercy be repaid with new loyalties from those he spared."

"That is our hope."

Matteo sat in his father's massive, dark-carved chair and watched as each remaining lord placed swords, daggers, and all manner of blades in the hall's doorway, then haughtily submitted to being searched by Eshda's guards. Corban sat on a bench to Matteo's right, near the restored footstool, which still sported the arrow spiked in its center. Recognizing his defender's now-familiar weariness, Matteo leaned forward and waved a hand to catch Corban's attention. Only half joking, he gestured to the wounded footstool. "If we survive, and if I gain control of Darzeq, I'll build an alcove for this thing in Arimna Palace and command a plaque engraved to commemorate your latest exploit—this arrow caught mid-air by the boulder-heavy footstool."

Corban shrugged, the motion drained of strength. "Your children's children will find some excuse to be rid of it eventually, Sire."

"I hope not." Of course, he presumed he'd live long enough to marry Dalia and have children. After Darzeq was finally at peace. Matteo brooded, watching the orderly search process at the far end of the hall. Who among these lords would ultimately support his cause? Perhaps by the end of the day, he'd have an accurate guess of his allies and his foes.

Thaddeus Ormr approached, unarmed and finished with his search. Where was his lord-father? His cousins? Was

Thaddeus the only member of the Ormr clan who remained loyal to King Jonatan's line?

Somber, the corners of his eyes and mouth etched with the first tracings of grim lines, Thaddeus kneeled before the dais, then bowed. "Sire. I apologize again for your lack of a welcome in Iydan."

Discomfited, Matteo motioned to Tarquin's childhood comrade. "No need for a second apology. Stand, Thaddeus, and speak freely. Where's your lord-father?"

"We argued, sir, and I travelled here without his approval. He forbade his brothers and our cousins to go, fearing the queen might send an army to attack us along the way."

"We're all taking risks with this gathering. I understand Lord Iydan's fear." Lord Iydan, Magni Ormr had ever been a fickle ally. Yet the Ormr clan was too wealthy to ignore or insult. "When you return to Iydan, tell your lord-father that I look forward to greeting him after Darzeq is at peace."

"If he's speaking to me."

"Will he bow to Cthar in Arimna?"

Thaddeus snorted. "If he does, I won't speak to him. Apart from giving Darzeq its late and worthy King Jonatan, she's done nothing else but spend our money."

Bitterness alone was enough to make Thaddeus an ally, but the heir of Iydan bowed to Lord Corban, who regarded him with a cool, wearied stare. "Lord Corban—I hope I've pronounced your name correctly. Thank you, sir, for saving our king and the Lady Dalia of Tragobre. Darzeq owes you an incalculable debt."

Corban lifted one hand, seeming more nonchalant than fatigued. "I'm opposed to injustice. And to scalns of every kind."

Thaddeus brightened and dug into his money pouch. "Thank you, my lord. Speaking of scalns, that reminds me ... I saved Iydan's copy of Dalia's note."

The muted squeak of iron hinges just beyond the dais caught Matteo's attention. Ekiael peered around the purple-and-gold curtain, studying the scene in the hall. Matteo called to him, "My lord-priest, is Dalia there? And Anji? If they wish to return and witness today's proceedings, I believe we're safe."

Thaddeus opened the folded parchment. "Thank you, Sire. I'll ask her to sign this parchment as my keepsake."

One of the southern lords approached the dais, sturdy, gray-haired, tanned from his journey and a bit disheveled from being searched. He kneeled before Matteo, grumbling dramatically, "Aw, what'll become of me when I'm finally too old to kneel, Sire? You'll have to lock me away! I doubt you remember me, O king, but your lord-father and I hunted together when we were young." He bowed. "I am Kemuel Talon of Lohe Bay."

"Lord Kemuel. Welcome. Stand, please." Even as Matteo nodded to the robust lord, a memory resurfaced. Father had mentioned Kemuel once, laughing heartily. Kemuel ... the scoundrel.

Dalia had returned with Lord Tragobre, her beautiful face so distressed that Matteo longed to kiss away her fears and console her. Before she could do more than bow to Matteo, Lord Kemuel said, "Tragobre! This is your daughter? By the Infinite's *great* mercy, she resembles her beautiful mother more than you!" He shook his head at Dalia teasingly. "Young lady, even in our quiet swamp at Lohe Bay, we've received a scrap of your reputed handiwork."

"May I say..." he reached beneath his cloak and dug out a parchment. "We appreciated this work mightily! Such heartfelt verses could be written only by one who sincerely loved our royal family. Someone who, perhaps, loves our King Matteo as well, eh?"

Dalia blushed. Lord Kemuel grinned, revealing a disarming gap between his front teeth. He winked at her, then glanced at Matteo. "I see."

Matteo smiled but remained silent. Why deny the truth? Yet he had no intention of officially proclaiming it either. Not until Cthar was brought to justice, and he'd ensured peace in Darzeq.

Thankfully, Kemuel abandoned his teasing and rejoined the other lords, who were gathering in small groups throughout the hall, talking as they waited for the guards to finish their searches. Aristo returned, bowed to Matteo and murmured, "I've placed additional guards throughout the hall and the outer yard, on the lookout for more suspicious activity."

"Thank you, Aristo. Please be seated. I'd welcome your opinion of our talks today."

Ekiael offered a prayer and a blessing to the Infinite. Then, without preamble, he removed a vial from his priestly belt and called out, "Lords of Darzeq, attend the words of your king, for according to the Infinite's laws and will, Matteo of Arimna rules you by right and law!" A shiver slid over Matteo as Darzeq's high priest approached, twisting the vial within his fingers to open the sealed stopper. His voice booming, Ekiael, cried, "Matteo! Son of King Jonatan of Arimna, today you are consecrated to the Infinite and to Darzeq! Rule with justice, humility, and devotion to your Creator as you serve your people with all your might!"

As Matteo sat statue-still upon his father's northern throne, Darzeq's high priest poured the vial's contents over Matteo's head. Golden oil seeped through Matteo's hair, trickled along his scalp, then slid over his forehead and down his face, dripping onto his garments.

Without another word, Ekiael proceeded to his designated place, a seat near Corban's bench off to Matteo's right on the dais. Anji, Dalia, and Lord Tragobre—all interested onlookers—seated themselves on benches to Matteo's left, just below the dais.

Matteo willed himself to remain calm—to resist thinking too deeply of his unexpected anointing in his lord-father's place. Matters must proceed. He cleared his throat and called out, "My lords, I command you in all civility and courtesy, state your concerns for Darzeq. I am listening."

With astonishing speed, Lord Kemuel raised one hand, saluted the Forum and Matteo, then stood, claiming the right to speak first. "Now, my lords, here we are again, not in Arimna as we expected, but in a far more interesting place—witnesses to interesting times. Yet I wish to resume our last debate and finish what we left undecided last spring."

He bowed toward Ekiael and Anji. "We granted Darzeq's only princess, the Lady Anji Rhiysa, permission to marry Darzeq's high priest. I believe we still agree that we made the right decision!"

Polite applause met his words, and more than a few Forum lords, including Kemuel, smiled at Anji and Ekiael, offering silent congratulations.

Kemuel's smile faded with the applause. He swept his mantle about himself more firmly and strode to the center of the hall, yelling, "But what did I say then, my lords?" He turned about, glaring at them all. Matteo straightened, intrigued. He'd been locked away in Kiyrem during the spring Forum. What had Kemuel argued for last spring that he was still irked enough to resume the argument now?

Kemuel bellowed, "I declared that the king's sons should be married for Darzeq's own good! Yet more than half of you argued over whom Tarquin should marry—with such vehemence that nothing was decided! Nothing! And look where our petty disputes have taken us! We are on the verge of losing our royal house! Only one son remains to Jonatan."

Bowing again to Matteo in the silence, Kemuel continued, "If our Lord Tarquin and his brothers had been granted permission to select their own wives last spring—as I suggested!—then we'd not be gathered here in Eshda today! The princes would have each been established in their own households, and granted their own territories upon marriage. What could that she-scaln Cthar have done then, eh? She'd not be on Arimna's throne now, I warrant you that!"

Matteo's thoughts reeled, and his stomach churned at the realization. If the Forum hadn't been so splintered last spring and caught up in their own petty rivalries, his brothers would be alive. Pestilence take these lords! Matteo seethed with the longing to strike at them all. He could almost taste bile as Kemuel raised a fist in defiance of the Forum. "You are all to blame for what's happened, and there's no changing matters now! Will we continue squabbling like old fools, or will we finally make some right decisions?"

One of the other lords—Demriys of Blekvell—called out, "Are you suggesting we reach a decision now?"

They all looked at Matteo, and he straightened, raising his eyebrows at them. "Not now, my lords! We're on the verge of war."

Kemuel's expression turned mournful. Thoroughly dismal. "Sire, if we lose you and you leave us no heir, we have only *her*. Unless the Lady Rhiysa battles her."

Matteo flicked a glance at his cousin. Anji frowned at Kemuel and shook her head.

Undeterred, Kemuel continued, "Either way, we'd have another great battle on our hands to seat your successor! My lords—" Kemuel Talon challenged the Forum, "who will suggest a wife for the king? Blekvell, you've an enchanting daughter. And you, Thaddeus Ormr, though you're no lord yet—may the Infinite preserve your absent father!—you have several younger sisters. What say you all?"

Matteo cut a glance toward Dalia. Her eyes were huge, and she appeared to be on the verge of confronting the Forum herself, except that Roi had one hand on her shoulder. Even as

Matteo watched Dalia, Lord Blekvell stood. "Tragobre! Your daughter's here, and it's no secret that she's risked her life to defy the queen-mother for the House of Jonatan. Have her marry the king if he wills it!"

Roi Hradedh released Dalia and stood. "Blekvell, you are too cowardly to offer your own daughter! You're all too willing to risk my only child to save your own!"

Matteo stood. "My lords, now is not the time!

Dalia called out, "May I speak?"

His voice overriding them all, Lord Kemuel roared, "My lords, all in favor of this marriage, *stand* and proclaim it decreed!"

Almost to a man, the Forum members stood and yelled, "Decreed!"

Roi Hradedh sat heavily on his bench and covered his face with his hands. Dalia hugged him fiercely, kissed the top of his head, and then ran to Matteo. She hopped onto the dais, clutched Matteo's hand and hissed, "They didn't even let me speak!"

"They'll never hear the end of it," Matteo groused.

Corban, evidently disgusted, shook his head, bowed to Matteo and then stalked from the hall. Below the dais, the lords clustered in groups, arguing with each other. Matteo gusted out an aggravated sigh. "No wonder my lord-father was so aggravated with the Forum's lords. They're all possessed of extraordinary emotion without enough foresight to anticipate the consequences." He bent and hugged Dalia. "Somehow, I'll save you from their impulsiveness. We'll marry later, when Darzeq's settled."

"What if it's never settled, and what if I don't want to be saved?" Dalia interlaced her fingers with his own. "No. I'm not afraid, Sire. However..." A wistful frown crossed her delicate face. "I want my lady-mother present. I'll write to her now."

Matteo bit down an argument he wouldn't win. An argument he didn't actually care to win. Not with Dalia holding his hand, and pressing such a sweet kiss on his lips. Both beyond resisting—the lady and her kiss. He gave up and enfolded Dalia within his embrace.

But he glowered at Lord Kemuel, who laughed, and approached, offering congratulations.

Dalia folded a list with her letter to mother, describing which clothes and jewels she wished to wear during the marriage ceremony. Mother would undoubtedly make some wise suggestions of her own and bring the whole lot to Eshda.

A thump sounded against the door. Father stalked inside followed by Matteo, both looking as if they were about to say words at her memorial instead of her marriage. Father slapped two pieces of parchment on Dalia's writing table. "This just arrived from Iydan. Your lady-mother sent a courier bird to Magni Ormr, begging him to send her message to us here. At least Ormr found enough courage to forward her note to us in Eshda!"

Dalia lifted the smaller note, which was curled after its journey within a courier bird's miniature bronze message tube. Mother's gossamer script filled the tiny strip of parchment. *My lord, do not return from Eshda unless you lead an army. Tragobre is besieged.*

Chapter 15

Dalia cupped the tiny note in her hands, as if by protecting it she could save Mother. Cthar had acted so swiftly. Obviously Dalia's identity had been too easily confirmed, and Cthar was determined to crush any breath of opposition. Who in Kiyrem had given those guards Dalia's name? One of the students? Parnemedes? Kurcus? "This is my fault! I should have surrendered to the authorities. I could still..."

Matteo squeezed her shoulders gently and bent to kiss her cheek. "No. You *are* with Darzeq's authorities. Cthar's the usurper, and you did nothing wrong."

"I thought I could remain anonymous. One of Kiyrem's teachers or students must have named me as the author of those notes." Dalia clasped one of Matteo's hands, but pleaded to Father, "Sir, what can I do to help?"

Roi snapped, "Remain safe and silent!" Dalia winced at his harshness, though she deserved it and far more. Father gentled his tone. "I'm worried for your mother, Dalia, don't mistake me. But I'm afraid for your safety as well. I meant what I said. You'll remain here and hidden—your mother would agree with me. Particularly when I declare that you should marry at once."

Matteo's hands tightened on Dalia's shoulders as he protested, "Sir, I say we wait until Darzeq's at peace."

Roi glowered at him. "My lord and king, there will be no peace in Darzeq if my wife and my daughter die because of *your* grandmother's ambitions!"

Father might as well slap Matteo—indeed, Matteo's hand twitched beneath her own. Fury lifted hot color to Matteo's face, and his eyes glittered darkly as he returned Father's glare. "My lord, do you believe I'd endanger them willfully?"

Would he fight with Father? Oh, One Who Sees Us, quiet them, I beg you! She stood, gulping for breath, fighting tears. "Please, sirs, don't quarrel! I love you both and can't endure it. Not now."

Matteo controlled himself. Dalia could almost hear her beloved counting, summoning patience within his thoughts. Matteo touched Dalia's cheek, making her look at him. "Your father fears for your mother's safety and for your own. I understand. Therefore, if, by marriage, I can offer help to Tragobre, I will. I'm far more to blame than you for this siege. Agree to marry me now, Dalia, and then your lord-father and I will return to the Forum and call for allies to save Tragobre."

This would be a test of Matteo's power as king. A measure of his hold on Darzeq. She nodded. "Yes. It's not the ceremony I've dreamed of, but yes."

Father turned on his heels and headed for the door, though he called over his shoulder, "Write a courier-bird's note to your mother, and we'll send it wherever we must in order to reach her. Tell her that we trust her decisions and pray and work for Tragobre's safety. May the Infinite bless and shelter her and Tragobre."

He stalked out. But Matteo lingered, clearly concerned. He slid his hand tenderly over Dalia's cheek, then wove his fingers into her hair, drawing her closer. "All the powers I can summon will march against Tragobre, my love! Continue being your courageous and honorable self and I'll be the most blessed bridegroom in Darzeq. With or without a magnificent wedding."

Matteo kissed her, his lips warm, gentle, and sweet, intoxicating even as he comforted her. Dalia leaned into his embrace and closed her eyes. "Sir, I love you. If I marry you now, it's because I truly love you—not primarily to protect my mother."

"Which is why I'm blessed." His beautiful golden eyes sparkled as he studied her face. "I know you love me, and that's a treasure worth fighting for—a treasure few kings can boast of. Write that note to your lady-mother and Tragobre. I'll send Anji to you, and I'll alert our Lord Aristo that we'll celebrate our wedding tonight."

Tonight?

Dizzied by the thought, Dalia sat before her desk, staring blankly at Mother's delicate note, and the letter she'd half-started for Mother. She'd fought for a love match and ended up as a political pawn in an appallingly rushed wedding, yet love remained.

She saw adoration and protectiveness in Matteo's beguiling glance and his caressing touch. In the enduring warmth of his kiss, and his reluctance to leave her.

She ran her fingertips over his subtly whiskered jaw, then returned his grin. "Go, my lord-king. I'm well."

"Forgive me." Matteo kissed her hair, then dashed from her chamber—a man with causes to pursue. And by her impulsiveness, she'd added to his list of causes, her poor darling husband. Well. She'd add no more. She would be prudent, remain silent, and hidden away from trouble until Darzeq was at peace.

As Matteo and Father wished.

Reaching for a fresh square of parchment, Dalia mentally composed her courier-note.

Mother, be encouraged! Father trusts your decisions, and we pray and work for Tragobre's safety. May the Infinite bless and shield you and Tragobre until our return.

Would it be wise to add the news that she was about to marry Matteo? Dalia rested her trembling hands on the table, calmed herself, then began to write.

Corban entered the whitewashed stone stairwell from the guest chambers, then paused. Footsteps echoed to him from the royal chambers above and from the hall below. Was he about to be overrun? Unlikely. Both sets of footsteps sounded distinctly light and quick. Feminine, he guessed.

Anji rounded the steps from below, her expression distant and preoccupied. Until she nearly collided with him and squeaked—the alarmed-rabbit sound and her huge brown eyes made him smile as she gasped. "Lord Corban!"

Before he could say a word, Dalia descended from the steps above and greeted them, flourishing a tiny parchment cylinder. "I thought I heard voices. I was just coming downstairs to give a courier-bird note to my lord-father. Have we planned a meeting unawares?"

Corban bowed to them slightly. "Forgive me, ladies, if I frightened you."

Anji sighed. "You gave me a start, sir, but you are not frightful."

"True," Dalia agreed. She flung Corban a wry little look that would have stolen him completely if he hadn't been so taken by Araine. "You'll never be frightful to me, my lord. Particularly not when you smile."

If she knew the truth, she wouldn't be so complimentary. Corban grimaced. "Thank you, lady."

A wistful expression crossed Dalia's exquisite face and she glanced at Anji. "You've heard my news? Tragobre's besieged and I'm to marry Matteo tonight, by my lord-father's command. He wants me to remain here, safe and hidden while he musters an army to save Tragobre and my lady-mother."

What? As Corban masked his shock, Anji nodded. "Yes, Matteo just told me—I was on my way upstairs to help you prepare for the ceremony. We'll pray for the army to be gathered swiftly."

Corban banished the mournful silence that followed. "May I guess who dares to besiege your home, Lady Dalia? The queen-mother?"

"Yes. Because of me." Dalia muted a sniffle. "Someone in Kiyrem named me as the author of those doggerel verses. I've caused such grief to my poor parents!" She fought tears, and Anji scrambled up the few steps between them to console her friend.

Seeking a graceful means of retreat, Corban muttered, "Lady Dalia, I would be honored to deliver your note to your lord-father, if you'd entrust me with it."

Dalia blinked down tears and held out the tiny note. "Thank you, my lord—you're so kind!"

He would kill to hear similar words from Araine in times past. To step back and change everything. Infinite, You Who See, if only this could happen! If only she'd grant me her forgiveness!

Unable to speak, he bowed and left the ladies to their commiserations.

Downstairs, in Eshda's great hall, members of the forum were already arguing. Matteo, in full regalia again, formally seated on the dais, lifted both hands and called out, "One at a time, my lords—and you must permit each other to speak without interruption! Kemuel Talon, Lord of Lohe Bay, how will you answer Lord Tragobre's request? Will you bring your men to stand against Cthar's army?"

"My lord and king, you know I will. The men of Lohe Bay are ever for the true sovereign! The queen-mother dares to attack your wife's family, therefore it's a strike against you, and verging on treason!"

Kemuel finished with a vigorous nod. The instant he sat down, another lord hopped up from one of the benches.

Matteo nodded to him. "Karvos Stradin, Lord of the Jizni Plains, what do you say?"

His tanned features tense, Karvos shook his head. "Majesty, and my lords, this siege is a private matter, and Lord Tragobre has the wealth and men to rout his enemies...."

Before he could finish, Tragobre bellowed, "Not an army of Arimna! Not decisively, Karvos, and you know it! Are you sentencing me to death for our past disputes in the Forum?"

While Karvos spluttered his denial, Kemuel yelled, "Make no mistake, my lords, this is the queen-mother's first show of force on a battlefield, and if we allow her to win, she will gather more allies! I say roust her forces while we can, and then surround Arimna! If you allow her to prevail, you hand her the crown! Is that what you want?"

The uproar escalated and Corban found himself rolling the parchment cylinder between his fingers—a gesture of frustration over his lack of a sword, and his lack of power in this foreign country. To work off his fury, he stalked along the hall's western wall, toward Lord Aristo, who greeted him, low-voiced to be heard. "Have you ever heard such an uproar, Lord Corban? Bear with us, I beg you...."

"We shall see." Corban held up the tiny parchment and leaned toward Aristo. "This is intended for a bird to be sent to Tragobre—from the Lady Dalia and her lord-father. Have you any options?"

Aristo accepted the parchment and nodded decisively. "I've friends in the courier's hall of Port Bascin—King Jonatan's favored retreat. I know Tragobre can be reached by courier bird from there. I'll send this immediately, then I'm off to arrange matters for tonight's ceremony. If our king is to marry his queen here, I'll not have Eshda disgraced."

"I'm sure everyone will be pleased," Corban muttered, as shouts deepened around them. What was wrong with these lords? They were all cowards, declining to fight. Kemuel Talon had spoken the truth. If they didn't act now, and decisively, the crisis would deepen and worsen. Darzeq could be enmeshed in a full civil war, causing more casualties in the long run.

Corban marched to the center of the hall and faced Matteo, who raised an eyebrow, then called out, "Lord Corban Thaenfall, what do you wish to say?"

The Forum silenced, all the lords staring at him, obviously unsettled. Lord Corban Thaenfall, the scaln-slayer, the king's living shield, had finally deigned to speak.

He scowled at the lordly wretches. "I'm Siphran, yet as a lord who protects your king, I will speak! I've been watching you all and listening to your squabbles. They're pointless! A country that can discipline itself can rule the world, but you, my lords, can scarcely rule yourselves. You must all agree to set aside your self-flattery and make rational plans tonight! If you assemble an army, I will bow to its leader and fight for him! Gather your courage and reclaim Darzeq before you lose control of your land altogether!"

They gawped and blinked like confounded toddlers. Well, let them. He'd learned his lessons in Siphra, and he would not stand by idly while avoidable disaster overtook this country. More to the point, he would not remain in Eshda with a pair of newlyweds. The thought was enough to roil his stomach.

Matteo nodded and called out, "Thank you, my lord! I will ride out of Eshda with you! What do you say, my lords? Who will ride with us?"

Roi Hradedh stood at once, and Thaddeus Ormr joined him. "I'm no lord, and I've few men of my own, but we follow the king and Lord Corban. We'll free Tragobre, whatever the cost!"

Kemuel pounded his fists on his allotted table and stood. "The men of Lohe Bay have already sworn to fight for the king! Lords of the south, join us! We can form an army even as we leave the forum! Remember that *she* dissolved our assembly! If she has killed her own grandsons and the Queen Valsignae and perhaps her own son, our King Jonatan, do you believe she'll spare you when she's done with you or when she covets your lands for her favorites? I vow she won't!"

Other lords stood, and buzzing waves of conversation flowed through the great hall. Even Karvos Stradin stood, though his expression remained unconvinced. He called, "Let us claim the victory and compel the queen-mother to accede and leave Arimna in peace!"

The man's tone struck Corban as off—a forced and ill-meant clamor. He slid a glance toward Matteo. The king remained in Eshda's magnificently carved ruling seat, and his expression didn't change, but one hand knotted into a hard fist as if he longed to clout Karvos Stradin and then attack the queen-mother.

Matteo of Darzeq craved vengeance—a longing Corban understood all too well. Yet he must beware. This same thirst for vengeance had poisoned Corban's reaction to Araine's "betrayal" and had nearly destroyed him.

Frowning, Corban sent his thoughts toward the Infinite. *One-Who-Sees, You saved me. But did You save her? Let me eventually find the truth!*

Meanwhile, he would help to secure this realm for Matteo of Darzeq. It wouldn't make restitution for his crimes, but it was a start.

Amid the Forum's buzz of conversation, Ekiael finally stood and walked to the center of the hall, facing the king. Matteo called out, "My lords, Darzeq's high priest wishes to speak. Let's hear what he has to say!"

The conversations hushed to whispers and a few coughs. Ekiael nodded and glanced around. "This is as it should be, my lords, and I pray the Infinite grants you all overwhelming success at Tragobre. However, one man has declared his intentions of riding off to war against the Infinite's sacred Word!"

Matteo frowned. "Who, my lord priest? Deal with him!"

Ekiael bowed to him and bellowed, "You, my lord-king! How can you ride out to battle when you've agreed to marry tonight? The Book of Laws forbids it! 'If a man marries, he must not go to war. Let him remain with his wife for twelve months and make her happy.' Sire, it is the Infinite's will that you remain here."

"No," Matteo argued. "A year's not practical, and there *are* exceptions, my lord-priest!"

His protest was drowned out by hoots and laughter from the Forum. Thaddeus called to Matteo, "Sire, let us win this battle on your behalf! You owe us an heir!"

Kemuel cupped his hands around his mouth and yelled, "Where's the bride? I'm ready to feast!"

Dalia wrung out her scrubbing cloth over a stoneware basin, then dropped the twisted fabric onto the stonework table and sighed. "I'm clean, but I don't feel like a bride. This isn't what I dreamed of, Anji. Remember how we talked when we were girls?"

Anji's lustrous dark eyes softened, misting with emotion. "I know. But obviously life in this fallen mortal world doesn't conform to dreams. Yet the Infinite's with us—I sense Him!"

Dalia rested her hands on the table's mosaic surface and closed her eyes, questing and praying with all her heart. One-Who-Sees ... thank You!

His presence enfolded her, calming, and beautiful as any bridal gown. She opened her eyes and smiled at Anji. "You're right. How can I be unhappy if He is present—a guest at my wedding. Why am I complaining? I ought to be dancing—I'm going to marry Matteo!"

They laughed and hugged each other. Anji kissed her cheek, exulting, "At last, I'll have a sister! Or a girl-cousin, and that's near enough! Now, let's find a comb and some hair oil. I doubt Matteo would want me to meddle with your hair too much—he loves you exactly as you are."

"Do whatever you think best for my wild mane. I'm at your mercy."

"Why do you always say your hair is wild?" Anji shook her head in gentle reproach. "Your curls are lovely, and I wish mine were like yours." A gentle tap on the heavy door summoned their attention. Anji called out, "Who is it?"

Lord Aristo's voice answered cheerily, "Lady, wedding gifts if you'll accept them for the bride. From Eshda."

Dalia swooped a cloak over her linen undergown and nodded. Anji sped to the door and admitted Lord Aristo Faolan. He bowed, his portly frame and face as gracious as any courtier could ever be. And he tenderly presented a linen-swathed bundle to Anji, though he spoke to Dalia. "For the bride to wear, or save, as she pleases. "These were gifts to my lady-wife from our Queen Valsignae, many years ago, following a royal visit. We were honored, for the queen selected these herself. My wife never wore them, but we've cherished them ever since, and Eshda humbly offers them to you now."

Aristo spoke of his wife as if she were yet alive, and his tenderness melted Dalia. Whatever he'd offered, be it musty and moth-riddled, she'd wear it for the sake of the love he still cherished for his wife. She offered him her warmest smile, blinking down heartfelt tears. "My lord, I'm honored. Thank you!"

Seeming robbed of words, Aristo bowed and retreated, shutting the door quietly. Anji unwrapped the parcel, murmuring, "What can it be? It's so heavy, Dalia, I'm afraid...."

Dalia gazed down at the parcel's contents, covered her mouth, and burst into tears.

Chapter 16

Matteo fought the impulse to pace about on the dais as he waited for Dalia's entrance. He must be patient. Regal. And wholly appreciative, for preparations he hadn't even considered ordering for his wedding were obviously afoot. Aristo had summoned musicians and commanded lamps lit throughout the hall at the approach of dusk.

The musicians were few—obviously recruited from the garrison—but they were all clean and neatly clad, and it was clear that they'd practiced together quite often for Eshda's enjoyment over the years. Their leader lifted one hand, tapped the air four times, and the harpists led, followed by the low-chiming dome drums, their delicate notes transforming the hall's entire mood.

Standing nearby, Ekiael's eyes brightened approvingly. He whispered to Matteo, "It's music from the Book of Praises! Well done!" As if he were in Arimna's Holy House, Ekiael lifted his hands, closing his eyes, his fingertips reverently moving in time to the added chimes and flutes, which rounded out the ethereal melodies of the harps and dome drums.

Corban, on guard just below the dais, turned—clearly listening to the flowing, perfectly harmonized notes. He glanced quizzically up at Ekiael, who remained lost in his worship, as Matteo should be.

Matteo closed his eyes briefly, praying beneath his breath. "Mighty One, be with us. Grant us peace, this one night!"

For Dalia's sake. Let her be pleased, despite this rushed ceremony and her mother's plight.

A creak of hinges to Matteo's right, followed by the rustling of garments, made him glance toward the hidden door. Ekiael turned as well. Anji glided from behind the curtain clad in her finest available clothes, her dark eyes shining, so brilliant that Ekiael stared at her, clearly bedazzled, as if he were the bridegroom. Matteo smiled, half-longing to shove his priest-friend and mock him for his addled wits—until Roi Hradedh entered the hall, looked around grim-faced, then raised one hand, evidently beckoning Dalia.

Matteo saw her small hand first, reaching for her father, clasping his fingers tight. Then Dalia stepped into the hall, and Matteo caught his breath.

No woman alive was as beautiful as his bride.

Dalia beamed at Matteo, though her huge eyes glistened with tears. Her every movement glimmered in the lamplight, her heavily embroidered garments and rich veil so gem-laden that she already looked like a young queen.

As she walked toward him, a murmur ran through the hall—the Forum's lords all whispering to each other. "The queen's colors! She's wearing the queen's colors."

Matteo stared. It was true. From her veiled hair down to the hem of her gown, Dalia wore Queen Valsignae's favorite soft violet, embroidered with gold, pearls, and amethysts. And as she stepped onto the dais, Matteo recognized the distinctive embroidery. His mother had undoubtedly embroidered that veil with her own hands, using her favorite self-created flower pattern.

An ache lifted in Matteo's chest. Dalia stood before him clad in his mother's handiwork, while he wore his lord-father's own royal robes. If his parents could not be here, he'd been granted touches of their presence this night. Swallowing hard, Matteo nodded to Roi Hradedh, who eyed him as if still unconvinced that Matteo wasn't worthy of Dalia, sole heiress of Tragobre.

Perhaps he was right.

Matteo looked Dalia in the eyes—those perfect gray eyes—adoring her.

Prepared to protect her with his life.

Dalia exhaled, willing her tremors to cease as she faced Matteo. He greeted her lord-father and then offered Dalia his dear lopsided grin—stealing her heart and her fear. His spectacular, long-lashed golden eyes glittered with hints of moisture, as if the sight of her had nearly moved him to tears. Had he recognized his dear mother's handiwork on the veil and her gown as Dalia and Anji had? She hoped so. His family had been so dear to them both. She would comfort him later, when they were alone.

One of the onlookers coughed roughly, and Ekiael lifted his hands to praise their Creator, his voice becoming a melodious blur, lost to her as she gazed at Matteo, her very soul seeming to skip as he clasped her hands and pledged himself to her, then removed his oldest ring from his smallest finger. The ring was simple, a small gold signet engraved with a royal shield, given to Matteo by his father several years ago. The signet slipped precariously about on Dalia's ring finger. Matteo hurriedly lifted her hand, holding the ring on her finger as she repeated her pledge to him.

She had no ring for her husband. She was about to whisper apologies to Matteo when Father nudged her, offering one of his own heavy rings embossed with Tragobre's crest of a tower. Holding her breath, Dalia tested it on Matteo's ring finger. Only slightly too large.

Matteo nodded and Dalia blinked back tears.

Ekiael rested his hands on their shoulders, blessed them, and then launched into a song of praise to the Infinite. Listening, Dalia closed her eyes, praising Him.

Corban studied the ceremony, absorbed by its mingled solemnity and joy. No Atean worship ceremony had ever been this reverent. All were raucous and focused on mortal pleasures; no Atean wedding had ever achieved this calm, beautiful dignity.

And as Ekiael, high priest of Darzeq, poured his powerful voice into a sonorous, musical blessing, all the hairs on Corban's scalp and arms lifted as his senses comprehended a Presence.

Corban steadied himself as his thoughts reeled in shocked recognition.

Infinite, You are here...

Aristo waited on Dalia and Matteo during the feast that followed. But each time he presented a dish, he tasted the food, then waited. Personally checking for poison, Dalia realized. She winced, studying Lord Aristo for the slightest sign of discomfort as he tested then carved the richly browned roasted lamb. Evidently satisfied, Aristo arranged the sliced meat on a broad silver dish and presented it with a golden sauce, which he'd also tested.

Dalia smiled at Eshda's lord. "Thank you, sir." But as he turned away, Dalia whispered to Matteo, "I'd rather test everything myself than risk his life. The last thing we want is for this good man to die of our wedding feast."

Matteo leaned down, his breath caressing her cheek as he whispered, "Death is the last thing he wishes for you, as the bride and his queen. Let him fulfill the task he's accepted and honor him by enjoying your meal."

She turned, facing her sweet husband almost nose to nose. If she tilted her head just slightly she could lean forward and kiss him. But their guests would howl and yell provocative taunts. She ought to tease Matteo instead and save her kisses for later. "Was that a lecture, my lord?"

"Of course it was." He grinned at her. "You're quite welcome to argue with me later. For now, however, we should eat before our food is cold instead of lukewarm."

As he cut their meat into bite-sized portions, she asked, "Is this how the future's to be for us, my lord? Fearing for our lives and our servants' lives?"

Matteo set down his knife, his gaze distant. "Yes. The best we can do is face matters with courage, and pray. Perhaps, by the Infinite's plan, we'll be spared."

Unlike his parents and brothers and their servants. Was Matteo remembering them now? Undoubtedly, by the shadowed look that dimmed his gaze and stole his joy.

Clenching her hand into a fist to prevent her wedding ring from falling off, Dalia nudged her husband into the present, smiled at him, and then forced herself to eat.

Freed from the feast and their guests' staring eyes, Dalia gazed about at Matteo's bedchamber. It was large enough to be called regal, yet surprisingly comfortable, with its faded tapestries and warm jumble of tables, chairs, storage chests, and the broad, heavily curtained bed. Beyond the bed, a tapestry-shielded window beckoned. Matteo's window surely opened to the west. Her previous chamber had opened to Eshda's eastern lands, with views of the castle's courtyards and mountains beyond. Would she see the stars if she looked?

Her wedding garments rustling, Dalia crossed the chamber, crept behind the small tapestry, then unfastened and opened the shutters. Stars shone at her, but so did a distant fiery glow at the far end of the valley that dimmed all heavenly lights by comparison—a glow multiplied by a sudden plume of fire that lifted and fell against the night, startling her even from this distance. Was the valley afire?

Behind Dalia, the chamber door thumped shut, the lock clattered, and Matteo called out, "Dalia?"

She leaned from behind the tapestry, meeting his gaze just as he spied her. He grinned. "There you are. Were you hiding from me?"

"I wanted to see the stars. But what's that fire?" She turned to stare out the window again.

Matteo edged in behind the tapestry to join her at the window. He wrapped an arm around her and kissed her cheek. "Lord Aristo said it's Lost Lake, though he doubts there was ever a lake there. Only a pool of molten stone."

"So the valley's not ablaze?"

"No. Remarkably, the pool's confined to a stone caldera. The lands beyond it, however, are the wilds, with Istgard farther north."

"I'd love to visit Istgard, but not if I have to cross prime scaln territories."

"Then, stay here, with me."

"I might." She threw him a teasing glance, admiring his eyes, which glimmered even in the night's dimness. He smiled, seeming truly carefree for the first time since she'd arrived in Eshda. Emboldened, she hugged his waist. "As if I would leave you, ever!"

Matteo leaned down, then lifted her in his arms. "You'd have to escape me first."

"I've no wish to escape you—I've longed to marry you for years! You're the one who'll plot an escape!"

She kissed him and lost herself in the warmth of his lips ... the joy of his embrace. Matteo nuzzled her cheek and murmured, "Your face is cold."

Without asking, he carried her away from the window and gently set her down near the bed. Somber now, he grazed his fingers over her face, then touched her veil. "How did you acquire this? I recognized my mother's needlework."

"Lord Aristo presented it to me on behalf of Eshda. He said that your lady-mother gave it to his wife years ago, after a royal visit; it's never been worn until now."

"It compliments you perfectly, and we'll treasure it always. Another debt we owe our Lord Aristo." Matteo's solemnity vanished as he looked her over. "Lovely as it is, that veil must be heavy. Do you need some help removing it?"

"No, thank you, Sire. I can tend myself perfectly, thanks to Kiyrem's severe schooling." In her best mimicking-Master-Tredin voice, she recited, "You have no servants here, young lady!"

"That's not true my love." Matteo clasped her hands and kissed them. "You have me. And by the Infinite's will, I'll remain your servant, even when we're very old."

Her ring slid, almost falling off her finger as Matteo lowered her hands. Dalia caught the fugitive silver circlet. "If you're determined to be so, my lord, then please help me secure this ring."

"How?"

"I need cordage of some sort."

He found some cordage in a storage chest and, following her instructions, he tied it around her wrist, then used the long loose ends to secure her ring. As Matteo tightened the knots, he sobered. "I know this ceremony wasn't what we'd hoped for. Nor did we plan for the siege to entrap your lady-mother...."

He cinched the final knot and wound his fingers together with hers. "But when Arimna's returned to my father's house, I'll make reparations to you and your family as best I can."

He meant every word. She saw it in his determined gaze, the set of his jaw. Was he blaming himself? She had to set his thoughts aright. "If anyone needs to make reparations, my lord, it's Cthar. She owes Darzeq for destroying your family and placing an unwanted crown on your head. But you owe me only what you pledged tonight: Your devotion as my husband for as long as we both live—and I intend to hold you to your word!"

She stood on tiptoes, flung her arms around his neck, and kissed him fiercely.

To make him forget all else but her for at least this night.

Summoned from a dreamless sleep, Matteo intuitively drew Dalia closer, and then opened his eyes. Gray light silvered the edges of the tapestry, announcing the dawn.

He'd slept. Not quite long enough, but better than any night since the massacre. And he held the reason in his arms—his enchanting, delightful bride. Living balm to his soul's wounds. In silence, he blessed the Infinite. Thank You for sending her to me!

Matteo smiled, watching Dalia's eyes flicker beneath her closed eyelids. Was she dreaming? Of their future perhaps. Could he now hope for a future? Dalia certainly gave him reason to anticipate the future. He pressed a stealthy kiss in her hair.

Infinite, protect her! Save her from Cthar ... from all my enemies....

Dalia inhaled, then stretched, evidently waking. Tempted beyond endurance, Matteo rained kisses over his wife's face and throat, making her laugh and cling to him, banishing the world from his thoughts.

Corban straightened in his saddle, then glanced over his shoulder at the Forum's army—Lord Kemuel, Thaddeus Ormr, and Karvos Stradin, among them, all following him and Lord Roi to liberate Tragobre castle. An army's worth of weapons clattering, horse-hooves splatting in the mud, men talking too loudly, bridles and saddles creaking....

Riding with an army was a new experience Corban didn't relish. Solitude suited him better. Only Araine had ever tempted him toward permanent companionship. Indeed, most of Darzeq's lords chafed his temper like sand over polished wood—particularly Karvos Stradin, who rode up to Corban's left, eyeing him as a man studies a freak.

Corban looked away from the importune Karvos and fought to maintain a veneer of civility. Certainly most of the forum lords could be trusted to an extent, but he doubted a number of them, including Stradin.

Matteo apparently shared his mistrust. He'd delayed sanctioning the loyal army's departure until the Forum lords had first departed, taking all undeclared enemies with them—leaving Matteo and his household secured within Eshda's walls and guarded by a devoted garrison. Corban silently applauded the young king's quiet delaying tactics; most promising for future battles, political and real.

Roi Hradedh drew back his horse and waited, raising one eyebrow at Corban then motioning to a blue-green range of hills. "My lords, there's Tragobre. You can just see the line of the fortress from here."

Corban studied the landscape, admiring its beauty, even as Karvos growled, "A pity we can't see the queen-mother's army from here—we could plan an appropriate attack and end matters quickly."

Tragobre's lord nodded, his gaze still fixed on the distant hills. "Perhaps I should send out a few spies."

Spy... The idea took hold within Corban's thoughts, unfurling as a plant springing to life. An idea he didn't necessarily welcome, though it promised adventure, not to mention time away from the Forum's army. Being a comparative stranger, he could spy upon the enemy more readily than anyone here.

Was he being a fool? Or did this inspiration have its roots in another source entirely?

One-Who-Sees, have You placed this wish within me? Or do You know me so well that You understood I'd wish to take on this role? Am I the sole instigator of my own folly?

Caution warring with battle-ready elation, he nodded to Roi. "I'll go."

Chapter 17

Dusk fell as Corban urged Ghost through the huge encampment. Travel-weariness and boredom faded as he eyed the soldiers who idled before Tragobre's fortress, glaring at him in turn. Corban acknowledged their stares with icy Thaenfall pride. Not one man challenged him. Indeed, several backed away.

Cowards.

Interesting. None of the men were attired alike, and their tents were equally cobbled together, some of oiled canvas, others of leather, several were plain lean-to's of fabric that promised little sleep in the looming autumn chill. Tragobre was besieged by an army of mercenaries. Had the queen kept most of her trained army in Arimna to shield herself against attack? It seemed so.

Corban studied the muddled assortment of tents, then grimaced against the stench of unkempt privy pits. By all that he'd been taught as a youth, this encampment of mercenaries was ripe for disease. Their lack-wit commander should be dropped into one of his own pits.

Stifling his breath, Corban rode toward the largest tent, which dared to flaunt Darzeq's pennants and banners—most boasting a fortress set above waters. Depicting Arimna Castle's origin as guardian of the land between Darzeq's twin rivers. If the queen mother, Cthar, wasn't here to command her own forces, then who had she sent in her place, bearing treasonously stolen colors? Royal banners she'd stolen by spilling royal blood.

He almost smiled at the irony. He, a Thaenfall, was insulted on behalf of a king chosen by the Infinite. His lord-father would have ordered Matteo and Corban roasted alive. As Corban might yet be if he failed to keep his wits now. He'd concealed enough weapons about himself, on his belt and in his boots to use if anyone attacked him. However, if this camp's commander ordered him thoroughly searched, there would be no meeting. No gathering of information to share later with Lord Tragobre—though Corban could speculate with some certainty that many of these men would soon be stricken with flux of the bowels and fevers matching their violent digestive unrest.

The guards ringing the tent eyed him warily, and a vaguely familiar Istgard-accented voice cut into Corban's thoughts. "Swiln-gut gouger!"

Ghost huffed as Corban reined him in, seeming to recognize his erstwhile foe even as Corban recalled the man's name. Corban glowered toward the Istgardian wretch and answered with cold, carrying blade-like sharpness. "Aki of Riyan. Do you believe I've forgotten you—you sniveling runaway stable hand?"

Aki puffed up like a defensive motley bird. "I'm free and no runaway!"

"You ran when I beat you to the pavings in Riyan." Disdainful, Corban warned the men seated around the startled Aki, as if the listening men were nearer his equal. "Guard your horses, sirs. This man will thrash them and demand that you pay him for injuring them—yet when he's struck, he whimpers and flees. Istgard's well rid of him. Who is your commander, and where is he?"

One of the louts edged away from Aki then nodded toward the tent's entry. "Lord Gueronn's there at evening meal."

Gueronn. Corban's senses seized upon the name, blade sharp and keen to fight. Wasn't Gueronn the palace guard who'd led the slaughter of Matteo's brothers? Corban foraged his memories for details from the king's retellings of the massacre. Had Gueronn been a lord before this siege? Not likely. Courtly life hinged upon matters of rank, and Corban would have remembered mention of a "Lord Gueronn."

Had the queen-mother merely rewarded a common guard for killing Darzeq's princes, or was Cthar heaping honors upon her unsanctioned favorite? If so, then undoubtedly Gueronn was setting himself up to rule Darzeq through the queen-mother. Overreaching felon!

Corban suppressed a snarl as he dismounted Ghost and lowered the reins onto the trampled soil. Not bothering to lower his voice, he commanded his horse, "Wait here. If anyone approaches you, alert me and then stomp him to dust."

He turned toward the butcher Gueronn's tent, stretched out his arms, and then lifted his chin, eyeing the guards, silently commanding them to search him. As they approached, he allowed them the thinnest smile in his arsenal and ordered the lead guard, "Tell your commander-general that Lord Corban Thaenfall of Siphra requires an audience—it will be well-worth his time."

The lead guard, no autocrat, bowed like a scuffling minion. Too easily intimidated, as were his lessor comrades. The lead made one meek request. "Your sword, sir? My lord."

Corban unbuckled his sword from his belt, but didn't hand it over. "This was my lord-father's sword, and I allow no man to touch it. I'll place it in the entryway where you may view it while I speak with your commander. I've one dagger in my right boot, the other at my left side."

The lead nodded and motioned to the others, who searched Corban, their motions too-wary, tentative as a pack of timid maidens. He wore two additional concealed blades and these wretches found neither.

The lead announced him in awed tones, then stepped aside. Corban swept past him, leaned his lord-father's sheathed sword just inside against the entry post, dropped the entry's curtain, then nodded toward the camp's commander, Gueronn, who betrayed his lowly origins by standing the instant Corban eyed him, and muttering, "My lord."

Corban smiled, noting his host's sumptuous attire—the fine linen, the rings on his fingers, his heavy new gold and gem-studded belt, the golden cloak, and the lordly golden circlet crowning his head. "You are ... Lord Gueronn."

"I am." Gueronn straightened, affecting a superiority that rested on him as awkwardly as a gossamer scarf settled upon a gladiator. His looks, brawny, tanned, and sun-streaked, would have gained royal attention in Siphra's former court—as they obviously had in Cthar's. Moreover, this Gueronn's table was covered with fresh linen, gilded silverware, and well-prepared food that half the men in his camp might kill for. Corban would wager his own life on his conclusion.

Gueronn was more than the queen-mother's guard.

Did the new-belted lord understand the risks he now faced as royal favorite? Gueronn studied Corban, not entirely a fool. "Who are you, sir? One of the foreign recruits?"

"I am Lord Corban Thaenfall of Siphra, offering my service to Darzeq. May I salute Dazeq's favored new lord?" Corban gave the man a courtly Siphran salute, even as his entire being protested the degradation. He straightened, then stood at ease, hands behind his back beneath his cloak, resting against his concealed dagger's hilt. To the Infinite, he thought, One-Who-Sees, be with me now—this time, I ask! Let me understand Your will for this man.

A sensing slipped over Corban as a downrushing air current and he smiled, fixated upon the favored guard-turned-lord.

Gueronn accepted Corban's formal salute with a grin. He relaxed in his chair and reached for his gem-chased silver goblet. "Darzeq's new 'lord' has only begun to rule! How might you serve me, Lord Corban?" The arrogant guard's eyebrows raised, he took a mighty swig of the wine, then set down his cup with gusto.

Splinterings of outrage stabbed within Corban's thoughts, expanding to fury against the opportunistic Gueronn. The man dared to step above his place and seize control of Darzeq. Dared to slaughter the heirs of the Infinite's anointed king! Dared to threaten Darzeq's new queen.

Corban eased his dagger from its sheath and slipped it around beneath his cloak. "Today, I formally pledge to serve Darzeq with all my soul."

Too late, Gueronn saw his intent.

Corban lunged and slid his dagger into the man's belly. Gueronn spewed wine, and Corban swiftly choked off any outcry, grasping the man's jaw with all his might, lowering him to the tent's carpeted floor, even as he pressed the blade deeper into the favorite's abdomen. Within two bubbling breaths, Gueronn's features went slack, his body exuded its dying fumes, and his eyes stared into an eternal void, horror-masked.

Leaving his blade submerged within the corpse, Corban rinsed his bloodied hand in a water pitcher, dried his fingers on Gueronn's fine linen tunic, then lifted the golden circlet from the favorite's head and crushed it flat. Gueronn's bejeweled dagger gleamed at him, and Corban took that as well, using the dagger to harvest a lock of the guard's sun-bleached hair. He hid the dagger in his belt, tucked the kill-tokens within his heavy coin-purse, then stalked outside, retrieving his father's sword from the entry. He must escape before that familiar and unwelcomed fatigue drained him of the ability to fight. Closing the entry curtain behind him, Corban nodded to the guards. "I'll return later. He doesn't wish to be disturbed—he's using the privy pot." Eternally.

The guards all bowed to Corban as he strode away, with Ghost following.

Seated at their encampment's fire, Lord Tragobre stared at Corban and shook his head in wide-eyed disbelief. "You didn't."

Corban sat near the fire adjacent to Lord Kemuel, sighed, then slid the favorite's crushed golden circlet and the golden dagger from his waistband. "I did. Then, I removed these pretty things from Gueronn's wine-soaked corpse. By the way, he was so heavily adorned with gems and finery that I'd wager my life he was the queen-mother's paramour."

Tragobre and the other Forum Lords stared, aghast. Tragobre coughed. "There've been rumors, but nothing's proven—except that the man wielded too much power, despite his lowly status."

Then Kemuel broke into a broad grin and pounded his fists on his knees. "Gueronn's dead! The golden toad's crushed!"

Thaddeus Ormr laughed. "Justice has been dealt to the man! More mercifully than he deserved, Lord Corban, make no mistake! Yet, we're grateful. I'd *pay* to tell the king this news, except that I'm poor now that my lord-father's disowned me."

"I'd pay for you," Kemuel retorted cheerily, "But by then it would be too late—I'd have told the king myself."

Corban lifted one hand, calling out, "To continue... The force set against Tragobre is mercenary—all hired men. Some will be true fighters, but I suspect that within two days, half the camp will be puking or too wearied to fight. The other half, if wise, will flee by dawn when they finally realize their commander is dead."

His eyes lit with ferocious glee, Roi Hradedh tapped his fingertips together—a man making plans. "Then we attack after dawn, when they've discover Gueronn's corpse and everyone's panicked. Once we've regained Tragobre, my lords, I say we gather our mutual forces, blockade the river—both branches, north and south—and surround Arimna!"

"We'll be there all winter," Lord Karvos argued. "I say we open negotiations with the queen-mother and convince her to leave Darzeq."

Kemuel reached for a steaming metal pitcher and a cup. "We'd be negotiating for years. I say we gather a raiding party, break into the palace, and drag her out."

"Suicide," Karvos muttered.

Thaddeus shot a quizzing look at Corban. "I'd go if you would, my lord. The Infinite's with you. Fighting under your command would be an honor."

Roi Hradedh grunted agreement as he reached for the pitcher. "To watch you fight, I believe, is the nearest we'll ever see one of the Infinite's warriors battle in our mortal realm." He poured a cup of steaming liquid, then studied Corban. "You're not as fatigued this time as you were when you defeated those scalns, my lord."

"I've been waiting for the exhaustion to strike," Corban admitted as Roi handed him the near-brimming cup. Had the attack on Gueronn simply been less draining, or was he becoming used to these divinely prompted bouts? Moreover, Lord Tragobre's comment about the Infinite's divine warriors ruffed all the hairs on Corban's scalp in wary unease. He hurriedly shifted the subject. "As far as joining a raid to wrest the queen-mother from Arimna ... yes, I'd be willing to go, but I know nothing of the place."

Karvos growled and shook his head. "It's foolishness! You won't get past the palace gates."

"I'd wager he will," Tragobre argued.

Ordinary fatigue mingled with boredom as Corban listened to the escalating quarrel. He sipped at his cup, helped himself to several handfuls of dried meat and sweetened grain-cakes, and then left the squabbling lords for the solitude of his own tent. But he called back over his shoulder, "Excuse me, my lords. It's been a long day, and dawn will arrive soon enough. Let me know what you decide!"

Whatever they decided, he'd do as he pleased, if the Infinite allowed.

A golden sunrise did nothing to brighten Corban's sour mood as he guided Ghost toward Darzeq's dominant Forum lords. They all greeted him, but said nothing to each other as they rode with their men toward the river road leading to Tragobre.

Corban masked a scowl and eased his shoulders beneath his metal-riveted protective vest. He should have stayed with these surly noblemen and finished their quarrel—their silence boded ill for winning a battle. Had they clashed beyond repair? Beneath his breath, he groused to the Infinite, "One-Who-Sees, do You see these lords? Deal with them as You've dealt with me! How can we prevail here if we're fighting among ourselves?"

His own dourness deepened as Lord Roi led them beyond the next curve in the river road—wrought by a bend in the river. Tragobre's town—blockaded and barred against the invaders—rested along the river road between the bridge and the fields near the approach to Tragobre's fortress. The fields where the mercenary army should have been.

Lord Tragobre himself called out, "Where've they gone? Beware a trap, my lords!"

They drew their swords and rode toward the castle above, amid a clutter of camp rubbish, badly trampled soil, abandoned utensils, and still-smoking hearths. Gueronn's tent still stood, but wide open and cleared of his corpse and his gear, as if his guards had removed all evidence of his existence.

Lord Kemuel turned toward Corban and shrugged eloquently, bug-eyed with wonder. "They're gone! All because that toad is dead—thanks to you, Lord Corban. My one disappointment is that I didn't have the chance to watch you fight this morning."

Even as Kemuel talked, the castle above was obviously astir, its inhabitants becoming aware that the besiegers had departed and that Lord Tragobre approached. Ram's horns blared in the distance, and shouts accompanied the din of the clattering, creaking gate and gears being worked as the castle was opened.

Lord Tragobre led them all up the steep incline toward his massive fortress. They rode through the gatehouse single file, then into a crowded bailey teeming with animals in makeshift pens, and the heady scent of manure piles, which steamed in the cold morning air.

A noblewoman emerged from the main building, obviously summoned in haste. Her dark, thickly curling hair billowed long and loose about her shoulders, and she'd clasped a noticeably uneven mantle around her linen gown. Yet for all her carelessness—or perhaps because of that graceful carelessness—Corban would have known her anywhere as a relative of Darzeq's new queen.

Lady Tragobre's delicate features predicted her daughter's own, and her glorious smile as she greeted Lord Tragobre was so reminiscent of Araine's that Corban bowed and glanced away.

In time to see Lord Karvos ride in one uneven circle around the courtyard before he led his men out of Tragobre without a word.

The royal messenger arrived and was admitted to Tragobre's keep after being thoroughly searched. Corban stood on guard nearby as Lord Tragobre greeted the messenger formally, never moving from his lordly high chair upon the dais in his great hall. The courier bowed then cowered before him. "My lord, I bring you a communication from Lord Karvos, who is in Arimna."

Tragobre's eyes widened, then narrowed in a frown that cut deep twin furrows between his eyebrows. "Arimna?" He glanced toward Corban and then at Lord Kemuel, who had just entered the great hall. "Karvos betrayed us!"

Kemuel halted. "How dare the cur sidestep us!"

Tragobre broke the note's seal, opened the crackling parchment, scanned its contents, and then cast them down onto the stones below the dais. He snarled at the messenger, "Out! Now!" To his own men standing in the doorway, he bellowed, "Take that man outside! Give him some food and lock him out! There is no reply!"

The doors' great bars rasped into place, sealing Tragobre's great hall. Roi snarled toward Corban and Kemuel, "Karvos has gone to 'negotiate' with the queen! He's destroyed all our plans and given us away completely—she knows everything!"

He stood and stomped off the dais. "She wants to meet with the king, and his new queen. I'm going to kill Karvos!"

Chapter 18

The fragrance of baking cakes permeated the long, narrow archery courtyard, and Matteo's stomach growled its longing for a taste of that aroma—toasted grain mingled with sweet fruit. Lessons hadn't even begun and he was already distracted. Footsteps sounded from the keep and Anji clattered down the steps, with Lord Aristo following and carrying a broad box. To the approaching Aristo, Matteo growled a feigned complaint. "My lord, why have you ordered the army's supplies to smell like actual food? Aren't rations supposed to be sawdust? I want to try some of those cakes!"

"So do I," Anji chimed in, her dark eyes sparkling as she rested her hands over her unborn baby, who was finally becoming large enough to be noticed. "But I have an excuse, cousin. You've none except your own appetite. Unless Dalia's with child and you're taking on her cravings."

Might his Dalia be with child? Matteo glanced at the far end of the courtyard where Dalia sat at an opened camp table, meticulously penning a tiny courier bird note for Tragobre—her answer to her parents' triumphant courier note, informing them of Tragobre's liberation and Gueronn's death. Dalia looked up at Matteo then, as if she sensed his glance, and her beautiful face lit with delight. She called to him, "My lord, how can I possibly concentrate when you're staring so?"

Matteo laughed at her. "I've much to stare at! Darzeq's queen is a wonder to be adored forever. However, if you can't concentrate, my love, then come learn this new bow my lord-father feared."

In truth, Dalia *must* learn this new weapon. Anji must learn. And Ekiael must also, as soon as he dragged himself away from his studies. Darzeq's royal family would add to its self-protective arsenal. Never must another massacre take them by surprise.

Dalia beamed at his invitation and immediately wiped her writing stylus, then covered the ink vial. "At your command, Sire—and gladly!"

If she was already with child... Matteo's heart constricted at the thought, half-fear, half hope, all overwhelming. *Infinite, bless You and thank You for granting me Dalia as my wife! You are the Mighty One, the One-Who-Sees! You saw my grief and offered me consolation....*

He smiled at her, and then toward Ekiael, who hurried down into the archery yard. "I apologize, but the Infinite's Word must never be neglected—particularly not by one of His priests, particularly as we approach the Season of Joy."

Matteo nodded. "I agree—though I'm shamed by your studiousness. I need to be more attentive and not allow life's cares to interfere." The Season of Joy marked the end of the year, and the beginning of the next, with the Five Observances scattered through the year's first five weeks: Gratitude, Repentance, Purification, Atonement, and Rejoicing.

Would he be able to observe all five without losing himself to grief over his family?

Resisting the pain of memories, he held out one hand for Dalia, who hurried toward them, asking Aristo, "My lord, is this a difficult weapon?"

Aristo bowed and smiled, clearly delighted with Darzeq's new queen. "Majesty, it is not. Which is why our good King Jonatan feared it. He said that anyone might take up this invention, this crossbow, and become a warrior—so long as that warrior had enough strength to draw back the bowstring."

Eshda's lord kneeled, placed the box on the yard's paving stones, and lifted the plain wooden cover. Inside, he'd stored two of the new bows and an ample supply of small, metal-winged bolts. "I shall demonstrate, and then all four of you may test the weapon for yourselves."

He offered the first weapon to Matteo, with a fistful of bolts, then grabbed the second weapon and stood. The weapon appeared deceptively simple. A sleek bow fastened to a long, smoothly polished wooden plank, with a groove carved down its length, set with a shallow metal-sheltered hook at the top of the groove and an iron stirrup at its base. Beneath all, a long metal latch rested within the base of the plank—evidently affixed through the wood to the slight hook above. Aristo cautioned, "Sire and ladies, beware. The slightest touch to this latch will fire the bolt, which will pierce anything in its path—even armor."

Matteo nodded. "We are excellent students, my lord. Advise us."

Grinning like a boy sent out to play, Aristo rested the weapon's iron stirrup on the pavings. Using both hands, he drew back the reinforced bowstring, which gave a satisfying creak just before Aristo latched it into the small, sheltered hook. He straightened, placed a small bolt flat within the long groove, then slid it backward toward the bowstring. Taking aim at the metal target set at the far end of the archery yard, Aristo squeezed the latch.

Before Matteo could even blink, the bolt shot through the metal target, pinging and leaving a perfect hole in the target's center. Dalia cheered, Anji applauded, and Matteo laughed. "Aristo, you're a champion! This is amazing!" With one slight problem. "Except that while you're busy drawing the string and setting the bolt, any plain archer can strike you down in turn."

"Exactly, Sire." Aristo nodded. "Which is why one is well-guarded or sheltered when using this weapon. No exceptions."

Dalia sidled up to Matteo and fluttered her lashes at him, a blatant flirtation. "My dearest lord, hurry and test the thing—I want to try it!"

Her plea tempted Matteo to kiss and torment her. He controlled himself, rested the weapon nose down, and planted his foot within the iron stirrup. "As you command, lady. Be patient." The bowstring creaked as Matteo drew it back and rested it within the hook. He straightened, clinked a metal bolt into the wooden channel, and slid it backward until its slight wings rested at the bowstring. Then, he held his breath, fixed his gaze on the dot of light left by Aristo's earlier shot ... and fired.

A second hole appeared in the target, accompanied by a vibrant ping that echoed through the courtyard. Matteo eyed Eshda's lord. "Thank you, sir. I approve, and claim this one as mine. Unless you've a better one."

"Now that I think if it, Majesty, your lord-father's was locked away somewhere in the armory. He never touched it. When we've finished here, I'll go search it out and have it restrung for you."

Aristo offered the second bow to Anji. Matteo was about to claim a kiss from Dalia when a servitor hesitated in the doorway. Matteo raised his eyebrows at the man. "Yes? Do you have news?"

"A courier's note relayed from Thaddeus of Iydan, and a courier's note from Arimna."

Aristo retrieved the note, still sealed within its tiny tube. Shifting the crossbow bolts within his hands, Matteo broke the tube's seal and frowned at Thaddus's miniscule script. *Karvos Stradin serves Cthar, who wishes to talk with you to discuss terms. All ploys and traps. Karvos told her all our plans. Be warned.*

Scowling, Matteo opened the second note and gritted his teeth. His grandmother's writing sprawled across both sides of the delicate parchment strip. *Matteo, my heart is broken and I weep. You, my only living blood, must meet with me and listen for your own sake, as the southern lords even now rally to my cause.*

Matteo roared his fury and cast the tube and bolts at a wall, making them ricochet back, clattering and ringing on the courtyard's pavings. "Ingrates!"

He raged to Dalia and the others, "She's spinning her webs around the southern lords, and they believe her! Did my father live and fight for nothing? Did my mother and brothers die for nothing? Karvos Stradin has defected to Cthar and she wishes to 'talk' with me. There's nothing to discuss! I want her dead—tortured as she's tortured others! I want Karvos hacked to pieces, and his estates in ruins! If the other lords do follow him.... They're traitors! I want to kill them all with my bare hands!"

Anji's face grayed with obvious distress, causing Ekiael to hold her supportively. Aristo retreated a step, watching Matteo as if he feared Matteo might turn against him, and Dalia's eyes went huge. She couldn't look more distraught unless he'd beaten her—which he never would. And yet...

Matteo turned away and pushed a hand through his hair. "Forgive me. How is it possible for me to hate anyone so much as I hate that woman and her toadies?"

Aristo's voice neared. "It is because her betrayal was too deep and against all that's right. Majesty, your rage is understandable."

Straightening in Ekiael's arms, Anji murmured, "It's the grief, Matteo. You've nothing to apologize for—least of all to me. I saw her betrayal as you did, and I'm angry too! Those who support her have no sense—"

As her voice failed, Ekiael said, "They're afraid Cthar will win the struggle for Darzeq because she has Arimna. Yet, according to the Infinite's promises from ages past, your line will continue despite her, and you're not wrong to crave justice."

All logical and soothing reasons to tell himself that he wasn't to blame. Nevertheless, a welling of pain and shadows lifted within his soul and darkened his thoughts. Trying to control his rage, Matteo stalked to the far end of the archery yard and stared down at the target, feeling heart-pierced as that metal plate.

Infinite, One-Who-Sees, I can become as dark as Lord Corban in despair. Darker. Angrier. Even now, I could kill her! Gladly ... too gladly!

Light footsteps approached. Beloved footsteps. Matteo braced himself to face his wife, his comfort. Before he could turn, she twined her arms around his waist and held him, her lilting voice soft. "You're too cruel toward yourself."

"No. I'm not." He half-turned, looped an arm around his wife's slender frame and drew her close. How could he even look at her? "The truth is that I could easily kill all who oppose me, if I allowed myself to be corrupted. Love, what if I'm ultimately corrupted beyond hope? It's in my blood! I'm like my grandmother—descended from a mortal fiend. I'm so full of rage that I must deserve to be where I am—no true home, and no true crown. I'd destroy a kingdom. Perhaps I don't deserve to survive. I'm too much like her!"

"No." Dalia touched his face, compelling him to look at her. "You're not like her! You've loved others, and you love them still, as you love me. She's loved no one but herself and those she perceives as portions of herself—yet even there, her love is conditional. Don't allow her to rule your emotions from a distance. In time you'll have justice for your family's deaths."

He allowed himself to be lulled, soothed by her tenderness, her love, and her cherished face and form. His beautiful little wife. Matteo grazed his fingers over her soft cheek, then murmured, "I would go insane if I didn't have you here, my love." But insanity would be too easy an escape, and he must seek justice for his family. He raised his voice. "We should rejoin the others. Perhaps our high priest will counsel me. *Won't* you, Ekiael?"

If Ekiael had been a dog or a horse, his ears would have perked. "Won't I what, Majesty?"

"Counsel me."

Darzeq's high priest grinned. "Here's my counsel, Majesty: Follow true wisdom. Seek answers from the Infinite. Find a true prophet and never ignore his or her words from our Creator."

Unlike Sheth. Sheth should have listened to Belaal's prophet. He should have ruled. He would have been a great king. Mighty One, call to me, as you called to Sheth through Your prophet, and let me hear and obey. Unlike Sheth—

Matteo tightened his hold on Dalia and closed his eyes. His last glimpse of Sheth and their brothers returned, attacked by Gueronn and his mercenaries. Because of Cthar. She must not prevail—Infinite, my Creator, do not allow her to triumph!

Above all, prevent me from becoming ever more like *her*.

Matteo opened his eyes and called out, "Aristo, do we have a courier bird who considers Arimna Palace as home? I must write a note to my erstwhile grandmother."

Cthar of Kaphtor. Murderess, your plea failed. I loathe carrying any taint of you in my blood. You destroyed my family, but I am my father's son! I will repay you for my mother's death and my brothers, you she-scaln! Consider yourself prey, and pray to the Infinite for mercy, for I've none! Matteo of Darzeq.

Finished with her latest note to her parents at Tragobre, Dalia fanned the parchment, and then slid a glance toward Matteo, who sat at his own writing table near their chamber window. A scowl marred his lean, beautiful face as he rolled and bound his own note into a tiny cylinder. Truly, he had every right to be furious and vengeful toward Cthar. And yet ... rage changed Matteo. Rage transformed him into a stranger whom she'd no wish to know.

A stranger she'd chase away whenever he dared to show himself.

Dalia quietly packed away her writing supplies and then crept across the chamber to pounce upon her unsuspecting husband and attack him with kisses. Matteo laughed and stood. He lifted her in his arms, kissed her fiercely, then held her, swaying and smiling as she wrapped her arms around his neck and rested her face against his wonderfully thick dark hair. Matteo murmured against her throat, "What would I do without you, my love?"

"You'd be quite unlike my darling Matteo. Abandon your writing, Majesty, and kiss me."

Evening sunlight streamed into Eshda's great hall from the high windows, pouring red-gold warmth over the dais and the evening meal like a blessing from the Infinite—a whim as pleasing to Anji's soul as the entire tranquil day. To her left, Matteo and Dalia where whispering obvious endearments to each other like the teasing pair of newlyweds that they were, and to her right, dear Ekiael ate perfunctorily while he read verses he'd copied from the Infinite's sacred Books. Beneath his breath, he murmured, "'...the Infinite hears when I call to Him....'"

Within her, the child stirred and stretched as if summoned by its father's voice. Or was it more than Ekiael's voice?

Spiritual recognition poured over Anji, warm as the evening sunlight, and she closed her eyes, absorbed by her Creator's presence.

One-Who-Sees, You see my child! But what is my child to You, Creator of the Universe?

Breath squeezed from Anji's lungs at the realization, joy battling fear. She rested her spoon in her dish of black rice, then clasped Ekiael's hand. "The Infinite claims our child."

How could she be ill over such an astonishing, divine realization? Yet nausea welled as it hadn't since the earliest weeks of her pregnancy. Ekiael met her glance, his lively gaze shifting swiftly from joy to wonder, then to a fear that matched her own. His voice so reverent that it must be a prayer, Ekiael breathed, "Infinite, what is Your will?"

His will? Anji swallowed, praying hard as she curved her arms around her unborn child.

Darzeq's future prophet.

Corban's breath misted in the deepening autumn chill as he urged Ghost northward, off the River Road. One more day's journey and he'd be in Eshda. Again. The place was beginning to seem like home—welcomed for its promise of comfort and rest, yet dreaded for the responsibilities he owed to its inhabitants.

Was Darzeq's new king and his exquisite queen well? Surely they'd been protected in his absence. For all of Aristo's kindly ways, the man kept fanatical watch over the king and Eshda. Knowing this, why did uneasiness settle upon Corban as a murky cowl?

He rode until just before dusk, when wise men sought shelter for the night. Until a promising tinge of food-scented smoke drifted toward him through the cool air. He peered ahead, eyeing a small town in the distance—a mild-seeming cluster of unwalled stone and thatch buildings. A town large enough to boast modest lodgings for travelers. Would the queen-mother or his enemies seek him if he stayed at an inn for the night?

The evening's growing chill made the risk one worth taking. He needed shelter, and Ghost needed food and care.

His decision made, Corban rode into the town, decided upon the most comfortable-seeming stables and paid for Ghost's lodging, food, and grooming—which he oversaw for himself, to the stable keeper's mild annoyance.

Yet the stable keeper seemed level-headed. He handled Ghost adeptly, clearly admiring him as any horse-lover would a superb charger. Corban flung the man an approving grin. "Thank you. Which inn here most meets with your approval?"

The stable keeper looked up from currying Ghost. "Eh. My own home's the best. If you must pay, however, The Vine is the cleanest and quiet, and its food is the best."

Corban placed a coin on a nearby stall—away from Ghost—and departed.

The Vine was the most distant inn, but worth the walk. Corban approved the green and gold sign, as well as the clean stone entrance and the well-oiled door. Inside a troop of men, all armed and journey-wearied, turned toward Corban, curious. He approached the heavy wooden ledge, sheltering the innkeeper's personal alcove. "Do you have a spare chamber?"

The innkeeper looked up from his ledger and eyed Corban. Apparently judging him as a man able to pay, he nodded. "Two, sir. The best is a quarter-weight of silver for one night—a full weight buys you a week. All meals are served here in the main room, but our food's the best."

"So I'm told." Corban glanced at the men, already eating in the main room. They seemed to be uniformly groomed and garbed—a trained force, such as kept by a nobleman to protect his household. "Has another lord paid for lodgings here tonight?"

"Another?" The innkeeper studied Corban with a bit more respect, then nodded. "Lord Losbreq rides to Eshda at dawn."

Losbreq. The lord of Qamrin who had refused the uncrowned Matteo refuge, and then rained arrows upon them, wounding Ekiael. Corban tamped down an impulse of fury—longing to crash into the rebel-lord's rented chamber and beat the nobleman to blood-streaked pulp.

What business did Losbreq of Qamrin have at Eshda?

Corban worked a half-weight of silver from his coin purse and clicked it onto the ledge. "My name need not concern you. Give me the best chamber remaining, for one night only. Send my evening meal to me, then leave me in peace. I'll be riding to Eshda at dawn, so don't disturb me." Perhaps by sunrise, he'd be calm enough to greet the lord of Qamrin civilly. Whatever happened, he'd be watching Lord Losbreq's every move. Let the man breathe one threat toward him or Eshda, and Corban would turn the man to dust.

Corban urged Ghost toward the inn, toward the uneasy shadowy cluster of men gathering outside. Golden light rimmed the eastern sky beneath a dark violet canopy still lit with stars, but Losbreq's men were stamping their booted feet, glaring at the cobbled pavings and grumbling low, surly complaints about the morning's chill.

Several looked up at Corban as he approached. He nodded to them coolly. One, a coarse-faced, keen-eyed shaven pole of a guard, half-bowed. "Sir? May we assist you?"

"I am traveling to Eshda today," Corban informed the man. "I'd prefer to journey with your lord and master. I've no wish to face an ambush of scalns alone—if there's one to be faced along the way."

"Wise," the coarse-face guard commented to the stones.

Wise? To the Infinite, Corban petitioned beneath his breath, "Yes, grant me wisdom."

If Losbreq planned ill toward the king and queen, he'd be minus a beating heart within his first traitorous instant.

Chapter 19

Losbreq, Lord of Qamrin, emerged from the inn as night's final hues faded amid a golden burst of sunlight. Tall and thin, with a lordly golden circlet crowning his dark hair, Losbreq mounted his restive silvery horse. He motioned his men forward with one gloved hand, then threw Corban a wearied, disinterested glance. "You are the honored guest traveling to Eshda?"

Corban nodded coolly, but caught and held a shocked breath. Losbreq's bearing, his self-importance, and those emotionless dark eyes might have been Thaenfall. Here was his father's arrogance mirrored in a foreigner's singularly raised eyebrow, the superior nod to his men, and the icy assurance that his life would ever be exactly as he'd ordered or others would suffer. "I am indeed traveling to Eshda. As for being honored ... that is debatable."

Losbreq studied Corban, a vague bafflement edging his bored tone. "Sir, have we met previously?"

"No." Corban loosened Ghost's reins. "I am Corban Thaenfall, a foreign lord currently without lands or fortune—a mercenary. If we'd met, I would remember you, my lord. You remind me of my lord-father."

Qamrin's lord huffed a muted laugh. "I fear the resemblance isn't entirely welcome."

"My father was formidable," Corban admitted.

"Was?" Lord Losbreq expression turned guarded. "He's dead then? I'm sorry for your loss. How?"

It might be best to shock this lord with the truth. Corban managed a half-smile. "He was executed for treason. I'm told he was unrepentant to his last breath."

Again, Losbreq lifted an eyebrow. He stared for one long instant, then gazed at the road ahead. "Now, you interest me, my lord. A similar situation's been much on my mind since I refused a noble visitor this past summer. Unlike your resolute lord-father, I've questioned my decision and repented it—something I rarely do."

Words Corban wished he could have heard from his own father. "I'll be direct, my lord. I accompanied the king this summer. Did you realize that your men wounded Darzeq's high priest while chasing off the king?"

Losbreq's expression didn't change, but his tawny complexion turned ashen. "Ekiael? I commanded my men to chase off the prince ... the king ... and his men until I knew the true situation in Arimna. I've my wives, my children, and slaves to consider. I'll be no party to treason—though it seems I committed something close enough. Is the high priest well?"

"I believe so. Though it took him a while to recover."

The multiple creaks and clinkings of riding tack melded with the thuds of horse-hooves, filling a brief silence. Losbreq asked, "What of the king? Might he excuse a wary and apologetic subject?"

"If the apology is sincere, he might. But if your apology is not genuine, my lord, I advise you to retreat to Qamrin at once. Three lords attacked the king during the Autumn Forum, and their remains now rot in the ravines below Eshda's bridge."

"I would expect no less. I allowed myself to be swayed by promises from Arimna Palace. Yet as much as our deceased king frustrated me, I knew his opinions. The queen-mother, however is proving herself less forthright. She promised me lands and honors to bestow on my children, requesting only my loyalty in return. Now, however, a price has been named and I believe that if I comply she will demand more."

"Is the queen-mother demanding a portion of revenues from your lands?"

"She's demanding a life." Losbreq cut a sharp glance toward Corban. "Two days ago, I received a courier bird with a message from the queen-mother. In order to claim the lands she's promised my children, my men and I must hunt down and kill a Siphran mercenary who dared to slaughter 'General' Gueronn."

He was being hunted so soon? Did Losbreq suspect his identity, or could Corban bluff his way out of assassination? Corban masked his surprise with a grim smile. "I've heard that Gueronn was her favorite guard."

Losbreq straightened in his saddle, then relaxed and lowered his voice. "Months ago, I heard, with some validation, that Gueronn was a slave who became her guard and then her secret husband. We lords of the Forum have exchanged so many notes these past few months that the air ought to be dark with courier-birds' wings. This week, I received a note from another lord, informing me that Gueronn did indeed arrange the royal massacre at Cthar's behest, and that our lord Matteo committed no treason, though the queen-mother previously implied to me that he had."

Lord Losbreq sneered, clearly offended by the memory. "The queen-mother's playing games with us all to tighten her hold on Darzeq. Which is why I haven't commanded my men to kill you, Lord Corban Thaenfall of Siphra, assassin of Gueronn. Which is also why I wish to bow to the maligned Lord Matteo and pledge loyalty to him as Darzeq's king. I did not like his father's policies, it is true. But Jonatan honored his own code, and I would far prefer to be ruled by a son of Jonatan than the she-scaln, Cthar."

Corban summoned a smile. "This, my lord, is why I'll not pray to kill you and your men."

"Is your strength all that I've heard, Lord Corban?" Losbreq studied him intently, a man trying to comprehend a potential foe. Or a possible friend. "That you slaughter troops of guards within a breath? Seven scalns within a heartbeat?"

"Five scalns, and a few misguided assassins. But no, the strength is not mine—it's granted by the Infinite. A year ago, I would have preferred to leap from a tower rather than bow to Him. Now ... I am His uneasy servant."

"You're not the only one who's uneasy, Lord Corban. I'm no perfect follower of the Infinite, but nor am I apostate." Losbreq glared at the road ahead. "Darzeq's been blessed with an excellent high priest, but we need a prophet such as Belaal's during these troubled times."

The too-familiar ache tightened in Corban's chest. Araine, prophet of Belaal. Was she his Araine? He'd give anything to know the truth and gain her forgiveness. Against his will, he spoke her name to Losbreq. "Araine, prophet of Belaal, sent a warning earlier this year. She warned one of Darzeq's princes, Lord Sheth, to instruct his brothers to flee Arimna. He didn't believe her."

"To Darzeq's sorrow. I fear many will die because he didn't believe the warning. Araine of Belaal, you said?"

"Yes." Corban's throat constricted. He'd speak no more of her. Pain and guilt raked invisible furrows within his soul whenever he pronounced Araine's name.

He rode on with the cagey Losbreq, neither saying anything of consequence.

At sunset, they reached the approach to Eshda, reassuringly beset with scaln-traps, their multiple wires and pikes filled with the crimson-fleshed, stinking corpses amid the broken steaming crevasses lining the road.

Corban said, "My lord, command your men to lower their banners. Also, they must relinquish their weapons inside Eshda's gates, for the king's safety."

If they refuse, Mighty One, You-Who-Sees, grant me the strength to vanquish them all.

Losbreq lifted a gloved hand, halted his men, and issued the commands with the strict superiority of a lord who expects obedience. When the golden Losbreq banners were safely furled and stashed away, Losbreq nodded to Corban. "Lead on, Lord Corban. But when we enter the fortress, please walk with me as I approach the king."

Corban cut a look at Qamrin's proud lord, and saw the tensed, self-strengthening look of a man preparing himself for death.

Aristo personally greeted Lord Losbreq, then watched as Qamrin's men obediently set aside their weapons and opened their mantles to be searched in Eshda's sunset-shadowed central stone yard.

Corban walked among the Qamrin men, watching them. Praying for discernment. Was he wise to vouch for Losbreq? For these men who might be a danger to Darzeq's new king and queen?

An impulse of wariness, of heaviness, halted him near three of Losbreq's men who were exchanging hissed comments between themselves. Beneath his breath, Corban prayed, "Infinite, enlighten me. What's here?"

One of the men folded his sword belt, but scowled as he placed it upon the growing heap of Qamrin's surrendered weaponry. The second glanced up and glowered, but the third froze, gazing at Corban in clear guilt. Absolute ice, Corban challenged him, judging him the weakest of the three. "You have a complaint, sir. Let's hear it *now*."

Darting a fearful glance at his sullen comrade, the guard said, "We don't all agree with our Lord Losbreq. Doesn't the queen control Arimna, thus all our trade? She can strangle Darzeq!"

Corban leaned down, glaring into the man's eyes, making him step back. "And you've a lord who issued his commands. If you disagree with him, then leave his service and his pay! You dishonor yourself by talking against him."

The first guard said, "We've rights in Darzeq. Your lands might be different, lord, but we've some freedoms here. The queen's promised lands and treasures to her allies. What's Matteo of Darzeq done for us? Nothing!"

Losbreq joined them, resting one hand on his emptied belt, as if infuriated. "Is this what you think, Abraxis? And you, Hiburin? Have I finally heard the truth? Well, know this: I won't be reviled as untrustworthy because one of my own men thought he knew better than me! You are dismissed. Leave Eshda. Now! And you, Iovis—fear makes a feeble follower. Go."

Iovis recoiled. "But, my lord, night's near, and Eshda's prime scaln territory. You'll throw me out to die!"

"You'll betray us all with your weakness! I'm no follower of Cthar of Kaphtor, but you whine against Darzeq's king. Out!"

The first rebel, Abraxis, lunged toward the pile of weaponry and seized his sword. Too slowly. Hiburin followed him, sluggish as a drunkard. Corban bashed both men to the ground, hauled them up by the hair, and then wrenched them toward the gate, goading the cowering Iovis with a kick that made the man yelp. "The last thing you'll do for Qamrin is obey its lord!"

His skin crawling with fury, Corban herded the men bodily through the gatehouse, Abraxis roared as his sword clattered to the stones. "Give me my sword!"

Corban snarled, "Your lord provided you with that weapon, but you're leaving his service. The sword stays!" He should strip them of their gear, right down to their under-linens. Arms flailing from Corban's next kick, Iovis shrieked out his panic while Abraxis and Hiburin thrashed and clawed against Corban's grip. Eshda's guards cleared the way as Corban stalked out to Eshda's arched bridge. There, he released the two men and shoved them onto the bridge's path.

Hiburin snarled his outrage and charged, wrenching a dagger from his belt. Corban hammered a fist into Hiburin's chest, directly over his heart. Hiburin's rage vanished, and death-blankness washed over his face, just before he fell like a toppled tree, taking Abraxis down with him. Abraxis grunted and scrambled, reaching for Corban's booted feet, obviously bent on tumbling him to the stones. Corban stomped the man's arm. Abraxis screamed and lifted his free hand, claw-like toward Corban.

Corban seized the man's proffered wrist, stepped off his crushed arm, then flung Abraxis bodily up into the air, sending him in a high flailing, screaming arc over the bridge. After some distance, Abraxis dropped, howling, into the seething abyss below.

Iovis ran along Eshda's magnificent stone bridge, fleeing like a terrified child. Straight into the scaln territory he'd feared.

Absolute silence ruled the gateway as Corban turned toward the gatehouse. Eshda's men were staring at him, their mouths agape, and Qamrin's men retreated into the fortress once more, all hushed and compliant.

Tremors coursed through Corban's limbs as he herded everyone through the gate, and as Lord Losbreq subtly bowed him inside Eshda's walls once more.

Why should Losbreq honor him? He'd just added another death, perhaps several, to his list of dubious deeds.

If he continued such a lethal and infamous course through Darzeq, he wouldn't leave this country alive. His journey to Belaal, to learn the truth about Araine and to beg her forgiveness, was a fading dream, lost in waking darkness.

Alone in her opulent chamber within Sulaanc's royal palace, Araine, prophet of Belaal, stared at the sacred scroll, seeing beyond it. Glimpsing a waking-dream fragment. Of a brutal man she'd prayed to never see again. "Corban..."

No.

Her heart thudding, heavy with dread, Araine stood, clutching the scroll.

No. He no longer existed for her. This dream-fragment didn't exist.

She turned away.

Chapter 20

With Ekiael and Anji standing to his right, Matteo sat in the regal chair on the dais, watching as Corban walked with Losbreq up the length of the great hall.

Corban's forbidding expression, edged with fatigue, gave nothing for Matteo to interpret. Was he angered by the guard's rebellion and death on the bridge? Did he actually trust Losbreq?

Losbreq seemed equally grim, but more chary than fatigued.

As cautious as his unexpected lord-guest, Matteo sent a prayer upward, beyond the hall's soaring whitewashed ceiling. *Infinite, hear me ... give me wisdom now. With forbearance and every attribute a good king must possess. How must I deal with Losbreq of Qamrin?*

To Ekiael and Anji, he muttered, "What are you thinking, my cousin and my priest?"

Ekiael whispered, "I forgive him, Sire, for I'm almost fully healed. As for trust, isn't Corban with him? Let Losbreq prove himself."

"I agree." Anji leaned toward Matteo, soft-voiced. "A royal pardon, if deserved, might reassure other lords who hesitate to commit to your service."

Several steps from the dais, Losbreq halted and bowed. "Sire." He knelt abruptly and removed the golden chaplet from his head. More humble than Matteo expected him to be, Losbreq placed the lordly circlet on the stones before the dais, clearly offering it to Matteo before he prostrated himself upon the stone floor. "I do not merit your forgiveness, Sire, yet I beg it of you, for the sake of my family and my people. I consider myself your prisoner until you declare otherwise. Furthermore, I give my word—my life—in pledge. I'd no wish to harm you or Darzeq's worthy high priest, nor to cause the Lady Anji Rhiysa such terrible distress."

"Stand, Lord Losbreq of Qamrin." Matteo glanced at Corban, who gave him an almost imperceptible nod. As Losbreq retrieved his chaplet and stood, Matteo asked, "Why beg my forgiveness now? What's truly brought you to Eshda?"

Losbreq flicked the gleaming circlet in his hand. "It would take all night to tell you everything, Sire."

"Then eat with us and we'll talk." Father would have approved his decision and his peaceable tone—Matteo hoped Losbreq would appreciate it and approve as well.

Beside him, Ekiael added, "Stay with us this week, my lord, to begin the Season of Joy—we are celebrating the Five Observances at Eshda instead of Arimna."

Losbreq shot the high priest a questioning look, clearly unconvinced that his pardon was genuine. "I'll celebrate for a week with you, my lord-priest, if you've forgiven me. I'm pleased to see that you've recovered. If you'd died, I would truly deserve condemnation."

Dalia entered the hall, drowsy from a nap, her sweet face imprinted with a pillow's crease that Matteo longed to smooth away. She smiled at him, banishing his cares with her presence. As she approached, Matteo reached for his wife's delicate hand. "Lord Losbreq, have the flights of rumors informed you that I married Lord Tragobre's daughter during the Autumn Forum?"

"No, my lord. My sources have failed me, congratulations to you both." He smiled at Dalia, openly admiring her, and reminding Matteo of this lord's reputation for pursuing lovely women. Losbreq was known to have agents permanently employed in Darzeq's key slave markets to purchase the most beautiful slaves for his own household—a self-indulgent practice that caused Jonatan of Darzeq to repeatedly and openly rebuke Losbreq, building their erstwhile enmity.

Matteo drew his wife close, studying her for signs of illness. "Do you feel better?"

She leaned against him briefly. "Yes, Sire. Much better, thank you. I simply needed to rest." She smiled at Losbreq politely, but her eyes brightened as she glimpsed Corban standing below the dais. "Welcome, my lords! It's a good day indeed, when we're blessed with your company."

Her delight set Losbreq visibly at ease. Qamrin's lord grinned and bowed, and even Corban relaxed enough to smile.

Over their evening meal, amid the lowering sun's ruddy glow in the windows, and Lord Aristo's ever-attentive presence, Losbreq tugged a scroll from beneath his overtunic and placed it on the table. "Before the queen-mother demanded Lord Corban's life, and the day before you appealed to me from Qamrin's gates, I received this from Cthar of Kaphtor. She implied that you were suspected of attempting to seize Darzeq. She offered me lands, revenues, and honors for my children if I would ensure your capture and bring you to justice. I doubted her motives and didn't accept her offer. But I also doubted you, Sire, which was why I didn't welcome you. Forgive me. Nevertheless, you're indirectly accused of the massacre."

Dalia hugged Matteo and huffed, as Anji gasped, "That's outrageous! Gueronn led the attack, and he was her guard—more than her guard if I believed the rumors among the Queen Valsignae's attendants."

Losbreq said, "Lady Rhiysa, I've heard the same rumors, and I believe them. I also believe that she's sent the similar notes to various lords throughout southern Darzeq. My lord and king." He bowed his head toward Matteo. "As an older player in Darzeq's politics, I advise you to counter her pledges with your own to draw Darzeq's lords to your side. Unfortunately, lands and money will win you more supporters than will your gratitude and royal heritage."

Matteo scanned the notes, his pulse quickening in fury as he recognized his grandmother's elegant, unmistakable writing. *Lord Losbreq of Qamrin, this is a war I must win to survive. Join me and you'll be repaid. I pledge wealth and honors to you and your children. My heart is broken to think that Lord Matteo might have effected such tragedy....*

Her writing, clear and concise, was remarkable, given her anguish, within mere days of the massacre. Matteo dropped the note onto the table and hastily flicked it toward Dalia and Anji lest he viciously tear the parchment to shreds, as he longed to shred Cthar. If she were here ... yes, he would have immediate and merciless revenge. He tamped down his murderous longings, struggling to preserve the evening's peaceable mood.

The instant he was calm enough, Matteo said, "Thus the kingdom's at war with itself, and I'm isolated. We must write again to the Forum lords. Remind them of their promises. I'll offer them equal incentives, but unlike the she-scaln I'll keep my word. If Darzeq's lords give me men for an army, I'll give you all shares of wealth. I'll scatter Cthar's estates among you all—not to mention any wealth she granted Gueronn. Cthar will never fulfill her promises to them; she loves herself too much."

Ekiael leaned over Anji's shoulder, perusing the note. He grimaced. "While we wait for the lords' responses, we pray and stand fast until the lords of the south become disenchanted. I'll send word to my most trusted priests to encourage their lords to see reason and beware the queen-mother."

Dalia released the note and clasped Matteo's arm. "This makes me so angry! My lord, please excuse me. I believe I've eaten and read as much as I can endure for one meal."

Matteo nodded, and Dalia fled. Losbreq glanced after her and smiled. "I also advise you, Sire, to proclaim the one thing that Cthar can never claim for herself—Darzeq's new queen is no foreigner who will betray our laws and scorn our traditions."

Dalia gazed into the glowing, softly crackling hearth and sipped from the warm cup in her hands. A tisane was all she could manage to calm her stomach. Indeed, a clear tisane was all she should drink. At sunset, the most holy time of fasting began.

She must forget about the treacherous Cthar and remind herself instead of the Observances: Gratitude, Repentance, Purification, Atonement, and Rejoicing. Yes, she could, in good conscience, declare all these things and rededicate herself to the Infinite.

The door opened softly, and Matteo entered. Her handsome husband. He grinned, crossed their chamber, and sat beside her, drawing her into his arms. "I thought you'd be asleep."

"No. However, I am tired, and with good reason." She leaned back in his embrace and looked up into his eyes. "My beloved lord-husband and king, I'm carrying our child."

Infinite, Creator of All, let the baby have Matteo's beautiful eyes....

Matteo stared at her, then laughed, rocking her, hugging her closer, his bewhiskered cheek and breath warm and perfectly delicious against her skin. "So soon! But it's wonderful. I wish my family were here to celebrate with us." His expression darkened, then he kissed her fervently. "May the Infinite bless us with many healthy children, though without my scaln-eyes."

Pouring all her love and tenderness into the words, Dalia argued softly, "May the Infinite bless us with many healthy children, who joyously gaze at life through eyes as golden as their royal father's! I'll never be tired of looking at your wonderful eyes."

Obviously disagreeing in silence, Matteo shifted the subject. "I pray that we're free to return to Arimna soon, and that this child learns of the coming war only through history lessons."

Dalia kissed his cheek. "How long do you suppose it will take to regain Arimna?"

"One day is too long! I want her *gone*."

Dead. Dalia's thoughts supplied the word, followed by a prayer. *Infinite, until we're free of our self-imposed prison, grant my dear husband peace.*

Until then, perhaps the child would bring them joy after this year's sorrows.

Anji smiled at the midwife, Yiska—sent to Eshda months ago, and strongly recommended by Lady Tragobre. Finished tending Anji, the midwife cooed and fussed endlessly over Anji's newborn son, Jakin, as if he were her own adored kindred. Lovely to see, but who had done the most work in this chamber this day? Anji begged, "Yiska, *please* let me hold him!"

Her long, earnest face aglow with delight, Yiska carried the warmly bundled Jakin to Anji's bed. "If I must give him over, Lady Rhiysa, then I must. He's as beautiful an infant as ever I've held—and I've held many."

Anji laughed and reached for her son. "I must accept the truth—he *is* beautiful." Jakin gazed up at her, his round swarthy face and dark dreamer's eyes so like his father's, that joyous tears misted her gaze. Though she glimpsed the heritage of Arimna's kings in her son's small, distinctive nose and chin. How could this tiny mortal bundle be Darzeq's future prophet? Was she mistaken?

She nuzzled her son tenderly, cherishing his warmth and petal-soft skin.

A light tap sounded at the door, and Dalia practically danced inside, scarcely showing her own pregnancy yet, but fully recovered from her morning sickness. "When will you be ready to hand him over? Ekiael is eager to see him, and so are the others. I've brought my mantle to wrap him in for his first journey downstairs. See?"

She lifted a fur-lined violet mantle from the crook of her arm, then swept it high in the air and cast it over the bedcovers beside Anji. "We won't keep him long."

No. Anji longed to say the word. To hold her newborn son forever, sheltered and untouched by pain. *Infinite, You-Who-Sees, how can I release him to this world that he must one day confront? Will they hate him? Kill him? Give me strength!*

Dalia leaned into Anji's prayer and kissed her cheek. "Come on! Be brave. You must give him up just long enough for me to take him to his lord-father. Ekiael's been pacing and praying all day—Matteo too. Have pity on them. I'll bring him back quickly; I give you my word. Particularly if he cries."

Ekiael ... yes, he'd undoubtedly be distraught, certain that something was wrong. Anji kissed Jakin's small forehead and relinquished him to the world beyond this chamber.

But, as Dalia lifted the edge of her violet mantle, Yiska frowned and scolded. "Not in that trailing thing, Majesty, above all, not as you go down those stairs. Queen you may be, but this child is my charge, and I intend him to be safe. As I will your own lordling when he's born, so step away."

Her slate-gray eyes huge, Dalia obeyed, leaving Jakin in Yiska's care. But she complained, "No wonder my lady-mother sent you—I'm sure you'd scare off an army! Which is a good idea. Why don't you lead an attack on Cthar?"

Yiska lifted her firmly rounded chin, a glint lit her eyes, shockingly war-like for a midwife. "I'd relish it, Majesty. But not until I'm sure this child's safe, so stand back."

As one of the lamps beside him threatened to gutter in the winter-gloomy great hall, Corban stretched and straightened, though his gaze and thoughts still rested upon the parchment scrolls opened on the high table before him.

Song-verses copied from the Books of the Infinite beckoned his attention—verses Araine had once written to him in paraphrase, applying them to his life while he was yet a nobleman of Siphra.

I pray good for your sake ... May your soul find peace ... Allow your thoughts to dwell upon calmness ... seek reason....

Her letters reached him during the anxious days after his lord-father's execution. Tranquil words worthy of contemplation, bringing peace and order to his torn spirit. He'd treasured her letters. Lived for the serenity they offered during those days of grief.

He'd welcomed their consolation. But he'd refused to see their source, which rested before him in these ancient verses—the Infinite's own words. Words he'd only begun to read in full at Ekiael's insistence.

One could not spend an entire winter locked up in a fortress with the Infinite's obsessively enthusiastic high priest and remain unaffected. One either longed to bash down the unrelenting enthusiasm and escape, or one finally surrendered and listened.

This day, however, Ekiael was more agitated than enthusiastic, waiting for definitive proof that his wife and newborn son were well. Ekiael was pacing in the shadowed hall, complaining to Matteo, "It's taking too long! I should just go up there and pound on the door—never mind what Yiska has decreed."

The far door beyond the dais opened, and Dalia glided out, bright-eyed, hugging a small bundle fastened about her in a plain linen sling—the sort of carrying sling that any common woman used to hold an infant while she tended her chores. If Darzeq could see its true queen, the entire country would surrender to Matteo.

Ekiael charged toward Dalia, his voice booming across the hall. "Is my lady-wife well?"

"Yes, and the baby is perfect! See."

The high priest laughed and crooned at his son, clearly besotted. Corban supposed any new father would be this smitten. But he, Corban Thaenfall, was no father, and likely would never be one. He tried to ignore the joyous chatter, Ekiael's laughter, Matteo's congratulations, and Dalia's cooing. Until Dalia finally approached him, the newborn still snug in her embrace.

Exactly as Corban had once thought he might eventually see Araine, holding his own child.

A dream he'd dismissed long ago, which haunted him as Dalia smiled at him—finally on her way out of the hall to return the baby to its mother. "My lord, isn't he wonderful? Look!"

Corban obliged, forcing a smile, which became genuine as he studied the infant in the lamplight. "He's a miniature Ekiael. Amazing."

"Isn't he?" Dalia beamed. "I pray my child's equally healthy." She glanced over her shoulder at Matteo and Ekiael, who were approaching because she'd stopped. Softly, she pleaded, "Lord Corban, if something happens to me ... if I don't survive my labor ... promise you'll protect Matteo and my child if I die."

If she died? Corban mentally crushed the idea. "You'll survive. Lady, don't ask me to stay."

"Only until he's safe, my lord."

"Kings are never safe, lady." Neither were queens. Nor were winsome young noblewomen facing childbirth. No. She must not die.

Matteo and Ekiael loomed behind Dalia, and she hushed as they laughed and admired the newborn again. Corban fought bleakness by taking refuge in the Book of Praises.

A Psalm of sleep: Hear me when I call upon you in righteousness, Infinite, my Creator...

Do not let her die!

Chapter 21

Matteo kissed his sleeping wife and then studied his newborn son, Benamir. Darzeq's heir—named by Matteo as Darzeq's "child of promise"—a living challenge to the now-barren Cthar.

The baby gazed up at him quizzically, his eyes dark, yet extraordinarily luminous, resembling two of his brothers, Alvir and Boas. Hopefully, Benamir's eyes would remain as dark as theirs. Yet Dalia and Anji both declared his eyes would surely turn golden, for he looked so much like Matteo.

Matteo grazed a knuckle along his tiny son's face, marveling at its softness. Its perfection. The baby grimaced, just as Dalia did when she doubted something, and Matteo almost laughed. Barely forming the words, Matteo whispered, "Don't doubt me!"

And don't let his eyes turn golden.

"Don't be like me."

Ever prey to his tainted blood, inherited from a murderous scaln-queen.

Cthar would kill his son without hesitation, just as she'd surely kill Matteo if she could get either of them in her grasp. No.

Matteo smoothed his son's tender cheek, then straightened. Now, more than ever, he had good reason to fight. He must persuade the southern lords to join him and throw off Cthar's poisonous talon-hold to free Darzeq and to save his son from a merciless foreign queen.

Anji turned, leaning away from the writing table as Matteo marched into her chamber. Her cousin looked happier than he'd been since Benamir's birth, almost eight months past.

Matteo grinned and raised a tiny, gleaming cylinder. "We've news from the south. Kemuel's been gathering complaints and making allies of those who're offended by Cthar. *At last* we'll have a true army to besiege Arimna!"

"Well." Ekiael rested his writing stylus on the edge of its gilded tray, then straightened, his voice dry. "It's only been—what?—fifteen months?"

Anji touched his ink stained fingers, cherishing his warmth and his scholarly distraction. "It's been more than eighteen months since the massacre, my darling, and you should be glad to be freed from Eshda after being locked up with me all this time. I'm surprised it's taken Cthar this long to break enough promises to turn her allies into enemies."

Ekiael smiled, his lustrous dark eyes conveying tenderness, melting Anji, particularly as he murmured, "A thousand years of being locked in Eshda with you wouldn't be enough, my love."

She laughed. "Remind me to kiss you later."

Matteo cleared his throat. "I'm here to talk strategy, and you two are flirting like newlyweds. Gather your wits and pay attention."

Anji lifted her chin, joyously defiant. "Sire, you're just as distracted when Dalia's in the vicinity, therefore I refuse to feel guilty or negligent."

Ekiael drew Anji's hand to his chest. "Agreed. Nevertheless, my lord-king, we are listening."

Matteo placed the tiny cylinder and its minute parchment scroll on the table, then held his hands over a nearby glowing brazier, talking as he flexed his fingers above the low flames. "According to Kemuel, we now have men and weapons pledged from every river port south of Arimna, and they're planning a blockade of the entire River Tinem, both branches, north and south, to intercept goods heading to Arimna from Kaphtor. Because we're still in the cold months, Cthar won't expect such a maneuver. No one will."

Ekiael released his hold on Anji's hand, and she leaned toward him to study the minute crisp parchment cipher. A blockade of the entire river, north and south? When had the river's lords *ever* trusted each other enough to agree on such a tactic? Never in Darzeq's history. "That's amazing! Has Cthar bespoken enough trade with Kaphtor to endanger her personal income if the river lords take it all?"

Matteo's triumphant smirk told Anji the truth. Cthar—feeling secure and triumphant, convinced she'd permanently exiled Matteo to Eshda—had apparently invested an overwhelming amount of money in trade with her home country. "Anji, she does as she pleases, according to her creed, and all her thoughts are toward Kaphtor not Darzeq. The river's been aswarm with ships from Kaphtor at the expense of Darzeq's merchants. It never occurred to Cthar that such favoritism would stir such resentment among the Forum lords and our own citizens."

Ekiael huffed. "It's never occurred to her that she needs favor with the Forum lords, *and* with the priests, and with the people above all. We're maggots in her opinion. She's going to give Darzeq to Kaphtor."

The chamber door opened further, and Dalia entered, lovely and ashen in her furred violet wool cloak, carrying seven-month-old Benamir.

Benamir's wide golden eyes lit up, bright in his handsome little olive-brown face, and he reached for his father, clearly eager for fun. Matteo kissed Dalia and swept Benamir from her arms. He rumpled Ben's glossy black curls and murmured to Dalia, "Beloved, sit down and rest."

Ekiael rushed to drag an X-framed chair near the brazier for her comfort. Dalia smiled and gratefully sank into the seat, drawing her cloak tight. Matteo flung a coverlet over her and tucked it in one-handed, delighting Benamir as Matteo jostled him about like a parcel.

Dalia's second pregnancy, just confirmed this past month, was draining her worrisomely and testing the limits of both Aristo's and Yiska's anti-nausea remedies. Matteo's distress was evident as he hovered near, stroking her flowing, wild curls, then gently tracing the line of her throat. Anji studied her dear friend's wearied tawny face, then scolded gently, "You shouldn't have trekked down here; we would have brought you news shortly."

A welcome glint of friendly mutiny lit Dalia's wide gray-green eyes. "Lord Corban brought word that we've good news. I couldn't wait. He's bringing Jakin along, but you know how Lord Corban is with the boys."

Anji hid a smile. Yes, if she wished to frighten Corban and make him behave like a fussy old dotard, she handed him Benamir or Jakin.

Darzeq's formidable royal champion sidled into the chamber, clutching the robust thirteen-month-old Jakin against one shoulder, while Jakin maintained a powerful two-fisted grip on the wary lord's rumpled dark hair like a tiny rider ruthlessly commanding a skittish horse. Corban cut a hopeful look toward Anji. She laughed and abandoned her seat to rescue the mighty warrior from her toddler-son. "My lord, bless you for risking your life over this little tyrant. Jakin, let go." Anji pried her son's fingers from Lord Corban's hair.

Freed, Corban exhaled his relief, then eyed Matteo. "Sire, when do we go to battle?"

Matteo grinned. "You'd rather go to war than tend babies, my lord?"

"We're into our second year of confinement," Corban reminded him, neatly sidestepping all discussion of babies. "Eshda's a comfortable and restful place, but we've been here long enough. It's time for Darzeq to settle matters and support its royal family."

Ekiael nodded. "Agreed." He motioned to his current heap of sealed notes, prepared for his contacts throughout Darzeq. "I'm sending word to the priests and their men to gather in Port Bascin. As soon as we've liberated Arimna, we'll purify the Holy House and plan the coronation."

Corban stretched his long hands over the brazier and taunted Ekiael cordially, "I'm eager to see your army, my lord-priest. Are they well-trained?"

"Yes, and they'll be praying every step as they march toward Arimna." Ekiael grinned, not the least offended. "For love of the Infinite, His Holy House, and all their loved ones in Darzeq, they'll fight with the best of the king's warriors. A man who knows only self-love won't fight for others, whereas a man who loves his family, his country, and the Infinite, will risk his life to protect all."

Ekiael's words settled in Anji's soul, heavy and troubling as storm-darkened waves against a gloomy shore. Ekiael might die leading the priests into battle, and indeed he would fight for his beloved Infinite. *One-Who-Sees, guard him, I beg You!*

She glanced over at his current note to one of the southern priestly clans, mentally translating the ancient priestly language: *Fight for the Word of the Infinite—yet let Him bring the victory if we are worthy. Spread the news among those who love Him: set your households in order....*

In other words, prepare for death.

Oblivious to her fears, Ekiael continued, "If Cthar gains the victory, we are all dead. Therefore, we'll use every weapon in our arsenal and then battle with all our might. Trust me, my lord, the priests are as eager to finish this conflict as any in the realm."

"Rest." Matteo bent over Dalia, his weapons clattering faintly against his belt as he tucked the covers more securely around her shoulders while she nestled in their huge bed. The last bout of nausea had left her trembling. According to Yiska, Dalia had one month left before the worst of her morning sickness would be gone. She looked so fragile, staring up at him, her hand so thin as she pulled it from beneath the covers to touch his face.

"My lord-king, my sweet husband, protect yourself and don't worry about me. You know I'll stay here and guard our family until the battle's won."

He kissed the palm of her hand, then covered it beneath another fold of the uppermost quilt. "I know you will. I trust Aristo and Yiska to help you. I've written to your parents. Your lord-father intends to join me in Port Bascin. We'll capture the palace there and use it as our headquarters."

It would be strange and difficult to occupy the royal residence where his lord father had last been seen alive. Pushing aside the thought, he concentrated on Dalia, willing her to thrive in his absence. *Infinite, our Creator, let her be safely delivered of another healthy child. Let us survive this new year, restored to Arimna Palace, with Dalia as queen.*

She would captivate Darzeq as surely as she'd charmed him. Matteo caressed his wife's flowing, richly curled hair, cherishing its softness. "I love you! Thank you for this past year—for our son! You've given me hope, and reason to fight and survive."

Unable to continue, he kissed her with absolute tenderness, and then fled.

To catch one last glimpse of his son.

He'd never expected to love anyone else as much as he loved Dalia, but Benamir claimed Matteo's heart—love causing Ben's shocking yellow-gold eyes to seem brilliant and perfect rather than a curse inherited from the she-scaln of Kaphtor.

Moving quietly to prevent a clatter of weaponry and plate armor, Matteo closed the magnificent bedchamber door, crept down the hall, and then into the spiral stairwell. He descended seven steps and stopped at a nondescript landing beside a plain-seeming door, whitewashed to blend with the stairwell's stone walls. To any uninformed person, this seemed a mere service door, perhaps concealing cleaning gear. Not the sort of door that should lead to a prince's chamber.

The first door opened to a second, which unlatched silently and glided open on its well-oiled hinges, revealing a small, warm chamber lit by a dim hearth and one lamp set safely within a wall niche. In the snug chamber's center, Benamir dozed peacefully within his carved cradle. But Yiska, asleep in the small cot beside him, instantly woke, turned and looked up as Matteo stepped into the chamber. Her initial glare made him grin—the woman seemed ready to attack anyone or anything that entered the chamber. A perfect attendant for his son.

Careful to avoid blocking the firelight or its warmth, Matteo knelt and gazed down at his sleeping son and prayed. *Mighty One, thank You for blessing me with Benamir! You-Who-Sees, Mighty One, guard him! Shield him from the savagery of his elders.*

Yiska rested one protective hand on the edge of Benamir's cradle, reminding Matteo that he'd startled her from sleep. He nodded his silent thanks, gave his small son the lightest possible kiss on his soft sleep-stilled face, and then retreated from the royal living quarters, nodding at troops of guards before joining Ekiael, Corban, and their men.

Amid the calm, protective hush of pre-dawn Eshda, they rode out to bring war against Arimna.

Followed by the king's men and Qamrin's forces, Corban rode after Matteo, Ekiael, and Lord Losbreq, their weapons clattering as they departed Qamrin's massive, sheltering walls. After two nights of solid rest within Lord Losbreq's domain, Corban fully appreciated the chary lord's self-isolating protectiveness. His wives, children, and unofficial wives—beautiful slaves—all seemed loyal and devoted to him, though impatient for victory. Qamrin's protective war-time defenses were useful against any possible attacks, but evidently paled in comparison to his other sprawling, less-protected mansions. As for Losbreq's children, ten sons and five daughters.... No wonder Cthar had attempted to lure him to her side with promises of gifts for his children.

Losbreq's love for his handsome tribe was equaled only by his ambitious plans for their futures. And Matteo and Ekiael had both pledged positions and tributes to Qamrin's heirs, which would be taken from Cthar's private estates and her personal treasury following victory.

Clearly, Losbreq trusted Matteo as king far more than he trusted Cthar's rule.

Qamrin's walls and rich riverside fields gradually gave way to wild lands, which adjoined rich forests, perfect for hunting.

For hiding.

Corban eyed the trees ahead, his senses sharpening uncomfortably. Beneath his breath, he demanded, "One-Who-Sees, why am I worried? What's ahead?"

Sight descended upon him in a down-rush. Shadows flickered within those distant trees, and scent washed over Corban—heavy, oily odors of unwashed bodies and mortal sweat. Corban shifted his crossbow higher on his shoulder, prepared to use it. "Sire! My lords—!"

He heard the arrows, then saw them slicing air amid the trees. Corban flung himself off Ghost and then reached up to drag Matteo and Ekiael to the ground beside him, both yelling as if he were an enemy instead of their defender. Before they could right themselves and stand, Corban leveled his crossbow and aimed around the horses, shooting one bolt, then another into the shadows.

Losbreq's arrow-hit horse squealed its terror, and Qamrin's lord dove for the nearby winter-dried bracken. Shielding himself behind a tree, Corban slapped bolt after bolt into his crossbow, sending each to a shadow-target in the trees beyond. The shadows fell like pellets in a hailstorm, heavy and fading and melting into the soil amid their final resting places.

Behind Corban, the king's men and Losbreq's forces took up their weapons and entered the fight. Just as Matteo joined Corban, crossbow leveled, a host of shadows broke free of the trees, rushing toward Corban. Two he took down with bolts, then used his crossbow as a club and a spear, alternating strikes against his foes.

To Corban's right, Matteo yelled, "Attack! Spare no one!"

Above them, more arrows sang through the air, and men roared battle cries.

Corban splintered his boltless crossbow against jaw after skull after jaw until his enemies became a heap, a wall to defend Matteo. When the crossbow fell to pieces, Corban snatched an enemy sword and slashed toward his foes, cutting down two, then four in wide-arced strokes toward their throats. The remainder fled, until they were taken down by arrows in their backs, shot by Losbreq's men.

As the shadows receded, Corban exhaled, then eased his shoulders. Matteo shifted behind him, bloodied, standing over a single body—his single challenge. Matteo eyed Corban warily. "Are you finished? Thank you, my lord, but I feared you'd throw me like a javelin!" He grinned then, and quipped, "You don't leave much for the rest of us."

"I'd prefer to." The immortal-seeming sight left Corban within a breath, and he sat in the bracken, his limbs quivering. Corban tightened his arms around his knees and bowed his head, fighting the dead-weight fatigue. He drew in a feeble breath and muttered to the king, "Yet the victory's not mine. If I'd tried on my own strength, I'd have been dead by the first arrow-strike."

Losbreq approached him and half-kneeled, staring. "Thank you, my lord. If you hadn't called out that warning, I'd be dead. Where would my family be then? I owe you my life."

Corban acknowledged him with a nod, then rested his face on his folded arms, praying. *Infinite, I confess that without Your sight I am nothing. I am a dim weakling fool.*

The others faded to shadows as they celebrated around him, claiming a victory the Infinite alone had granted. Too weak to correct them, Corban endured until Ghost finally breathed on him, and then nudged Corban to stand—to rejoin the mortals.

Matteo, riding just ahead of Corban, lifted a hand and halted the procession near the evening-darkened crest of a hillside pass. As Ghost grazed, Corban surveyed the broad river valley before them.

Port Bascin's royal stronghold sprawled over the highest hillside opposite the mighty river, its lower walls stark-white, its towers crowned with gray slate that gleamed purple-hued in the dusk. Corban studied the fortress, approving its vantage-point over the river. A magnificent place with equally splendid woods rimming the small city at the foot of the fortress. Below this fine vista, twelve ships moored at extraordinarily crafted stone docks, manned by numerous workers who appeared minute from this distance. A relaxing scene and a fine city. No wonder this had been King Jonatan's favorite retreat from Arimna.

Could this fortress be taken?

Matteo turned to him. "We want a bloodless victory here, if possible. My lord-father loved this place and I don't want to harm its citizens." He nodded southward along the river. "There's our first approach, and Port Bascin doesn't even notice it yet."

Corban followed the king's gaze along the river to a tranquil-seeming punctuation of ships tucked here and there near the shores, none seeming related to the others. Matteo continued, "More will gather overnight and close the port. Our targets are ten of those ships—the ones with the golden flags. They're floating treasure-houses of Kaphtor. We must capture them all." Drawling now, with a mild-humored menace that caught Corban's interest, Matteo asked, "Lord Corban, how do you feel about a secretive mission aboard a tiny, vulnerable watercraft?"

With the promise of treasure that might ultimately pay his way to Belaal and Araine?

Corban smiled. "Sire, I was raised along rivers near the ocean. Command me, and I'll fight."

Chapter 22

A tap at the door drew Anji's attention away from her delightfully chubby Jakin and little Benamir, who were playing, bellies down on the carpet, both laughing as Jakin built small unsteady towers of his wooden toys, and then tumbled them to clattering disorder. Anji smiled toward the door. "Yes? Enter!"

Jakin chirped, "Yes!" Lord Aristo marched into the chamber, and Jakin clambered to his feet, and charged Eshda's noble caretaker, his eldest comrade in play.

Aristo caught the toddler and laughed as he set Jakin on the carpet. "Here's proof that Eshda's food is sufficient! Little lord, you're heavy as if you're made of iron!"

"See," Jakin urged, pointing to his heap of toys. He tugged Aristo toward the blocks. "See?"

"You say you want me to build you a tower?" Aristo beamed. "With your lady-mother's permission."

"Of course." Anji nodded to Aristo.

Eshda's lord-governor sat down, captured the crawling, ever-busy Benamir in one arm, and then—out of Benamir's reach—he stacked four ships upon eight blocks, then crossed them with miniature beams. Finished with the base, he offered two blocks to Jakin. "Cap the tower, my Lord Jakin. Steady, now."

Jakin studied the blocks, his solemnity such a reflection of his father's that Anji blinked against sudden tears. While the little boy set the first block totteringly on the tower, Aristo murmured to Anji, "Lady, all's barred and closed for the night—I've checked each entry, and called upon you to wish you good rest. The queen's complexion seemed less gray today.

Yiska and I've hope our remedies are finally taking effect and she'll soon regain her health."

"I'm praying so, for the sake of the baby. Is she asleep? I was about to carry the boys upstairs to share prayers and say good night."

"Lady, the queen is awake and will surely welcome a visit."

Jakin placed the second block atop the tower and the tiny edifice toppled with a muted clatter over the carpet. Benamir laughed, Aristo chuckled as the boys both shrieked their delight. Aristo bowed to Anji and offered her Benamir. "With your permission, Lady Rhiysa, I'll carry Lord Jakin."

"Permission granted." Anji bent and kissed her son's dark, curled hair. "He is heavy."

Anji took the squirming Benamir into her arms—his golden eyes reminding her of Matteo. Of Sheth and King Jonatan. She refused to admit Cthar's name to the list. Benamir was nothing like *her*. Anji kissed Benamir's softly rounded face, then tucked him into a carrying sling. "Darzeq would love you, if only you could be seen!"

Holding Jakin, Aristo bowed Anji and Benamir through the doorway. "I continue to pray for the day when it's safe to open our gates, and the king's received in Arimna. Until then, Lady Rhiysa, as a further precaution, I've ordered Eshda's gates closed to everyone. Visitors will be welcomed only within the outer court until the war's well-ended and your lord-husband returns to take you home."

Ekiael.... Anji's heart fluttered with longing. Her husband had been gone for fewer than ten days, but it felt as if a year had passed. "Let the war end well indeed."

Anji hugged Benamir close, nuzzling his lustrous hair and crushing down her fears. *Infinite, our Mighty One, I look to You! Give my husband and my cousin all they need to conquer their enemies, and Yours!*

In the pre-dawn darkness, Corban braced himself against the lift and sway of the Tinem North's currents as his conveyance, a small fleece-padded skiff, glided silently toward one of the ten Kaphtorian vessels that floated tranquilly amid its moorings alongside one of Port Bascin's stone docks.

The instant the skiff rested gently against the ship's stern, Corban hefted a jug to his shoulder and stood—a motion replicated by other loyalists in a fleet of small boats converging on the now-quiet port.

Cautious, controlling his movements, Corban raised the jug and dribbled the oil along the ship's massive tight-wound rope girdings that bound and reinforced the ship's timbers. The ropes subtly eased, soaked but not dripping. Good. Lord Kemuel had provided the oil, yet supplies were limited, and they couldn't afford to waste a drop.

Corban sat down again, and the skiff's commander motioned his men toward the opposite end of the ship. Exhaling, Corban repeated the anointing at the base of the ship's high, curved wooden prow. Kaphtor's elaborate carvings certainly lent themselves well to holding the fuel....

A creak from beyond the vessel's timbered sidings froze Corban in place. The men with him, who steadied the skiff, huddled down beneath their dark cloaks, undoubtedly not daring to breathe. Aboard the ship someone coughed. Corban waited, gritting his teeth as he lowered the jug to his shoulder again. The cough wasn't repeated. Instead, a bubbling, muted snore took its place. Clearly, the men aboard these ships felt safe in Port Bascin.

Dawn would tell the truth.

Corban eased himself down into the skiff once more, tapped the crew's leader and motioned them away in silence.

As the soldiers worked the oars, and the skiff glided onward to the next ship, Corban exhaled, his breath mist within the chilling darkness.

One-Who-Sees, let this work!

As the current lifted his borrowed skiff, Matteo glanced southward along the river, studying the blockade yet again. Ferocious joy melded with relief as he surveyed the armada's full strength—rows of ships forming a bristling, heavily fortified wall from one side of the river to the other.

Did Cthar realize that she'd amassed so many enemies? Her ploys and stratagems had won her more time than Matteo would have liked, but surely this dawn marked the beginning of her end.

Or his.

No. For Darzeq, Dalia, and Benamir, he must survive. Hadn't the Infinite pledged to maintain his father's line forever? For the sake of His own name, He'd vowed to extend grace to Darzeq and all the known world beyond. Surely, as Ekiael proclaimed, the Infinite's promises were eternal—as everlasting as His Name.

Yet these reassurances didn't mean that Matteo of Arimna would survive this conflict.

Seated behind Matteo, Ekiael breathed, "Let this clash be His! Who is like Him? There is no one here, nor in the heavenly realms, who can claim His place! His glory is forever."

A line of skiffs glided up to Matteo's, and he grinned at the waterborne procession's leaders, Lords Kemuel, Corban, and Losbreq.

Lord Kemuel offered Matteo a toothy grin and a bow from his seat—so stalwart that he nearly knocked his head on the skiff's low wooden rail. "Sire! I beg the honor of calling your challenge to the Kaphtorians in Port Bascin. Don't I have the loudest voice among all your lords? Grant me this favor!"

Matteo laughed. "Granted, my lord! With all my thanks for everything you've done. When I am crowned, you will stand near me with Lord Losbreq and Lord Corban. I pledge this."

With Dalia, Anji, Ekiael, and Lord Aristo—all who'd supported him during his exile from Arimna.

Beneath his breath, Matteo prayed as the line of skiffs turned and slipped over the river's gently rippled surface. "Mighty One, guard us! Let our plans succeed. Let our enemies be quelled as You protect my allies."

Would it be greedy to pray that this conflict might bring him more allies? Matteo nodded to his boatmen and they turned his skiff, cutting across the current to follow the others—for the lords had forbidden him to risk his life, and Matteo didn't relish the genuine risk of being dragged ingloriously from a skirmish by his overzealous lords.

Matteo gazed ahead at the skiffs and prayed, planning his tactics.

Corban drew in a sharp, bracing gust of air and muted a smile as his skiff glided forward in the dawn-hued waters. One skiff among perhaps seventy, all lit with torches and lamps and bristling with archers who'd volunteered for this attack. Behind the line of skiffs, a secondary force of larger ships waited, their crews undoubtedly anticipating the clash ahead.

Mornings rarely promised wonders, but this dawn the very air about Corban pledged a change. Port Bascin gleamed before him, all its outlines crisp, and struck with a sparkling frost that glinted along each stone building's carved edges.

Ahead of Corban, Lord Kemuel stood in his torch-and-lamp-lit skiff as a giant from an old legend, and he bellowed across River Tinem's waters, "Awake, you slime-gummed rotting whelks of Kaphtor! Come out and face us! Your puny sea snail's hearts are about to fail you all!"

Here and there, foreign seafarers poked their heads above the ten Kaphtorian ships' carved rails, all of them bleary and sleep-fogged. His movements grandiose, clearly confident, Kemuel motioned toward Corban and the others in their adjacent skiffs and roared, "Archers, set and fix your marks!"

Corban lifted his bow, its arrow-tip's hollow cage packed with oiled waddings, tow, sulfur and charcoal, all glazed with stabilizing incendiaries. He rested its caged metal point over the nearest torch and gloated as it caught fire. All the men with him followed suit, several aiming gleeful taunts at the sailors from Kaphtor.

"C'mon you sniveling chaplet-worms! Run, all of you! Rot-tripes! Jump!"

Aloud, Corban prayed, "Infinite, send these arrows down fast to the oil, and let them fuel terror into those Kaphtorian hearts."

For the first time in his life, Corban rued his lackluster marksmanship with arrows. If only two of his ten hit an oiled girding and set it aflame, he'd be pleased and count it good. As one, he and the men in his skiff aimed at the central ship—the agreed target for all the skiffs. Corban held his breath against the harsh fumes and waited, his gaze fixed on the ship.

Kemuel bawled, "Fire!"

Arcs of blazing arrows lifted in hissing, flaring flights from all the skiffs—an extraordinary firestorm. Corban tensed, his gaze fixed on his arrow's glowing flight. A perfect arc. Impossible. It landed solidly against the oiled rope girdings bracing the low-slung ship. Another impossibility. A puff of smoke wafted from amid the girdings, followed by flames that sped over the oiled ropes like one of Eshda's appalling fire-spills pouring from its wounded soil. Screams lifted from the

Kaphtorian ships, answered by whoops and shouts from Kemuel's forces. Corban laughed with the others, and howled as Kaphtor's sailors, one after another, jumped from the besieged ship, splashing heavily into the icy current.

Corban drew another incendiary arrow, aligned its nock to the bowstring, then lowered it to the torch affixed at the skiff's prow.

Of the dozens launched, only six arrows puffed out amid plumed arcs of gray smoke.

As the trade ship's mast took flame, Lord Kemuel bellowed, "Surrender, Kaphtor! Abandon your ships, all of you!"

Some of the sailors fled, but others stared and shook their heads, while several sent arrows toward Kemuel. The doughty lord ignored the arrows, though one pierced the water before him. He lifted one hand and called out, "Next target! Set... Fire!"

A second firestorm fell over the next agreed-upon Kaphtorian trade ship. Howls and screams lifted in the storm's wake, and as if by some unseen signal—a singular sweep of panic—Kaphtor's sailors abandoned their ships, diving into the river or charging toward the pier.

Kemuel called to the waiting secondary string of small ships, "Advance! Take them all! For Matteo of Arimna and the House of Jonatan!"

His sword flashing in the morning sunlight, Matteo stepped out of his skiff and ascended stone steps onto the stone pier to join Kemuel and Corban's forces on the walkway above. Battle trumpets reverberated from the fortress above as a battalion descended to protect the river port. Kemuel and Corban bowed, and Kemuel greeted Matteo with a cackle of glee.

"Now, Sire, let's see what they're made of—these pampered Port Bascin darlings!"

Matteo snorted. True, Port Bascin was quiet for a river town—to the point of sluggishness sometimes. Yet he'd loved this place ... loved it still. He cut a mock-angry look at Kemuel. "Hold your insults, my lord! Remember, I spent much of my childhood here."

"You couldn't help that misfortune, Matteo of Arimna and Darzeq. Nor could your noble father, yet there's time to remedy Port Bascin's feebleness."

Ekiael laughed. "Agreed! Sire, confess; Port Bascin's nothing to Port Zamaj, Qamrin, or Lohe Bay. I pray the city finds courage today—in our favor." He lifted his sword and bellowed to the city ahead, "Awake, Bascin! Awake, and greet your king!"

His battle cry sent a chill over Matteo's scalp and back. Would they spill blood here this day? He surveyed the massive stone walkway where he and his brothers had played and fished as children. Where he'd pretended imaginary battles, never dreaming he'd actually lead an invasion on this beautiful river town.

Victorious, thus far.

Not one sailor or commander from Kaphtor had risked remaining with the captured ships. The few who had resisted floated, arrow-spiked, in Port Bascin's frigid harbor—fallen of wounds he'd not wish to inflict upon anyone else in Port Bascin. Beneath his breath, Matteo pleaded with the Mighty One: "Give me swift conquest! You-Who-Sees, grant me this prayer. Spare us a bloodbath. Bring us favor."

Flanked by Ekiael, Kemuel, Losbreq, and Corban, and backed by two-thirds of all the men from the ships and skiffs, Matteo strode along the cold, oil and fish-scented pier. A clangor of swords and shields reached him from the pier's entrance. Matteo braced himself. Would he and his supporters die now?

A troop of soldiers stormed into his path, blocking off the pier like a wall, their shields and emblems of office shining in the morning light.

At their head, Port Bascin's constable, Jorim Goldensleeve, brandished his sword and a pike, a grayed warrior, whose gaze was as sharp as ever. Jorim, who'd trained the Dreaded Seven, from Tarquin down to Matteo.

Goldensleeve looked Matteo in the eyes, and recoiled visibly, as if faced by a slavering scaln. If Goldensleeve wished to kill Darzeq's uncrowned king and claim the glory before Cthar, he need only hurl that pike.

Courage.

Matteo lifted his chin. "Goldensleeve. I'm here to claim Port Bascin, and to avenge the House of Jonatan. What will you do?"

Chapter 23

Goldensleeve stared at Matteo, as if gazing at a dead man returned to life. "My lord ... Sire!" For an instant, the corners of Goldensleeve's mouth weakened. But then his expression hardened. He knelt, placed his weapons on the ground and removed his helmet. As the men around him also knelt, some appearing baffled, others struggling to suppress grins. Goldensleeve yelled, "We're defeated! Overwhelmed! Sir, have pity and spare us—we surrender! Port Bascin is yours to command, only spare our lives!"

Was this a self-protective strategy? Was Matteo and his army safe? Perhaps. But it wouldn't hurt matters to offer incentives for loyalty. Matteo called out, "Commander, take the three unburned ships nearest the pier to share with Port Bascin, as restitution for the harm I have inflicted. Cease your rebellion, surrender, and I'll spare you all!"

A gleam lit Goldensleeve's eyes and brightened his face. "Sire! I've prayed for this morning! May the Infinite bless your way to Arimna!"

By the jubilant looks traded among Goldensleeve's men, Matteo knew he'd won them—or at least he'd bought their loyalty.

Had he ever lost their loyalty to begin with?

Perhaps not. But it would be best to reward his allies and earn their gratitude for the future.

He motioned to Goldensleeve. The man was a wellspring of gossip, rumored to pay for clandestine news among the royals and other nobles of Darzeq. Goldensleeve approached and knelt, bowing his silvered head over Matteo's hand. Matteo whispered, "Clear the streets as soon as you've secured your three ships. Please oversee dividing the spoils with your men and the city. Let everything be done openly. Now, I must take the fortress. Who commands the fortress?"

Goldensleeve moistened his thin lips. "Lord Karvos. In theory. He's in Arimna this week as a guest of the palace. I've heard he's loath to interfere with his own comfort and therefore bows to the queen-mother."

"So I've heard." Matteo muted his fury. A death order would certainly interfere with Karvos Stradin's comfort, once Arimna was conquered.

Clearly encouraged by Matteo's outward calm, Goldensleeve straightened and looked him in the eyes. "Please excuse my boldness, Sire, but I advise you to send orders to the garrison above to surrender. Most are loyal to you, but enough of the commanders belong to Karvos that there will be resistance. Test them."

Wariness tinged Goldensleeve's advice, and understandably so. Cthar would have the commander's head for his actions today. Best to leave him out of the initial approach to the fortress. Matteo muttered, "If I'm granted an easy entry, I'd suspect an ambush. But if they bar the gates against me, Commander, what's the surest way to gain access to the fortress?"

Accompanied by Kemuel and Losbreq, and brandishing Darzeq's piked purple and gold pennant, Corban stood before the closed fortress gates. Near enough to be heard, but not so close that Cthar's louts could barrage him or Kemuel and Losbreq with sling-stones. "Guardians of Port Bascin, open your gates and welcome your king! Matteo of Darzeq pledges you his protection!"

A brief tumult of noise gave way to one commander's bellow—resonant enough to match Kemuel. "Matteo of Arimna is a traitor to Darzeq, and a dead man! Take your buzzing elsewhere, you insects!" The commander shifted away, calling, "Archers! Mark your targets! Ready...."

"Mighty One," Corban breathed, "save us!"

Fury-driven, Corban turned the pennant's pike, aimed, and sent the makeshift spear hissing upward at the commander, skewering him before he finished the lethal command. Several archers peered over the crenels, openmouthed. But one had the gall to finish his dead commander's order. "Aim and shoot!"

Corban snagged Kemuel and Losbreq by their scruffs and rushed them downslope as arrows thudded at their heels. He dropped both lords and himself before Matteo and Ekiael and shook his head, catching his breath.

Kemuel sat up, growling as he rubbed his neck and scalp, but Losbreq yelled to the skies, "That was payback for my misguided defense of Qamrin, wasn't it?"

Corban snorted. "Your earlier offense never crossed my thoughts, but if you complain, I'll chase you within arrow range again!"

Qamrin's lord brought his icy gaze down to meet Corban's. "I wasn't complaining at you, I was complaining to the Infinite, and obviously He's more merciful than you, Lord Corban of Siphra."

The man sounded completely Thaenfall. Corban returned Losbreq's glare, then addressed the not-quite-smirking Matteo. "What's our next plan?"

Corban stomped his makeshift cleats solidly onto the inclined stone slope, huddled in the moonlit darkness against the fortress's southern foundations and held his sword readied, though he'd rather hold his nose as Goldensleeve's men pried off the tunnel's protective grating. The iron bolts crumbled, falling away in a rain of rust. If the upper grates were this aged, then the king's men should be able to enter the pits above the conduits, and from the pits, invade the fortress. If.

Beside Corban, Matteo shifted higher to check the conduit. Beyond him, Goldensleeve huffed, "This is the first item I'll order repaired when we claim the fortress! I'd no idea these grates were in such bad shape."

"It's to our advantage now." Corban kept his voice low, but he muted a snarl of frustration. Were these waste conduits truly the only way into the fortress above?

Warm fetid air puffed out at Corban's face like a humid moldering cloak flung from the conduit's gloom. Corban hid his inward flinch. At least Goldensleeve was in on this befouled attack. And Kemuel, Ekiael, and Losbreq were leading similar sorties against the other conduits funneling into the fortress just above. No one was spared this privy pit indignity, not even Matteo, who edged up beside him, his sword upraised.

Matteo nudged Corban—clearly eager to help him lead the begrimed charge. "Are we ready, my lord?"

No. Corban fought a scowl. A manure march had never been mentioned during initial battle plans. Yet he'd go. The first Thaenfall to enter battle through a tunnel of sludge and steaming filth. He hoped his share of the spoils was worth this—enough to take him to Belaal and Araine.

"Aw!" One of the men who'd hunkered near Corban half-retched and then dug his wooden cleats into the slope with a ferocious double-stomp. "Nah, I'm not going in there!"

Corban tugged a dark scarf over his nose and mouth, then leaned into the man's field of vision and stared coldly, steadily, predator waiting to claw apart weakling prey. The man flinched in the deepening night. He bowed and tugged his own scarf over his nose and mouth. "Lord Corban and Sire, please forgive me. I'll go. I vow I'll follow you without question."

"Be sure you do," Corban murmured. He regarded the others, maintaining the emotionless Thaenfall stare—his lord-father's most formidable expression. "I'm prepared to fight the instant we reach the upper courtyards. For Darzeq's king."

To a man, they bowed their heads, covered their mouths and noses, and checked their swords.

Onward. As Corban drew a deep breath of chilled untainted air and then released it, preparing to enter the foul conduit, Matteo spoke through his own gray scarf, "In a few years, we'll laugh together as we remember this night."

"Sire, I pray we do." But first they must survive this conduit.

Corban lifted his sword and ducked into the tunnel, steadying himself with one hand against the curved stones above, and praying as he stomped, nearly blind, through the oozing stench of fermenting waste.

His eyes burning and watering amid the tunnel's fumes, Matteo blinked back moisture as he followed Corban's shadowed form into the dim waste duct. Matteo skidded in the ooze, then ground his boots' metal cleats—pieced together with wires from an old chainmail vest—into the sludge and set a stomping pace. Filth spattered heavily upward over his leggings, chunks of waste pitched from Corban's cleat-nailed boots as the Siphran lord tramped ahead. Matteo winced at the thought of inadvertently bespattering Goldensleeve with waste, but the commander remained protectively close behind him, despite the sludge.

How his brothers would laugh at him now. Even as they cheered him on through this filth. Even as they urged him to learn the truth behind their lord-father's death.

Avenge them, Infinite! Bring all truth to light.

Ahead of him, Corban paused and shifted in the tunnel. Feeble hints of light slipped reassuringly around his tall form. They'd reached the tunnel's end. Corban shoved against the upper grate and hissed to Matteo, "Sire, are you ready?"

"Yes. Goldensleeve and I will lead." How many times had he visited the privy pits above as a boy? Never in his privileged existence had he dreamed he'd be trekking into the fortress from these privies, a renegade in his own realm.

Corban glanced back at him, his eyes gleaming visibly above his black scarf. "We'll kill the rebels with our stench." For an instant, he closed his eyes. Then he grabbed the filth-encrusted grate and shoved it mightily.

The grate broke away as if made of a child's twigs. Corban bolted upward into the pit above and then reached back to haul Matteo from the conduit. "It's clean."

Behind Matteo, Goldensleeve groused, "I said it would be!"

"And I bless you for it, Commander." Matteo grabbed Corban's wrist. Corban hauled him up within a breath and then reached for Goldensleeve. Matteo helped the commander through—a weakling effort compared to Corban's—and then steadied himself amid the dank straw on the giant privy pit's stone floor. While Corban and Goldensleeve hoisted the other men from the conduit, Matteo caught his breath, lowered the scarf from his face, pried the cleats from his boots with his dagger, then looked around. The reservoir pit had indeed been cleared—with only small piles of excrement and straw at punctuated intervals beneath the wooden privy seats set in the stones above.

Incongruously comforting ... the light streaming from the unoccupied privy holes above. Were Port Bascin's guardsmen all at evening meal? Most likely.

The other men were scrambling clear of the conduit below, wrenching off their protective scarves and doffing their cleats, clearly glad to escape the dark conduit. Unordered, they hurried to the wooden seats above—though several men grumbled as they tromped through fresh waste piles to reach up and shove aside the wooden seats. Corban vaulted himself up through one of the broken seats, then clambered into the privy chamber above. Through the opening, Matteo saw him glance around, and then nod, evidently satisfied. He reached down and hauled up Goldensleeve, followed by several guardsmen, lifting them by their arms or vests as if they weighed nothing.

Striving to avoid the manure pile, Matteo waited his turn, then lunged for the opening above. Corban snagged his boiled leather vest, hoisted him through and set him down—so quickly that Matteo's senses spun. "Sire, if we hurry, we'll reach the others soon enough."

Goldensleeve snapped, "Outside and to the left."

Matteo gulped at the clear air and nodded, remembering the fortress's layout. They were at the southern wall. If they hurried to the western wall's privy for Lord Losbreq and his men first, they wouldn't pass the heavily guarded gatehouse to the east. From the western privy, they could charge to the northern one, meet up with Ekiael, then rejoin Kemuel's men at the eastern pit. By then, surely the fortress would be alarmed and prepared to fight.

Sword readied, Corban rushed through the privy chamber's open doorway. Matteo scrambled to keep up with him. Beside Matteo, Goldensleeve panted, "I fully understand why you asked him to lead us—the man's a single-souled army!"

Matteo gasped agreement, "Yes. An Infinite-spurred army I can never fully repay." He followed Corban, slipping through the shadows at the wall's base until they reached the western privy. Inside, Losbreq's dung-smirched men were binding up a prisoner, a bug-eyed young guard, who cringed away from their stench as much as their muted threats. Losbreq wrenched off his scarf and glowered at Matteo. "For this, Sire, you'd best be

Darzeq's greatest king! I'd never tramp manure for a lesser one."

Matteo fought dark amusement. "Let's pray that your share of those merchants' ships will calm your annoyance."

Corban smirked as Losbreq pried off his cleats with a short sword. "Do you need help, my lord?"

Losbreq raised a defensive hand. "No! *You*. Stay. There!"

By the time they reached the northern wall's privy, watchmen were brandishing ram's horns and bellowing battle cries. Ekiael was outside the privy, wheezing, "I'll never be clean again! Never..."

An approaching cadence of soldiers' boots drew Matteo's gaze to the western wall—just as a battalion rounded the corner tower. Matteo yelled, "Form ranks and run for the east!"

Kemuel ... they had to rejoin with Lord Kemuel.

They met up with his men, who'd vanquished six guards. Matteo heard Kemuel roar above the din, "You rot-tripes! Where are the king's men? Join us!"

Matteo turned and took up his cry, yelling toward the approaching battalion. "Join us! For Darzeq and Matteo of Arimna! Who stands true for the king?"

Corban and Ekiael echoed him, and the battalion splintered as it approached. More than half the soldiers slowed their attack and then turned on the remnant who'd dared to charge Matteo.

Caught between Matteo's forces, and the garrison's loyalists, Cthar's outnumbered defenders fought, then fell. Matteo parried one man's attack, and then cut him down. No others reached him—walled off by Corban's raging attacks, and Kemuel, Goldensleeve, Losbreq and Ekiael.

When the clash faded to scufflings and the cries of the wounded, Matteo called to Corban, Ekiael, and Goldensleeve, "Where's the fort's commander? Take the keep!"

Instantly the conflict shifted to the magnificent tower as loyalists within battled to unbolt the keep's massive doors. Corban flung himself into the fray, followed by Goldensleeve. The doors groaned open, and men spilled out, several fleeing as others screamed, "House of Jonatan!"

Matteo edged around the uproar and sped after Corban and Goldensleeve, into one of the tower's spiraling stairwells.

Did the current commander have the effrontery to actually live in the royal quarters? Evidently not. Goldensleeve veered out of the stairwell just before reaching the uppermost level, and charged instead toward the keep's administrative chambers.

Corban and Goldensleeve bashed at the lock with a decorative stone urn until the urn and the door broke. Together, they rushed inside, just as a gold-cloaked man released a courier bird from the far window.

A message warning Cthar in Arimna?

The gold-cloaked man dropped to his knees and lifted his hands in surrender. As Corban and Goldensleeve bound the man, Matteo rushed past him to the window. The courier bird had, of course, vanished within the darkness.

Dread welled as Matteo's thoughts sped toward Arimna more swiftly than the bird's flight.

He could see Cthar's proud, beautiful face tensing, her long gold-shielded fingernails clicking relentlessly against the nearest marble tabletop. The way she glared up at Arimna Palace's vaulted gold and amethyst roof while plotting her own devices to bring about her wishes, whether they be prudent or not.

Whatever her reaction, he must be prepared. He must make plans to wrest Arimna from her grasp and to declaw her permanently. Until then—

Matteo turned to Corban and Goldensleeve. "Thank you! We'll secure the fortress and offload those ships, divide the spoils, then use the ships to sail against Arimna.

Meanwhile, as they prepared to attack Arimna, he would question Port Bascin's garrison and servants to learn the truth behind his lord-father's death.

Had Cthar killed her own son to grab Darzeq's throne?

Queen Cthar's elegant handwriting dominated the parchment, commanding the lead warrior as surely as her proud voice. *She is your goal. Do not fail. Not if you and your men wish your families to survive.*

Chapter 24

Anji smiled and rested her writing stylus over the crystal ink vial as Dalia crept into the chamber. Brightened by her afternoon walk, her eyes shining, her complexion radiant, Dalia glanced at the boys, who were sleeping on Anji's bed. A contented smile softened her face as she tweaked the boys' coverlets. Obviously satisfied that the children were content, Dalia skittered toward Anji and settled into her cushioned X-framed chair. She slid a piece of parchment from her writing box and murmured, "Our babies are perfect!"

"Of course they are." Anji bit down a chuckle and dabbed the stylus into the vial. She'd finish this letter to Ekiael in Port Bascin, and then nurse Jakin—surely he'd wake soon. Yiska had tucked both boys in for a nap after midday meal and then requested the afternoon off. A lovely request, for Anji never tired of tending her son and Benamir. Here was a blessing: Being confined to Eshda, away from the royal court, she could see her son as often as she pleased, without waiting upon ceremonial delays. Softly, she asked, "What news did the messenger bring from your lord-father?"

Dalia's eyes sparkled as she lifted the gilded lid off her vial of ink. "Father's gathering troops from the north and preparing Tragobre's boats and ships. Now that Port Bascin's secured and home's no longer threatened, he and Lord Losbreq will meet in two weeks to organize a another blockade north of Arimna to cinch in Cthar. Oh, and my lady-mother sends her love. Here..." She leaned against Anji, hugged her fiercely, and kissed her cheek. "From Mother."

A pang of longing shot through Anji, almost tangible enough that it hurt. It wasn't just that she missed Lady Tragobre's gentle presence. She missed everyone. Her beloved, ever-warm Ekiael's embrace, King Jonatan's doting smile, the Dreaded Seven's endless teasing, darling Valsignae's sweet attentiveness, and even her own lady-mother, who'd often kissed her as fondly before a fever stole her away, not to mention her royal father, whose thin face and frail form was a barely recalled blur from her earliest years. His was the first royal funeral she remembered. King Jonatan had wept for his fragile younger brother...

Anji sighed to Dalia, "How blessed you are to still have your parents!"

Dalia's joy misted, becoming tender sympathy. "My parents would love to borrow you and Jakin. They'd ever-wanted a keep full of children. Instead, they ended up with only me."

"I daresay you're enough," Anji whispered. "However, you'll take Benamir to visit Tragobre as soon as Matteo's established in Arimna."

"You'll come with me," Dalia insisted. She touched her writing stylus in the ink and began to write her letter, sighing as she scratched the stylus over the parchment. "Until then, we'll write. Sometimes I feel that half the kingdom's held together by parchment and ink—we've written so many letters. Victory's certain before summer. Father and Matteo are convinced of it. The Forum lords are fed-to-the-gills sick of Cthar's games."

Might they really leave Eshda by summer? Anji's melancholy vanished at the thought. Eshda had become homelike indeed, and Lord Aristo was as doting as a kindly and watchful grandfather. Yet they'd been confined here for so long that she'd become impatient to ride south.

A soft tap at the door disrupted Anji's thoughts. She motioned Dalia to stay seated and she crossed the chamber.

Lord Aristo bowed as soon as she opened the door. He smiled, but his eyes remained solemn. "Lady, three priests have journeyed here from the south to speak with your lord-husband. They're grieved to learn that they've missed him—their journey was so prolonged. One of them is ill with cramps and vomiting. I've allowed them only into the gatehouse. If you wish to speak with them, let me know."

"If one of them's ill, then I can't risk speaking to them, my lord. What if I bring the contagion into the keep and the boys are stricken?" Anji shook her head. "Tell them that I pray the illness is brief and the recovery swift. They can rest in the gatehouse until they've recovered enough to travel south. How did they miss my lord-husband's messages to the southern priests to meet him in Port Zamaj?"

"How indeed?" Aristo fretted his grizzled eyebrows. "Perhaps they set out for Eshda before his instructions arrived for the priests in the south. I'll order that they be tended to, Lady. Rest at ease."

"Thank you, Aristo." Anji smiled, allowing the genial lord to see her fondness for him. He sighed, bowed again, and then turned toward the stairwell. Anji closed the door gently, just as small complaining noises sounded from the bed.

Benamir squirmed and then floundered amid the furred coverlets, waking Jakin, who sat up, ruddy, rumpled, and bewildered. Hopefully not wet. Anji laughed at Jakin's expression—one dark lifted eyebrow and his wry mouth puckered, so like his father's.

Well, he looked quizzical enough for a future prophet. Now, however, he was simply her sweet, rowdy little boy. Particularly as Benamir dragged at his arm and shoulder in an effort to sit up. Jakin yelled and both boys fell over. Anji hurried to dig them out of the puffy coverlets, teasing, "Oh-my! Oh-no! Where's Jakin? Where's Ben? What did you do? Where *are* you?"

The boys laughed and burrowed deeper into the covers, hiding their faces. Dalia rushed to help Anji, cooing over their sons before asking, “What news from Lord Aristo?”

“Three travelers are resting in the gatehouse. One’s ill, so we won’t be meeting them. I’ve sent my regards. They’ll be well-cared for.”

“I’ll pray the illness is nothing,” Dalia murmured. “We can’t allow a plague inside these walls.” She lifted Benamir dotingly and then skewed her lovely face to one side—a comical, over-exaggerated grimace. “Ugh! Such a huge stink! Little man, you could slay a scaln with your stench! Phew!”

Ben laughed, his round face dimpling with hilarity, distracting Anji with his delight. She mustn’t mar their joy with her fears of contagion, brought to Eshda by wandering priests.

Amid the glittering gold and amethyst splendor of Port Bascin’s royal apartments, Matteo nodded, welcoming his brother Tarquin’s best friend. “Thaddeus, it’s good to see you.”

Clad in quilted fleece and a scuffed, boiled leather vest, Thaddeus Ormr bowed before Matteo, yet he shook his head. “Sire, I’ve tried again to bring my family to your side, but they won’t move without my lord-father’s permission. He’s forbidden me to support you openly.”

“Yet you’ve defied him again, risking your inheritance. Why?”

“Some causes are worth risking life and limb for.” Thaddeus grinned. “What good is my inheritance if Cthar kills us all first? I’ve brought my own boats. All three of them, for what they’re worth, and twenty men.”

Thaddeus had turned against his powerful lord-father, Magni Ormr. For him. No, against Cthar. "Anything and everyone's welcome to help us pry Arimna from Cthar's grasp."

Thaddeus turned bleak, unamused. "Agreed. Tarquin and the others did nothing to deserve death, however much they loathed Cthar."

A mutual loathing, now ripened to poisonous hatred. Matteo scowled. "For all her quarrels with my lord-father, I've found no signs that Cthar planned his death. It's as Ekiael said—his death freed her to do as she pleases in Darzeq. She felt she owed us nothing. Not even our lives."

"No normal grandmother would do such thing," Thaddeus said.

A thump at the door startled them both. Thaddeus stood, one hand going to his dagger as his gaze narrowed. He looked ready to attack any intruder. Matteo stood, trying not to share his friend's alarm. Kings must always be vigilant. Always be aware that their lives were in peril, even during seemingly quiet intervals. "Yes? Enter!"

Ekiael strode in, his full, flaring robes adding to his considerable presence—at odds with the way he carried and offered Matteo a sealed parchment scroll, held pinched between his thumb and forefinger as if the thing were soiled. Corban followed him, looking grimmer than usual. Ekiael said, "I was just about to leave for Port Zamaj when this arrived. From Arimna Palace. Guess who?"

Guess? Matteo scowled at the parchment's seal. The royal seal, undoubtedly set in that golden wax by his erstwhile grandmother. He longed to tear the thing to shreds, unread. Exactly the fate he wished upon Cthar. His bloodthirsty impulse made him clench his jaw. He accepted the parchment with a frustrated nod to Ekiael and the others. "What does she want? I've nothing to say but that she deserves to die for her crimes."

He slid a short dagger from its scabbard at his side, sliced apart the seal's cordage, unfurled the crisp, pale note, and scanned Cthar's elegant script.

Matteo of Eshda, my own grandson, congratulations on your recent victory.

You please me with your restraint in not gloating overmuch upon the dung heap you've conquered and the trinkets you've confiscated—I approve your regal conduct. I also perceive your plan, but I warn you that you will lose.

Arimna cannot be taken, but you can. Nevertheless, I wish to spare you.

Indeed, I wished to spare you from the first. Did I not summon you that morning to speak to you? Yet I perceived your potential defiance of my will and gave you up as lost to me. Nevertheless you've survived. Therefore, understand, Matteo, that what happened in Arimna at Gueronn's hands was vital. I was fighting for my future, yet you and your men are destroying my life as ably as ever Tarquin and Sheth had pledged to do. I cannot permit this. Am I not allowed to defend myself? Yet even now, if you bow to me and stand at my side, you will be my heir.

Who else do I have? No one?

Matteo nearly crushed the parchment in his fist. All lies, bluffery, and deplorable excuses. Furthermore, she was completely ignoring Benamir's existence. And Dalia's and Anji's and Jakin's. Did she plan to take their lives as well?

Stiff-armed, he gave the parchment to Ekiael.

Darzeq's high priest scanned the parchment and glowered as if he'd like to reach beyond it and snatch Cthar through to face them all in this chamber. The instant he glanced up, Matteo said, "I'd wager anything that this is a ruse. She's trying to open talks to buy time. Perhaps to better prepare Arimna against the coming siege."

Ekiael shook his head. "Who can say? It's Cthar, and only the One-Who-Sees can fully comprehend her soul. By your leave, Sire, I'll depart for Port Zamaj at once and gather my own forces. The priests are prepared to fight in Arimna for the Holy House."

"Thank you." Matteo landed a fist on Ekiael's shoulder. When had the high priest become like another brother to him? "My prayers are with you and your men, for your safety. When we learn of Cthar's plans, we'll send word to you at once. I need spies. I need information from Arimna."

"I'll go," Corban offered.

"No." Matteo shook his head. "You're a plague to Cthar since Lord Karvos betrayed our scheme to steal her from Arimna. You've a price on your life."

The Siphran lord grimaced, unmoved. "Yes, save for Istgard, I'm a sought man in every land I've entered. However, the queen-mother is nearly destitute if she's truly sunk by the money she invested in those ships."

Matteo had to smile. "Yes, she's probably been in raving fits, after losing her treasure."

The spices, the gems, and rich fabrics they'd removed from those ships. Port Bascin's merchants were joyously glutted with loot to resell throughout Darzeq, and he and his comrades were secure monetarily for the first time since Cthar had stolen the throne. They'd take Arimna and rebuild Darzeq and their lives with Cthar's personal fortune.

He would bring Dalia and Benamir to Arimna Palace and arrange the coronation—with Dalia crowned beside him.

Dalia... Matteo ached to see her. To hold her. Soon. He nodded to the others. "Let's walk downstairs to bid Ekiael farewell, and then we'll finalize our plans to retake Arimna."

Thaddeus grinned. "I live to avenge Tarquin and your family, Sire. I'll give my whole inheritance just to see Kaphtor's game-piece queen taken down."

"She's more than a game-piece. She's utterly corrupted," Matteo pointed out. "Why was I born into that woman's line?"

Catching the king's furious glance, Corban said, "I've learned that being born is something you've no control over. But how you chose to live will be your answer to her crimes."

"Yet her cursed blood is in my veins." Matteo finished buckling his sword, though his fingers shook with the violence of his rage. "I wish I could burn it out—physically remove it forever!—and yet that same corrupted blood craves the joy of personally killing her."

"Her blood's only one drop amid all the generations of blood in your veins," Corban pointed out.

"Yes, but it takes only one drop of strong poison to kill a man, my lord." Bitterness laced Matteo's words, tasting harsh and metallic in his mouth. "And I've been poisoned."

Thaddeus shook his head. "Nothing you've done thus far indicates you're tainted, Sire. If you kill her, it is a justifiable deed, to be applauded. Only unjustified killings would make me question your supposed corruption. You judge yourself too harshly."

"No, I don't." Closing his eyes hard, Matteo added. "And, the day I start killing honorable citizens, my friends, you must kill me. Until then, let's work to free Darzeq."

Drawing her furred violet cloak tighter, Dalia exhaled in Eshda's vast courtyard, her breath emerging as vapor. When would winter's chill finally break and release spring's warmth? Lord Aristo's bootsteps crunched beside her own and she shot him a mock-distressed glance. "My lord, can't we open a few of those underground fire pits around the castle and warm the air a bit?"

Aristo laughed. "Now, Majesty, there's an idea! How might I do so without risking our men?"

They approached the gatehouse, and Dalia glanced at the men above, whose backs and posture indicated that they were on watch, guarding the gate's mechanisms and the stronghold's entryway.

Aristo followed Dalia's gaze and nodded approvingly. He bowed slightly to Dalia, and they prepared to turn for the keep again. Until one of the guest priests wandered into view, caught sight of them, and bowed. Smiling, he straightened. "My lord. Majesty, good news! Through the Infinite's mercy, the fever broke last night. Our friend is walking about and we're well. By your leave, my comrades and I will depart tonight or tomorrow."

Dalia returned his charming smile. In some ways this priest reminded her of a mix of Ekiael and Lord Corban. Dark, yet trim and civil. And by all the gatehouse reports this past week, they'd been quiet, genial guests, deeply and prayerfully concerned for their sick friend. Dalia approached, accompanied by Aristo, the gatehouse's shadow falling over them. "Good sir, I'm glad for your news and I pray you all remain well. Our high priest will certainly welcome you to Port Zamaj."

Aristo interposed, genial, compassionate. "Do you have enough supplies for the journey? Speak to my men tonight and ask for what you need."

"Restorative medicines would be welcomed," the lean priest murmured. "Our friend has lost strength, yet he's worried about the delay. Perhaps some..."

His voice faded and Aristo drew closer, ever-interested in health remedies. "Ginger root if his stomach's still touchy, with honey and perhaps a touch of cinnamon. And eggs. If we've any to spare, I'll order them crated in straw for you."

Relief washed over the thin priest's face and he half-bowed to Aristo and Dalia. "Thank you! Your kindness has personified all that Infinite expects of us." He clasped Aristo's arms in supplication, then embraced him.

Eshda's lord flinched, gasped, and then recoiled. Swift and silent, the priest swung Aristo into a shadowed stone corner within the gatehouse. Aristo sagged and cast a wide-eyed look at Dalia, then his glance faded, his eyes glazed, lifeless.

Dalia retreated from the priest, but he swept an embracing arm about her—breath-swift, and muffled her screech with one of his long sleeves, nestling her close.

Sickly sweetness clogged her nostrils, and filled her lungs as she drew breath.

As the world faded around her, the priest kissed her cheek.

Chapter 25

Covered and muffled, unable to move her arms and legs, Dalia squirmed, struggling to steady herself against a vicious headache and an onslaught of jolts and wit-jarring bumps. Was she in a wagon? If only she could see! An unexpected thump tossed her helplessly into the air, and she landed with a breathtaking whack that echoed hollowly of wood.

Pain stabbed—bruising aches, stiffness, and countless needle-stuck stabs scourged her hands and feet. No doubt she was in a wagon. Scaln's breath! She was being stolen.... Rolled in a swath of canvas like one of Aunt Pinny's old unwanted carpets. Thick, heavy fabric rested too near her face, almost smothering her. She strained, fighting to turn her gaze toward dim light, as she worked for air. A thin current seeped over Dalia's face, and she closed her eyes.

She must calm herself. She must escape and return to Benamir and Matteo. Aristo... That priest had killed him! Wretched man! False priest... Poor, darling Aristo.

Dalia turned her head within her canvas confines, found a slightly larger breathing space, and wept. A mistake. Her nose dripped, and the drying tears irritated her skin, and she couldn't lift a hand to mop herself. But poor Aristo. He'd deserved so much better! He deserved a tranquil passing after a long life, many years hence. Not murdered by a false priest—a mercenary.

The cart or wagon bumped again, jouncing her pitilessly, and a subdued voice declared, "That's far enough. Gather everything, and let's make haste." A big hand clamped over

Dalia's ankle, making her shriek through the cord-gag in her mouth. She squirmed, longing to kick the offender. Murderer!

His grip tightened and he dragged her across the cart's wooden slats like a bundle of old rags. The muffled voice chuckled. "She's awake and fighting mad. Or only mad. Thoughtful of Matteo of Arimna to marry such a slight female—not much heavier than an actual tent."

They'd rolled her in a tent tarp? Well, if she emerged victorious from this battle, these vile men wouldn't live to pack another tent, these ... these living boils!

Grinding her teeth into the cordage, she prayed. "Dear Infinite, save me if You will it, but bring these vile pit dwellers to the end they deserve!"

Sharp tugs wrenched the bindings over her arms, hips, and feet, and the canvas lifted away from her face, allowing her to breathe the misty, chilling air. Allowing her to glare at the malefactor who'd killed sweet Aristo and stolen her from her family. Imposter priest! If she could repay him—

He smiled that false show of teeth, just as he'd done before killing Aristo. "Ah, lady, you do look angry. Wait. I've something to cool you off."

He tugged the carved plug from a waterskin and dashed water over her face, which chilled instantly. Water clogged her nostrils and throat, blocking air. As she coughed, the false priest lifted a corner of his cloak and wiped her face, rough as a resentful servant. "It wouldn't do to present you to the queen with that grubby face."

He turned Dalia over his arm and hammered bruises between her shoulders until she gasped and wheezed in sharp stabs of air. Pain goaded her to pray. "Beloved Infinite, give me a sword and a chance to punish him! And to escape Cthar." Oh, mercy.... They were taking her as a prisoner to Cthar.

No reason to panic. Not yet. Not if she could escape.

The two men with him, tall, fur-cloaked and watchful, yet amused, unhitched the luggage cart and brought their horses around. The huskiest of the three mounted his horse and nodded to Dalia's tormentor. "Ready, Murchadh."

Murchadh, the false priest, handed her up to the husky horseman as if she were nothing more than a rolled blanket. The horseman settled Dalia roughly against his chest and muttered, "If you need to visit a privy hole, you'll have to wait."

Murchadh and the third man dropped their horses' reins to the road and then rolled the small cart to the road's edge and pushed it over the precipice into the rocky gorge below. Murchadh grinned and nodded to his comrades. "Good job. Let's be off before they catch up to us."

They. Eshda's soldiers? Dalia squeezed her eyes shut in ferocious prayer.

Infinite, let us be caught!

A distant clatter and vague hissing drew her attention. One of Aristo's scaln traps had done its job and held a snared, dying beast. The scaln's brilliant crimson-colored leathern skin was purpling, its black tongue lolling from its gaping, jagged-toothed mouth. Venom drained thinly from its lips and it hissed softly, moving feebly as they rode by.

Dalia gazed at the dying beast and her heart contracted. Poor scavenger, hated for its allotted task in this fallen mortal world, to end in such appalling misery—much the same fate that Cthar undoubtedly planned for Dalia, wife and queen of Matteo of Darzeq.

Benamir squawked in Yiska's arms, and Jakin dragged at Anji's hand as she watched a formal company of soldiers enter the hall at a dirge-pace. Between them, the soldiers carried a cloak-draped litter. One of the soldiers was blinking, his broad face contorting as he fought tears, which defied him and glided down his face. The other soldiers remained hard eyed and grim, clearly fighting for calm. They placed the litter before her and reverently drew back the cloak, revealing Aristo Faolan's ashen, mottled face.

Anji swallowed bile, but she couldn't swallow her weeping. Sweet Aristo—valiant, gracious man! She dashed a hand over her face, fighting for composure. "What happened?"

"Murder, Lady Rhiysa. We—"

"No!" She'd lost enough beloved ones for a lifetime. This slaying could not go unanswered. Anji spoke through gritted teeth. "Who *dared* to attack one of the king's most gallant subjects? The killer will hang from Eshda's walls!"

"We found him in the gatehouse, in the chamber he'd allotted to the priests. It seems he was checking on their welfare and they killed him. We've sent men after them, lady. We'll bring them to justice."

Anji shook her head, a sickened knot tightening her stomach. "He was doing more than checking on their welfare—he was walking with the queen, guarding her. Where is she? Wait!" Anji kissed Jakin and chased him toward the tower steps along with Yiska and Benamir. Anji ordered the shocked midwife, "Yiska, go! Hurry. Bar yourselves in my chamber and don't open the door until you hear my voice. Do you hear? No one else's!"

"Yes, lady! It'll be done." Yiska swooped the puzzled Jakin toward the door as Ben squirmed in her other arm. She rushed the boys into the stairwell and swung the door shut. Anji exhaled prayers, hearing the heavy clunk of the barred lock behind the door. "One-Who-Sees—Mighty One—I trust You to guard them!" She turned to Eshda's commander. "Are Eshda's gates locked? Who last saw the queen? Search everywhere, and hurry! If they've taken her, send a company of men to reclaim her and deal with the murderers!"

Seated on the bare, frosty evening-shadowed ground, Dalia shivered and winced as the reprobate Murchadh finally tugged the knotted gag from her dry mouth. At least her jaw wasn't dislocated. But she ached fiercely, and she needed to bind her foundation garments tight. It was long past time to nurse Benamir, and she was suffering for it. Oh, her sweet little Ben. Surely Anji would feed him—a kindness she'd granted him often these past few months, as Dalia's strength and milk had dwindled.

"Amazing," Murchadh's voice grated, unpleasantly genial. "You're free to speak, and you've nothing to say? That's unnatural, isn't it?"

Frosty as the air, Dalia glowered at the unshaven brute. "What should I say to a murderer?" But Aristo's final fading glance resurfaced in her thoughts and she raged at Murchadh, "You killed a *good* man! One of the best—the finest of Darzeq's lords! Why? Are you under orders from that she-scaln in Arimna Palace? For half a copper mite, she'd have you butchered and you should be smart enough to know that!"

Murchadh grinned, and taunting dimples creased his long face. "I'd my reasons, lady, and they were far more than a half-mite."

"Oh, let me guess your reasons!" Dalia snorted. "The traitor-queen-mother promised you silver! Perhaps even full-coined gold nobles. She'll never pay you. I didn't know mercenaries were so trusting."

All three stared as if she'd guessed their secret—fascinating, because she'd called them mercenaries as an insult. "You poor dupes! I spent enough of my childhood in the royal courts to know that Cthar does nothing unless it pleases her, and it rarely pleases her to fulfill her promises."

One of the men—the most sharp-faced and sardonic-looking—sneered. "It'll please her if we're within ten paces."

A laugh, dark and mirthless, escaped Dalia before she could suppress it. "You'll never be within ten paces of her again—much less bearing weapons. Her guards would slice you down within a blink."

Murchadh shrugged. "I'm hearing nothing but your venomous temper, lady. But, spit all you please and get over your rage. We've a long journey ahead."

Long enough for her to escape somehow. Dalia huffed, "I'll never get over my rage at what you've done! I'll never forgive you!"

"Ah, but 'never' is such a short time for you, lady. I'd wager this journey's all you have left of life."

She glared. "Better my short life, well-lived, than your putrid existence in any measure—you mold-witted fool! And anyone *you* claim to love probably wishes for a short life!"

The tallest of the three churls pretended gape-mouthed shock. "Well, listen to her! Lady, where'd you learn to slap around words?"

From her lord-father. Not to mention five of the Dreaded Seven, excluding Matteo and Sheth. Poor Sheth. And darling Matteo...

Grief-spiked longing pierced her, sharp enough to make her flinch inwardly. Oh, to see her husband's gorgeous face and to catch him in an eternal embrace. What would he do when he heard that she'd been stolen? First, he'd rage. Her fierce beloved. He'd lash out at the world, and then seize weapons to steal her again. In her thoughts, she warned him, Beware the risks! Your life's worth far more than mine.

Best to be realistic. Unless she could escape, she'd die. Her life was over. Yet, her duty was done. She'd borne Benamir, a son of the Infinite's promise to Darzeq. If Darzeq would abide with Him.

"Dear Infinite ... One-Who-Sees ... remind Darzeq of its pledges to You! Save Matteo and Benamir!"

She had every reason to believe Matteo would survive Darzeq's chaos. Hadn't the Infinite sent Lord Corban to defend Matteo? And her. Would it be too much to hope that He would save her and her unborn child? No. Until the last breath of her life, she would trust Him.

And she would defy the killer Murchadh and his reprobate comrades.

Matteo slid his lord-father's strongbox into its storage space within the stone wall in the royal apartments. No matter how many times he'd read Jonatan's letters, his unsent diatribes against Cthar, and her terse, snide responses to the few letters he'd evidently written and sent to her, he saw no threats against the king's life.

Nothing in this entire fortress—from the testimonies of the servants, to his father's last half-written portion of a letter to Mother—indicated that Cthar had killed Jonatan. But had she managed to infiltrate his household?

If he could learn the truth...

A tap at the door jolted Matteo to the present. He closed and locked the narrow vault, then swiftly replaced its shielding tile. "Enter!"

Corban and Thaddeus entered the chamber and bowed. Matteo nodded to them. "Good news, Thaddeus?"

Thaddeus had sent another petition to his family for permission to command the Ormr clan's significant forces in their planned attack against Arimna. If the Ormr clan officially joined Matteo's forces, he'd have an excellent chance at taking Arimna by force. Thus far, the squeamish Magni Ormr had refused, and he'd gone off on a mission as ambassador to Belaal.

Thaddeus shrugged and lifted his long arms in frustration. "No reply to my petition yet, Sire. I continue to hope. Until then—" He nodded at Corban, who offered Matteo a slender courier-note vial and muttered, "From Eshda, Sire."

A note from Dalia? Sweet, engaging, delectable wife! How he longed to see her.

"Thank you." Matteo grinned and pried open the tiny metal cylinder. Anji's familiar, minuscule script noted: *Cthar's men killed Aristo and stole Dalia from Eshda. They're taking her to Arimna. Soldiers in pursuit. Full details soon. Note sent to Tragobre. Ben is safe & well.*

Air vanished, crushed from Matteo's lungs by a hammer-blow of pain. This had to be a mistake. He read the note again. Anji's words didn't change. Didn't waver.

He dropped into his father's chair, sucked in a harsh breath, and then rasped, "Cthar's captured Dalia!"

Corban and Thaddeus stared as if he'd lost his mind. And he would lose is mind if Cthar killed Dalia. His Dalia ... in Cthar's claws! He'd tear Cthar to mincemeat with his bare hands!

Fury-wild, Matteo pitched the courier's note toward Corban, then stood and stormed to his personal storage chest. He plotted aloud as he flung open the lid and reached for his sword-belt and its baldric. "Eshda's been attacked, and Aristo's dead. Though we've few men, our attack begins *now*! We must rescue my wife before Cthar's men cross the river to Arimna. This is Cthar's revenge. Her strike against me for Port Bascin. What won't she do? Are you two coming with me to steal back Darzeq's queen?"

Corban half bowed. "Yes, Sire. Even if you command us to stay here. Between Eshda and Arimna, where should we gather to watch and wait?"

"And," Thaddeus glanced at the crossbows in their stands against Matteo's chamber wall, "What weapons should we use?

The crossbows will be ideal—if half our men shoot bolts while the others reload."

"Gather crossbows, longbows, swords, whatever you please," Matteo commanded. "But use the weapons only if the queen's not trapped amid the fight." Matteo strode to the far wall and lifted his favorite crossbow from its stand. "I won't risk her life in our attack. We also need ships. Not those wide heavy merchants' ships, but small warships—light, fast, and well-armed."

"I'll send word to Kemuel," Thaddeus offered. "As well as Losbreq and Lord Tragobre. If they can each command at least one ship to patrol the northern river roundabout Arimna, we'll have a good chance at intercepting her."

"I pray we do!" Matteo loaded his entire arsenal of crossbow bolts into a knapsack and began to add his hunting gear. "If Cthar kills her..."

He couldn't finish the thought. He would go insane.

Dalia wrinkled her nose and huddled, shivering on Murchadh's horse, averting her face from the tickling descent of early-spring snowflakes. But hiding her face in her cloak wasn't much better. After almost a week of rushed, unscrubbed travel—with no fires, few rest stops, little sleep, and no time nor means to so much as comb her hair—she stank like raw rotting meat cast onto a steaming dung heap. Although a steaming dung heap might be warm, and certainly more wholesome than Murchadh's loathsome grasp.

At least he hadn't tried to kiss her again. Bound or not, she'd make him regret such folly, and then she'd be beaten for it. She peered at the road ahead. They'd soon reach the city of Tvirtove Gate—one of her rest stops between Tragobre and Kiyrem during her school years. Might she somehow escape

Murchadh inside the city? If Eshda's soldiers were indeed pursuing them, as Murchadh believed, she could hide and watch for them. Murchadh unsettled her thoughts with a shove. "Sit up and look pretty, Queen! We're approaching Tvirtove Gate—your presence is expected."

Surely he didn't mean that Cthar was in Tvirtove Gate's stronghold. "What do you mean 'expected'?"

"Your escort to the river, and then downstream to Arimna."

An official escort could only mean Cthar's men. Had she sent a royal barge?

Murchadh's stoutest comrade, Kalnir, called out, "Good! Expected or not, I'd refuse to sleep in the wilds tonight. Not with this snow. My blood's still too thinned out by the purges and emetics I've taken. I'd freeze to death."

The third man shook snow off his cloak and drew it tighter over his shoulders. "Agreed. After all, she's to be brought to Arimna alive."

"Alive?" Dalia huffed. "The queen-mother might regret her—"

Murchadh shook her to silence. "Hush, I'm hearing horses."

Horses? Had Eshda's soldiers caught them at last? Dalia straightened. As Murchadh turned, she caught a glimpse over his shoulder. Soldiers, a full company, charging toward them from the north. Murchadh snarled, "Kalnir! Call a warning to the guards—before we're overtaken!"

The grubby Kalnir raised his hunting horn and blasted a frantic trump-call toward the city. The instant the call faded, Dalia screamed over Murchadh's shoulder, "Eshda!"

Murchadh swore and cuffed Dalia's ear—a vicious clout that shot pain through her skull and left her deafened to everything but a low, ominous hum. Before she could re-gather her wits, Murchadh kicked his horse into a full gallop that nearly unseated Dalia.

Her senses spinning, Dalia clung to the saddle's high-built pommel and struggled to appraise the city ahead. Tvirtove Gate stood stalwart above Darzeq's great river-valley, a walled gathering of slate-roofed stone buildings, with a massive double-gate that opened, spewing forth horsemen.

They rode out in haphazard fashion amid a tumult of weaponry and sloppily donned cloaks, all of them wearing Cthar's badges, or carrying her household's pennant.

So many men. Eshda's men would be outnumbered and slaughtered. Despair sent tears gliding down Dalia's face. She leaned over Murchadh's arm. "Stop! Turn back to Eshda! You'll be killed!"

Her warning cry was lost amid the reverberations of their charge.

Chapter 26

Eshda's soldiers overtook them, screaming battle cries that pierced through the dark humming in Dalia's ears. Within a breath, Murchadh's comrades were cut down—so swift and violent that Dalia gasped. Murchadh's grip tightened around her waist and he wrenched her close. Dalia squirmed, fighting to unseat herself.

Until a violent thud jolted Murchadh. He gasped and dropped his sword.

Before she could blink, one of Eshda's soldiers snatched Dalia from Murchadh's slackening hold and dragged her onto his horse. Over her head, the soldier cried, "To Eshda!"

As one trained force, Eshda's soldiers turned, forming a living shield of warhorses and men around Dalia. She'd no chance, no breath to warn or thank her rescuers, and this huge horse's gait was so ragged that she was badly jounced. Leaning forward, she hung on tight, weaving her fingers into the horse's mane. Just as an arrow whisked past her protector. He bellowed, "Majesty, remain low while we fight them off!"

Obedient, she huddled over and prayed with all her might. "Mighty One, defend us!"

Though the warhorses continued at full gallop, metal clashed against metal as the two forces fought. Dalia's guard hissed to his horse, and the beast surged ahead of the others as the men around them slowed to fight amid the roar their battle cries.

Dalia hugged the warhorse's massive neck, fighting nausea, averting her gaze from the dizzying blur of the ground beneath the beast's big hooves. She managed one glance back, just as one of Cthar's soldiers charged—sword upraised, then falling against her protector.

A thud and a breathtaking impact struck her shoulders ... consciousness vanished.

Everything swam, rocked, making her stomach churn. As Dalia swallowed hard, a man's voice rumbled, "There. Her eyelids moved, and she swallowed. Didn't I say she was alive?"

Alive. Her limbs heavy as fallen posts, her thoughts sluggish and inept. Dalia pressed her hands against the swaying give of canvas. How'd she come to be carried on a litter like a corpse? Who carried her? When she finally dared to open her eyes, she saw blood. Spattered over her garments, her hands, her disheveled hair.... Blood, everywhere.

Was her baby alive? She tried to move her hands, but weights held them down. So much blood. Two men gripped the litter at either end, and Dalia studied their drab attire for some designation. Whose men carried her? Eshda's or Cthar's?

Another man leaned into Dalia's line of vision, his stone-gray gaze acute. His heavy cloak flaunted Cthar's colors—the reverse of King Jonatan's. Deep gold with intense purple edges. Wide edges, denoting a commander. Dalia closed her eyes, hit by a muddled sweep of panic. "Are Eshda's men ... dead?"

"Yes," Cthar's commander growled. "All are dead. As they should be."

Feeble streaks of tears slid down her cheeks, trickling into her hair and ears. *Dear Infinite, I prayed! Did You not hear? Am I so unworthy?*

Darkness slid over her thoughts, muting them. Stifling her senses. She welcomed nothingness without a fight.

A chill brought her back to consciousness—a wet cloth swiped her face, then hands unfastened her mantle. A woman's sharp voice snapped, "If you're not her husband, then back away!"

"As the queen's commander, I'm ordered to guard her," a man argued from Dalia's left. "On pain of death."

"Is that so?" The woman huffed. "Well, guard her, but on pain of death, you'll face the wall, not the lady. I'll not scrub another drop of blood off her until you've turned away!"

Dear woman ... whoever she was. Dalia longed to thank her, but only managed to open her eyes instead—to a matronly and disgruntled woman, who glared at Cthar's commander. Dalia stared at the man until he noticed her and turned away. He snorted. "Hurry, then!"

The matron gusted out a furious breath. "I do my job properly, which means I'll take my time. You want this poor girl cleaned and tended, then give me leave to do so! It's not as if she can run."

Indeed not. Pain encompassed Dalia's body as if a giant had squeezed her in his mighty fist and then flung her against a wall. Dalia grimaced as the woman finally met her gaze. "Thank you."

Still livid, color blooming in her olive-skinned face, the matron nodded. "Course, lady." She scrubbed at Dalia's face again, and then dabbed at her snarled black hair. The rag stained crimson. Eshda's blood. As Dalia sniffled back tears, the matron murmured, "I remember these curls and your big eyes. You're Lord Tragobre's daughter—I've seen you stop here on your way to and from Kiyrem. You wrote that insulting-grand poem."

"Yes." The poem that had earned her Cthar's absolute hatred. Dalia moistened her lips and tasted blood's metallic thickness. Was this blood from the soldier who'd tried to save her? Those dear men! Poor Aristo.... All dead because of her.

She sobbed, and the matron patted her as she wept.

"There now. You go ahead and cry, lady." Sounds of splashing water, wringing of a cloth, and water dripping into a basin met Dalia's ears. The unknown woman dabbed at Dalia's face and throat, then unlaced her bloodied garments. So softly that Dalia barely heard her, the woman murmured, "I'm Iva. Tell me now—I've heard rumors—were you in Eshda all this time?"

In less than a whisper, Dalia said, "Yes. I married the king, Matteo of Darzeq. I bore him Benamir, our sweet son."

Iva blinked, then nodded and continued checking Dalia's arms, ribs and limbs. "I believe you, lady. *Majesty!* I see you're wearing nursing linens. Filthy of those louts to take you from your baby, just as it was of the others to attack you. I fear you suffered a blow to your head. Any severe pain anywhere? Broken bones?"

Dalia flexed her hands, feet, arms, and legs. "No. But, I'm queasy. My muscles are all torn." And a death-deep chill dragged at her ebbing strength.

"Stop!" the guard commanded. "Enough whispering!"

The matron yelled, "I'm a free woman of Darzeq, talking female to female as women should! Do you have some girl-wisdom to add?"

Whirling about, his boots rasping grittily against the floor, the commander snarled, "I ought to beat you!"

Iva rested one hand on the heavy water basin, obviously ready to fling it like a weapon. "Turn away, lord-commander, or you'll explain bruises to your comrades—my aim's true!"

The commander's face purpled and he strode toward Iva. "For threatening me, you'll be fined and—"

Dalia reached up and clasped Iva's arm. She might be a prisoner, but surely her requests carried some weight even now, and she must protect Iva from her own temper. Dalia offered Cthar's commander a pleading look. "Sir, I beg you, there's been too much violence because of me—be merciful. Grant a truce." With time to grieve.

The commander snorted and turned away in disgust. As tears brimmed, burning Dalia's eyes, Iva bent and hugged her. "Courage, Majesty! Let me help you sit up to finish scrubbing, and we'll change your gown. I've warm, clean robes for you, and I'll find fresh linens. Surely they'll grant you a few days to rest before going to Arimna."

"A day," The commander said, not turning around. "She may have one day of rest while we bury the dead."

Iva flung him a condemning look. Beneath her breath, she promised Dalia, "Fear not, Majesty. I'll tell your lord-father, and everyone, what's happened!"

"Tell them..." Dalia hesitated, choosing her words. "Tell them, I've courage to die, but every reason to live."

Matteo, Ben, her parents, and Anji and Darzeq were all reasons to live. Silently, she prayed, "One-Who-Sees, Mighty One, though I'm unworthy, save me."

When would this springtime snow ease? Corban frowned at the lowering gray skies and then studied the river valley below. Just beside him, clad in weighty, subdued hunting garb—as was Thaddeus and the company of men behind them—Matteo observed, "At least the river's not frozen. Tragobre and Kemuel should make it through by morning. Perhaps Losbreq too. Until then, we pray that Dalia hasn't yet been taken into Arimna. If she has, and we're too late, we'll need to invade the city itself, and we don't have enough men to claim a victory."

"May your enemies be destroyed," Corban said, the words almost a prayer. Let this conflict be finished! He'd seen enough chaos, and so had Darzeq. And the sooner matters were settled here, the sooner he could journey to Belaal and seek Araine's undeserved forgiveness. Let him at least have forgiveness. If his life was demanded in Belaal as punishment for his crimes, then he would give himself over without a fight. Nothing Thaenfall about that.

In truth, everything Thaenfall ought to be purged from his soul. Corban could almost see Ekiael grin at the thought, ready for a debate. Something about facing one's history and the past, making restitution, and acknowledging the unworthiness of all before the Creator.

Oh, the irony of counting a high priest of the Infinite as one of his few true friends. Corban allowed himself a bleak smile. His father would have killed Corban in absolute fury at the mere thought.

Yet Ekiael was a friend. As was this brooding, uncrowned king standing beside him.

With the Infinite as their sovereign.

Infinite, You see my heart. Give me this one mercy. All that I have and all that I am, I dedicate to You.

The prayer departed from him, unseen, yet felt from his very soul. Matteo shifted, sighed, and looked upward, as if sending a silent prayer alongside his own, and then he nudged Corban and nodded to Thaddeus. "Come on. Let's set watchmen for the night and lead the men back to camp."

Corban half-bowed. "I'm your servant, Sire."

And Yours, Mighty One. Let us save the Lady Dalia and capture Arimna.

On the inn's steps, Cthar's commander, Brune, swept an appraising look over its small courtyard at his gathered men and nodded. Then he glanced down at Dalia, clad in her clean gown, mantle, and a borrowed fur-lined cloak so heavy that it dragged her already-wearied steps. Dalia lifted her chin at him.

"You've your orders, Commander, so let's continue. We can't disappoint the queen-mother."

Brune opened his mouth and then closed it as if trapping inappropriate words. Did she detect a flicker of approval in his glance? He grunted. "Can't fault your courage, Majesty. I suppose you've much to say to her."

"I've already written more than she can endure," Dalia reminded him. "If I say what else I think to her face, she'll slay me with her own hands."

"Let's be truthful, Majesty, you're dead anyway—we both know it. What would you say?"

"To the she-scaln of Kaphtor? She's poisonous enough to kill all Darzeq as well as the House of Jonatan, and Darzeq ought to be warned. Death probably fears her, which is a shame."

One corner of Brune's thin mouth curled, and then eased. "Lady, you ought remain silent and wait for the executioner—he'd do the deed more mercifully than she would, hearing you say such things." Brune guided her down the steps, one hand gripping her elbow, keeping her near as any death-pledged man might do. As Murchadh had done.

Unlike Murchadh, however, Brune didn't command an easily overwhelmed pair of cohorts. More than twenty men waited at attention in the court, and Dalia glimpsed more cavalrymen mounted and waiting beyond the inn's small stone gate, with a distant trump-call evidently summoning more soldiers to duty. To his men, Brune bellowed, "Laggards! Let's move! Onward to Arimna!"

Dalia's stomach clenched at the words. For all her supposed courage, she was certainly holding tight to fear. Dragging the heavily furred cloak nearer, she stepped forward, temporarily obedient to her enemy.

Brune helped Dalia onto a horse, bound her hands before her, then took the lead reins. And he warned her with an unmistakable taunt. "Try to escape, Majesty, and you'll likely fall."

Dalia smoothed her stabbing rage to benevolence. "Commander, I'm proud of you for not sounding as smug as you might."

He quirked an eyebrow at her, as if trying to decipher her meaning, but then he turned away, though not swiftly enough to hide his furtive smile.

As they passed the waiting horsemen—a formidable cavalcade that would surely intimidate Arimna's citizens—Brune ordered their commander: "Wait here, long enough to recite your pledge of service to Darzeq twenty times."

To his credit, the cavalryman didn't so much as blink. Smooth-voiced, he began, "To Darzeq, I pledge my life, my honor, my unfailing service. May the Infinite be witness...."

Dalia pondered the order. Why delay the cavalrymen? Why didn't Commander Brune lead his entire force toward the river in one appalling show of might?

One-Who-Sees... Dalia pleaded silently, *Be our witness indeed. Act on Darzeq's behalf!*

Matteo reined in his horse and peered through the trees at the broad hillside thoroughfare, wearied of the wait, yet praying. Were they too late to intercept Dalia's abductors? He'd thought they would ride through the previous day, at the latest, on their way down to the river. Yet not a sign of their approach.

To his left, seated on the magnificent Ghost, Corban briefly lifted a hand and then leaned forward, clearly listening to some distant sound. Calming himself, Matteo concentrated. And heard ... horses. Many horses. Also a double-timed cadence of foot-soldiers—sounds he recognized from a childhood of attention at military drills and ceremonies. Heartbeat quickening, he nodded to Corban. This had to be an official procession.

The first soldiers tramped by, stoic, clad in Cthar's colors—gold stamped with purple—the opposite of Darzeq's field of purple with gold. Several horsemen rode through, one leading ... Dalia!

Matteo's throat constricted as he glimpsed her distinctively rumpled hair and her fragile, superb profile, so dignified and calm despite her predicament. His brave love. This night, he'd hold her again, after he'd freed her from Cthar's grasp—their forces looked more than equal to the challenge.

Matteo lifted a longsword—indicating their preferred weapons for this attack—and signaled his men forward. Corban's usually cool eyes gleamed as he slid a cutting blade from a scabbard at his side, and he pointed Matteo's forces ahead through the trees, baring his teeth in a savage grin.

Without a warning cry, they rode down the slope to the road, a living current of men, horses, and weapons. As planned, Corban led the charge against the forces behind Dalia's captor, and—followed by Thaddeus and his men—Matteo sped to retrieve his wife.

Ever quick, Dalia turned and looked directly at him. Her beautiful eyes widened, and she smiled, elation and adoration mingling within that single look. Then, she gasped, glanced up the hillside thoroughfare, and screamed, "No! It's a trap—leave! Leave!"

Chapter 27

Corban led the charge, allowing Ghost free rein down the wood-sheltered hillside. In his mettle, Ghost crashed through the final thicket, snorting his battle-readiness. Amid the by-rushing blur of ground and air, Corban leaned down to swipe at three startled soldiers, wounding one's shoulder as the others broke ranks and fled to the trees on the opposite side of the thoroughfare.

The Lady Dalia's cry broke through his attack, "No! It's a trap—leave! Leave!"

Corban glanced at her. Dalia flung a brief, horrified look up the thoroughfare, and Corban followed her gaze.

Cavalrymen rode over the hillcrest and down the sloping road, in numbers far exceeding Matteo's forces. Dalia screamed, lifting her bound, clenched hands, "Go! Please!"

Her captor spurred his horse, drawing Dalia's small horse away while his men rushed into the gap cutting off Matteo's path, weapons readied to attack him. Matteo roared his outrage and—flanked by Thaddeus' men—slashed at the nearest troops, all of them too absorbed with fighting to notice the danger. If Matteo pursued Dalia, he'd be surrounded and taken down. Corban yelled and swerved Ghost toward the king.

Dalia flung him a look and cried, "Flee! All of you!"

Mighty One...! Corban sent the prayer-fragment skyward, desperate to reach Matteo, who now recognized his predicament as Thaddeus and his men fought to cut an escape route from the thoroughfare. Corban pressed his knees into Ghost's sides, urging him along. Too slow—

Corban bellowed his family's battle cry, adding, "Thaenfall!"

His very name seemed to break the opposition. Many of Cthar's soldiers drew back, some feinted attacks toward Corban, but their widened eyes and enfeebled motions communicated only fear and shock. Several gathered courage and aimed swords and javelins at him. Corban slashed them all away in fury, protecting Ghost as he stormed toward the king.

He reached Matteo, and Thaddeus bellowed, "Go!" Baring his teeth viciously, oblivious to a trail of blood scoring his face, Thaddeus called out, "For the king!" He slashed another foe back and drew his men away.

Before Matteo could join them, Corban lunged and dragged him over to Ghost. Gripping the king's nape, Corban nudged Ghost's silver-gray sides. "Go!"

Ghost cut from the road at a full gallop, scaring off their final attackers. Matteo flailed, then brandished his emptied crossbow, enraged. "Let go! Circle back!"

"Yes!" But not until he knew Matteo was safe. If need be, he'd knock the king unconscious, then try again to retrieve the Lady Dalia.

Gritting his teeth, all his senses alerted to any pursuers, Corban held Matteo in a relentless grasp and sped Ghost into the sheltering woods beyond the road.

Dalia trembled, biting down sobs. Had they escaped? Oh, please let it be so! Dear Infinite, protect them! The clash was too much like the previous ones—her defenders overwhelming her captors, and then overrun and slaughtered in the ensuing fight. "Please, please, let them escape!"

Brune jerked her horse nearer, almost unseating her. "Why such fear? Was your husband among them? Eh?"

She snapped out, "I'm praying no more men die! Isn't that enough to fear?"

Brune snarled to his men, "Go back! Find Matteo of Arimna and bring him to the queen!"

Dalia shot him a furious glare. "Queen? Did you mean me, or that she-scaln, Cthar?" She turned upon Brune's men. "*I'm* your queen, and you're all sop-witted cowards! Since when do valiant men follow a murderess from Kaphtor instead of their rightful king? Come to your senses and follow him as well!"

Several of Brune's men actually faltered and glanced from her to their commander. Brune hesitated, then yelled, "Go back! Find Matteo of Arimna and bring him to me!"

Plagues!

Violent tremors shook Dalia so fiercely that Brune noticed. He reached over and gripped her arm, steadying her. "Calm yourself, Lady. Nothing'll be helped if you die of your own foolishness."

"*My* foolishness?" Dalia longed to spit at him. "You're all perfect examples of 'good' men taking bad orders! Worse, you're taking them from a spoiled foreigner who'd squash you for half a mite! Where's your wits? She has power only because you've allowed her to take it! Gather your courage and defend your king!"

Brune scowled. "If only the situation were so simple, Majesty. Now hush!"

Dalia growled and hushed. What was the use? *Infinite, One-Who-Sees, clear their wits! And help Lord Corban protect the king!*

Matteo crouched behind a shielding natural screen of brambles and evergreens. To be within a glance of her, and then torn away. He must be wounded—bleeding inside. Corban dropped to the ground beside him, and Matteo fought resentment against being rescued. "If I lose her, I have nothing!"

"You have your son—and hers," Corban argued quietly as he unfastened a waterskin. "Nevertheless we'll save her. We will. We simply have to find a safe route out of these hills."

He didn't say what they both knew. They were separated from his men. Had Thaddeus managed to escape?

If only he could see the river. Kemuel's ships, and Tragobre's. If Losbreq's ships arrived, they might manage a rescue.

Let it be so.

Sucking in a sharp, bracing breath, Matteo prayed, then closed his eyes.

Hide and wait.

Seated in the center of a broad, flat-bottomed skiff that cut over River Tinem's current much too swiftly, Dalia hugged her bound hands over her unborn baby, trying to still her persistent tremors. If only she could be far away, resting secure in Matteo's arms, with Benamir and the unborn baby nested between them in drowsing peace. What torture it was to see her gorgeous, sweet Matteo—to have been so near to rejoining him!

She gritted her teeth against the torment. Matteo must certainly blame himself. Anguish squeezed her breathless at the thought. The words noiseless, she prayed, "Dear Infinite ... Mighty One ... don't let that be my last sight of him!"

Distracting herself from the heartache, she focused on small things. The lamps in each skiff to light their evening passage. The gleam of lowering sunlight over the water. The ferocious concentration of the oarsmen in their small convoy, all intent upon guiding their skiffs across the chilly river. As a single force, the rows of men glided the oars flat over the frigid river, then cut sharply into the water, casting precise splashes that bespoke years of working together. All the skiffs perfectly timed to the same recurrent beat. Dalia watched the icy water droplets fall riverward again, studying the swift-fading rings and whirlpools.

So much better to dwell on small details such as the fleeting sparkle of water droplets, the lovely sloshing of water about the skiffs, rather than contemplate life's larger details.

Such as dying in Arimna.

How would Cthar kill her?

Or would Cthar hold her captive—sparing her just long enough to use as bait to lure Matteo to Arimna?

Dalia sent a silent rebuke to her husband. *Don't you dare place yourself with Cthar's reach! Don't even think...*

Men's screams lifted from the skiffs to her right, their piercing cries blotting out her silent scolding. Dalia turned and looked, just as a small, sleek, sharp-keeled ship sliced over a nearby skiff, tumbling its oarsmen and guards into the water—all thrashing against the bitter current. Another ship, larger, weightier, collided with the skiffs ahead, and a third ship followed.

One collision was mischance. Two revealed a plan. Three ships weren't just an attack—this was a rescue. Her rescue! Were there more ships on the way? Dalia squirmed about in her seat, straining to see.

Brune clawed his big hand into Dalia's shoulder, his grip crushing as a falcon upon a prey sparrow. As Dalia gasped, he roared, "To arms! Bowmen, the arrows!"

The arrows? Against their attackers. Her rescuers. Who...?

Echoing her unformed thought, Brune snarled at Dalia, "Who are they? *Who?*"

"I don't know!" Yet she could guess. The smaller, sleeker ship was of a southern design, cut for speed. Most likely from

Lord Kemuel's cherished Lohe Bay. The larger ships.... Tragobre colors fluttered in a far pennant.

"Father!" Dalia's jolt of delight vanished as she glimpsed *the* arrows. Cage-tipped arrows, packed with incendiaries, which flared to burning life as the soldiers touched them to the lamps Dalia had admired earlier. "No!"

Brune held her down on skiff's slat seat. "Steady! We've borrowed this tactic from your lord-husband, lady. At Port Bascin." To all his men, Brune yelled, "Fire to the ships!"

As the burning arrows hissed toward the ships, Dalia lunged away from Brune. If Father's men retaliated, then she'd give them a clear path to Brune. Clearly loath to part with his shield, Brune snagged Dalia's mantle, wrestled her onto the bench again, and then dragged a short sword from his belt. He angled the blade along her face and jaw, then yelled, "Tragobre! See your daughter? Call off your men and let us pass! Do you hear me? Kill us and she'll go down too! Back off!"

Aboard the ships, Dalia heard men yelling orders as they struggled to douse the fire. Above their shouts, she heard her father call, "Dalia! Are you there?"

She struggled to see him, and Brune physically turned her about on the seat. Partially concealed by a mast, Father watched her from the nearest ship. His eyes were so huge ... so worried. Dalia gulped against the tightening in her throat. Brune snapped, "Answer him!"

"My lord, I'm here!" She longed to call to him, 'As is your grandchild.' Instead, she managed, "I love you—I'm not afraid!"

Brune shook her. "Tell him to retreat!"

Dalia clamped her lips together and realized that her nose was running. No, not running, bleeding. Brune yelled, "Fire to the ships at will!"

She stomped both of her feet onto his, and then twisted her hands, struggling to free herself. Brune swore.

A veritable firestorm of arrows soared from the eight remaining skiffs—volleys Father's men retaliated against only toward the outermost skiffs. Obviously they feared she'd be killed. Screams of alarm and agony reached Dalia from the ships. Brune shook her again, and she felt the blade skimming her cheek. She froze, calming herself. Until acrid breeze-borne smoke billowed toward her from Roi Hradedh's ship. Brune muttered, "Ours are no ordinary fire-arrows. These are Kaphtor's incendiaries, which cannot be quenched until their fuel's spent. Those ships are lost."

Proof of his words spiraled upward in black flame-pierced columns from Father's ships, and Lord Kemuel's ship. Would they be sunk? Taken out in flames with the ships? "Father, retreat! Protect Benamir! Lord Kemuel, hurry to shore, I beg you!"

Perhaps later, they'd find another chance for escape.

As if realizing that the fires would quickly overwhelm and sink them, Kemuel and Father withdrew their ships. Dalia watched her father until his form vanished. Already the ships rode lower in the waters, and the flames burned brighter. Agonized screams lifted from the ships, and Dalia raised her bound hands to her face, shutting her eyes tight. Praying. Not bothering to sop her bloodied nose or to wipe her tears.

Brune sneered, "Who's that, so late to our party?"

Four small ships approached from the north, gliding straight toward the burning vessels, clearly intent upon rescuing crew members. Brune laughed as if watching some humorous play. Dalia sniffled at another trickle of blood and turned to glower at him. "Commander, I already want to kick you from here to the river's mouth. Don't make me wish worse."

Brune looked interested. "Is that all, lady?"

She refused to answer. Wisdom forbade mentioning her wish to gut him before kicking him away.

As his men pulled their skiff toward Arimna's docks, Commander Brune eyed her face. "Let's clean you up, and hope your nose isn't broken. Arimna's queen is odd over appearances."

"Is she?" Dalia sniffed, and rubbed her bloodied nose on her cloak. "Well, Arimna's queen might be odd over appearances, Commander, but I promise you, *Darzeq's* queen is not!"

Commander Brune laughed, then sobered and gave her a warning look. "If you wish to preserve your life for as long as possible, Lady, don't taunt *her* with your true status."

"You confess my rights as Darzeq's queen."

Brune leaned over and gripped her arm to drag her from the skiff. "Lady, you never heard a word from me."

Some details of palace life hadn't changed a whit. Timorous maidservants announced that Cthar wished to see Dalia promptly, but not before she was presentable, scrubbed and wearing proper ceremonial attire. If only food had been part of the schedule. As the young women rushed to comb and cleanse Dalia, a sad-eyed attendant placed fresh linens and two heaps of heavily embroidered and bejeweled robes and veils on a nearby table—in Queen Valsignae's colors. Were these some of Valsignae's stolen garments? Most likely.

Cthar wouldn't waste new items on Darzeq's renegade queen. Indeed, Cthar would find perverse pleasure in seeing Dalia wear the vanquished former queen's clothes. Yet here was reason to be thankful; just seeing the exquisite soft violet garments gave Dalia courage.

She'd speak for Valsignae and all of King Jonatan's family if given a quarter-chance. To the Infinite, she mouthed a silent plea, "Grant me calm. Clothe me in courage with these garments—you know how I loved their owner."

Cthar's maids braided a thin gold circlet into Dalia's hair—and then stitched the weighty veil in place. They checked her face, hands, and her gold-sandaled feet, straightened her robes one last time, and then led her outside to the lavish amethyst-paved and pillared corridor.

Brune waited beside the nearest pillar, somber-faced until he saw her. He straightened and bowed as a subject bows to a royal. Softly, Dalia warned, "Cthar might punish you for that bow, sir."

His dour expression returned. "Reflex, lady. I'm a citizen of Darzeq—not one of those mercenaries."

He seemed so proud of not being a mercenary. What did that matter? The outcome was the same; she was Cthar's prisoner. "Time to face the queen-mother. Lead on, Commander."

Matteo descended the slope, stumbling in the half-darkness as he watched the burning ships slide further into the Tinem North's waters. Here and there, beneath the water's surface, quench-resistant flames blazed through the liquid like an immortal dreki's eyes, described in the Books of the Infinite. Symbols of pride and glory gone down to darkness.

Had he lost his perfect Dalia? Were Kemuel and Lord Roi dead? If so, he wouldn't recover.

Behind Matteo, Corban exhaled, and Ghost huffed in the darkness. Farther down the slope, rustling sounded, lifting to Matteo, halting him in his tracks. Metal clinked, and was muted. Still farther down, shrubs quivered as if jostled or kicked. Matteo drew back, lifting a hand to alert Corban.

Had Cthar's men found them?

In answer, a hissing sound whisked past Matteo—air sliced by a javelin, which thudded into the ground just to Corban's right.

Clutching his crossbow, Matteo crouched and waved Corban back. The Siphran lord slapped at Ghost, sending the mighty beast into the woods to their west, and undoubtedly praying as the magnificent animal drew a volley of arrows in its wake. Hoof-beats fading, Ghost vanished amid the trees.

All his senses heightened, Matteo crept through the shrubs along the slope, following Corban. When the unforgiving light faded from the burning ships, they scurried upslope into a thicket of trees.

Stalked like prey.

Chapter 28

In Cthar's glorious golden chamber, a maidservant poked at a snapping, glowing fire, rustling the embers dryly. Dalia longed to curl up beside the hearth. She clenched her hands into fists beneath the ceremonial mantle and willed her shivering to cease.

Willed herself to eye Cthar, who waved out all the servants except Brune, who bowed. She smiled—a plaster-faced smile that didn't brighten her expression in the least. "Commander, thank you for bringing her here so promptly. Was she much trouble?"

"Somewhat, Majesty. She gave herself a bloody nose while trying to escape during the river crossing. Otherwise, no."

"Nevertheless," Cthar warned gently, approaching soft footed, "Keep her in hand now. If she takes even one step forward, kill her."

Dalia shrugged. "I'd rather step backward, Lady. Isn't that what a wise person does when approached by a venomous creature?"

"Mm." Cthar clicked her gold-shielded nails together as she neared. "You enjoyed writing that mediocre bit of poetry. I'm so glad. But be careful to not quote it in Arimna, Lady. I might yet cut off the hand that wrote it. You wouldn't need your hand anyway. You won't write anything else, ever, now that I've brought you here."

"I'm sure you're delighted to think so."

Cthar smiled, her golden eyes glittering—and sporting wrinkles that Dalia didn't remember. Her hands, too, looked older. Still elegant, but knotted, the bones showing visibly. And deep crescent lines framed her mouth, running down almost to her jawline, where the skin hung in tiny sags, tattling her true age. "Yes, I am delighted. You're bait to lure your husband, and you're Darzeq's gift to me, a living apology to dispense with as I please. The instant you set foot in Arimna tonight, I sent word to our beloved Lady Rhiysa, inviting her to join me. I'll give her this one chance to pledge her loyalty to me."

"I wish I could see her reaction," Dalia murmured, failing to sound pleasant. "I wonder how she'll respond to the woman who ordered her cherished cousins murdered along with their lady-mother. Our Queen Valsignae didn't deserve to die, nor did our King Jonatan."

Cthar's golden eyes widened within their black outlines, and her black-crescent eyebrows lifted high. "I did *not* kill my son."

Dalia read truth in her tone in her eyes. Cthar lifted her chin. "He died of internal injuries after a hunting accident in Port Bascin. My informants hid him at my bidding, then brought him here by night, packed up like freight from the river. But as soon as he was dead, Tarquin and the others *had* to die. They wanted to have me imprisoned or exiled, so I had no other option."

How logical she sounded. How convinced that she'd acted rightly. Dalia shook her head. "You could have returned to Kaphtor."

Cthar turned, glided back to her chair, and sat, elegantly, the shadows kinder to her face than the light. "Return to Kaphtor? I was sent here to serve my people by wielding power in Darzeq, and so I have. Return indeed! I'm no tame fool. I'm no Valsignae."

"Valsignae was loved throughout Darzeq."

"And I am not," Cthar countered, smooth-voiced. "Because foolish young women write malicious poems, while audacious young men and over-reaching priests believe I'm unfit to rule.

Yet I've ruled well, and will continue to do so—as I deal with my enemies. Really, that's all you need to know. I sent word to your mother today that her precious daughter will die in a few weeks, and that her power-hungry lord-husband is dead in the river."

"You don't know that!" How dare she taunt Mother! How dare she proclaim Father dead! It wasn't true. "You're—!" Dalia caught herself from stepping forward, just as Brune tugged sharply at the back of her mantle. Warning her.

Dalia landed her heels firmly in place and glowered at the she-scaln, who sat proudly in her chair, smiling. Cthar clicked her golden fingernails together delicately. "I'll tell you what I am. I'm bored with Tragobre's spoiled little heiress. Commander Brune, take her out. The servants will show you where she's to be kept—with everything befitting Darzeq's little queen. If you cherish your life, you'll guard her well. Go."

As an early spring gale bashed at Eshda's barred, tapestry-draped shutters, Anji re-read the courier bird's note. Trust Cthar to be so brazen!

My beloved and only granddaughter, know that Dalia of Tragobre has arrived safely in Arimna. To celebrate, I invite you to serve me during my dedication ceremony in six weeks. Attend and live.

Cthar of Kaphtor and Darzeq

Attend? As if she would. No, she'd remain, safely locked in Eshda, living on its stores until the war ended. Darzeq's future king and the future prophet would be protected. And loved, as they deserved. If Cthar triumphed and dared to execute Matteo and Dalia, then Anji, Darzeq's Lady Rhiysa, would lead the next revolt, with Ekiael beside her. Together, they would place Benamir on Darzeq's throne. They must.

To her husband, Anji pleaded in silence, *My beloved lord-husband, claim this victory! Live and thrive for the Infinite's sake.*

Anji studied the parchment again, pondered her options, then spat on Cthar's words. Taking a fresh piece of parchment, she pressed it over the offending note to absorb the moisture, carefully smearing all the edges. While her work dried, she helped Yiska bathe the boys, and she mentally composed her reply.

Cthar, I refuse your command as illegal. Who ordained that you should rule? Not One. Also, the parchment you hold was soaked with my spittle. No longer your granddaughter, Anji.

From the cover of evergreen brambles within the woods, Corban peered between the trees at the neglected field beyond. At Cthar's soldiers who were stabbing the moldering haystacks abandoned by some hapless landowner. Half-kneeling beside him, Matteo glowered through the snarled brambles at the men and tightened his grip upon his readied crossbow. Remarkably alert when they'd both been deprived of food and sleep for so long.

Several soldiers neared the far section of the field, and Corban held his breath. Why must Cthar's men be so efficient? Corban nudged himself backward from the brambles ... and startled a hedge-sparrow, which shot from the leafy brambles like an arrow, over the field.

The soldiers approached, and Corban formed a noiseless prayer. "Infinite, conceal us."

Beside him, Matteo waited—until the soldier saw them and bellowed, "Here! Commander, they're here!"

All three soldiers charged the hedge, javelins and pikes set to skewer Corban and Matteo like speared fish. Matteo squeezed the crossbow's release lever and took down the first, and then dashed from the hedge. Corban pierced the second man, who collapsed writhing onto the briars. The third man roared a battle cry and flung a javelin, which tore into the shoulder of Corban's boiled leather vest and knocked him flat. Fiery pain streaked down his left shoulder, and as Matteo rushed to help him up, Corban's hand went numb.

In a frenzy to reach them, the third soldier wielded sword and shield to hack aside the brambles and press them down. Right-handed, Corban snarled and wrested the javelin from his vest. Fresh agony sliced from his left shoulder down his arm, and his own blood dripped from the javelin's razor-sharp point. Shielding his wound, Corban spun the javelin about and flung it at the third soldier, who fell back into the field.

Matteo seized Corban's uninjured arm and yanked him away.

Blood slid down Corban's side as he ran. Pain blurred his vision as he prayed. *Infinite, Mighty One ... send me Your strength! Save us.*

Mist descended in a sheltering haze as they stumbled into a decrepit clutch of farm buildings. Matteo cast a backward glance at Corban, who'd said nothing since the attack. The Siphran lord was lagging, his gaze vacant to their danger, instead turning inward to his own thoughts.

He'd tucked his arm within his leather baldric, using the heavy strap as a sling. Matteo hissed, "Sir, you should have said something! Your wound's worse than I thought."

Corban met his gaze, reassuringly acute. "It's no matter. I'll tend it when we're safe."

Matteo looked around at the sagging buildings. Sodden, icy leaves heaped against doorways. Moss and lichen frozen in ragged green-and-gray-patched blankets over the slumped roofs. Abandoned buildings would be perfect. If...

He listened hard, hearing only his own breath, until Corban said, "I've heard nothing for some time—and it's not because I'm old and deaf."

Matteo shouldered his crossbow and then grabbed Corban's free arm. "When you of all people start to make feeble jokes, then I'm worried. We need to rest and bind your wound. I think we might risk sleeping here for tonight—in one of the central buildings, if we can cover our tracks."

A childhood filled with forest chases and creating impromptu camps served him well. He'd learned from his brothers how to cover his tracks. How to build fires. How not to vomit while eating fried grubs on a dare. He could do this. He chose a smaller building and shoved the door inward. It gave just enough room to let them squeeze inside. Matteo double-checked the mat of leaves outside, covered a muddied boot-print, and then shut the door. Inside, pallid hints of light slipped through breaks in two of the walls and a hole in the roof, promising a cold night. Matteo coerced Corban to sit down. "Rest, and don't argue. Since a fog's descending, I'm going to risk a fire. A small one."

Blessing the Infinite for giving him a father and brothers who loved to hunt and camp, he prowled through the hut and found old pine cones, bark, slivers of various types of wood and a heap of chips. Had this been a wood-working shelter? He found a small central hearth and propped the cones, chips, and small slivers of wood within it, then tucked fistfuls of ancient straw into the gaps. Small clumps of wood fungus shadowed the pale bark. Matteo pried them off with his dagger, set them on a solid piece of old wood, and then fished his flint and iron kit from his hunting pouch.

Corban sucked in an audible breath, slid his wounded arm from the baldric, and began to clumsily unbuckle his vest.

Matteo concentrated, landing sparks on the dark fungus, blowing them to glowing life on the rough-dark clump of rot. He wedged the smoldering fungus into an open pine cone, and then blew at the ember until he was half-sick, coaxing the flames to build over the cone. Satisfied, he nested the blazing cone within the straw, flanked it with other cones, set the tinder, and then turned to Corban.

An ugly gash had lifted a wedge of flesh from Corban's shoulder, exposing torn muscle. Drying blood stained Corban's shirt, turning the white linen crimson with brown at the edges. Corban shivered, but spoke calmly enough. "I need to rest, and my left hand's still numb, but I'll live."

"Unless that becomes infected." Matteo cut a strip from the hem of Corban's ruined shirt and fashioned a clumsy bandage.

Corban held his hands near the fire, chafing the left one fiercely. "We won't discuss that until we've reached safety." Lowering his voice, he admitted, "I'm shocked that I'm wounded."

Uneasiness gnawed into Matteo's thoughts. Corban, a hitherto unconquerable fighter, had suffered a wound, which was disturbing enough—the Infinite had ever shown favor toward Corban. Until now. What if he was crippled? What if he, Matteo, couldn't help his friend?

Mighty One ... am I judged? Have You found me lacking?

It must be true. Within a few hours, he'd seen his dearest friend, his wife, stolen away—perhaps to die—his father-in-law and one of his staunchest allies sunk in burning wrecks in the river while he was cut off from reaching them or rejoining his men, and now his most fearsome fighter wounded, perhaps taken from future battles. Perhaps even taken from life.

Had he, Matteo of Darzeq, lost almost everyone he loved and his country's future by his own failures? He bound Corban's wound, offered him his waterskin, and then covered his friend with his own cloak. While Corban rested, Matteo stared into the small fire, seeing desolation amid the ashes.

The beasts emerged from a green-black sea, immortal giants, their colors garish beneath sullen storm clouds lit by lightning. A golden-winged aeryon, a crimson-hued scaln, a black lindorm, and a crested blue dreki, all arrayed against Araine as an undying army—until the scaln raked the wings from the aeryon, then turned upon it. The lindorm joined the feast, but the scaln savaged the giant serpent, tearing it to bloody shreds. Yet the scaln finally weakened as the dreki grew, its darkening claws becoming mighty talons, its teeth like rows of merciless blue azurnite blades, glinting as the beast turned its bloodied gaze toward Araine and the souls sheltered within her care.

Araine leaned against her desk and covered her face with her hands, drawing in deep breaths of warm, gently humid springtime air. Infinite, bless You! Let me ever serve You. But what does this dream mean?

The vision faded, and unbidden unwelcome memories opened within her thoughts. So real that she sprawled, almost feeling her father tightening the ligature around her throat as he wept. She fought to breathe—fought to save the Books of the Infinite from destruction. "Infinite, no!" Hands tightened around her shoulders and she struggled against her noble accuser, Corban Thaenfall. Betrayer! Murderer... "Infinite!"

"Araine!" Nikaros, her husband, held her. But his embrace was too similar to Corban's possessive grasp. Araine flung off his arm and sat up straight.

"Infinite, why am I reliving this again?"

Nikaros leaned over Araine and rubbed her back gently as if she were a frightened child. His handsome face tensed with worry. "Araine, what's wrong?"

"I'm unsure." She stared into her waking vision as it shifted, revealing death. Innocent victims in Darzeq—a massacre she'd predicted last year, to the disbelief of a Darzeq prince. For his skepticism, the royal family of Darzeq was all but destroyed.

Araine put a hand to her throat, trying to breathe without weeping. Why was she seeing this carnage again? "Infinite...? How is Corban involved with the massacre?"

Hearing His answer, Araine leaned into her husband's arms and wept. As he smoothed her hair and held her, she pleaded, "Pray for me! The Infinite commands me to speak to Corban once more."

His voice tight with protective disapproval, Nikaros said, "I'll go with you. When?"

"I don't know." Never, she hoped. A futile wish indeed. And ... she must go alone.

Chapter 29

Hunger growled Corban to consciousness. To the smoldering fire and an instant of peace. Opposite the small hearth, Matteo slumbered, though one hand rested on his crossbow as if to use it at the first hint of trouble. "Just don't shoot me," Corban muttered.

He rubbed his eyes and then his still-numbed hand. If a full night's sleep hadn't restored him, then he must count himself as a doomed fighter. It was, after all, no more than he deserved. His failings presented themselves, alive in his mind as he'd first lived them.

Insolence and arrogance toward authority. Resentment against his lord-father. Licentious self-indulgences that he'd never regarded with remorse until this past year. Above all, his loathsome fury and destructive behavior toward Araine and her grandfather for believing that she'd betrayed him—which she hadn't. He saw the truth.

He deserved no mercy from the Infinite, even if the Infinite had forgiven him. A price must be paid for his crimes.

Matteo stirred, lifted his hand from the crossbow, and then stretched. He sat up, eying Corban. "You look a shade or two better. We need to find food. How's your hand?"

"Still numb. However, it's not my sword hand, so I stand at least half a chance in battle."

"We'll find a doctor," Matteo pledged. He stood. "You were injured because of me; I won't rest until I see that you're cured."

"If a cure isn't forthcoming, then we must accept it," Corban countered.

"Speaking of cures, how is the wound? Infected?"

Corban lifted away his clothing, and then peeled back the layered makeshift bandage. Surprisingly, the flesh wasn't festering, yet it ached, and movement brought searing pain. Nevertheless, he hauled himself to his feet and returned Matteo's cloak to him. "I'll be fine. Here. You'll need this. The question is, where should we go? To the river, or Port Bascin?"

Gloom crossed the king's face, and he let the cloak drop. "Whichever way I chose, it'll be a question of survival. Your wound might not be festering, yet you're still weakened, and I don't want to risk your life in a skirmish. We ought to stay here until nightfall, when darkness will cover our retreat."

Stay in this drafty wooden hut and starve until dusk? No. Corban donned his own cloak, then drew his sword. "I can fight, Sire."

Matteo shook his head, obviously resolute. "No, we'll stay here 'til dark."

A breath of air gusted into the aged hut. With a flash of light that revealed a young woman as perfect as the Lady Dalia, but with gold-streaked hair and clear blue eyes. In her hands a slender staff glowed with ethereal light.

How...? She'd appeared from nowhere, without opening the door. Just *there....* Corban blinked, but the young woman didn't vanish. Instead, she glanced up at Matteo, then at him, seeming as startled as they were.

Araine? Corban flinched and stepped backward aligning his drawn sword against his face in a non-combative stance, his shock warring with wonderment.

Araine, lovely as ever, caught her breath visibly when she saw him. Her eyes widened and she clutched the light-formed staff closer, as if it could protect her. "Corban."

Infinite... He'd forgotten how truly lovely she was. And how brave. Despite her visible fear, she didn't retreat. She held her ground, valiant and stunning. He'd been such a fool. He'd never deserved her. If this was Araine. Corban shook his head. "This cannot be true! Araine?"

She swallowed and straightened slightly, bracing herself for battle. In her hand, the branch shimmered, and she pleaded, obviously praying aloud, "Infinite, where am I?" Within the same breath, her eyes flickered, and her gaze became absorbed as if listening to someone else. She glanced from him to Matteo. "Your Creator sees you both. Do not think you are forgotten."

Matteo glared, as if certain that Araine was taunting him. "What are we to think? All hope's gone! Who are you, and how did you get in here?"

Corban cut in, more wary. And skeptical. "Araine, are you actually alive, or a specter sent to haunt me for my failures?" If this truly was Araine.... How could he look her in the eyes without shame? Yet, he had to know...

Araine looked him in the eyes, equally mistrustful. "I'm alive, sir. Not some specter."

If she was real... Corban stepped toward Araine. She slammed the staff between them, its base thudding on the dirt floor. "Stop! I've been brought here by the Infinite, but you will not touch me!"

Was she still ruled by her fear of him? Corban knelt and placed his sword before the glowing staff—a gesture of surrender, of humility. He must reassure her ... beg her.... "Forgive me! Araine, I promise you, I've thought of you every day since your disappearance from ToronSea. Wherever I've been since that night, I've remembered you! And your grandfather..."

Araine whispered, "I can't discuss him." Tears brimmed in her lovely eyes. "Instead ... the Infinite sent me to speak to you both. I am His prophet to Belaal."

His prophet. Corban lurched backward, trying to absorb the implications of her status. Rumors were one thing, but to hear her say the words.... "It's true?"

Matteo leaned into the conversation, almost accusatory. "*You!* You're the prophet who warned Sheth of the murders!"

"Yes. If he'd listened, he would be alive, and Darzeq would be at peace. As for you..." Araine studied Darzeq's uncrowned king as if seeing his very soul. "Matteo of Darzeq, why are you hiding?"

Matteo gawked, and then shook his head. "Why do you ask, Prophet? Undoubtedly you know—just as you foretold Sheth's fate. We've lost! My wife..."

Araine frowned, and her delicate voice carried a gentle rebuke. "Did you ask your Creator?"

She sounded so authoritative. So different. As Corban studied her anew, Matteo pleaded—fresh hope revitalizing his face. "Does *He* dispute what's happened? Dare we hope for victory if we attempt an attack?"

"The Infinite hears your prayers, which is why I've been brought here to warn you. Now, obey Him. Leave this place and fight or you'll be captured, both of you." She looked at Corban again, still wary, yet impressively commanding. Not the gentle little Araine he'd remembered. "And you, Corban Thaenfall, the Infinite sees your heart. Do what you know you must, and bow as His servant."

He stared at her, unable to move. Who was this young woman, really? And yet, he had to know, *had* to ask, "Will you forgive me? Araine, please!"

She swallowed and hesitated, as if debating. He couldn't blame her; she had much to forgive. At last, she nodded. "I ... do forgive you. But you must go, *now*. Both of you. Escape and fight!"

His impulse exactly—thank You, One-Who-Sees! As Corban stood to obey their Creator's command, another current of air stirred within the hut. Delicate wisps of light hair drifted and played over Araine's exquisite face. She bowed her head toward Corban. Even as she vanished within a breath, Araine added, "Seek peace, my lord."

The air in the hut became lackluster. Enfeebled and intolerable without her presence. Or was it the Infinite's presence?

Matteo slung his shoulder over his cloak. "Let's go. I cannot believe you're actually *acquainted* with her."

Corban affected a sneer and bent to smother the hearth with dirt. "This from Darzeq's king. Who would guess that I'd ever be an acquaintance of yours? Yes, although I never deserved Araine. At first, she was another lovely name on my list of bad intentions. But I made the mistake of living with her family for a few weeks, and I fell in love with her sweet spirit as much as her beautiful form. I couldn't admit the truth to myself. Particularly not when I believed she'd betrayed me by abandoning Atea—our goddess of mutual worship—to follow the Infinite."

Stamping out the final embers, Matteo threw him a blaming look, clearly taking Araine's side. "How is her trust in the Infinite such a betrayal?"

"She had the gall to write the Infinite's verses to me, when my lord-father had recently died while fighting against Him."

"So you were grieving and regarded the Infinite as your enemy." Matteo headed for the door. "Whatever you did, she's still afraid of you, and I don't want to know why."

Good. Because right then, telling Matteo the full story would be intolerable.

They fled through the morning mist, spurred on by Araine's warning. As they entered the sheltering woods, Matteo nodded toward the west. "Port Bascin, though we'll watch the river along the way. Perhaps we'll meet up with the others."

Guided by the sunlight breaking through the canopied trees, they made their way to the river. Until a warning clink of metal halted him in his tracks.

Within a breath, a gold-wool-cloaked soldier stepped into Matteo's path. Matteo lifted his sword, ready, but the soldier looked him in the eyes and nodded toward the south. "Move on, Sire, but be chary. Soon, others will search along here, and they mightn't be as friendly. By the way..." The soldier grinned. "I've served the Lady Cthar's household for a year now, therefore I say, 'Long live your queen!' She's finer than a thousand Cthars."

He nodded at Corban, then hurried toward a fresh clamor of weaponry and voices in the distance.

The man had met Dalia? And she'd won his loyalty. Let her win over Cthar's entire army! Matteo fought a short laugh and hurried on.

As they wove their way onward, Matteo frowned at Corban, who'd again resorted to using the baldric to support his wounded left hand. He muttered, "Can you endure a prolonged trek?"

Corban nodded and fixed his gaze south. Toward the Tinem North, and Port Bascin.

Within the trees above the northern river road, Corban braced his feet against the slope, and paused. His shoulder ached and sent stinging whips of pain down his arm as he eased his wrist from the sling and flexed his numbed hand. At least his fingers still moved at his bidding, but they remained numbed and unsure.

Ahead of him, within the tree line above the river, Matteo stopped and waited, eager to continue their journey, yet unwilling to proceed without him. Low-voiced, he asked Corban, "What do you think of eating raw grubs."

"I'll starve, thank you, Sire."

"I thought so. However, I'm almost hungry enough to risk swallowing the creatures whole." He nodded toward Corban's arm. "Is it worse?"

"The same." And talking wouldn't restore his hand. Corban rested his wrist within the baldric again, prepared to march onward.

But Matteo propped himself against a tree and rested, staring down at the river, then along the road. Corban resisted the temptation to sit on the slope; he might be too tired to drag himself upright again. Moreover, if he sat down, he'd remember Araine again, and he couldn't withstand his thoughts yet. As they watched, two small ships appeared in the east on the Tinem North, their white sails full-rounded by the breeze. At last, Matteo shook his head. "If you're ready, let's move along. At this pace, we'll reach Port Bascin in two days."

Corban groused, "By then I'd be willing to consider the grubs."

"Wonder how they'd taste roasted."

They continued on, threading their way through the tree line until approaching hoof beats warned them to hide. Corban ducked inside an overgrown thicket of drooping tree branches and evergreen gorse bushes. Matteo burrowed beside him, then cautiously parted the spikey tangle of gorse and branches.

A group of riders cantered toward them from the east, a rag-tag procession—the men looking over their shoulders too often to be unconcerned travelers. What were they watching? Were riders following them?

Matteo checked his crossbow. "If we're caught, are you certain you're prepared to fight?"

"Always, Sire."

"Good. Give me your crossbow."

Matteo pulled back the bowstrings of each crossbow, set the bolts, and then returned Corban's weapon. They descended the slope, and approached the road, then crouched within a dense stand of grasses. Corban studied the riders as they approached. Matteo huffed out a relieved breath. "There's Thaddeus!"

They charged from the thicket, through a snow-edged ditch, and then on to the river road. Matteo stood in the road's center and raised a hand to halt Thaddeus and his men.

Thaddeus drew his horse to such a sharp halt that the beast reared and threw the other horses into confusion. Several of the men saw Corban and Matteo and whooped. Thaddeus warned, "Sire! No time—we're being pursued. Though now we'd best fight here. Losbreq's on the river!" To the others, he ordered, "Thaenfall's here! Turn and attack! Roar for all you're worth!"

Corban ground his teeth. His name was cried up for battle before these men knew he'd been crippled. "Infinite, help us!"

Matteo ran along the road and yelled, "Those who've crossbows, use them!"

Several men drew back their crossbow strings, lifted the weapons, and set the bolts. Their pursuers were within range. Corban hurried to stand beside Matteo. Willing his numbed fingers to work, he propped the crossbow with his left hand and aimed at the approaching yellow cloaks. Holding his breath, he pressed the release with his right hand.

One of Cthar's men cried out and fell. Behind him, evidently hit by Matteo, another man threw his hands in the air, dropping a short sword. Another fell, hit by one of Thaddeus's men. Cthar's troops halted in brief confusion as Thaddeus and his men attacked, screaming harsh war cries.

Unable to reload, Corban dropped his crossbow and drew his sword, praying as he ran. "Blessed be You, Mighty One! Help us now!"

Time blurred and his targets slowed, seeming confounded by the sudden onslaught. Hunger and fatigue fled as Corban screamed, "Thaenfall!" He cut the first man from his saddle, then flung him bodily into the ditch. The next soldier seemed incapable of anything but a slack-jawed look of shock. Corban bashed him to the ground flat-sworded and finished him with one swift stroke.

Within mere breaths, the clash ended. The surviving yellow cloaks fled—four in all, escaping while they had breath. Thaddeus whooped, flung himself off his horse, and charged Matteo. "Sire! You're alive! Infinite, thank You! We'd lost hope—I was near to giving myself up as gallow's food!"

He nearly bruised Matteo with a triumphant hug, and then knelt in the muddied road offering him a proper bow. "Sire, with your permission, let's take you safely to Port Bascin. But first—I'll show you why we feared you'd died."

He stood and forged into the tumult of wearied, elated men and reemerged leading a tangle-maned, disgruntled gray. Matteo exhaled as at least one regret unwound itself from his knotted stomach, and Corban rushed past him to greet Ghost.

Dalia risked a spoonful of thick steaming bread soup, then set down her spoon to evaluate. No, her throat wasn't closing off, her mouth wasn't burning, she wasn't drooling or vomiting uncontrollably, nor did she need a privy pot. Her stomach wasn't the least affected, and she sensed no odd fatigue, dizziness, or agitation that might indicate she'd been poisoned—if she believed Kiyrem's medical texts.

Evidently Cthar's orders included fattening up Dalia lest Darzeq criticize her for starving Matteo of Arimna's wife. Matteo. Dalia's heart squeezed as she thought of her husband, his dazzling eyes, his beautiful smile, and the way he gazed at her when they were alone together, as if she were the most incredible sight in all the world. Which exactly mirrored her expression whenever she gazed at him.

In her thoughts, Dalia implored her husband. Attack Cthar. Wipe out her mercenaries, and command this palace! And ... find Father and Lord Kemuel, alive, please.

Meanwhile, she'd decide how best to serve the king from within Arimna. From the confines of this tiny cell-like room. A room with no windows, and no hidden passages that she knew of—though she would check for those later. In Arimna's palace, secret rooms must be expected in odd places, even in what she could only presume was a gloomy office, or a trusted servant's sleeping area.

At least there was a fire in the small stone-wall hearth. However ... Dalia slid a glance over her shoulder toward two women standing behind her like glowering figureheads from Kaphtor. The forbidding pair kept watch over her while she ate—ready to challenge her every unexpected move. Sadly, there'd be no unexpected moves this night. She would lull everyone into absolute complacency by pretending mind-numbed dullness.

Dalia finished eating and then rested her folded hands in front of Matteo's unborn baby. Precious little one, already embarking on adventures with such an unfortunate mother.

As soon as the servants let down their guard, she'd create havoc to help Matteo.

Chapter 30

Followed by Corban riding Ghost, Matteo spurred Goldensleeve's glistening two-year-old sorrel along Port Bascin's stone pier, praying as he eyed his destination. Losbreq's ships rested uneasily at the end of the pier, just anchored with most unwelcome news and grievous cargo. A funeral... The grandest Port Bascin could muster under such short notice.

Already, six of Losbreq's men were carrying the purple-draped litter down the ramp from the ship to Thaddeus, who'd reached the ship first. Matteo dismounted and met them with a salute. The men placed the litter on the stones, allowing Matteo room.

One-Who-Sees, give me strength. He reverently lifted the heavy purple pall and gritted his teeth. Kemuel's scorched and bruised features were tensed as a man caught in a bad dream—never the way he'd appeared in life. A living link to his lord-father ... gone. And Matteo of Darzeq was to blame.

Matteo honored his doughty ally by committing his battle-scarred face to memory, and he gripped Kemuel's death-bound hands. "Thank you, my friend!"

Corban knelt beside Matteo and sighed. "Here's a day I never wanted to see—and a man I was honored to know is gone." Because of him.

He covered Lord Kemuel slowly, reverently, managing the heavy fabric well, despite his still-numbed hand.

Furious tears blinded Matteo's gaze as he stood. This should never have happened. Cthar must be repaid! She should have been banished years ago—as Tarquin insisted—returned ingloriously to Kaphtor. So many deaths would have been avoided. But Jonatan of Arimna felt duty-bound to honor Cthar as his mother.

By then, Losbreq and Tragobre had descended the stairs, Tragobre limping and raw-skinned, looking nearly drowned with grief and fury. He bowed to Matteo, then stood, his squared face working with emotion. "Sire, we're blessed that you're alive. Help me to save my daughter from that woman!"

That woman. Exactly what Aunt Pinny had always called Cthar. Matteo nodded. When he could speak, he rasped, "If it costs me my life, I'll save her and the baby! Come on—" He greeted Losbreq with a nod and a fierce one-armed hug. "My lord, thank you! I wish you could have found both alive, but at least the queen and I've been spared mourning for her lord-father."

"Sire..." Losbreq's lean, wary features twisted, revealing deepest guilt. "If only I'd been able to arrive sooner and save her as well!"

"You tried," Matteo reminded him. "You saved Lord Tragobre, and we'll give thanks for that. Now, let's set aside what might have been. Kemuel deserves every honor we can grant him, and then we've an invasion to plan. Ekiael has sent word that he and his army are on their way from Port Zamaj. Let's be ready when they arrive."

Losbreq nodded, but Matteo caught his uncertainty, which magnified visibly as he watched Corban rest his injured hand within his baldric again. No one had spoken the prevalent fear, but Matteo understood it all too well.

Lord Corban of Siphra was most likely permanently injured, which proved he was as mortal as any man drawing breath.

Cthar would rejoice when she heard. Worse, her mercenary assassins would take courage and stalk Corban, stalk all of them, bent on slaughter. Perhaps he'd be wise to follow Anji's lead from Eshda, and lock himself and his men safely away until his army was fully gathered.

Slouched near the hearth in the main hall of the Port Bascin fortress, Corban flexed his numb fingers, willing them to retain sensation and strength. He was sick to death of the king's concern, his physician's uncertainty—and of reading misgivings into others' kind words and sidelong glances.

Yes, he comprehended their worries. His wound and continued weakness proved that his brief stint of glory as the king's unofficial champion was ended. He was forsaken by the Mighty One.

Was it true? Should he leave Darzeq? His share of the spoils from Kaphtor's merchant ships were locked in his chamber to be used as he pleased. Belaal, however, was out of the question. Moreover, he couldn't leave Darzeq until the Lady Dalia was freed. He'd be forever haunted if he abandoned Matteo and the young couple died.

Honor. Corban scowled inwardly. How base of him to even consider leaving until matters here were settled.

Thaddeus Ormr raced into the great hall, wild as a schoolboy released from his master's rule. Corban flung him a sour look. "What's afflicted you?"

"No affliction, my lord." Thaddeus halted and waved a parchment at him. "Good news! I've word from my lord-father. Belaal's prophet convinced him to join our cause—he's ordered troops to follow me while he's detained in Belaal."

His lord-father was acquainted with Araine? Corban straightened and stared. Thaddeus laughed. "I've your serious consideration now, don't I? Here's proof." He handed Corban a fold of parchment that contained a smaller slightly curled strip of parchment—a courier bird's note.

Thaddeus, as warned by the Prophet Araine of Belaal, I give you charge of all of Iydan's available fighting men. Lead them in defense of the king. Magni Ormr, Iydan. Written in Belaal.

The larger note was also to Thaddeus, written in the delicate style affected by many noblewomen.

Thaddeus, my beloved son, you will excuse me for opening this script from your lord-father, because I am even now sending out word to every hide of land granted to Iydan since our family first claimed royal honors in Darzeq. I bid you wait patiently in Port Bascin, for Iydan's men will arrive there, each from his own holding to fulfill service owed to your lord-father. With this happy news, I also send your full allowance for this past winter—forbidden until now at your lord-father's command. I implore you to be wise and frugal and cause no...

Corban handed the full page of maternal admonishments to Thaddeus. "Good news indeed. Listen to your mother, by the way, and be glad she's scolding you."

Corban's mother had been too busy struggling to cope with Corban's lord-father to be concerned with errant children.

Thaddeus shrugged. "My mother worries about everything. If Belaal's prophet were here, I'd kiss her, and gladly! I've heard that she's lovely."

"She is, and you won't kiss her. Furthermore, if you're wise, you'll never speak of her again so casually. I considered marrying her while I was yet in Siphra."

Before he'd tried to kill her.

Thaddeus practically stuttered. "Y-you? Marry her?"

Unwilling to speak of Araine—his life's greatest loss—Corban stood and stalked from Port Bascin's great hall.

At least she'd forgiven him. He must learn to be content with the dregs of his life.

In the seclusion of the royal apartments, Matteo skimmed the courier note and Lady Iydan's message, then handed them back to the elated Thaddeus. "This would be good news if we could afford a delay, but we can't. Not while Cthar holds my wife."

"Sire," Thaddeus protested, "Isn't it better to wait and be certain of a full army and victory than another chance battle that might cost us your life, and hers?"

Yes. But would Dalia survive in Cthar's custody for another month? He needed spies! If only he could reverse time and return to Arimna, three years past. None of this would have happened. He shook his head at Thaddeus. "How I wish my brother Sheth had obeyed the prophet as your lord-father obeyed her. My brothers and mother would still be alive." Perhaps Father as well. Yet, after weeks of scouring, he'd found no evidence that Cthar had murdered her only surviving child.

Might Cthar have actually honored the parent-child tie?

Pulling himself from brooding, Matteo nodded to Thaddeus. "Thank you for telling me. You're right; we should be patient and gather our forces. Now, back to work. If we're to wait and plan a successful invasion, we need informants from inside Arimna—preferably the palace itself."

Thaddeus scrolled the notes together and tucked them into his money pouch. "Perhaps my lady-mother can petition her contacts in Arimna for news. Does Port Bascin have any courier birds that home-roost in Arimna?"

"No. The last were sent off when we captured Port Bascin."

"I'll send our request and thanks now, Sire." Thaddeus bowed, clearly prepared to take leave. But then he paused. "Lord Corban's in a dark mood. Did you know that, years ago, he wanted to marry Belaal's prophet?"

The prophet's beautiful, wary face appeared in Matteo's thoughts. Fearful, though Lord Corban bowed and repented before her. "He never said so, but I know that he loved her.

Loves her still. Be wary of taunting Lord Corban, Thaddeus. He's wounded, it's true, but he's not vanquished."

Not yet, Matteo hoped.

A fanfare of trumpets from the gatehouse announced welcome visitors. Who? Perhaps another prospective ally.

Matteo motioned to Thaddeus, and they hurried out to greet their visitors.

Corban almost grinned as Ekiael dismounted in the fort's central yard. Ekiael's eyes gleamed—a scoundrel plotting mischief. He slung a heavy leather knapsack over his shoulder and approached Corban, bellowing for the entire city to hear, "There you are, Siphran! What is the latest? I see your hand remains stubbornly affixed to your wrist. Clearly you're not rotten enough that it should fall off!"

Was that a joke? Before Corban could answer with a churlish snarl, Ekiael pounded Corban's good shoulder cheerily, and then nodded him toward the keep. "After you! Valor must be honored."

"You find manners just when I've decided to hammer you flat with my one good fist," Corban groused.

"This is what I like about you, Siphran. You're not intimidated by my sacred rank—though you should be."

"I am intimidated," Corban admitted. "I was prepared to die the instant I bashed you."

Darzeq's high priest laughed. "I thought you had more brains than that. I'm disappointed."

"Now you've learned the truth, lord-high priest."

"No, tell me the actual truth. What are your thoughts concerning life?"

The truth? "I'm feeling trapped and trampled—cast into a refuse heap."

"Well, then you are mortal indeed, and you may grumble and snarl all you please and I'll listen."

"There's nothing else to say."

Matteo and Thaddeus emerged from the great doors just as Corban started to the steps. Ekiael greeted the king more solemnly. "I've received word from my beloved wife that she's locked herself in Eshda with the boys, and she intends to conquer Arimna herself if we fail. May the Infinite save us all!"

Matteo grimaced as they climbed the broad stone steps. "If Anji is forced to attack Arimna, we'll certainly be dead beforehand. Tell me that you have good news."

Darzeq's high priest actually lowered his voice to something near a whisper. "I pray you think my news is good. Our invasion of Arimna has begun. One soul at a time, slipping through its gates and ports to reclaim the chambers beneath the Infinite's House. From there, we'll branch out into the city to await our king."

Priests as shadow warriors, infiltrating Arimna. Corban cut a look at Ekiael. "I wish I were among them now."

"But you're here," Ekiael pointed out. "Therefore, from this place you serve Him."

Aware of Matteo and Thaddeus, both looking away, Corban lifted his deadened hand. "How can *this* serve Him?"

"It will serve Him when you give Him leave to use your misery and weakness for His work—His glory. This decision is yours, Lord Corban. Do you trust Him? Are you His servant?"

If only he could hate Ekiael for those sharp words. But it was impossible to hate Ekiael. "Then He hasn't forsaken me?"

"Why should He? He's worked to bring you here, my lord, therefore He will finish what He's planned. Just because that plan isn't what *you* imagined, doesn't mean it's canceled." Changing the subject, Corban asked what the king was undoubtedly wondering. "Do your shadow-priests plan to free the queen from Cthar's hold?"

"If there's the least chance without risking her life, yes. Until then, we plan and pray. Which reminds me—" Ekiael tilted his head toward his knapsack. "I've some more writings for your studies, and we've other details to discuss regarding the king's formal investiture."

"What formal investiture?" Matteo leaned into their conversation, his eyebrows almost meeting together in a frown. "About all these plans you've made regarding my wife and me ... I would have liked to be included."

"You know as much as you've needed to know, Sire. Until now. Feed me, and we'll talk."

Dalia woke from her nap, wearing gloom like a cloak. Another day faced with her three unhappy, unspeaking attendants. No wonder she'd been sleeping almost since her arrival in Arimna Palace. Opening her eyes proved too unbearable. If she remained asleep, she'd see Matteo's handsome face, Ben's sweetly dimpled baby grin, and she'd hear Anji's gentle voice. Truly, she could live in her dreams.

A rasping at the door snapped Dalia awake. Brune muttered fierce words as he worked the lock and then opened the door. His words as roughened as the lock, Brune snapped at someone in the hall. "Hurry, you!"

A servant scurried inside, not looking at Dalia, his arms full of kindling and split wood. His face, though averted, arrested Dalia's attention at once. Matteo's childhood servant, Abiah. Did he remember her? Was it safe to talk to him? She sat up. Abiah flicked a glance her way and then prodded the sullen ash-dusted coals to life in the hearth. He worked efficiently, as if he'd always been a fire-setter, not the highest-ranked servitor to a prince. She'd at least risk courtesy, and allow him to see that she recognized him. "Thank you."

Abiah nodded and turned just long enough for her smile, but then he scurried out. He'd recognize her, no doubt. Was he well? Beaten, or...?

Brune scowled at Dalia. "The queen requires your presence soon, so make ready."

"Commander Brune, I am Darzeq's queen."

"Tell *her* so and she'll have me carve out your tongue. Hurry, now. First, eat."

Eat?

Another servant marched inside, thunked down a wooden tray, and then vanished as Dalia's two gloomy attendants stood to keep watch over her every move.

As if she could incite a revolution with a wooden bowl of bread-soup and a spoon.

Could she?

And why had Cthar summoned her?

Dalia scowled. Perhaps she ought to keep the spoon and sharpen it for a blade. Just before she crowned Cthar with a dish of cold bread soup.

Chapter 31

Schooling mutiny from her face, Dalia sat in her designated chair in the formal writing room adjoining the royal apartments and arranged her heavy blue courtly robes. How many times had she and Anji written notes at this very table, laughing and whispering to each other as they wrote? Only to be shushed by dear Valsignae from a nearby table, or by King Jonatan, who often worked in his adjoining chamber and loved his quiet.

Sweet, cranky King Jonatan. And Anji...

The door swung open and Cthar entered, her layered white gown showing in fragile contrast to a heavily embroidered crimson mantle held in elaborate folds by two bejeweled clasps at her shoulders. Her golden eyes were rimmed with stark black paint, and her lips and cheeks flaunted crimson to match her cloak. She lifted one stark eyebrow at Dalia and muttered, "Have your gown exchanged—I'll not endure thrice-worn rags. Now, however, you will write to your lord-father—"

"He's alive?" Dalia looked Cthar straight in the eyes, mutiny and thrice-worn indignities forgotten. "My lord-father's alive!"

Cthar narrowed her golden gaze, resentment tightening her regal face. "Yes. Do not interrupt, Dalia of Tragobre, or I'll have you whipped like the schoolgirl you should still be. Command your lord-father to cease gathering his militia, or I'll be forced to deal with Tragobre again—with Kaphtor's weapons this time, not merely with a show of force."

"Kaphtor's incendiaries?" Dalia shifted her gaze to the polished amethyst-stone tabletop, fighting down memories of the unquenchable arrows setting Tragobre's ships ablaze.

Cthar seated herself stiffly opposite Dalia, her words clipped—every syllable edged with loathing. "The details needn't concern you. Just warn your lord-father that I've an entire arsenal of incendiaries and I won't hesitate to use them on Tragobre's great hall, once I'm certain your parents are inside."

One-Who-Sees, is it wrong to hate someone so much? Dalia lifted a silver stylus, touched it into an inkwell, and then glided the first word onto the paper. *Dalia, Queen of Darzeq to her beloved parents and Tragobre. Greetings....*

Cthar snatched the parchment from beneath Dalia's hands. "You'll write what you are. 'Dalia of Tragobre, to her parents. Greetings.'"

"I am a married woman," Dalia reminded her. "I will use the title my lord-husband and king bestowed upon me."

"He's a traitor and your marriage is illegal. You'll use no title at all."

Dalia folded her hands in her lap. Could the baby feel her inward tremors? Cthar's eyes fixated upon her, scaln-like. Even to the blood-shot veins lacing themselves about her golden irises. Dalia met her gaze with Hradedh dignity. "My marriage to your only surviving grandson was witnessed by the Autumn Forum and blessed by the Infinite through Darzeq's high priest! Furthermore, my lord-husband, *your* king, is not the criminal. If I'm not permitted to write the truth, then I'll write nothing."

The pupils in Cthar's golden eyes dwindled to two tiny black dots. She leaned back in her chair. "Do you think I can be talked out of this? I won't answer you with mere words, so don't test me. Write to your lord-father. Then you will write to the Lady Rhiysa, in all courtesy, and tell her that if she wishes to appease me, she will travel to Arimna."

How nice that Cthar could be so concerned with courtesy, having such bloodied hands. Dalia smiled beatifically, hoping she wasn't overdoing sweetness. "I prefer to be realistic, Lady. Here's the problem with your beloved Chaplet theology. According to your beliefs, we are all gods in flesh, and life is given to us to seek joy and to do what we deem as good, or needful and pleasing. What if none the other little 'gods' in flesh agree with what pleases you?"

Cthar stared at her, unblinking. Her loathing almost palpable, filling the writing room with its murderous presence. Raising her voice coolly, she beckoned the guard. "Khvel."

Silence answered. Cthar stood. "Khvel!"

Dalia smiled. "Whoever Khvel is, he's doing as he pleases." And hopefully he would now run, because Cthar was ready to kill. Genuine color bloomed beneath Cthar's spots of facial paint. She stormed through the open door and into the hallway.

Alone, Dalia eyed the nearest door—Valsignae's. Smiling, she snatched the slippers from her feet and hurriedly crept off, blessing Valsignae's sweet spirit for refusing to have locks installed in her apartment's well-oiled doors. "Dear Infinite, One-Who-Sees—let me see no reminders of her death!"

Dalia closed herself inside Valsignae's thankfully clean, linen-draped chamber, and then raced toward the secret panel. She pushed up on the carved hidden latch, slipped into the narrow stone tunnel behind the false wooden wall, and closed the secret door.

Just as Cthar screamed in the distance, "Dalia!"

Dalia was pleased not to answer. Instead, she dashed toward Aunt Pinny's rooms—the dear and irreverent Princess Pinae-Sonem, who must surely be cheering her on. Dalia slid open the door, crept into Aunt Pinny's former domain, then carefully closed the door and caught her breath. Whatever she did, she must hurry.

Where was the nearest storage area?

Her slippers carefully muddied to dullness, her hair coiled and knotted beneath a drab linen towel, and her scorned ceremonial robes ingloriously tied up beneath a servitor's protective overtunic, Dalia merged into a line of servants waiting to exit the palace. In her arms, a linen bundle of draperies from Aunt Pinny's rooms, which hid her courtly mantle.

Matteo would be proud of her—she looked as drab and servant-like as she'd ever appeared in Kiyrem. Several tradeswomen clustered together ahead of her, lugging baskets and bundles of fabric. Dalia approached them, her gaze on their worn sandals and boots as she joined the fringes of their ranks.

Ahead of Dalia, one of the women sighed and shifted a basket from her arm to her fabric-crowned head. "The wait's longer today." She eyed Dalia. "Haven't seen you 'bout. You've a heap to carry through. I thought they'd stopped sending out laundry."

Dalia affected a bored sigh and a Tvirtove Gate accent. "Mendin'." Her usual assigned task at Kiyrem.

"You good with 'broidry?"

"I am. 'Prenticed two years north o' Tvirtove Gate."

"Name?"

Dalia smiled and offered the nickname bestowed upon her by Matteo's brother Sheth. "Lia."

The guard was waving them through, clearly convinced by Dalia's guise. The tradeswoman beckoned Dalia again. "You seem right enough. I'm Glenna. If you're lookin' for more work, we need a 'broiderer at Gold Needle in the weavers ward. Be there at first light."

"Thanks, an' I will." Dalia bobbed a polite 'Lia agreement and watched Glenna walk away.

Placid, as if she'd walked the same lane for years, Dalia turned east, toward the city's main gates.

Taking his usual place in Port Bascin's great hall, Corban slouched into his cushioned chair, and studied the ancient Book of Praises in the evening light. *Hear me when I cry to You, Infinite, Lord who grants me righteousness. You have upheld me in my suffering; reveal Your mercy now, and hear my prayer.*

The words settled within him, calming as a night song, yet alive. The tranquility that had once permeated Araine's letters to him returned as he read these verses. Finished, he closed his eyes.

Hear my prayer. Infinite, allow me to...

Goldensleeve swept into the hall, harried, his squared face drawn with concern. "Another courier bird's descended upon the receiving tower. It's our day for news. I'm off to tell the king."

Corban opened his eyes and left his selfish prayer unfinished. Restlessness descended upon him again, unwelcome and exasperating. Nevertheless, the king might have received news of the Lady Dalia.

He sped across the great hall after Goldensleeve, and marched up the spiraling stairs toward the royal apartments. On the broad upper landing, he paused as Goldensleeve rapped on the king's door. A rush of footsteps descended the spiraling steps from the tower loft above, where the courier birds were fed and sheltered. A servitor bowed to Corban, then kneeled, pleading, "My lord, it's from Arimna! I beg you to present this to the king. If it's bad news, I'll never shake the disgrace of being its messenger."

"As you please." Corban accepted the thin gold-painted tube and waved off the servitor. "Run."

Goldensleeve grunted. "You've more courage than me, my lord. The king's called us to enter." He stepped aside and bowed Corban through.

Corban bowed to Matteo and Ekiael, who stood on opposite sides of the huge writing table. Corban offered the gold cylinder to Matteo, mask-calm, but praying fiercely.

Infinite, grant my unspoken request, and this one: Let the queen be well!

Matteo passed a hand over his growing beard, accepted the message, broke its wax seal and read the tiny note. Then he laughed and shouted to the carved wooden ceiling beams, "Yes! My wife will rule all! Listen!" Grinning, he read aloud, "'The Queen has been well and this morning escaped the palace. Yrs from Arimna.'"

Ekiael snorted in mock scorn. "That's all?"

"It's enough for now!" Matteo kissed the note and tucked it within his coin pouch. "Infinite, shield her until we can gather our army!"

So be it. Corban exhaled and dropped into a chair near the desk as Goldensleeve laughed and bowed in the doorway. "With your permission, Sire, I'm off to tell Port Bascin that our queen's slipped the she-scaln's claws."

Dalia kept her gaze lowered, trained on her bundle of fabric. Ahead of her, a quarrel erupted at the city's gate. A merchant haggling with the guard. "An eighth-weight of gold? Do you think I'm the king?"

"No," the guard quipped. "The king has no money for a pass fee. But you—by the looks of your garments and horses—have more than enough. Measure out your gold or leave."

A pass fee. Dalia winced. She'd forgotten about money for a pass fee. But wasn't this illegal?

No money, no pass-through from Arimna, and too much attention from the guards to be risked. She sidled from the line, not bothering to hide her dejection.

Where to now? The longer she wandered in the open streets, the more certain she was to be caught. Between the spice market and the bakers' ward, Dalia skimmed the city's beautiful stonework spires. Gleaming golden light reflected from crown of the Infinite's House, catching her attention. Dalia smiled. The Infinite would surely welcome her for one night's refuge in the outlying courts of His Holy House. Was it entirely locked?

Perhaps she could even somehow reach the secret chambers Matteo had described that the priests had adjourned to on his last night in Arimna. From there, she might escape to the River Tinem without needing to pay the pass fee.

A coarse voice bellowed directly at her: "Lady!"

Dalia jumped, hugging her bundle tight. She'd been caught. *Oh, One-Who-Sees, no ... please save me!*

Dalia glanced toward the voice, awaiting her doom. A young man smiled and winked at her—a baker's apprentice by the look of his dusted garments and that basket in his hands. "Last of the day's cakes—given for the taking."

Dear man, he was giving out samples of his master's work. Or perhaps his own efforts. She smiled at him, all her relief and delight undoubtedly visible. The apprentice blushed and his grin widened as he held out the broad basket of golden cakes. "For that kindly look, lady, you'll take several."

"Thank you, sir, for your kindness." *One-Who-Sees, thank You for seeing my approaching hunger!* She shifted her bundle and accepted two cakes.

"Of course," the apprentice murmured. But he was looking at her wedding ring, all gilded silver, bound by the rich but stained cord fastened by Matteo's hands on their wedding night. An odd expression passed over the young man's face, and he gave her a sidelong look before turning away.

Dalia hurriedly tucked her ring and the cakes beneath the tunic's sleeve and walked on. Any instant now, she would hear voices calling her to halt.

None called. No one else paid her heed as Arimna prepared for the evening, and the night to follow. Dalia trooped through the paved streets in the slanting evening light, winding her way toward the Holy House.

She reached the grand outer courtyards, tired enough to risk a rest behind the shadowed crenels of a mighty pillar. Leaning against the bundle, she chewed on one of the dense, lightly sweetened cakes, then placed a hand on Matteo's unborn baby. Just beginning to show—though most would still never suspect. Almost inaudibly, she whispered to the baby, "With the Infinite's blessings and mercy, we'll live! I'll see your sweet face."

Heartened, Dalia scooped up her bundle and skirted the edges of the vast temple complex. To the south, the priests' homes, all emptied and locked, formed a stone maze of secluded streets, with gardens lining walls. A beautifully woven and gilded gate revealed itself as she rounded an overgrown evergreen hedge. She nudged the woven metal and it swayed beneath her touch.

Unlocked.

Might she gain entry to the chambers below? "Beloved Infinite, forgive me if I'm trespassing. You see my heart, my wish for sanctuary."

She crept inside, closed the gate, then made her way through the outer courts. Testing doors. Checking every wall and ingress for some unmarked entrance into the caverns below, rattling some of the smaller bronzed doors and drainage grates amid her growing frustration.

Throughout the night, Ekiael's men checked the temple's hidden hoards and kept watch, listening as the underground complex echoed with odd noises. As if their hidden presence had become known. The distant rattling of a grate unnerved one of the younger priests enough to mutter, "We should climb up and chase off whoever's there!"

"You'd give us away," an elder hissed. "Then how could we prepare for the king's arrival? Obviously it's no priest acquainted with our ways. Stay here and keep quiet!"

Dalia sat within the sheltering leaves of blooming odora shrubs, their tiny fragrant blossoms perfuming the air while the last scraps of nighttime unwound and yielded to dawn. The heady fruit-pine scent and fresh leaves pledged true spring, strengthening Dalia's resolve. She finished the second cake, and then whispered to the baby, "We'll go to the embroiderers and earn our way out of Arimna."

Blessing her embroidery lessons with her mother and Sophereth in Kiyrem, Dalia retraced her steps through the Holy House complex, then out to the city beyond.

To the shop of the Gold Needle in the weavers ward.

The marketplaces were already awake and astir. With more than merchants calling out their spices, fabrics, and foods for sale. Here and there, soldiers lurked, eying Arimna's citizens.

Looking for her?

Dalia veered unhurriedly around the traders' stalls, avoiding all mortals.

But Commander Brune's familiar voice almost stopped her cold as he bellowed, "By order of Lord Karvos, at the command of the Queen Cthar, these premises are to be searched. Stand clear!"

Oh, indeed, she'd stand clear. Not merely stand, but stroll away to the weavers' ward. Why must Brune be so stinking dedicated to his duty?

And Lord Karvos! Was he still in favor with Cthar? Dalia almost huffed beneath her breath, recalling the man's scornful, olive-drab face. Her own lord-father's enemy—such a bitter word-stung loser.

Well, search as he might, Karvos wouldn't find her. She hoped.

Brune bellowed in the distance, "Halt! You there..."

Dalia strolled on as if she hadn't heard, then rounded a corner and scampered—a young woman rushing to her day's work.

Chapter 32

For the hundredth time, Anji returned to her writing table. To study the perfectly cut strip of parchment, skewered to the table with Anji's own hair pins. She hadn't dared to touch the courier's note for fear the parchment was imbued with poison. Cthar would certainly try poison if her own selfish Kaphtorian life mightn't be risked—and perhaps she'd found a way.

You have received the last courier bird of Eshda. No more exist in Arimna. Nor will they be needed. I am your sovereign, and no further mercy will be granted. Cthar of Darzeq.

Anji scowled at the note. A smear of blood, daubed at the lower right edge of the note, bore a fingerprint that could only be Cthar's. Had the woman sealed an unspoken vow in blood? It must be so.

One-Who-Sees ... Mighty One ... Infinite, be our Counselor and shield. You alone know the truth. What must be done?

Yiska, seated on a carpet and wrestling Jakin into a fresh tunic, sighed loudly. "Lady, you've stared at that she-scaln's scribbling so many times these past few days, that you must have memorized every tinge of shading in its very parchment and ink. I *won't* think of that fingerprint. The blood ought to be black or venomous. I beg you ... burn it."

"Thank you, Yiska, I will." But what was Cthar's full intent? To slaughter everyone in Eshda? Most likely. Brooding, Anji sat with Yiska on the carpet. Benamir crawled toward her, his golden eyes so beautiful, so innocent. So unlike Cthar's. Anji gathered the baby in her arms and settled him beneath her mantle to nurse him. He and Jakin were worth every fearful breath, every drop of despair, even if their imprisonment should last for years.

Distant horns and warning trump-calls from the watch towers made Anji look toward the window.

A rough clattering of boots and weaponry in the stairwell made her stand, hugging Benamir close beneath her mantle. Yiska rushed to answer the fretful rhythm of fists hammering against the door. Commander Jindrich, Lord Aristo's reluctant temporary successor, leaned inside, his rough-whiskered face intense. "Lady, forces have been sent from Arimna. I'm guessing they're not the king's."

"You're correct. The queen-mother is determined to capture me or kill me."

"That won't happen," Jindrich promised. "Not while the last soldier here draws breath."

"Yet I will die to protect the children." Anji hesitated, loathing the fact that she'd even thought to ask a question with such horrifying implications. "Commander, when was the last time the scaln traps were cleared and replaced?"

Jindrich's eyes widened, and his dark skin took on a brief ashen hue. "Eh, not since the week after the queen was stolen. They've been forgotten."

Sickly horror brought bile. Anji swallowed. "Warn everyone. And reinforce the gates, then double-check all of the conduits that drain wastes from the fortress. Please be sure they're secured and guarded."

Bless sweet Ekiael for writing all the wretched details from their invasion of Port Bascin. She'd already ordered the conduits cleaned, checked, and rendered too narrow and unwelcoming for soldiers to crawl through. Unless Cthar's soldiers relished shedding their armor and gear while confronting razor-rims of metal spikes in the conduits.

Faced with death-orders from Cthar, one could never be sure.

Jindrich bowed and hurried downstairs. Benamir's small, precious body sagged, fully relaxed in her arms. Sound asleep, the darling boy. She carried him to Ekiael's bed and nested him in its center, kissed his petal-soft cheek, then whispered, "Sleep soundly, my little lord. You're safe."

Turning to Yiska, she smiled encouragingly. "We'll survive."

For Darzeq's sake, they must.

Glenna leaned over Dalia's shoulder and nodded at the emerging tapestry. "Pretty. That'll sell at a fine price for sure."

Tvirtove Gate accented, Dalia said, "Aw, thanks!"

Two weeks with Glenna's family had earned her their trust and a tiny sleeping closet near their kitchen. As long as Glenna's dreadful cooking didn't bring down the residence in flames, she'd survive. Tomorrow, she'd be paid and she and the baby would buy their way out of Arimna the day after.

Then nothing would stop her from speeding down to Port Bascin and Matteo. She would...

Fists thudded at the workroom door, and a soldier shoved his way inside, making Glenna and the other girls gasp. "All out into the streets! By order of Lord Karvos, at the command of the queen, these premises are to be searched. Clear the way!"

"Scaln's breath!" Dalia tucked her needle into the edge of her tapestry, mulling over her options. Run the instant she hit the street, and call attention to herself, or cut an extra door into the back of the work room. Neither choice would work this instant. Therefore, she'd try to behave normally. She smoothed her tunic and glided both hands over her headscarf. Good. Curls hidden, drab attire, eyes properly downcast, she followed Glenna tamely into the street and merged with the crowd of weavers and embroiderers in the ward.

Horse hooves threw vibrations through the pavings beneath Dalia's slippered feet. She risked a glance then averted her gaze as Karvos himself guided his purple and gold chariot toward the crowd, staring them over, his upper lip curled contemptuously as if considering how to rid his city of some virulent mold.

His men scattered and entered the first four shop-houses on the street. Every weaver, mender, and embroiderer standing on the street's pavings winced as splintering crashes accompanied the search. Beside Dalia, Glenna mourned, "Oh ... if they're breaking the looms..."

Karvos urged his horse onward, guiding his chariot up and down the street then halting some thirty paces away. "All of you listen to me! We're seeking a fugitive—a woman! Give up anyone who's taken shelter with you in the past three weeks, *now*!"

Swallowing, Dalia willed herself to remain calm. Glenna and her family stood perfectly still, and not one person on the street offered so much as a peep. Not that they'd much to say. Few knew of Dalia's presence in Glenna's home; she'd deliberately remained inside and working.

Clearly irked by the quiet, Lord Karvos snapped at two guards, "Take a girl prisoner and bind her!"

A young woman shrieked as the guards dragged her from amid the workers. An older woman screamed and slapped at the guards until Karvos himself lifted his whip to lash her face.

Dalia yelled in her true voice, "Lord Karvos, I forbid you to torment those women!"

The great lord lowered his whip, then turned about within his fine chariot, looking and listening, intent as a dog on a hunt. "Where are you?"

If she must give herself away, then she'd do so grandly. Let all of Arimna hear! Dalia kissed the shocked Glenna's rounded face, then threaded her way through the crowd of workers, yelling as loudly as her lord father, or any of Matteo's brothers. "I am Dalia of Tragobre, Eshda, and Darzeq! Wife and queen to Matteo of Darzeq, and mother of the young lord Benamir of Darzeq! Lord Karvos, you will release these women and pay for any broken wares or looms!"

Karvos laughed and brandished his whip again. "I owe no one anything!"

"I say you do!" Dalia charged the chariot and cut between him and the stunned, tearful women. "Don't you *dare* touch them again!"

"Hush, you!" Karvos snatched her up bodily and tossed her into his chariot. His guards closed ranks about them. Karvos gripped Dalia's shoulder hard, and pulled the linen off her hair, which immediately unwound in frothing black curls. "I'd recognize you anywhere, lady. You're too much your father's daughter."

True. But she was Mother's daughter as well, and Mother, despite all her sweetness, wouldn't be meek now. Dalia bellowed over her shoulder, "Arimna, remember your king! Pray for me—your queen—held captive by Cthar of Kaphtor! Avenge the house of Jonatan!"

Hisses cut through the crowd and one of the weavers yelled, "Save the queen!"

Amid the growing tumult, Karvos growled and whipped his horse into a rackety pace, sending the chariot thudding along the paved streets ahead of the mob. Dalia caught her balance and hung on to the chariot's side rails, praying with all her might.

Infinite, save me from his wild driving!

If Karvos slowed enough, she might be able to shove him into the street. Unfortunately, he might take her down with him. Would she and the baby survive a hard fall and possible trampling by a mob?

Dalia gripped the chariot's rail and gasped as Karvos veered around a street corner, the chariot's wheels scraping and squealing above the screams of the mob. Oh, mercy! Either way, she was going to die.

Within the central courtyard of the palace, Karvos drew his winded horse to a halt. The chariot teetered precariously for one last breathtaking instant before it settled with an iron-rimmed thud.

She'd survived.

Trembling, Dalia uncurled her hands from the chariot's built-in holds. Karvos faced her and raged, "What possessed you to aggravate the commoners? We could have both been killed."

Dalia stepped from the chariot as proudly as her wobbly knees allowed. "Righteous wrath, my lord, that's what possessed me. If I'd the strength and a third arm, I would have shoved you into the street and let the mob deal with you."

Karvos muttered harsh words beneath his breath, then snarled and grasped her by the arm. "You're worse than Tragobre ever was!"

"And you are a bully, and a coward, and faithless—still here in Arimna Palace waiting on *her*! Traitor!"

"I'm guarding my interests!"

"Does your wife agree with your plans?"

Karvos gave her one long, cold stare, then nodded at his rattled guards, who formed ranks about them both. Karvos gripped Dalia's arm. "I'm taking you to the queen this instant, before I'm tempted to kill you here and now!"

"I am your queen."

"You've no crown. Nor will you, if I've anything to say."

"Traitor's words." Dalia bit down further taunts. Was Karvos planning to ultimately seat himself on King Jonatan's throne, in Matteo's rightful place?

Rage blinded, she marched with the traitor and his soldiers along the amethyst corridors to Cthar's rooms. A guard rapped at the door, and Cthar called out, "Enter."

She remained seated at her parchment-strewn table as Karvos led Dalia inside, but her black-lined golden eyes widened. She looked Dalia up and down, then frowned at Karvos. "My lord, no one is to be brought into my presence unless cleaned and attired befitting my rank and theirs. Furthermore, she's not bound, as I commanded."

Karvos protested, "Majesty, this one detail escaped me, though she did not. I beg your forgiveness. Also, if I'd paused to bind her then, the mob would have swarmed me."

"Mob?" Cthar stood. Her tone could have frosted every pillar in the palace as she hissed at Dalia, "If you gloat that you incited a mob in my streets, I'll have you beaten!"

Well, then. Dalia pressed her lips together.

Cthar gusted out a furious breath. "Very wise. How did you escape us so quickly?"

"Through unlocked doorways, when you turned away, lady." Cthar needn't know which doors.

The queen-mother glowered. "Never mind. Whatever games you've played, they're ended. My realm will remain at peace, and you will be Darzeq's offering to me soon enough—my validation as their sovereign. Where will your schemes be then, lady? In the void. Or, as other people say, the nightlands."

Dalia braced herself. She must not react. Her death sentence had been pronounced. "When?"

Smiling, Cthar seated herself gracefully, and then silently waved them out—including Karvos. He bowed, but Dalia glimpsed a wash of crimson tinging his olive face. Karvos drew Dalia backward with him from the chamber, and the guards closed the great gilded bronze doors. Expressionless, Karvos guided Dalia toward her small, stark room.

For a man who'd just been sorely snubbed, his composure approached admirable. Dalia sighed, unwelcome sympathy stirring. Gently, she warned, "My lord, I fear you're doing yourself no favors here. She's not the least bit grateful."

"You concentrate on your own worries, lady, and I'll tend mine."

Flanked once more by the guards, they continued down the corridor, watched by startled servants. Several, including Abiah, Matteo's servant, looked dismayed. Proof that she had sympathizers in the palace.

As they turned from the gleaming amethyst-and-gold wing, where the royal family had once lived, a cadence of boots drew Dalia's attention. Commander Brune approached, leading a small contingent of soldiers. He bowed to Karvos and slid a wary glance at Dalia as they halted. "My lord, I've just returned from searching the northern section of the city that we discussed this morning. But I see that you've found her."

"Yes, Commander. No thanks to your laggard search techniques these past two weeks! Return to your usual duties." Karvos motioned his men onward and muttered, "And *that* was more thanks than I received."

"It's likely my grubby appearance distracted Cthar from thoughts of thanks," Dalia murmured. Her words pacified him a little. Perhaps enough, to risk her next question. "Lord Karvos, When am I to die?"

Testy as any of her teachers during the final weeks of school, Karvos sneered his scorn for her question. "In two weeks, by the sword, as befitting your rank. Where, I don't know, so don't expect details; accept your fate."

"No, thank you." But when he locked her into her small, windowless chamber with its tiny hearth, gloom settled in, weighing upon her soul in funeral dread. She rested one hand on the subtle roundness of her unborn baby. "Sweet little sojourner, if only you'd been born with your brother."

Would it do any good to tell Cthar and ask for six months of clemency? It would give her a few weeks, perhaps a month, to nurse the baby before...

But Cthar had ordered her grandsons and the gentle Valsignae murdered. Why would she be merciful to her enemy's unborn child?

When her two dismal attendants, Aneta and Trina, were finally propelled into the chamber and the door locked behind them, Dalia worked up a false-bright smile. "Don't worry. In two weeks, Darzeq will be rid of me, and you'll both be free again."

She'd be dead. Unless Matteo or their allies freed her. Trina stared, and Aneta blinked, absorbing her meaning.

Closing her eyes, turning away from their reluctant pity, Dalia prayed. "You alone, O Infinite, are my safety."

With the boys asleep and guarded by Yiska, Anji donned a dark cloak, hurried up the spiraling stairs, and slipped outside, onto Eshda's rooftop terrace. Why did she torment herself so? Yet each night, she'd come up here alone to pray that Cthar's forces would retreat, driven away by fear, isolation, and winter-starved scalns.

There weren't enough sturdy shelters for all of those soldiers.

Anji gazed into the darkness, beyond Eshda's mighty walls, and picked out Lost Lake and all the familiar fires marking the landscape. Then one edge of the ring of fires surrounding Cthar's troops. If a fire dwindled too low... If the scalns were particularly hungry... She shuddered. "Mighty One, let the soldiers retreat before more die!"

Distant screams lifted beyond the walls, in the valleys below—several conveying agony so piercing that Anji covered her mouth and sobbed as she stared into the darkness.

Into the abyss of torments that Cthar had inflicted upon those poor men.

Closing her eyes, Anji wept and prayed, listening to the screams.

Chapter 33

She's recaptured. In good health and calm, tho' somber. Too closely watched for escape. Execution planned within two weeks. Priests sighted within the city. Cthar's name hissed. Gather your forces!

In Port Bascin's huge courtyard, Matteo clenched the note in his fist, blessing the unknown messenger while longing to deny the news. Yet refusing to accept the facts would change nothing. She'd been recaptured, his brave love, while Anji stood guard at Eshda.

Matteo sucked in a sharp breath and shoved the note into his coin purse. Dalia ... if he lost her to Cthar, and if Eshda fell, losing Benamir, he might as well kill himself at Arimna's gates. He'd little else to live for except his wife and children.

What had happened?

Why hadn't the priests tracked Dalia and whisked her into hiding as they'd planned? In his thoughts, Matteo traced the soft lines of his wife's perfect little face and held her close. When he liberated Dalia and the children, they'd never be more than a few steps away from him again.

Surely liberation would come soon enough. Tragobre's army would join up with his own and—bolstered by Ekiael's priests and Ormr's troops—they'd retake Arimna.

From the keep's steps, Thaddeus sent up a sharp, beckoning whistle. Behind him, Corban stalked from inside, his expression masked and austere, his numbed fingers curled in a fist within his baldric. He'd lost much serving here, though Darzeq wasn't his own country.

Why should he, Matteo of Darzeq, mope like a sulking child? Corban lived as testimony to perseverance despite overwhelming prospects, and Matteo ought to take lessons from the man.

Some ten steps away, Thaddeus halted, blocking Corban's path. "You've bad news?"

"The queen's been recaptured."

Thaddeus ran one hand over his face and stared, then growled his frustration. But Corban shouldered aside Thaddeus. "When will we be ready?"

In his chamber, Ekiael touched Anji's brief message, wishing the note had brought his wife with it. *Eshda's beset by Cthar's army. Arimna's defenses are weakened—seize this chance! Beloved, secure the king and queen, then think of me and the boys.* Arimna first. *I bless the Infinite for you. A.*

How like his Anji, his own princess, to insist upon duty before her own safety. Ekiael sat at his table, snatched a parchment scrap, then jabbed a quill into ink. *Beloved wife, yes, I will see Matteo restored and Dalia saved, even if it costs my life, freely given. Isn't this the Infinite's will? I kiss you and the boys. Ekiael.*

He kissed her note and hid it within his knapsack—beneath the concealed ancient crown.

Dalia woke and stretched, and a slice of pain warned her to ease off. Overnight, the baby had blossomed within her, becoming fat and vigorous, pulling at all her abdominal muscles, the little scamp. But why should she be surprised? She'd little to do but eat, sleep, and pray. She'd never been so lazy in all her life.

Gently, Dalia stood then straightened, rubbing at her sides through the light linen gown. At once, Trina and Aneta stood, ready to pounce if she headed for the door. As if she would.

Aneta hesitated and then looked Dalia over. Dark eyes wide in her sickly face, Aneta said, "Lady, I'd guess you don't suffer from bloat from last night's cabbage."

Aneta's dismay and Trina's wincing look were incomparable. However, if they'd been truly observant, they'd have realized her condition several weeks ago. Dalia smiled at them, proud that she could speak with only a small tremor. "I hope his eyes are golden, like his lord-father's. It would have been lovely to see him."

Trina's mouth opened and closed, gawping as if she'd forgotten how to breathe. "Shouldn't we tell the queen?"

"Trina," Dalia reminded her, "Darzeq's queen knows her own condition, as does the king. But Cthar of Kaphtor won't care a mite. She didn't spare her own grandchildren, so why worry about an unborn baby who'd possibly contend with her for the throne? I command you to say nothing."

Aneta lifted both hands, pleading, "But..."

Dalia clasped the woman's hand and silenced her with a stern-quiet look. "*No.* If I'd any hope that a plea would save my baby, don't you think I would have kneeled before the she-scaln and begged? No. All I can do is pray for some sort of reprieve." Or an uprising.

Might she stir rebellion again in Arimna's streets? No, she mustn't count on victory through her own efforts. She covered her face with her hands and prayed.

Infinite, my Creator, Ruler of the Universe, One Who Sees Me, we are Yours to rescue or take according to Your will and Your plan.

If she must die, let it be quick. Let her die as Darzeq's queen should die.

Above all, let Matteo survive, victorious and safe ... and crowned king, with Benamir as heir.

She'd count her life as well-spent if they were protected.

If only her baby could be saved....

In the distance, morning gilded Arimna in violet and gold, the glowing dawn also illuminating the deliberately scruffy armies surrounding Matteo, riding with him from Port Bascin. According to his informants, a host of priests awaited him within the city, ready to break open the gates if need be upon his arrival. His hope, however, was to enter the city disguised as a rather grubby minor landholder. Tragobre rode at his left, and Ekiael at his right, with Lord Corban and Thaddeus following, praying and on guard, each of them clad in rugged, humble garments.

Matteo gazed at his home city, then lifted a hand and halted his men. "It's time. Scatter, and remember to play the part. We're here to celebrate the queen-mother's triumph. Take no offense if my name's cursed by her true followers."

Roi Hradedh snapped, "I'll spit whenever I hear Cthar's name—plague take her! I'm going to find out where she's hiding my daughter and then finish her plans."

Matteo stalled his father-in-law briefly. "My lord, guard yourself and remember to enter the Holy House before nightfall. Otherwise, I'll search you out myself."

Tragobre nodded grudgingly. "I know what I'm doing, trust me."

Lord Losbreq rode up beside Tragobre and half-bowed to Matteo. "I'll keep watch over him, Sire. It won't do to free the queen, only to break her heart by losing her lord-father."

"Thank you." Matteo sent them off with a swift salute, but gritted his teeth, watching Tragobre charge ahead. Matteo's own guards and priests, all deliberately rough-clad and impoverished in appearance, dismounted and surrounded him. Matteo swung himself off his horse.

"Mighty One," the coarse-clad Ekiael implored aloud as the remainder of the army flowed past them, scattering in their various guises, "Speed our steps! Cover the eyes of our enemies, and dull their sight, but not our king's." He removed ointment and a tattered strip of linen from his scuffed knapsack. "Ready, Sire?"

Ignoring Corban's dubious sidelong glance, Matteo stood at attention. "Ready."

Ekiael slathered the crimson-tinged ointment over Matteo's eyes, then tied on a linen strip. Matteo wheezed, then coughed as the initial pungent fumes burned his nostrils and throat, while crimson ooze slid down into his overgrown beard. Within a breath, the stinging settled to tolerable herbal acridness. "This won't blind me, will it?"

"It's my mother's remedy against pink-eye. Made with honey. Cruel stuff, Sire, just grit your teeth and endure." As planned, Ekiael turned Matteo toward a small cart and helped him inside.

While Matteo rummaged the cart's straw into a less uncomfortable heap, Corban's voice lifted, each gruff syllable sounding wrenched from his throat. "Bind me as well."

Matteo almost laughed. "I forbid you to suffer such an indignity, my lord. You've no scaln's eyes that must be hidden."

"I've been blinded enough by my own self-importance," Corban argued. "Furthermore, two wounded men being waited upon by a gathering of impoverished priests ought to convince the guards that the Infinite's own are on a mission of mercy. Wrap my arm as well, lord-priest. Please."

Ekiael evidently complied—Matteo heard Corban gasp and grumble beneath his breath as the ointment hit his eyes. At last, Ekiael spoke dryly. "Try to look beaten and defenseless, my lord. For once, I encourage you to cultivate your natural sullenness and gloom."

"As you command." Corban dropped into the cart beside Matteo, and obeyed, donning an oversized cloak's worth of taciturn bitterness.

Despite his attempts to joke and commiserate with Corban over their apparent shared ailments, Matteo counted exactly three words from the Siphran Lord during their final approach to Arimna. At last, Corban's gloom overwhelmed Matteo. He shut his eyes and prayed.

One Who Sees, guard us in our blindness. Let this not be my death journey.

Darzeq and Dalia must be released from Cthar's claws.

Jarred by yet another break in the river road's pavings, Corban closed his eyes beneath the tattered linen as Matteo offered a third polite remark on the road to Arimna. "Perhaps by tomorrow at this time, we'll control Arimna once more."

"Perhaps." King or not, Corban wished the young man would hush. Was he talking to cover his nervousness? He ought to be praying.

The cart thudded heavily, and Matteo lapsed into silence. Corban exhaled quietly against the stinging ointment, and willed his thoughts to rest within the verses of Praises from the Books of the Infinite.

Children of Dust, will you see My glory as shame for a lifetime? Will you ever love vanity and sell yourselves to the highest bidder?

...You whom I love. You whom I will redeem as My own. Have I not promised you gladness and peace beyond measure? Turn again to Me, Child of Dust, for I have set you apart as righteous, you who commune with Me in harmony....

Too soon, Corban felt the city's nearness and oppression threading into his prayers and reflections, intruding upon his peace—the spiritual calm Araine had sought for his rebellious soul.

Peace he'd resisted and resented. He'd never deserved Araine, the courageous and lovely prophet. Recalling her fear during their last conversation, Corban loathed his past anew. Why should a murderer plead for forgiveness? Why should forgiveness ever be granted? Yet...

Infinite, all that I've been or will become, I give you. My shame for Your peace. Your righteousness. Forgive me. Let me serve you ... reveal Your Glory.

A voice called out, "Names and reasons for visiting."

Ekiael answered, peaceable as a Corban had ever imagined a priest ought to be—to the point of meekness. "Eki of Tinem North. I'm bringing survivors of the attack on Port Bascin's ships here to recover and to celebrate the queen's triumph."

"Eh?" The guard's voice neared. "Survivors, you say? Are they of Darzeq or Kaphtor?"

"Darzeq." Ekiael's smooth swift answer was as natural as breathing—as it should be. Ekiael hadn't slathered his own face with insufferable ointment.

"Darzeq?" The guard huffed scorn. Corban turned slightly, listening. Beside him, Matteo lay in the straw, unmoving—as might a man without hope. The guard evidently believed their portrayals. He rapped at the cart. "Go on. The queen's not interested in Darzeq's victims. A pity they aren't some of the lost merchants from Kaphtor. She'd likely meet them once their eyes stopped oozing."

"A pity indeed." Ekiael sighed. "I suppose we'll ask for funds from others instead of the crown. What about you, sir? Will you give money for their care?"

"Later." The guard's tone cooled. "I've none now. Move on."

Corban muttered, "May you never be maimed and begging."

If the guard heard, Corban couldn't tell. Yet he listened, all his senses turned to any hints of threat against the king. *Mighty One, see for me! Defend us.*

Matteo listened for the guard's sudden snarl, or a challenge to Ekiael's credentials at the gate. Nothing. Not a whisper of threat stopped them. They merged into the city's clamor, and Ekiael muttered, "Leave your bandages on until we reach the Holy House."

The city's noises and smells assailed Matteo from all sides. Porters bawling threats to clear their paths, vendors calling out the first harvests from their early-spring gardens, the sizzle of meat grilling at street corners. The rattling and squeaking of other carts and chariots that glutted the streets. At last, the noises and scents faded in the distance, and one of the priests muttered a complaint. "Look at all the weeds we'll have to chop back."

Another said, "We've shutters to mend, and some of the houses have been vandalized."

"We'll make repairs later," Ekiael told them. "We've more important matters facing us now. Let's take the king down to the shelters." Gates creaked open, and the cart clattered over uneven stones, then bumped to a stop. Ekiael said, "Off with those bandages, Sire and Lord Corban. Unless you now prefer life with them on."

Matteo pulled off the linen strips and blinked hard. Other priests were emerging from doorways and inner gates enclosing the Holy House. Attuned as birds in flight, they swept around Ekiael, Matteo, and Corban, and tugged at their sleeves urging them toward the nearest portico, into a storage room beyond, then down a lamplit flight of stairs.

Down into the cavernous chambers Matteo remembered from the pain-blurred night of the massacre. Amid flaring torches and lamps, one of the older priests called to Ekiael, "My lord, we've a visitor—a refugee from the palace."

Matteo's heart skipped in a violent, hopeful beat. Had they actually saved Dalia?

But a man's shadowed bowed to him, thin and silvering. Not Dalia. Matteo summoned a smile. Whoever the refugee was, he might have news. The man straightened, and Matteo glimpsed his tears reflecting light. "Abiah!" He rushed forward and greeted his servant with a hug. "What news do you have?"

Abiah shook his head. "I wish I'd more and better to say, Sire. She's well for now, but will be executed tomorrow afternoon. Where and when, no one knows. The queen-mother will decree the time and place as she pleases."

"Then we must guess accurately and launch our attacks accordingly. But thank you for sending me the courier notes."

Confusion skimmed Abiah's thin face and he shrugged a pained denial. "Sire, I sent no notes. Let us hope that others are planning our queen's escape wisely, for—I heard rumors that the Infinite's priests had returned. I came to warn everyone and plead for help—her guards have been ordered to kill her immediately if the palace is attacked."

Chapter 34

Dalia summoned herself to wakefulness. Too-brief sleep misted her senses after a night of prayer. Nothing had changed. Despite her brief dreams of freedom, she was still in her dim cell, the lowering coals her only light. Aneta and Trina bestirred themselves, calling for guards to bring food and water.

Food for them all, and water to bathe the queen—to prepare her for death.

A sharp tap brought plain bread and hot water. And a softly layered white tunic, paired with a silver-embroidered green overgown befitting the daughter of a lord, not a queen. Evidently, Cthar had ordered the garments herself as a visual denial of Dalia's rank. A guard pushed the garments at Aneta. "She's commanded to be ready and waiting for the queen's instructions."

Dalia sat up in her cot. "When, sir?"

Without answering, the guard closed the heavy door and slammed the lock in place.

Oh, how Cthar loved her little games. Keep everyone guessing, then kill Dalia when she pleased. While Aneta brought the fire back to crackling life, Dalia forced down a piece of bread, and then scrubbed herself as much as the water allowed.

Aneta and Trina ate their bits of bread, and then carefully combed and plaited Dalia's stubborn curls. They pinned the braids high on her head, secured the simple layered tunic over Dalia's undergarments, then helped her into the robe. As they fought with the front closure, Trina complained, "It's too small."

Dalia looked down at her unborn baby's distinctively rounded linen-draped presence showing through the robe's green edges and she smiled. "No, the fit's perfect. Leave it be."

Darzeq would realize and forever remember what it had lost.

Roi Hradedh strode in at dawn, followed by Losbreq. Haggard in the lamplight, Roi glared at them all, as wild as Matteo to save Darzeq's queen. "How can we tell what that madwoman's intending to do? She's built no scaffolding in the palace, nor in her precious Chaplet Temple. What if she's already killed my daughter?"

"No." Matteo shook his head, refusing to consider the thought. "She won't. Cthar considers my wife to be her enemy and my weakness. I am her chief target, and Dalia is my lure, yet she wants to keep us in disarray ... scattered and weakened as we try to rescue her. We must gather our men and attack Cthar herself. The question is, where will she be?"

Losbreq passed one long hand over his fatigue-drained face. "Rumors are spreading that she's summoned her supporters to join her in a public celebration today."

Matteo could almost see his grandmother's coolly beautiful, aristocratic features skewed into a smile as she planned to celebrate her triumph. "Her vanity won't allow anything less than civic endorsement of her behavior. I'd guess that she will attempt to punish my wife publicly."

"Then...?" Thaddeus caught their attention, drawling, "What public place would she most love to consecrate with enemy blood?"

They all traded glances. Roi and Thaddeus nodded as Ekiael said, "That accursed Chaplet Temple."

Corban scowled. "Where is it?"

Dalia glided out of her cell, her heavy ceremonial gown's beaded silver embroidery glistening in the morning light—much too showy for facing one's own execution. However, if she must die this morning, then she ought to maintain dignity. Matteo's Aunt Pinny, the Lady Pinae-Sonem, always championed icy courage, whatever the situation. Mother advocated graceful defiance. Father would insist upon a fight.

Dalia pleaded beneath her breath, "Infinite, send me all three!"

She turned in the corridor and caught Commander Brune staring at her rounded form, stunned as a man bludgeoned by an unexpected opponent. He closed his mouth, then glared at Aneta and Trina. "You two knew she was in this condition! Why didn't you say something?"

"Because," Dalia interposed as Aneta quivered visibly and Trina fought sobs, "I ordered them to be silent. My condition will mean nothing to Cthar."

Commander Brune sighed. "Lady, you are ordered to remain silent."

Dalia threw him a sweetly defiant smile. "Of course, Commander. I believe I won't need to say anything." No wonder Cthar trusted Brune. The man was a scold in soldier's gear.

Willing herself to walk steadily to her execution, Dalia lifted her chin as Brune guided her down the corridor. Beneath his breath, he hissed, "Be observant, Majesty. If I say 'move' or 'stop,' please do so."

"Don't I usually, Commander? And since when do you call me 'Majesty'?"

"Not soon enough, Majesty. To Darzeq's sorrow."

Ekiael's army of priests opened the temple, and four watch-keepers called the faithful to the temple with their accustomed trump-calls. Armed with his sword, and gripping his crossbow, Matteo willed himself to stand quietly between the door's pillars, lest Ekiael chain him in place. Beneath his breath, Ekiael muttered, "This won't take long. Be patient."

Be patient while setting out to rescue Dalia? Did Ekiael think he was made of stone? And why—while clad in his most formal robes and gem-studded breastplate as high priest—did Ekiael still carry that scuffed, old, leather knapsack?

When the first curious onlookers ventured into the forecourt, Ekiael raised his sonorous voice to high-priest level. "Matteo, son of Jonatan, this day, by the Infinite's will, you are consecrated to His service as Darzeq's king!"

Matteo blinked as Ekiael pulled a golden vial from behind his breastplate and poured its gleaming contents over Matteo's forehead. Ekiael tucked the drained vial into the breastplate again, and then opened the knapsack, revealing an obviously antique gilded rim of worn iron. "Bear the weight of this most ancient crown with the solemnity it deserves, as did Darzeq's kings before you!"

He placed the circlet on Matteo's head, resting it securely over his temples. In the forecourt, most of the faithful—random witnesses from Arimna's streets—whooped and slapped each other's shoulders, though several ran away. As Matteo longed to do.

At the foot of the stone steps, his comrades applauded, and even Tragobre nodded approval. The assembly of priests, called out praises to the Infinite, and drew their swords, prepared to fight as the watch-keepers blared the longer trump calls summoning Arimna to war.

In the distance, trump calls echoed from the palace, signaling royalty departing from its gates.

Where was Cthar? Had she really departed during the trump calls?

Dalia exited the palace and looked around the courtyard. Ranks of guards waited—an elite company armed with spears, swords, and helmets gleaming in the morning sunlight. All night long, she'd lived this scene. She'd expected to die here in this courtyard, but no scaffolding awaited her. No gawping witnesses, no executioner, and no gloating Cthar.

"Oh, mercy..." Dalia swallowed as Brune guided her down the final steps. She was going to suffer a public execution. Were they planning to simply skewer her, or gut her publicly before cutting off her head? Her darling baby...

The world swayed around Dalia until Commander Brune shook her from faintness. She gripped his arm. "Thank you, Commander."

He grunted, then looked around as if seeing a problem, for his frown deepened. "Where *are* they?"

Dalia frowned up at the man. Why was he so agitated? He wasn't the one being marched to his death. "Where are they—who, Commander?"

Brune surveyed the ranks of men surrounding them—Cthar's own elite guards—and he shook his head. "A futile question from a laggard subject of Darzeq, Majesty. Never mind. Hope promises nothing today."

"You may abandon hope, sir. I won't until my last breath."

The dour commander muttered, "Exactly as Darzeq's queen should be. Come along, Majesty, before these fanatics become impatient. Again, be watchful." He led Dalia down to a massive military chariot that boasted four harnessed horses, and helped her to step up onto its enclosed platform. Two guards stepped in behind Dalia and lifted their shields defensively as Brune took the reins.

The waiting company of guards formed ranks around the chariot and the gatekeepers unbarred and opened the gates. The horses surged forward, clearly restless and eager to be away. To take her to be publicly executed. Time unwound itself as Dalia gripped the chariot's handholds. The crowds in the street passed in a blur, until she forced herself to take a breath. She was behaving like an addled soul, not Darzeq's queen. She exhaled. Chin up, shoulders back, and flaunting her round, linen-draped belly, she looked Arimna's citizens in their faces, willing them to see her.

To remember.

Perhaps later, to finally turn upon Cthar.

Mounted on his horse and followed by Ekiael, Tragobre, Thaddeus, Corban, Losbreq, and their mingled forces, Matteo rode past the palace gates, past crowds of gossiping citizens, who scattered when they saw his approach. In his wake, voices lifted in triumph and alarm. "The king! The king!"

Riding to Matteo's left, Thaddeus yelled, "Make way!"

At Matteo's right, Tragobre cried out, "Save the queen!"

Dalia walked into the Chaplet Temple's arena, practicing graceful defiance and courage as she stared up at the crowd. Cthar's adherents—too many of them noblemen of Darzeq, as well as Kaphtor—cheered as she walked into view. Undoubtedly not because they were pleased to see her, but because they were delighted to witness her death. Did they think they'd prosper under Cthar's rule? Beneath Kaphtor's grasping might?

Cthar—ensconced in the purple-canopied seat of honor in the upper tier of the Chaplet Temple—smiled down at Dalia as if they were attending a social gathering. But then her smile stiffened like paint on a mask, and she leaned forward, clearly displeased as she studied Dalia's rounded form.

Dalia watched the queen-mother's gold-shielded fingernails flash as she rested them claw-like on the rim of her balcony seat. She turned her head slightly toward Lord Karvos, who nodded to whatever Cthar had muttered.

If only Karvos could be persuaded to dump Cthar over the balcony.

But Cthar sat back, perfectly safe and sheltered beneath her royal canopy. And she motioned to Commander Brune, who led Dalia toward a wooden platform in the temple's paved center.

Toward the stoic executioner, who waited with his sword.

Matteo halted his horse at the Chaplet Temple complex, swung himself down, and set his crossbow's bolt. Thaddeus, Ekiael and the others surrounded him, swords drawn. Matteo bellowed at onlookers, "Where's the queen?"

Several pointed inside, then skittered away as a battalion of armed guards approached. Tragobre ordered them, "Bow to your king, then stand back or die!"

One of the guards flung a spear, which whistled past Matteo toward Corban, who lunged aside and yelled, "Defend your king!"

More than half the guards turned about, defying those who dared to challenge Matteo. Several skirmishes erupted, then scattered as Matteo ran inside the elegant temple, leading his army between its graceful entry columns and down the steps toward the white-paved central ground. Toward Dalia, who was kneeling on a guarded wooden platform ... before her executioner.

Dalia turned toward the din, the echoing clatter of swords and shields. Toward Matteo who was running, leading Ekiael, Thaddeus Ormr, Father, and an army of priests and ragtag fighters into the temple's arena.

Dalia scrambled to jump from the platform, but Brune lunged and swiftly dragged her down, just as the sword's shadow arced over their heads. Screams echoed from the crowd, and two of the priests' spears threw the executioner backward off the platform.

Up in her royal purple seat, Cthar shrieked to her guards, "Kill them! Traitors—cut them down!"

Brune crouched beside Dalia and drew his sword. "About time they showed up! I sent word!"

Matteo and Father sprinted toward the platform. Father half-knelt beside Dalia, looking ready to kill anyone who touched her. But Matteo halted directly in front of Dalia, shielding her as he lifted his crossbow and aimed up at Cthar. He'd made himself a target to protect her—not what she wanted. Her heartbeat speeding with panic, Dalia leaned nearer to Father and peeked around Matteo's booted legs, praying, "Mighty One, save him! Save us!"

In the upper tier, guards lurched forward to defend Cthar, one throwing a javelin toward Matteo, the other holding his shield before Cthar. The javelin rang loudly against the paving stones before Matteo, who stood his ground, aimed and pressed his crossbow's lever.

The bolt flew upward and punched through the guard's extended shield, as if guided directly to where the usurper's heart ought to have been.

Karvos screamed at Cthar's guards, and the world shivered around them.

His senses sharpening, heightening with his unspoken prayers, Corban stood beneath the temple's stone crown, seeing the edifice for what it was. A rim. A giant's too-vulnerable toy, sheltering the king's enemies, but encircling Matteo, Dalia, and their allies. This was the Infinite's intent—and Corban's chance to end this conflict with one strike. To protect them all, and to repay the rebels who'd endangered him and his friends. "Infinite ... Mighty One ... let me serve You, even to death!"

Peace flowed through him, and all movement stilled but his own. His numbed hand obeyed and he shoved the left pillar beneath the stone rim, which teetered. Corban looked up, grinned, and then threw himself against the pillar to his right and bowed, taking it down with his prostrated body.

Matteo tracked the upper tier's initial movement backward, to its source.

Just as Corban grinned in ferocious delight and threw himself against a pillar, then bowed at its base, bringing the Chaplet's upper tier down upon himself like brittle clay. Too late, Matteo called to him, "No!"

Behind Matteo, Dalia screamed, her cry becoming lost in the shuddering, thunderous din as Matteo's men rushed to shield him, and the Chaplet Temple fell around them, burying Cthar and her supporters.

Dalia placed the golden circlet of a Darzeq lord upon Corban's covered body, then stepped back, swiping at fresh tears. Father touched her shoulder in consolation, and then Matteo kissed her, sharing her misery.

Buildings could be rebuilt, and wealth gradually replaced. But nothing could restore a valiant friend to life.

Beyond Corban's temporary resting place in the palace, fires marked the city. For two nights, Arimna lived a mimicry of Eshda, as Cthar's hired mercenaries stole whatever they pleased, then fled.

But this morning's sun had lit a quiet sky, and calm swathed Arimna, promising an end to the chaos. Cthar's body lay rotting among those of her staunches allies, buried with her beneath a cairn of Chaplet stones, toppled by one downfallen Siphran Lord. If only he'd survived so they could repay him. No monument, not even the spectacular tomb and plaza Matteo was planning, could equal the measure of their gratitude and admiration for Lord Corban Thaenfall of Siphra. For Aristo of Eshda, and Kemuel of Lohe Bay ... all who'd been lost to Cthar's ambition.

Dalia returned to the bier, and kissed Lord Corban's covered forehead. "One Who Sees, You know his heart. Thank you for granting him peace."

Matteo wrapped his arm about her protectively, and drew her away, to face the crowds in the streets. And to retrieve and comfort Ghost, who lingered at the Chaplet temple, mourning near the broken gate where he'd last seen Corban alive.

In the stairwell below Eshda's receiving tower, Anji accepted the courier message, handling it warily until she recognized her husband's seal stamped upon the cylinder. Hands trembling, she opened his note and read, *Beloved, the battle's won, and*

Cthar is vanquished. Arimna offers its allegiance to Matteo, and I am hurrying to bring you all home. Dalia and Matteo beg you to kiss the children. Ever His servant, E.

She sat on the stone steps and wept for the lives stolen by Cthar's ambition. At last, composing herself, Anji descended the spiraling stone steps and returned to her chamber, startling Yiska, and making Darzeq's heir, and the Infinite's future prophet both laugh as she kissed them and hugged them close, blessing their Creator.

Ekiael sat in his rented room within the posting house, too restless to sleep. Half the night lurked between him and daybreak, when he and Lord Losbreq could lead their men toward Eshda and his family. Yet this darkness would not be wasted.

He smoothed a fresh piece of parchment, prayed over it, and then wrote: *In the last year of King Jonatan's reign, the Infinite sent a warning to Darzeq through Araine, the prophet of Belaal...*

Corban turned amid eternal calm, resting within the answer to his soul's quest.

This was the place he'd sought. A realm he'd first glimpsed through Araine's letters, inspired by the Infinite's words. Araine had struggled mightily to reach him within the mortal realm—to lead him toward peace. Yet she hadn't been the One who truly sought him.

One-Who-Sees-Me—praise You forever—You alone hunted me, to save me from myself!

Comprehending the Infinite's Spirit, Corban smiled, his immortal soul soaring, exultation speeding his thoughts toward the Infinite. Yes, he would remain here forever content.

Infinite, bless You…!

Amid his praise, a presence caught Corban's attention—a slender form he instantly recognized as mortal, and familiar. Belaal's valiant time-bound prophet paused in the distance, clearly a visitor within the Infinite's realm. Before Corban could even wonder why she should be there, the Infinite's Spirit poured eternal orders through his soul.

Corban smiled, bowing to Him.

Araine closed her eyes and stepped into her dreams, into a vision of darkness she couldn't fathom.

Cold, gleaming cities, nearly wild with chaos. Oceans of blackened blood birthing creatures of fire … a monster-dreki beyond her imaginings, its red-and-gold scales lit from within by the fury of hate, as souls cried out to the Infinite for rescue.

"Infinite, what is the truth about these creatures—about everything I've seen?

What do all these things mean?"

These are not for your generation, but for times to come. Don't be afraid, My Child of Dust.

As ever, her forays into future realms were almost too terrifying to endure, much less battle and then describe. Nevertheless, when she awoke tomorrow, she must think clearly and pray and strive for the Infinite's words as she wrote down everything she'd seen, for future mortal realms to study.

To declare His will and all that He'd decreed before time itself existed.

From the edge of her vision, Araine spied an immortal warrior approaching, tranquil, yet alight with joy and the

Infinite's reflected glory. Araine looked into the warrior's eyes and retreated, glimmers of recognition stirring fear. But Corban smiled at her, an ally in the Spirit. "Don't be afraid. I am His servant. His eternal warrior! And while you're here, we've a battle to wage."

He motioned her toward the chaos, shielded by their Creator's might, clearly prepared to walk with her...warrior, comrade, and guardian as the Infinite had forever seen him.

To Araine, the Infinite murmured, *Take up the weapons I have given you, and follow.*

Armed with the prophet's branch and His golden Word, Araine followed Corban, into the vision.

Into His realm, the branch glowing reflecting her soul, alive in the presence of her Creator.

Follow Me.

DownFallen Acknowledgements

Thank you dear readers, I appreciate each and every one of you. Love to my dear, patient husband, who cheered me on through a hectic six months and did housework while I wrote DownFallen on my days off. Hugs to my beloved sons, and kudos to my talented daughter-in-law, Katharin Gramckow, who drew and redrew the ink-on-parchment map for the Infinite series.

Scott Rodgers and the Falcon 1644 team, hey, what can I say? You're the most awesome crew! Thanks for putting up with me.

Pastor Tim Norris, thanks for your inspired sermons—definitely food for thought!

Readers, thank you again for your notes and your questions, and for all who have stopped by at my Facebook page and on Pinterest to monitor my progress as I wrote Exiles, Queen, and DownFallen! Keep after me, all of you! These stories are yours, and I'm blessed to write them for you.

Ever yours,

R. J. Larson

P.S. Catch me on the web!

http://www.rjlarsonbooks.com

https://www.facebook.com/RJLarson.Writes

https://www.pinterest.com/rjlarsonbooks

Don't miss out!

About the Author

R. J. Larson is the author of numerous devotionals and is suspected of eating chocolate and potato chips for lunch while writing. She lives in Colorado with her husband.

Read more at www.rjlarsonbooks.com.

Made in the USA
Middletown, DE
09 July 2019